I0604538

THE GODS ARE BASTARDS

D. D. WEBB

Podium

Podium

THE GODS ARE BASTARDS

PROLOGUE

"The gods are bastards."

The scene of the death was quite beautiful, now, years after the fact. A small creek cut through a little hollow in the prairie; the bowl-shaped depression had probably been a crater centuries ago, before rain and wind had blunted its edges and nature filled it with field grass and singing cicadas. In the exact center, in a vaguely star-shaped swath of emerald-green moss interrupting the golden tallgrass, stood a stone marker bearing the carved sunburst of Omnu, the victim's name, and the dates bracketing her pitifully short life.

She knelt before the tiny monument, apparently studying it, but in truth, merely listening as he approached. The crunch of his boots and the rattle of spurs had given him away long before he spoke.

"You can feel free to tell Father Reyfield I said so," the man went on, coming to a stop at the lip of the little crater. His shadow loomed beside her, an elongated figure in a ten-gallon hat, hands tucked into his belt with the stationary swagger of a man who kept order in his little town by sheer force of personality. "That old fart and I don't see eye-to-eye on much anyway. Here's little June Witwill, just plain the *best* girl in the province, near enough. Sang in the choir, donated all her pocket money to the local mission. Always spoke respectfully of emperor and country, and up to her eyes in everything that ever went on at the Church. She once got caught up in a stagecoach robbery when she was twelve and talked one of the bandits into turning himself in. He went on to become an Omnist monk, used to send June letters all the time." The shadow of his hat oscillated as he shook his head slowly. "Just . . . best kid I ever knew, is all. And there she was, walkin' out to catch crawdads in the stream, and just . . . burned. Went up like a goddamn firework. Town's almost a mile away, and we heard her scream like it was happening right there. What the hell kind of thing is that, except an act of the gods? And why the hell would they wanna pick on one of the sweetest things they ever created? Yeah, I ain't been to Church since. They're just plain bastards, is all, and I've got enough of those comin' through my town as it is."

His steps resumed crunching in the dry grass, more loudly as he picked his way down the slope toward her. The woman rose gracefully to her feet, brushing off the knees of her trousers.

"I doubt you can imagine what that did to a little town like this, where everybody knows everybody and their business," he said, drawing abreast of her. "And now, three years on, just when it's all starting to finally scab over, here comes some nosy elf with a big-city accent, snooping around, asking questions about poor June Witwill and generally opening old wounds. This town doesn't need that kinda grief, and the Witwills sure as hell don't. Ma'am, I can't honestly imagine what it is you're after, and I do not care. Speakin' with the full authority of my office, this is me tellin' you to knock it off. Coach leaves for the Rail depot at Saddle Ridge tomorrow at nine sharp. I think you oughta be on it."

"Wish you hadn't followed me, Marshal," she murmured without looking up at him.

He grunted. "Just bet you do. Now, are we gonna have any difficulty over it?"

"Three and a half years ago, in various places across the empire, four girls between the ages of fourteen and nineteen spontaneously combusted." She began pacing in a slow circle around the mossy area, peering at the ground. The swath of green was decorated here and there with tiny stands of *versithorae*, conical flowers in brilliant shades of yellow, orange, and crimson. Elf candles, the human settlers called them. They grew only in the aftermath of fire, where ash nourished the soil. "All four on the same day, and I'd bet my ears at the very same moment. And I should clarify that four is merely the number of cases I've verified so far. I'm almost positive there were others. I met the one girl who lived—she's to start my class this fall."

"Class?" He eyed her up and down, taking in her brown trousers and avuncular vest over a blousy, green shirt. "You're a schoolteacher?"

"Professor," she corrected absently, still circling. "I've found no common thread between them at all, except that each was struck down while she was alone, isolated, outdoors. In Shiver Gulch, a mining town in Calderaan Province, it was a sixteen-year-old who'd been in and out of more trouble than a privateer on shore leave. She was passing through a graveyard on the way to join a few other ne'er-do-wells who were waiting with a bottle of whiskey and a whole *bushel* of glittershrooms."

She straightened, stretching her neck, and met his eyes for the first time. He watched her warily, as he might a large prowling dog of uncertain intentions. Then she resumed her pacing, staring at the moss. "On the outskirts of Madouris, it was a poorly closeted lesbian roaming the backroads to hide from the town bullies. She was struck down as she crossed a footbridge and fell into a creek, which was vaporized on contact. In Lasa Vallas, another frontier town much like this one, it was a studious young lady of good parenting who worked at the local library and volunteered her time at a stable. Loved animals and reading. It hit her as she walked across an open prairie to the nearby elf grove to return a book she'd borrowed from one of the druids."

"Which one survived?" he asked quietly. She glanced up again, noting that the bluster had faded from him entirely, revealing a fairly young man trying to accept responsibility for his whole narrow world, while suddenly under pressures that came from well beyond it.

She came to a halt again in front of the memorial for poor June Witwill, whose faith had not saved her. "It's never the one you'd expect," she whispered. "The unfortunate Miss Witwill was attacked by a demon, Marshal. An extremely high-ranking demon, of a caliber not seen on the mortal plain since the Third Hellwar. It attempted to possess her, but a human body proved a wholly inadequate host, resulting in the destruction of the girl and, luckily, the creature. We know this because the survivor was able to integrate the demon into herself, preserving both."

"You're letting a girl possessed by a *demon* into your class?" he said incredulously.

"The situation is . . . complicated, even just the fairly small slice of it that I understand. The Church and the empire have both been involved in this, but I don't trust either to investigate their own butts using both hands and a mirror, especially not when they begin tripping each other up. So I'm after my own answers."

"Right, well . . . nobody in this town has your answers, Professor Elf. It was crawling with priests and imperial agents for a full year after the incident. If they didn't turn up anything when the scene was fresh, you won't now."

"Ah, but I doubt the investigators thought to ask the Black Wreath."

"The *who*?"

"The Black Wreath," she said patiently. "A cult dedicated to Elilial. They're secretive, mostly masquerading as—"

"I *know* who the Black Wreath are, lady! That's something else you're not gonna find in this town. Business like that goes on in the cities, not out here among ranchers and farmers who don't have *time* for demon worship, even if they have the inclination."

Wordlessly, she pointed upward.

Raising his eyes, the marshal started violently, cursing. The rim of the crater was ringed by figures in hooded, ash-gray robes; there were nine of them, nearly encircling the two below. He snatched up the two wands holstered at his belt, aiming each up at the menacing figures. Beside him, the professor rolled her eyes.

"All right, that's close enough," the marshal snapped, grasping for control of the situation. "We're all neighbors here; nobody needs to get zapped. Let's lose those hoods. Slowly, now."

"This is why I wish you hadn't followed me," said the elf mildly. "Now I have to keep *you* alive, too." He spared her a withering side-long glare.

"Sorry about this, Marshal," said one of the hooded figures, his voice muffled. "Always did like you, but you're in the wrong place at the worst possible time. The elf needs to go."

"You know how tricky it is to ask *exactly* the right questions, make it plain you already know too much when you don't actually know anything?" the professor asked idly, pitching her voice low. "The first two towns had no significant Wreath presence; the third one, I let slip who I was and spooked them into running. I've worked hard on this trap, Marshal, and I have no more leads, so kindly don't screw it up."

"All right, enough!" the marshal shouted, raising both wands higher; he was beginning to look rather frazzled. "Hoods off, hands where I can see them. *Now!*"

Four of the cultists moved, including the speaker, but they reached into their robes, not for their hoods. The marshal cursed and squeezed the switches on both his wands; their muted *clicks* were lost in a tremendous *CRACK* as bolts of lightning sprang from the tips, striking down two of the robed figures. Only two; the two others had pulled wands from their hiding places and returned fire.

Lightning bolts sparked harmlessly against a bubble of blue light a few feet from the two in the crater, prompting obscenities from above.

"*Do* try not to kill them all," said the professor, then bent her legs slightly and leaped fifty feet straight up, somersaulting over the heads of the startled cultists to land gracefully in the tallgrass beyond the depression. She gestured with both hands and two more of them went bowling cowl-over-spurs into the depression, all except for the speaker, who stood at the lip of the crater as if frozen; the rest scattered.

The professor strode unhurriedly after them; by the time the marshal had dragged himself up from below, she had pinned two more down under a mass of what looked like giant spiderwebs and felled a third with another invisible bolt of force. He paused at the rim, aiming both wands at the immobile cultist.

"Leave him be; he's not going anywhere," the elf called over her shoulder from up ahead. "That one seemed most likely to have useful information, so I fixed him in time."

"Fixed him in—" He started to reply, confused, then tore his gaze from the pacified cultist to her, breaking off what he'd been about to say. "Watch out!"

A dozen yards beyond her, the sole remaining robed figure had doubled over, nearly hidden by the waving grass. His robe began to ripple as though blown in a high wind. He let out a low groan, which grew rapidly into an ear-splitting shriek, then with a great ripping of fabric and flesh, seemed to explode, blood splattering the grass around him.

From the ruins of the cultist rose a bronze colossus, draped in scraps of gray cloth, blood, and viscera. Spiny wings sprang from its shoulders; it was proportioned like a gorilla, with stubby legs and hugely powerful arms, and covered in coppery scales that gleamed blindingly in the prairie sun. Lacking a neck, its lump of a head sprouted directly from its torso, with a gaping mouth extending halfway down its chest. Even neckless, it easily stood eight feet tall.

The creature weakly fluttered its wings once, swiveled its whole body back and forth as though looking for something, then fixed its gaze on the professor and emitted a howl that was more of a roar.

"Oh, fuck me," groaned the marshal.

"Hmm," said the professor. "This complicates matters."

Not waiting for any further commentary, he raised both wands and mashed the switches, unleashing blast after blast of lightning directly at the monstrosity. It roared in fury, but gave no sign of falling; the magic bolts left swaths of scorched prairie grass in their wake, but splashed harmlessly across the creature's hide as it charged them. He carried on firing relentlessly—it was the only thing the marshal could think of—until the elf tackled him from the side, pushing them both into the ground.

The earth shook as the monster ran right past them, howling. The marshal froze, the elf's meager weight half on top of him; one of the creature's bronze feet went by so close he could have reached out to grab it. But they were hidden by the tallgrass, for now, the brute stomping and roaring in frustration terrifyingly close by, seeking its lost prey.

It occurred to the marshal that the thing couldn't be very bright. Not that that would help anyone if it went for the town.

"That's a baerzurg," the elf breathed in his ear. "A lesser class of demon, but its skin is quite impervious. You'll only draw its attention with your wands. Stay put a moment."

Then she was gone.

For a tense moment, the only sounds were of the demon's snorting and snuffling, then suddenly the professor's voice came from several feet away.

"Hey there, handsome!" There was another roar and the pounding of heavy feet, followed by a light laugh from the elf. "Oooh, so close! Go on, have another try."

She continued to taunt the creature, leading it progressively farther from the marshal, the Witwill memorial, and the town, which was just visible in the distance. As the sounds of her laughing and the creature's increasingly frustrated yowls drew farther away, the marshal carefully rose to a crouch, removing his hat and peeking up through the upper fronds of the grass. He could barely make out the flicker of movement that was the elf, but the demon continued to stomp back and forth after her, roaring.

"Are you seeing what I'm seeing?"

He cursed and almost threw himself flat again at her voice, which came from just behind his shoulder. She winked at him from inches away.

"But . . . you . . . over there . . ."

"Illusory decoy," she explained. "Now, Marshal, don't lose your head. Anyhow, it looks like we're in luck. Our boy's a slugger, not a caster."

"I think I'm just gonna sit here and wait for everything to make sense again," he said woodenly.

"Oh, relax. Baerzurg are hierarchal; some of the upper castes are quite smart and can use magic, but this one's clearly nothing but muscle. That was all I needed to know."

"That thing looks like it could demolish a building!"

"We'd best not lead him near any buildings then, eh? Watch."

The professor stood and calmly made a lifting motion with her hand. The illusory decoy vanished, and the baerzurg bellowed as it suddenly ascended straight into the air.

"You can come out, Marshal," she called. "It's quite safe."

Slowly, he rose to his feet. The demon hung suspended twenty feet in the air, roaring and swiping at the elf, who stood almost underneath him, well beyond his reach.

"I'll need to concentrate for this bit," she said cheerily, "so kindly busy yourself elsewhere. Perhaps you could round up the rest of our visitors? Here." She handed him a sizable coil of slim, silvery rope, which she had definitely not been holding a moment before.

The marshal did as he was told. At least it was something he understood.

No matter how he steeled himself, each face he uncovered was a punch to the gut. These were his neighbors, in some cases friends. People he was responsible for . . . and they were apocalypse-worshiping demon cultists. Hamlet was a tiny village, hence the name; everyone knew everyone. But he was the marshal, and so gut punches or no, he did his job. Removing their hoods, dragging their bodies into a line, tying their wrists together in preparation to place them under arrest once they woke.

He had to use his jackknife to extract the two under the spider-webs, and even so, they were left covered with a sticky mess that he didn't bother to try removing. There was no need to restrain the two felled by his own wands. Some imperial marshals carried customized wands that could deliver varying degrees of power; some were even amateur enchanters who crafted their own to personal specifications. His were standard imperial issue and cast standard-issue lightning bolts, which were functionally identical to those that came from the sky. A person *could* survive a direct hit from a bolt of lightning, but it was a noteworthy event when it happened. It hadn't happened today.

Just as he began to reach for the hood over the figure still frozen upright at the lip of the crater, a heavy *thump* shook the ground. He spun to behold the professor walking toward him and the smoking body of the baerzurg lying in the grass behind her.

"Don't touch him till I release the spell. He's stuck in a pocket of slow time; even small impacts could damage him quite a bit."

"What's the story with that thing?" He jerked his head at the fallen demon.

"Oh, don't worry, it's thoroughly dead. Burned to a proverbial crisp."

"I thought you said it was invincible."

"Only the skin. Anything will die if you incinerate its internal organs." She grimaced, wiping her hands on her trousers. "Not a very kind way to die, but that's the price you pay for superficial invulnerability. All right, keep a wand out; I don't expect much trouble with this guy, but they've already surprised us once today."

He didn't see her so much as wiggle her fingers at the last cultist, but the man suddenly twitched as though waking from a heavy sleep. "Take her down! They'll—eh?"

That was as far as the confused man got before the elf pointed at him and he went tumbling over backward, unconscious.

The marshal sighed. "Why didn't you just do that in the first place?"

"I like certainty. Let's get him tied up to the rest of them."

She did so, while he removed the man's hood and the scarf wrapped over the lower part of his face. The marshal let out a defeated sigh at beholding the refined features of Jackson Towerwell.

"Ooh, I know him," the elf said, a tone of interest in her voice. "Clerk at the town hall, right? We spoke when I arrived. Perfect guy to have on your side if you're up to shenanigans."

". . . Right."

"Well, then!" She rubbed her hands together. "If you're sure of those knots, let's see what our wayward neighbors have to say for themselves." Leaning forward, she lightly touched Towerwell on the forehead. He started violently and tried to sit upright, succeeding only in entangling himself with the woman next to him. The elf quickly ran down the line, awakening each cultist with a touch.

"Afternoon, Jackson," the marshal said gravely.

". . . Marshal," the clerk replied in the same tone. He managed to look dignified, even sitting in the dirt with his hands bound behind him and being tugged about by the tension on the rope as each of his coconspirators awakened and struggled experimentally. "Well, I'll confess this is a mite embarrassing."

"You're not going to shoot us, are you, Marshal Ross?" asked Marie tremulously, glancing at the two fallen cultists and then back up at him.

"Not if I can at all help it, Miss Upwell, which will be contingent upon whether you choose to make it necessary. Needless to say, it's jail for the lot of you till I can send a scroll to the capital. This is imperial business now."

She burst into tears. The marshal tightened his jaw and kept his face impassive. This was the job. It usually involved drunks and the odd petty thief, not demon cultists, but . . . it was the job.

"Well, there is one bit of good news," Towerwell said with weary joviality. "I meant what I said, Marshal; really didn't like the thought of having to kill you. It sat poorly with all of us, in fact. Disappointing as all this is, I feel a good bit better that we missed that particular chance."

The professor snorted disdainfully, and Towerwell fixed a glare upon her.

"I see your companion doubts my sincerity. Do you think all members of the Wreath are necessarily wicked creatures who love nothing but destruction, girl? You're a fool. We're the last hope for humanity, the few willing to stand against the tyranny of the gods themselves. Would *you* dare to tread a mile in our shoes? A great doom is coming, and when it arrives, you'll wish you'd joined us."

She nudged him in the chest with her boot. "Don't lecture me, you presumptuous tadpole. I've *met* your dark goddess, and frankly she would find you embarrassing. Now, I'll need you to provide some answers concerning those girls your glorious cause casually murdered. So, we're going to play a game called 'First Person to Talk Doesn't Get Burned Alive like June Witwill.'"

"Now, hold it," the marshal snapped, drowning out a few muted exclamations of fear. "These folks are imperial prisoners, *Professor*. Nobody's laying a hand on them till I get backup out here."

"Boy," she said very calmly, "after all we've just been through, surely you don't imagine you can stop me from doing whatever I damn well please?"

He locked his gaze with hers, refusing to back down an inch. The fact was, she was right. But some things were more important than practicality. He had an oath, and a duty, and an agent of the Tiraan Empire did not throw that aside for anything.

"Who are you?" asked Towerwell quietly, peering up at the elf.

She tore her eyes from the marshal's, turning to study the prisoners dispassionately, then smiled. "Well, since we're all going to be such good friends, I suppose there's no harm in you knowing at this point."

So she told them her name.

The marshal took a reflexive step backward, and a new round of struggles and shouts resonated along the row of bound cultists. Jackson Towerwell bared his teeth at the elf in a feral snarl, furiously twitching and shifting his arms, which were still bound behind him.

"By all means, wear yourself out," the elf said dryly. "I have all the time in the world. We will discuss—"

"Wait," said the marshal suddenly, shouldering her aside. "That's not struggling, he's . . ."

Even as he knelt to look more closely at Towerwell, the man convulsed violently, his eyes rolling up behind his lids, and he tumbled over backward, taking Marie down with him. He thrashed in his bonds, beginning to foam at the mouth.

"Oh, *shit*," hissed the professor. "Their hands, Marshal. Grab their hands! Stop them!"

They were too late. All up and down the row, the imprisoned cultists had begun to writhe, a few groaning in agony. Each of them appeared to be suffering some kind of seizure.

The elf produced a gleaming saber from midair and unceremoniously slashed Towerwell loose from the others. She rolled him, still twitching, over onto his front, revealing a small, brass-bound glass tube tucked into his left hand. Upon closer inspection, the marshal saw that one end bore a needle, which was pressed into his opposite wrist.

The elf snatched it out of his grasp, but the damage was done. Already, Towerwell had fallen still, and the others were faltering fast. The marshal dashed around behind them, seeing the same little needle-tubes pressed into each of their wrists.

"What do we do?" he shouted. "What can we do?"

"Nothing." Her voice was like ice. She straightened slowly, glaring down at the glass tube clutched in her hand. "There are half a dozen poisons this might have been, and I don't have antidotes for any of them."

He cursed helplessly, clutching Marie Upwell by her shoulders as she twitched weakly, foam dribbling from her perfect lips, then finally went still. He held her, numb, for a few long moments, before lowering her gently to the ground alongside the others. Not one of them still breathed.

"What is that?" he asked, surprised by the calm in his voice.

"It's called a hypodermic syringe. One of the new dwarven inventions. Made for delivering medicine; it's held in the tube here, then you press the needle into someone's skin and push the plunger, which sends the fluid right into the bloodstream. They must've had them up their sleeves, above where you'd check to tie the wrists. Rather ingenious, really."

He dropped his gaze to Marie's face. It was an awful sight, her cheeks flecked with foam, eyes rolled up into her skull, mouth twisted in agony. Carefully, he pulled the hood of her robe out from under her head and draped it over her face, then began moving down the line, doing the same for each of them. He didn't look up from his task as he spoke.

"Was it true, what you said? You're really her? Arachne Tellwyrn?"

"You're really *she*," she corrected, "and yeah, I am. For all the good my infamy did here." She threw the syringe to the ground in disgust. "Congratulations, Marshal, you're now a member of a very elite group who've seen the great Professor Tellwyrn made a fool of. Fewer than a dozen have joined in the last century. In fact, I think you may be the only one currently alive."

She knelt and, with surprising gentleness, draped Jackson Towerwell's hood over his face, just as the marshal reached the other end of the line.

Finding himself without something immediately to do, he simply stood there, staring at her. She sighed heavily, knuckling the small of her back, and turned her head toward the distant town.

"I just . . . I don't believe it. Demon worshipers, in my town."

"That's not so shocking," she said dismissively. "The Black Wreath is everywhere. Mostly just folks looking to spice up their lives with a bit of the illicit occult, and a couple of true believers to keep them motivated. No, what's disturbing is that *this* circle had a suicide summoner and shiny new tech from the dwarven kingdoms on hand, and every one of them had the will to end it rather than risk being made to talk. Usually, you can count on a few cowards not to realize which is the easier way out. This is *not* what I expected from a small group of cultists in some backwater town. I must have been very close . . ." She sighed again, then shook herself. "Well. I'm staying at the Willowbranch Inn."

"Oh," he said numbly. "Yes. Right. I'll need to get a statement from you, after I . . . do something with . . ." He trailed off, sweeping his gaze across the row of dead cultists, who minutes before had been friends and neighbors he had sworn to protect.

"Statements, sure. Look, I've just been embarrassingly thwarted and seen months of investigation go up in smoke. I now have to start over from scratch, as if I have the bloody time for it, which means *hoping* another lead into another grisly death will surface. I owe it to my faculty not to come home this frustrated; they've enough stress on their shoulders with the semester starting in two weeks. As such, I intend to get thoroughly drunk and laid before catching my coach in the morning. Find my room before ten o'clock tonight if you wish to be part of any of that."

With that, she walked away, leaving the imperial marshal sitting amid the carnage left in her wake.

CHAPTER 1

Glad as she was to be off the caravan, Trissiny stepped into a scene of such chaos that she froze, struggling to take it all in. The Rail station at Calderaas was bigger than the entire abbey back home, but vastly open and apparently made of *glass*. She'd have thought the metal framework which supported it was some kind of empty cage, except that rain was pounding on it at the moment. Worse, the huge station was crammed with people—shouting people, shoving people, and people dressed in a variety of costumes such as she had never seen. A mere majority of them were even human.

She inhaled deeply, trying to orient herself. The Hand of Avei would not be paralyzed by indecision, nor peer about stupidly like some sort of bumpkin just in from the sticks. Truthfully, that might be a fair description, and Trissiny had little in the way of personal ego, but she was terrified of being an embarrassment to her goddess. She could do this.

Behind her, someone cleared his throat loudly. Blushing, she mumbled an apology and quickly lugged herself and her trunk out of the path so everyone else could leave the caravan. Apparently, the Hand of Avei *could* freeze like a spooked rabbit and hold up traffic.

Judging by the level of pushing and general rudeness going on around her, that more gentle reminder had been very special treatment. Well, even if people didn't know the significance of the silver finish on her armor, it was still recognizably a Silver Legion uniform; few would seek to irritate her. She took up a position to the side of the caravan steps, out of everyone's way, and fished out her travel itinerary from her belt pouch to look it over again. Not that she hadn't memorized the thing long since, and anyway, it wasn't that complicated, but it was a tiny bit of familiarity.

People back home weren't all that homogenous, or so she'd thought. Viridill had been settled by humans from every part of the empire, and even today was home to humans of every color, shape, and description. But, with the exception of the odd elven traveler and the lizardfolk up in the mountains, they *were* all humans and mostly adorned themselves in the same humble style. The people here in the station were a cross section of the entire empire, or so it seemed to her; olive-skinned Tiraan predominated, unsurprisingly, but she saw dark-complexioned Westerners and a few Stalweiss as pale as herself. Plus others who might have been from anywhere. And their attire was *mostly* familiar, but the costumes of cultures she'd never heard of were on display as well.

However they were dressed, the humans couldn't command most of Trissiny's attention. There were more elves than she'd ever imagined seeing in one place, mostly keeping to themselves and moving within small pockets in the crowd, as if their neighbors were reluctant to touch them, even by accident. Dwarves she knew only by description, but she recognized more than a handful here. A couple of very small people passing by on a goat-pulled cart had to be gnomes. Through gaps in the crowd, Trissiny glimpsed a small group of lizardfolk seated against one wall, a battered hat set in front of them. That sight was troubling; she'd rarely dealt with the lizardfolk back home, but she thought of them as too proud to beg.

She was gathering stares of her own, as well; none hostile, but many were in awe and some rather fearful. Apparently, quite a few people in Calderaas *did* know what silver armor meant. There might even be some present who could sense her innate divine magic. Trissiny schooled her expression, tucked away her itinerary, and set off in search of Platform Ten. There hadn't been a paladin of Avei in thirty years, and she surely hadn't been called upon now to make a spectacle of herself in the Rail station.

Five minutes later, she had to give up and reorient herself again. The layout of the station was confusing; platforms were interspersed with Rail lines that could only be reached by collections of wrought-iron footbridges, which arched over the Rails themselves. Her trunk had a handle and wheels, which she'd thought a great luxury when it was first given to her, but that was before she'd had to drag it up and down half a dozen sets of stairs. The platforms weren't labeled in the most helpful manner, either. She ultimately had to stop in the middle of one of the footbridges and crane her neck around to find the signs, which revealed she had been going in the wrong direction. With a sigh, Trissiny turned back and made her up-and-down way, gritting her teeth against the constant bumping of her trunk, to Platform Ten.

She was a good twenty minutes early to catch her next caravan, but made certain to consult the board posted by the stairs to verify that this would be the one going to Last Rock. With little else to do but wait, she tucked herself as out of the way as she could on the bustling platform and fell back to studying her environment.

Between her general nervousness, the roiling in her stomach from the Rail ride she'd just escaped, and the anticipation of her next one, people-watching was all she had the inner strength to do right now. Riding the Rails was one of the most romanticized experiences of the modern age; in practice, she found it rather like being sealed inside a barrel and rolled down a hill.

"Hey, Blondie! Yeah, you, girlie. I'm talkin' to you!"

It took a couple of repetitions for Trissiny to realize she was being addressed. No one in her life had ever spoken to her that way, and since she had gained her sword and armor, most people who possessed any sense would not have dared.

The man, grinning and eying her up and down, approached in a manner that nearly made her reach for her sword. He was garbed like something out of a penny novel, all dust-stained denim and flannel, with snakeskin boots and a ten-gallon hat, which he tipped at her. "Mighty pleased to meet you, missy," he said in a prairie drawl, his grin becoming an outright leer. "If you got a bit before your car comes, mebbe we can find a shady spot to have a drink? My treat."

Trissiny was too astonished by the sheer effrontery to react as she otherwise might. That bought her a moment to reconsider her first impulse; thrashing this fool would almost certainly lead to trouble, no matter how much he deserved it. At the very least, she'd miss her caravan.

"No, thank you," she replied stiffly. Was this guy *serious*? As he leaned in close enough for her to smell the whiskey on his breath, Trissiny reminded herself forcefully that she couldn't just punch men who lacked respect.

"Aw, don't be like that, darlin'. Why, I bet you'll find me the best company you ever—oof!"

A second cowboy, dressed similarly and strongly resembling her admirer in the face, shouldered him roughly aside, then turned to her and tugged the brim of his hat. "My apologies, ma'am. My brother ain't been off the ranch in half a year, an' sometimes he forgets he wasn't raised by wolves." He cut off the protest forming on the first man's face by swatting him upside the back of the head, forcing him to catch his flying hat. "Won't happen again. Scuze us."

"Turn loose a' me, Ezekiel!" the first cowboy said furiously as his brother grabbed him by the arm and began dragging him toward the nearest set of steps. "I was just havin' some—"

"You shut the hell up. Land's sakes, boy, if you gotta be embarrassing, couldja at *least* not be suicidal? Don't you know a paladin when you see one? You ain't *that* shitheaded!"

They were halfway up the footbridge, but their loud conversation remained clearly audible on Platform Ten. "Paladin? That ain't no paladin, dumbass. That girl ain't more'n fifteen."

"Jebediah Jenkins, if I weren't such a good brother, I'd send you back over there to finish what you started, an' spare myself the trouble of whuppin' your ass for botherin' a girl you think is *fifteen*!"

Trissiny would have liked very much to sink into the platform and vanish. Or maybe kick a certain pair of cowboys in front of an oncoming caravan, but mostly the first thing. The brothers Jenkins were acquiring stares, which were quickly transferred to herself as people discerned the source of their quarrel. Against her will, her cheeks heated. Hopefully the onlookers would take it for righteous anger, selflessly suppressed. Yeah, and if hopes were coins, Avei would have a temple in every hamlet in the empire.

A well-dressed man with the silver gryphon badge of an imperial agent pinned to the breast of his coat, and another decorating his hat, shouldered quickly through the crowd, moving purposefully in the direction of the loud brothers. His wand remained holstered, though he held a hand conspicuously near it and kept his gaze fixed on the two cowboys. He paused before Trissiny to tilt his hat respectfully. "Blessings, ma'am."

"And to you, Sheriff," she replied gratefully, inclining her head. At least someone took her seriously without having to taste her blade. She did *not* look fifteen!

He proceeded after his quarry, and she fixed her gaze stiffly on a point above everyone's head. It was funny how she could *tell* people were whispering about her, despite the ambient noise in the station.

And there she stood, for fifteen interminable minutes, while the caravans roared by on their Rails and people gazed curiously at her, often pausing their own business to do so, as if she were some kind of exhibit. Trissiny practiced her situational awareness, keeping her gaze rigidly fixed on empty space but trying to maintain knowledge of her surroundings through peripheral vision. It was the only thing she could think to do, aside from weltering in her own discomfort.

There were too many people, too little that was familiar. Trissiny had never experienced such a crowd, so many curious stares—and the glass and iron surroundings were so alien compared to the ancient stone temples, and even more ancient round hills, of her home. But she was a *paladin*, and could not let herself be swayed by mere discomfort. This was her duty, even if she didn't understand why.

She was first to move when the caravan slowed to a stop next to Platform Ten. The Rail itself, a single raised line on spokes—like a banister—that extended into the distance in both directions, began to hum and glow arcane blue with the caravan's approach. The train that arrived to take her to Last Rock had eight passenger cars, twice the size of the one that had brought her here. They looked the same, though—tiny bits of glass and steel looking like a single squared tube with so many in a line. This caravan also had four larger, boxy cargo wagons affixed after the passenger cars, and another angular enchanter's post behind that to match the one at the front. She wondered if the added weight meant it needed a second enchanter to keep it going.

Trissiny edged back from the Rail with the other passengers as lightning sparked along the rim of the platform with the energy of the caravan halting itself. The tiny hairs on her arms and the back of her neck stood upright.

She stood back to let the passengers disembark, most of them looking as stiff and disoriented as she had after her previous Rail ride, then moved quickly to claim her seat in the frontmost car, just behind the enchanter's post. Nobody complained or tried to slip in ahead of her. Trissiny supposed it was all right to benefit from a healthy respect for paladins, as long as she wasn't intimidating people on purpose. If folks thought the Hand of Avei might smite them for pushing in line ahead of her, well, there wasn't much she could do about that.

She stowed her trunk under the seat as she'd been shown on the last caravan, strapping it in securely, then unslung her shield and laid it on the bench beside her, before taking her seat. This car could have been a duplicate of the other, except that she had it to herself. The padded benches were wide enough to seat three; she took the one facing the front. Riding the Rails was rough enough without doing it facing backward.

It was like being in a little glass bubble, and she enjoyed the solitude after the crowded platform. People weren't hurrying to join her, but that would probably only last until someone came along who hadn't seen the paladin duck in here. She enjoyed the breather while it lasted, literally. Proper breathing was essential to both combat form and meditation, and Trissiny had been storing her gathering tension in her chest. She took advantage of the time to center herself with a breathing exercise. Slow and deep, in and out . . .

At least she'd regained enough calm not to be overly perturbed when a man entered her car, ducking his head to squeeze sideways through the low hatch.

"Good day!" he said cheerily, straightening. He was an older gentleman, well dressed and very round about the middle, with a jowly face accentuated by bushy, steel-colored sideburns. "Ah, a legionnaire! Excellent, I was just wondering why a pretty girl was sitting alone in a car. Usually the lads would be all over you. Don't mind if I share, do you? It's filling up back there, and a man of my great physical fitness is less welcome where the seats must be squeezed into." He chortled, patting his plump belly.

"The caravan is open," she said politely, forcing a smile.

"Many thanks, my dear, many thanks." He grunted as he lowered himself onto the bench opposite her, sliding over so as to grip the handhold bolted to the wall of the caravan. "Whoof! As often as I ride these things, you'd think I'd grow accustomed to the acrobatics it takes getting in and out of them. Heywood Paxton, imperial surveyor." He extended a hand to her. "I'm the emperor's eyes on the frontier! Of course, the emperor has more eyes than a nest of spiders, and do please remind me of that if I start to sound like I think I'm important." His pale eyes twinkled with good humor.

"Trissiny Avelea," she replied, shaking his hand. His eyes flicked over her and she tensed, but it was nothing like the gaze Jebediah Jenkins had dragged across her. In fact, Mr. Paxton seemed to be looking at her armor, not her body; she saw the moment when he realized it was silver rather than bronze.

"Omnu's breath," he exclaimed, settling back in his own seat and regarding her wide-eyed. "Forgive me if I'm being impertinent, Ms. Avelea, but . . . would you be the paladin? The new one?"

"I am." She forced a small smile. At least he knew the proper way to address a Sister of Avei. He was the first man she'd met since leaving home who did.

"Bless my old soul!" he enthused. "I'd heard that Avei had finally called a paladin, but . . . Well, this is a rare privilege, ma'am! An honor, it truly is. Wait'll I tell the grandchildren I rode the Rail with a paladin!" He laughed aloud. "Now, you be sure to tell me if I'm bothering you, Ms. Avelea. I do tend to let the old mouth run away with me sometimes."

"I don't mind," she replied, and found that she meant it.

Trissiny was not used to men. Obviously, she'd been around them before; as the Sisters of Avei were not a cloistered order. But briefly or at a distance, usually, and those men who weren't shy about being around Sisters had been strongly encouraged to keep away from the novices. Still, Heywood Paxton was one of the least menacing individuals she'd ever met.

"And would you be on a quest, then?" he asked enthusiastically. "Not that you need pay any mind to old me, of course! I shall gladly shove off if told to. But I'm heading out to Sarasio on the emperor's business, and I should be glad of the company, I don't mind telling you. If there's any place that could benefit from a taste of Avei's fist, that's it for sure."

"No," she said with some hesitation, and a small twinge of guilt. "Actually, I'm . . . going to college. At least for now; that was the goddess's command. I'm sure she has good reason."

Why did she feel the need to explain herself to this stranger? It wasn't his business; it wasn't even hers. If Avei chose to send her paladin to university rather than to the battlefield, well, she was entitled. No matter how chafed Trissiny was at what felt like a waste of her calling.

"Goodness me, to college? This line is heading straight out of the civilized territories! Nothing but the Golden Sea, tribes of wild elves, and a few frontier towns where we're . . . Ohhh." His expression cleared and he nodded sagely. "Last Rock, then?"

"Yes, to Professor Tellwyrn's University. You've heard of it?"

"Indeed I have, Ms. Avelea, indeed I have. You don't last long in my line of work without knowing the biggest players of the great game. Omnu's breath, I should've put that together the moment I noticed you in that armor. My brains are getting as droopy as my jowls, I declare." He grinned at her with such genuine good humor that she had to smile back.

A sharp retort like the crack of a whip resonated through their little chamber, and the caravan lurched. Then, it began smoothly moving forward; Trissiny found herself pressed back into her seat, while Mr. Paxton had to cling to the handlebar and surreptitiously braced his leg against the bench beside her to keep from being poured out of his.

"My goodness, they don't give us much time to get settled, do they?" he said cheerily.

It was only moments before the acceleration finally leveled off. The surveyor grunted, settling himself back into his seat, now that he didn't have to brace himself into it. "Whew! Every trip an adventure. You know, the Rail cars that service the interior provinces have buckled belts on each seat for passengers to strap themselves in. It seems there's no budget for upgrading old frontier equipment just yet."

Trissiny nodded, unsure whether she would prefer that. It would be nice not to be tossed around, but she wasn't at all certain she'd care to be strapped in, either.

"Oh, here comes the wide arc around Mirror Lakes," Mr. Paxton said, peering out the window. "Best brace yourself, Ms. Avelea, we're going to—"

And then the caravan curved so sharply to the right that its left wall became the new de facto floor; Paxton was tossed against it with a grunt. Only Trissiny's trained reflexes saved her from a pummeling. Spinning on the bench, she stuck one foot against the wall and the other on the seat opposite, grabbing her shield as it tried to fly across the car.

"Almost!" her fellow traveler cried with a grin. "More than a dozen trips on this line; one day I'll have that timing down exactly." She grinned back. The man's good humor really was infectious.

The car leveled out so abruptly that they were both tossed back in the opposite direction. Paxton slid along his bench, this time very nearly tumbling to the floor; Trissiny managed to pivot in midair, never releasing her hold on her shield, again bracing herself with a foot against the opposite seat.

They blinked and stared at each other, both pale, and then at her boot, which had struck down directly between his legs on the edge of the bench. Had he slid six inches farther, he'd have come to grief on her greave.

"I'm sorry!" she blurted, quickly folding herself back into her own bench.

"Hah, no harm done," he reassured her, pulling a handkerchief from his waistcoat pocket and mopping his face. "Though that's a nearer miss than I usually have!"

"Are they always this bad?"

"Well, depends on the Rail you ride. They try to lay them in the straightest lines possible, but there are some things that cannot be carved through. It's when the Rail has to dodge obstacles that we have trouble! But that's the price we pay for speed. You know, when I first started out in the emperor's service, the journey from Calderaas to Last Rock would have been weeks. Now, we should be there within another five minutes, and I'll be safely at Sarasio not more than fifteen after that."

"I believe I like that idea of belted seats very much, the more I think about it," Trissiny said, shifting on the bench seat. "Why didn't they put those in the caravans in the first place?"

"Ah! You see, the enchantments that make these beauties run are still newfangled enough that much of the older generation doesn't trust them, my dear. When this caravan was built, there was nobody to ride it but soldiers, imperial agents, and adventurers heading to the frontier. You know, the sort of folk who aren't apt to put up a fuss about their safety or comfort." He edged toward the opposite wall, getting a good grip on the handlebar and bracing both legs against Trissiny's bench. "Common folks riding the Rails is a pretty new event, considering, and few of them take these outer lines." He glanced out the window and then renewed his grip on the seat. "You'll want to brace yourself, Ms. Avelea. We're coming up on the worst stretch of this particular journey."

She slid her shield against the wall opposite him, sat down on it, gripped the bar, and placed a foot against the far bench. Not a moment too soon; the caravan changed course with a wrench that drew a grunt from her, even as it flattened Mr. Paxton against the other wall of the car.

What followed was even worse than her first trip down from the mountainous territory of Viridill. The Rail dodged back and forth around apparent obstacles, yanking them first one way and then the other before they had time to compensate. She couldn't spare the attention to try to study the passing scenery, keeping her arms and legs constantly tense against the forces seeking to toss her about the car. Paxton kept his grip on his handlebar, though at one point lost his seat and was flung full-length across the bench, and only recovered his position upon being shoved back into it. Trissiny quickly lost track of the passage of time; her arms and legs were growing sore, and even her jaw began to ache from the effort of holding it closed. Letting it bounce was a sure way to bite off a chunk of her tongue. At least she was managing, thanks to years of physical training; the longer this went on, the more worried she became about the much older and less in shape Mr. Paxton.

As suddenly as the chaos had begun, it ended. The caravan sailed along in near silence and perfect balance, its two shaken passengers blinking at each other.

"Is it over?" she asked uncertainly.

"For the moment," he replied, heaving himself back onto the bench with a grunt; he'd not managed to avoid a tumble to the floor in the last few moments. "Whew! They really should post warnings. That's one of the worst stretches in the entire Rail network, you know. Not much else is even half so bad." He shifted about on his seat, straightening his rumpled clothes.

"What exactly were we dodging around?" She resettled herself, stretching tensed muscles. Trissiny felt a moment of envy for her trunk, safely lashed in below her seat.

"Why, that's the Green Belt, so they call it. It's a whole network of elven groves, separated by fairly small stretches of open grassland. They've been there since long before the empire." He chuckled, dabbing sweat from his face again. "So, when the first surveyors came to find a route for the Rail, they ran into ill luck. Oh, the elves were very polite, as they always are, but dead set against letting the Rail come through any of their woodland. Finally, one poor fool lost patience and told them it would have to be done whether they liked it or not." He laughed aloud, shaking his head. "As I heard it, they politely told him to invite the emperor to try it."

"I'm a little surprised he didn't," she replied. "The empire conquered every other human nation on the continent, after all. Aren't elves a bit . . . primitive?"

"Well, yes and no!" He smiled broadly, clearly enjoying his role as storyteller. "They're not primitive in the sense that they lack magic and sophistication of their own; they just choose to live a little closer to nature than we do. It's been a long time since imperial agents chose to mistake the one for the other. For all our new magics and enchantments, the elves are something the empire does not care to provoke, particularly after that debacle with the Cobalt Dawn tribe some years back. Makes for a ghastly muddle, with them living in their own enclaves all across imperial territory. The surveyors finally chose to mark off the elven provinces as 'reserves,' and leave 'em alone."

"Hm." Absently, she ran a hand along the edge of her shield, pondering. "I seldom met any back home, and then only one or two at a time. They seemed rather standoffish, as a rule . . ."

"Anybody'll act different traveling in foreign lands than they would at home, surrounded by kinsmen."

"Professor Tellwyrn is an elf," Trissiny mused.

"That she is!" Paxton nodded, grinning. "An old one, and one of the most notorious people alive of any race. Not had the pleasure of meeting her myself, and for that I can't decide if I'm grateful or disappointed." His eyes shifted to the window and, as before, he braced himself, warning her what was coming even before he spoke. "Ah, we're coming up on the last stretch of our run, Ms. Avelea. Hold tight now!"

She swiftly followed his instruction, but it was not nearly as bad as before. The Rail curved in another long sweep to her right, but this one much more shallow. Trissiny got a good grip on her handle and had no trouble staying seated, though the force tried to tug her back across the bench.

"If you crane your neck a bit, Ms. Avelea, you can see your destination! I recommend it; Last Rock is quite a sight from a distance."

Indeed it was. She had to press her cheek to the glass to manage, but the view was worth it. They were long past the hilly region surrounding Calderaas, and even the elven forests; here was low, rolling scrubland, fading before her eyes into the Golden Sea up ahead, the huge and very magical stretch of prairie that occupied the heart of the continent. The empire had encircled it entirely, but the Golden Sea was much larger within than without; some theorized one could travel into it forever, and never reach the other side. It was a territory that could not truly be explored, much less conquered, but the emperor did the best he could, establishing a perimeter of forts and settlements along its frontier. One of these was the tiny town of Last Rock.

The town itself was a small cluster of buildings dwarfed by the mountain from which it drew its name; rising straight up from the plain with not so much as a hill within sight, the rock itself was tall enough to be taken seriously in most mountain ranges and seemed utterly colossal in its flat environs. Wedge-shaped, it formed a rising prow, cutting into the Golden Sea itself, falling sharply in rocky cliffs from its highest edges, but sloping up gently from the other side, in an incline that was no steeper than the average staircase. It resembled a long, narrow plateau tilted up with one edge sunk into the ground.

Now, a path ran from the town of Last Rock up toward its peak, and the upper quarter of the mountain was covered with the spires and terraces of the University.

Her home for the next four years. For some reason.

Trissiny eased back into her seat, against the force of the curve. They had already drawn too close for her to get a solid look at anything, and she didn't care to look like an overeager child with her face mashed against the glass.

"Not bad, is it?" her seatmate said with a grin. "Ah, the things there are to see along this frontier. And all over the empire, for that matter . . . Well, no rush. I expect you of all people will become plenty acquainted with it in time."

"I expect so," she murmured. As the curve of the Rail leveled out, she slid along her bench away from him, gripped her shield in one hand, and braced both feet against the seat opposite. As if on cue, the caravan decelerated sharply, seeking to pitch her face-first against the front wall.

Trissiny didn't let out her breath until the caravan finally came to a full stop with a muted squeal. Paxton sighed in unison with her, again straightening his coat. "Well, I believe this is your stop, ma'am. May I just say again that it has been an honor."

"I appreciate your company," she replied, this time with a genuine smile. "And the information."

"Oh, pishposh, just an old man's ramblings about all the things he's seen. Trust me, you'd find it much less interesting if you had to endure it more than once."

She bent to unfasten her trunk and pulled it out from under the seat, exchanging a grin with him one more time as she slung her shield onto her back.

"Still . . . it was a much better journey than the last one—the Rail line down from Viridill is a lot more . . . vertical. May I offer you a blessing, Mr. Paxton?"

His grin vanished at once into a nearly awestruck expression. "Oh! Well, that is . . . If—if you feel it's . . . I mean, I'd be honored."

Smiling, Trissiny reached across the narrow compartment to place a hand on his brow, not minding the sweat in his hair. A soft golden glow rose about them, seemingly from the air itself; she felt her own aches washing away in proximity to the divine power, though it was merely being channeled through her, and into the man beneath her palm.

"Justice be upon you, friend," she intoned softly, hearing the resonance in her voice of the goddess echoing, "and Avei watch your path."

Trissiny let her hand fall, enjoying the serenity that always came in the aftermath of calling on Avei. Heywood Paxton's face held an expression of almost childlike wonder.

"I . . . I swear you took ten years off me. Ms. Avelea, I don't know how to . . ."

"Just be as kind to the next person you travel with, as well," she replied.

"Oh, that I shall. This has been a real gift, ma'am . . . A very rare privilege . ." He trailed off, seeming at a loss for words for once.

With a final smile for him, Trissiny pushed open the compartment door and stepped out onto the platform in Last Rock.

CHAPTER 2

Once again, she landed in chaos.

Trissiny's mental picture of a frontier town admittedly came from the few comics and cheap novels that slipped past the abbey's defenses; she should hardly have been surprised to find that Last Rock was not a single dusty street lined with wooden buildings. Cobblestone streets fanned out from the Rail platform, framing solid and quite elegant structures of well-dressed stone that wouldn't have looked out of place in a medieval village. Really, that only made sense, positioned as the town was at the base of a mountain with no trees in sight.

She barely had a chance to appreciate the town, however, as a roar of pandemonium had gone up as soon as she stepped off the caravan. The streets and the edges of the platform were thronged with townsfolk apparently in their church-day best, cheering and applauding as though greeting victorious soldiers just back from the front lines. Somewhere nearby, barely visible through gaps in the crowd, an enthusiastic but clearly unpracticed brass band struck up a sprightly tune. Colorful streamers and buntings were draped everywhere, wreaths hung from darkened streetlamps, and strung across the main avenue directly ahead of her was a huge banner reading:

WELCOME, FRESHMEN!

And below that, a slightly larger one read:

WELCOME BACK, ASSHOLES!

That was troubling. Not just the needless vulgarity so prominently displayed, but . . . Was that how the townsfolk felt about the University students? Then why were they *cheering*?

Before she'd decided how to react to all this, a door was flung open two cars behind her and a boy came staggering out. Trissiny gathered only an impression of dark, tousled hair and a long black coat before he stumbled to his knees and was loudly, violently sick. At this, the cheering on all sides intensified.

She scowled, letting go of her trunk and turning toward the poor boy. Riding the Rails the first time without the benefit of a lot of physical training must have been a nightmarish experience; even she would have come out of the Green Belt bruised if it had not been for Mr. Paxton's warnings. And it was *not* right for people to treat someone's misfortunes as entertainment.

A second young man, casually dressed and with a very dark complexion, had emerged from the same car and now knelt by his fallen companion, ignoring the crowd. Trissiny hesitated; if she were in that situation, she'd rather people gave her space and not acknowledge her discomfort so publicly . . . Avei expected her to render aid wherever it was needed, but Trissiny was not a healer by calling. Divine magic had healing power, yes, but medical expertise was another—

"You there! You, girl, in the armor!"

Warily, she twisted back the other way in time to see an old woman in a black gown—nearly a century out of fashion— approaching her directly, and as fast as she could manage while leaning on two canes.

"You're that paladin, right?" The old woman grinned broadly, and Trissiny forced herself not to flinch; the woman's teeth, those that remained, were as brown as old wood. "Paladin of Avei. Finally the gods are sending us a message again, yeah? Finally the paladins are coming back, and they're both coming here! That's you, right?"

"I am the Hand of Avei," Trissiny said carefully, having to pitch her voice a little louder than she would have liked to be audible over the crowd. Several of the closest bystanders immediately cheered even more loudly at her; nobody offered up any of the rude commentary they'd thrown at the boy who'd lost his lunch. She glanced over at him; he was standing, weakly, with his friend's arm about his shoulders, and the pair were being pressed in upon by several of the locals carrying small trays. More detail than that she didn't manage to catch before the old woman in front of her let out a loud crow like a cockerel.

"I knew it!" she chortled, thumping one of her canes against the stone platform. "It's about time, is all! Yes, time for the gods to send someone to straighten out that nest of iniquity and vice up there on the hill. Elves and wizards and perverts, the lot of 'em! You'll fix 'em good, won't ya, paladin? Eh?"

"Ah . . ." Trissiny glanced around again. What exactly did this woman think paladins were? Over a dozen pairs of eager eyes were upon her; she was surrounded by grins. At least they were all ogling her and not the sick boy now.

"Oh, Mabel, give the poor girl a moment to get her boots on the ground before you start preaching," said a new voice in a throaty purr that really seemed too soft to carry as well as it did over the noise. Trissiny spun again and found herself almost nose-to-nose with a strikingly pretty black-haired woman. Only as an afterthought did she realize it was an elf.

Weren't elves all blond? Trissiny hadn't met many and had never been this close to one; she decided to keep her ignorance to herself. This woman was of slender build, her eyes were on the large side and her features rather pointed, but not enough to seem out of place on a human face. Trissiny herself had some of those traits. Only the long, tapered ears poking up through her hair marked the elf for certain.

"Hussy!" screeched the old woman, clobbering the elf with a cane, to no effect. Apparently, there wasn't much strength in those bony arms. "Freak! Harlot! Painted trollop! I know what you get up to, over in the taverns! Subhuman thing from Elilial's bosom! You get away from that girl. She's a good girl, she is! And you!" Trissiny jerked back as a cane was pointed directly into her face. "You smite this heathen slattern! She's of the Dark Lady's own stock, she is! Do yer duty, girl!"

"I see you've met my fan club," said the elf airily, ignoring repeated blows from the cane. "It's such a pleasure to meet you at last, Trissiny. Welcome to Last Rock. I have something here I think you'll like." Smiling disarmingly, she produced a small, flattish wooden box from within her coat and opened it; a golden pendant formed in the eagle symbol of Avei rested upon black velvet within.

"Do I know you?" Trissiny asked loudly, resisting the urge to grip her sword. Symbol of her faith or no, something about this woman set her on edge; she smiled just like that oily man who sold the abbey spare parts and building materials.

"I know *you*, my dear, which will do for a start. Everyone knows about the new paladins joining the student body this year. I'm just a simple enchanter and purveyor of magical trinkets, and purely honored to make your acquaintance. I'd like you to have this as a gift, from me, at no charge." Smiling broadly, she pressed the box forward again, then had to jerk it back as the crone tried to swat it out of her hands.

CRACK!

Even the band faltered. Townspeople who'd been pressing ever closer to her scuttled back, revealing a man in denim and flannel, with a wand pointed skyward and—oh, thank Avei—a silver gryphon badge pinned to his shirt. In the confusion, she hadn't even seen the lightning bolt, but the tip of his wand still smoked faintly.

"Okay, folks, that'll do. Show's over. Let's all take a step back before I have to feel disappointed in somebody."

"Sheriff," Trissiny said desperately, cocking a head at her two admirers. Tugging the broad brim of his hat to her, he ambled over.

"Omnu's breath, you two, were you raised in a barn? Do we have to go through this *every* year?"

"I was raised in a tree," said the elf with a grin, once more pushing the box toward Trissiny. "And unless it's suddenly illegal to talk to paladins, nobody's doing anything wrong here. Ms. Avelea, here. Please take this."

"Don't you pull that attitude on me, Master Samuel Sanders!" squawked the old woman, brandishing a cane. "Just because you've got a big fancy badge now doesn't mean you don't have to respect your elders! And taking a god's name in vain, for *shame*! I know your poor mother, Omnu rest her soul, raised you better than that."

"Well, you've caught me dead to rights, Miz Cratchley," the sheriff said easily. "It'd serve me right if you went and wrote a letter to the editor about my deplorable behavior right this minute."

"You see if I don't, you young hellion!" She waved the cane at him once more, then began the complicated process of turning around and ambling off, still shrilly complaining. "Young people these days. *No* respect. None! In my day, we knew how to pay respect to the gods, yes sir. And to our elders!"

"Welp, that takes care of the one I'd feel bad about shootin'." He raised an eyebrow at the elf, who fluttered her eyelashes at him.

"All right, all right, keep it in your pants, Sam. Trissiny, if you'd just—"

"No, thank you," she said firmly. "I don't need jewelry. Of any kind."

"Oh, but I know what a young adventurer needs! Trust me, I deal only in the most magical of—"

"That will *do*, Prin," said the sheriff, all humor gone from his voice. "She'll be here all year. You can bide your time and make a pest of yourself when the poor girl's had a chance to settle in. Move along."

The elf closed her box with a loud *snap*. For just a moment she glared daggers at Sanders, then turned an amiable grin on Trissiny. "Well, the man's not wrong. It's wonderful to have you in town, Trissiny. I look *forward* to seeing you again." Bowing, she backed away into the crowd.

"Thank you," she said with feeling. The sheriff smiled at her.

"Not at all, ma'am, that's why they pay me the big bucks. Can I offer you an escort past the town?"

"I appreciate your help," she said a little stiffly, "but I don't require any man's protection."

"I am well aware that you don't, ma'am, but there's more to life than what a body requires. I thought you might like a little protection anyway. See that?" He cocked a finger at the crowd where the two boys had been moments ago. They were gone now, either to medical care or because the fallen one had recovered enough to escape the crowd. In their place stood half a dozen well-dressed people carrying trays of snacks, toys, and baubles, all eyeing her hungrily. "My beloved constituency. Good folks, as a rule, but you should know up front that they view you and the rest of the students as walking coin purses. They'll leave you alone if you're with me, but if you'd rather not . . ." He shrugged. "You can always beat 'em back with your sword, I guess, but then we'll have to have an entirely different kind of conversation."

Abruptly, the fine hairs along Trissiny's arms stood on end; her scalp tingled distractingly. Then, with an earsplitting crack of arcane energy, the caravan behind her began moving along the Rail. Its acceleration was a frightening thing to behold; it was over the horizon in seconds. How had she survived riding that wretched thing? How did anyone?

"When you put it that way," she said carefully, bending to grasp the handle of her trunk, "I think I would appreciate an escort."

"I live to serve. Shall we?"

The sheriff was as good as his word, conducting her politely through the town all the way to the base of the mountain and wishing her good luck with the semester. From there, the mountain itself loomed above her.

Trissiny stared at it, at the ascending staircase rising up into apparent infinity, the spires of the University itself barely visible from this angle. A flat path was available, too, crisscrossing the staircase in a long set of switchbacks, which would at least triple the entire journey; though, she'd be able to roll her suitcase on it rather than dragging it up the steps.

A mountain. They expected her to climb a *mountain*, right after getting off that Rail contraption. It wasn't *much* of a mountain, in either total height or steepness, only looking as impressive as it did because it was so isolated out here on the prairie. She'd grown up in Viridill, a territory that was *mostly* vertical; Trissiny had been bounding up and down mountain stairways since just after she could walk. She was legionnaire-trained even before her calling, and had been trained as harshly as the Sisterhood could manage in the three years since. For some reason it had always been hard for her to put on muscle, but she'd put in the work and knew she was deceptively strong for her lean build. Plus, she had *excellent* stamina, and always had, even before her military training.

She could drag a suitcase up a mountain.

It wasn't that. It was . . . Trissiny stood with an absurd journey behind her, and before her . . . a school. *Why* was she at a school? What was the point of a paladin being sent to . . .

Realizing what she was doing, she set her jaw, gripped her suitcase, and began to climb. It was not for her to question the goddess's plans. Her place was to put one foot in front of the other, for as long as it took, until she arrived where Avei wanted her to be.

If only that was the last time she had cause to question.

After ascending the mountain—not exactly a *light* workout, though her training brought her to the top only slightly sweating and not even winded—Trissiny made her way through the campus, only having to ask directions once, and followed a series of helpfully placed signs to the first-year girls' dormitory.

This path brought her to the very edge of the mountain, and the worst surprise yet.

A wall surrounded the perimeter of the University to keep people from accidentally wandering off the cliff, though the buildings weren't perched right on the edge. The signs pointed to a gate in the wall, which opened onto a stone footbridge bordered by tall iron Railings; a plaque right by the gate proclaimed this the way to

Clarke Tower. She stopped at the foot of the bridge and stared in horror.

The bridge was gently arched, about thirty feet long, and terminated at the top of a colossal stalactite at least four stories tall. It tapered to a jagged point aiming downward and had a flat top, upon which a thick, round tower was built with a conical roof that had a huge clockface inset. And the whole island just . . . floated in midair, above a nauseating drop to the prairie far below.

Hesitantly, she crept across the bridge. It certainly *felt* solid. In her rational mind, Trissiny knew this all had to be perfectly fine. This was a University run by the most powerful sorceress alive. Arachne Tellwyrn was more than capable of making a tower levitate. They wouldn't have built a building on this island and housed students in it if it weren't safe.

So her rational mind frantically whispered while she stepped across a thin bridge to an island in the sky, on which they apparently expected her to sleep. In her heart of hearts, Trissiny *knew* she was about to plunge to her horrible death. Only by keeping her eyes firmly fixed on the door to Clarke Tower did she make it across the bridge, and that despite the strong breeze which seemed to perpetually flow across it.

Trissiny decided she was beginning to hate this place.

She raised her hand to knock, then shook her head. If they expected her to live here, she wasn't going to mince around. Grasping the handle, she pulled the door open and dragged her trunk inside.

"Oh! Hi there!"

Blinking, she surveyed her new surroundings. It was a comfortably furnished living room lined with overstuffed chairs surrounding a coffee table, with a battered couch along one wall and a grandfather clock ticking away in one corner. There were no windows, Avei be praised.

Upon her entrance, a woman rose quickly from one of the chairs and bustled toward her, beaming. She was a head shorter than Trissiny and at least twice as broad, her plump frame squeezed into a very fancy corseted gown of black and purple silk that displayed a dizzying expanse of cleavage. She wore a heavy layer of makeup that made her lips and eyes seem almost to pop off her rouged face; Trissiny was aware of cosmetics in theory but had seldom seen them used, and couldn't help staring. Waves of glossy ebony hair were wound around the woman's head in an elaborate bun, decorated with sprays of purple feathers.

"And you must be Trissiny!" the woman gushed. "Oh, it's so good to meet you at last! Imagine, a paladin staying under my roof. Arach—that is, Professor Tellwyrn's told me all about you. You're one of the first to arrive, dear."

"Uh. Thank you?"

"I'm Janis Van Richter, the house mother. Please, just call me Janis! I'm here to look after the place and you girls, make sure everyone's comfy and right at home. Any problems you have, just come to me and we'll get it all sorted, okay? Oooh, this is going to be such a good year! C'mon, I've put you in the upper room, so let's not waste any time getting you settled in."

Janis seized Trissiny's free hand in both of her own—they were plump and bedecked with far too many rings—and beamed up at her.

"Welcome to the University, Trissiny. Welcome to Clarke Tower. Welcome home!"

CHAPTER 3

"Thank you," Trissiny said weakly, trying not to dwell on what was under her feet, and what wasn't. "Did you say . . . upper room?"

Janis clucked her tongue, practically radiating sympathy. "You poor dear; I know, I know! More stairs, right after that awful hike up the mountain. And you wearing armor! But it's almost over, I promise, and this'll be *much* easier on your feet. We've got just the *best* carpeting on these steps. C'mon, I'll show you!"

She led an unresisting Trissiny across the room, where two doorways occupied a corner. One, into which Janis immediately climbed, led to a spiraling staircase, twisting upward into shadows. As she passed by, Trissiny glanced into the other; it led into a short hallway, in which all that was visible was a closed door and another arched doorway that didn't appear to have one.

"It's a bit cozy here, but with only six girls, Clarke Tower's *just* the right size," Janis nattered on as they climbed. "You saw the parlor, of course. On the bottom floor there's also the kitchen. Here's my door!" she said as they arrived at a small landing. "The tower narrows a bit after the first floor, so it's only one room per level from here on up. Now, you can knock on my door any old time you need anything, dear; I'm here to help with whatever problems you may have. Don't be a stranger!"

Trissiny kept silent, following her hostess. Janis had been right about the stairs; they were covered in the thickest carpet she'd ever seen or imagined. It was like walking on dense moss. Aside from being easier on her tired feet, her steps were completely silent and even the thumping of her trunk against the stairs was muted, and didn't seem to vibrate her arm as much. A dour corner of her battle-trained mind noted that anyone sneaking up to her room for any nefarious purpose would have the advantage of complete stealth; she'd never hear them coming.

They passed two more doors on their climb, at which Janis informed her that her housemates assigned to the third floor had not arrived yet, and that one of the fourth-floor girls had come in that morning, much earlier than expected, and had already departed to explore the campus a bit.

"Of course, I've got everyone's travel schedule, dear. I like to be as prepared as possible. I'm so sorry you had to come in alone! It's ever so much nicer to meet new friends as you're moving in. But there'll be two more Rail arrivals just after yours, and the rest of the girls are sup-posed to be on them. They're probably on the way up the mountain right now! So, it's about to get rather hectic, I'd imagine, but that's just as well! A full house is a happy house, I always say. Ooh, and did I tell you about the attic? Well, it's not exactly an attic, more of a study. Or music room. There's a pianoforte on the top level, under the roof, and our little library; not much in the way of textbooks, but I like to keep a stock of some lighter reading. It can't be all study all the time, or we'd all go mad! And here we are, Trissiny dear—your new room!"

Stopping in front of the next door they came to, Janis opened the heavy wooden door and ushered her inside. Trissiny paused in the doorway, taking stock.

The staircase occupied its own little turret on the back side of the tower, leaving the main building open. Her room was much larger than she'd expected, almost circular and perfectly symmetrical. A straight wall across the side opposite the door interrupted the curve of the outer walls, with another door set in its center. On either side of that, two beds stood flat against the straight sections of the wall; marching along the rest of the perimeter were two wooden desks and two towering wardrobes. Four narrow windows were spaced evenly along the walls, admitting the golden light of late afternoon. A line between the two doors could have been a mirror; both sides of the room so perfectly reflected each other.

Janis bustled past her and opened the opposite door. "Bathroom's in here, dear; the tower's only about twenty years old, so it's fully rigged up with plumbing. Imagine that! Cold *and* hot running water, all the way to the top! Oh, it's more common now, I hear, but when all this was put in, it was unheard of. Professor Tellwyrn's always on top of the newest trends, which you really don't see often in the really old elves. Omnu's breath, don't tell her I called her old!" She laughed, making her bulging cleavage bounce alarmingly. "I know it's not much, but of course you're welcome to decorate it however you like. Small, yes, but cozy! I'm sure you'll be very comfortable."

"I'm used to sleeping in a barracks with eleven other girls," Trissiny said slowly, still blinking in the doorway.

"Good heavens! This must seem like the lap of luxury, then!"

She nodded, keeping silent. It *did* seem luxurious to her, and that wasn't necessarily a positive thing. Avei's followers were not to indulge themselves in excessive comfort, nor take more than they needed. Truthfully, indoor plumbing was something she'd only heard of, but she wasn't about to say that and look like an unschooled hick.

"Now, you take your time getting settled in, Trissiny dear. We're going to have a little get-together in a bit, down in the parlor, but not till everyone else has arrived, of course! Forgive me for leaving you so soon, but I had best go man the door and make sure to greet everyone as they get here. Dear me, I may not have the chance to show everyone else around individually . . . Ah, but here I am still blathering on! Sorry to rush out . . ."

She hurried over and swept Trissiny into an impromptu hug. "Oof! Goodness, that armor isn't joking around, is it? Now don't you worry about a thing, dear, and remember, don't hesitate to come find me if there's anything you need, anything at all. Ta-ta for now! We'll all see you later at the meeting!"

"Thank you," Trissiny said belatedly as the house mother bustled back out; she couldn't make out words from the cheery reply, as Janis was already out of sight down the stairs. For such a stout woman, she certainly moved energetically.

After glancing back and forth a couple of times, Trissiny wheeled her trunk over and set it down by the bed on the right. The choice of sides made no difference that she could see.

She took a bit of time to investigate the bathroom and its fixtures. They were mostly self-explanatory, though there was a faucet above head height in the bathtub, which, though its purpose was apparent, struck her as incredibly indulgent. Another window provided illumination, but there was also one of those glass bulbs she'd seen in the stairwell, currently darkened. After a little experimentation, she learned to handle the light, too; it could be turned on or off by pulling a small lever attached to the wall by the door. There was another of these in the main room. Good to know.

The view out the windows was breathtaking, until she made the mistake of poking her head out to look down. Apparently, Clarke Tower had a small outdoor terrace on the bottom level; it would have been a lovely little spot if it weren't hanging terrifyingly in midair. Trissiny gulped and ducked back inside, then went quickly around the room pulling the curtains closed. They were flimsy things of pale blue lacework, not much of a barrier, but it was something.

Unpacking helped distract her. She owned little, having few personal needs, and all of it was within her trunk, plus a bit extra. Her spare clothing was quickly tucked away in the wardrobe; from this she learned that it lacked the proper accouterments to store armor correctly. There had to be somewhere in Last Rock she could buy an armor stand. In the meantime, she could make do arranging it carefully on the floor by her bed, as per camping procedure.

The wooden fixtures for her sword and shield, a parting gift to her from Mother Narny, were enchanted to adhere to any surface. In short order, she had them both displayed above her bed.

Trissiny was standing back, studying her handiwork with some satisfaction, when the door to her room burst open with a *bang*. She spun, dropping into a fighting crouch and reaching fruitlessly at her waist for the sword she'd just put on the wall.

"PREPARE TO BE BOARDED!" roared the new arrival, who then swaggered in, grinning at her. "Whoa with the fists, girl. Naphthene's tits, I'm kidding! Let's not start off with a scrap, eh, roomie? Maybe you need to work off a little tension, but after dragging my ass up this mountain and then this crazy damn tower, I sure as hell don't."

"Sorry." Trissiny straightened slowly, unclenching her hands. "I'm a little on edge. That was . . . quite an entrance."

"Only kind I make, babe!" Her apparent roommate was a somewhat plump girl, a head shorter than herself with oak-brown skin; she was dressed in an ankle-length coat of brown leather, over a midriff-baring shirt that seemed made of ruffles, baggy trousers, and knee-high boots. A sword was belted on over her coat, an ostentatious rapier with an extravagantly bejeweled gold handle. Topping off this ensemble was a wide-brimmed hat, bristling with a spray of colorful feathers. Striding into the room, she swept this off and executed an elaborate bow, revealing black hair in a tight braid, and a tiny blue gemstone somehow affixed between her eyebrows. "*Princess* Zaruda Carmelita Xingyu Sameera Meredith Punaji, commander of all I survey, and your new bunkmate. My friends call me Ruda, those of them I let live." She straightened, replacing her hat, and grinned.

"I'm Trissiny Avelea." She extended a hand, hoping her growing uncertainty didn't show on her face. "You're a princess?"

"And you're a paladin!" Zaruda crossed the room in three long strides and clasped Trissiny's wrist in a warrior's handshake, still wearing that subtly maniacal grin. "I guess we should both be honored, eh? Should be an interesting semester."

"I . . . suppose. Didn't you pack anything?"

"Course I did; you think I'm an idiot?" Releasing Trissiny's hand, she tugged on her lapels. "Got everything I need here in my pockets. But unpacking later—tonight, we *party*! Last chance before we gotta waste time studying and shit, right?" She nudged Trissiny with her elbow, winking broadly. "The nice lady with the rack said we're having some kind of get-together down in the front room. Sounds about as exciting as tea with the emperor's granny, but we might as well put in an appearance, eh? Check out the competition, at least. TO ARMS!"

With this bellow, she pointed at the door as though command-
ing a charge, and swaggered back out. Trissiny tried to swallow the
sudden sinking feeling that she wasn't going to be getting much sleep
this semester. She elected to leave the cumbersome shield behind, but
grabbed her sword before following. There wasn't likely to be much
danger here, but its weight at her side comforted her. Besides, Zaruda
wore hers around.

There was something new in the spiraling stairwell—music. The
soft sounds of a harp echoed off the curving walls, a gentle melody
that made Trissiny think of the small mountain streams back home.
Ahead, Zaruda half turned to give her a thoughtful look, but didn't
speak. Trissiny didn't want to make any sounds to cover the music,
either; it was a relief to learn her new roommate wasn't completely
infatuated with the sound of her own voice after all. Their boots silent
on the plush carpet, they followed the steps down, soft chords growing louder with every step.

At the next landing down, the door was now flung wide open,
revealing a scene of chaos. Posters had somehow been tacked up
on the stone walls, showing a variety of magical carriages, the new
kind that needed no animals to pull them; Trissiny had seen a few
of those over the years, but the ones depicted in the room's artwork
were much more extravagant, fancifully shaped and lavishly painted.
A music stand stood in the middle of the floor, laden with pages, a
large floor harp under a window, and two cases appropriately sized
to hold a guitar and violin sat beside one of the beds. Clothes were
strewn *everywhere*—draped over the desk chairs, scattered on the bed,
hanging from the open doors of a wardrobe, piled on the floor. From
what Trissiny could see, they were all men's clothes.

Sitting on a heap of coats on the edge of her bed, a girl was bent
over a gilded lap harp, her fingers gliding deftly across its strings,
seeming to caress them and producing that otherworldly music. She
had brown hair cropped boyishly short and was dressed in the height
of men's fashion, with crisply pressed slacks and a sharp coat over a
waistcoat and white shirt, its collar hanging open where a necktie
would ordinarily go. Though Trissiny wasn't well versed in clothes,

especially men's clothes, she could tell these had been tailored to their owner; they hugged her figure in such a way that despite the hair and the suit, she would never be mistaken for a boy.

Zaruda and Trissiny both stopped just outside the open door; the girl with the harp played on, apparently oblivious to them. The notes glided by, golden as the harp, feeling very much like the streams of Viridill used to when she would let them wash away the weariness from feet tired after a day of drilling. Even Zaruda stared silently, wearing an appreciative little smile, totally unlike her bombastic demeanor so far, which made Trissiny warm to her slightly.

It ended rather suddenly, the soft arpeggios slowing and terminating in a single chord that swept all the way across the harp's strings. For a moment, silence reigned, then the harpist drew in a soft breath and let it out in a sigh.

"Woo!" Zaruda ruined the moment by hooting and applauding; the harpist started violently, clutching her instrument, then relaxed just as quickly when she saw them in the doorway. "That's amazing! Do you do parties?"

"I guess? Is there going to be one?" Carefully laying the harp down on her pillow, she rose, straightening her slacks, and walked over to them with a smile. "You must be the upstairs girls. I'm Teal. Teal Falconer. Let's see . . . you've gotta be Trissiny." She turned a warm grin on the paladin, who smiled back, then turned to Zaruda. "And . . . I'm sorry, I didn't get everyone's name yet."

"Oh, I see how it's gonna be. There's a paladin on campus, so I'm gonna be upstaged everywhere." Zaruda grinned amiably as she spoke, though, taking any bitterness out of the words, and grasped Teal's hand, rattling off her long string of names again. Trissiny listened closely, fearing it might take a few more repetitions before she got them all down.

"And now everyone's introduced!" Zaruda proclaimed. "We're headin' down to the house meeting that's supposed to be . . . I dunno, about nowish. Wanna come with?"

"Oh yeah. Sure, I'll just . . ." Teal turned to look around her messy room. "I'll just finish this later, I guess. No sign of my roommate yet . . . She may as well learn up front I'm not the neatest person alive."

Zaruda let out a boisterous guffaw and clapped Teal on the shoulder as she pulled her door shut. Trissiny only forced a smile and moved ahead to continue down the stairs, the others a step behind her.

This time the footfalls were not so silent; a loud slapping noise accompanied each of Teal's steps. Glancing back, Trissiny noticed for the first time that she was wearing cheap rubber sandals in a garish shade of blue. What an odd thing to pair with her obviously expensive clothes . . .

She turned her attention forward again just as they reached the third-floor landing and met another person coming up. Trissiny had only a moment to gather an impression of slate-gray skin, white hair, and pointed ears before a burst of adrenaline flooded through her.

"*Drow!*" she shouted, whipping out her sword and falling into a ready stance. A blaze of golden light sprang up around her, filling the dim staircase with an almost physical force. Behind her, Teal let out a *yelp*.

"Whoa, whoa, whoa! Put that thing up, you loon!" Zaruda exclaimed. "We're not gonna be invaded here of all places. That's another student!"

"She's a—"

"Yeah, I can *see* that. Use your head, Triss—an assassin wouldn't be strolling up the stairs like she owned the place, and if we were under attack, there'd be more than one. Anyway, there's no underworld entrances anywhere in this province. What would a drow be doing here if she wasn't attached to the school?"

"One of the drow city-states is allied with the empire, y'know," added Teal. "Can you . . . maybe turn that light down a little?"

"I . . . suppose," Trissiny said reluctantly, lowering her sword a fraction. "Is that the case?"

The dark elf had stopped at the other edge of the landing, squinting, with one hand raised to shade her eyes. She was short and slight, Trissiny saw, unlike the tall, lanky elves she'd seen before now. Odd; drow were supposed to be more muscular than their surface cousins.

"I am a student, yes." Her alto voice was serene and only faintly accented. "You may call me Shaeine. I believe this is meant to be my room?"

"Oh. I . . ." Trissiny swallowed, sheathing her sword. The glow faded from her; Shaeine lowered her hand, and Teal breathed a faint sigh of relief. "I'm so sorry. I just . . . reacted. That was unforgivable of me."

"Few humans seem so willing to express contrition," the dark elf replied with a small, polite smile. "I have experienced numerous such misunderstandings since coming to the surface, and expect many more. May they all be so quickly resolved."

"There, see?" Zaruda clapped her on the back, nearly earning herself a backhand from the still-twitchy paladin. "We're all friends here. Is the sword your default reaction to everything?"

"Not everything," Trissiny said tersely. "I'm sorry, Sheen. I'll just get out of your way . . ."

"Shaeine," she enunciated carefully, "but that was a good try."

"Sha-ayne," Teal said, drawing it out.

"Very good! Shorter, though. It is one vowel which changes pronunciation midway through."

"Uh . . . I don't think that's how vowels work," Zaruda commented.

"It's called a triphthong," Teal said with a grin. "Elvish is an interesting language, though I've gotta say, I'm not very familiar with the underworld dialect."

At this, Shaeine's smile broadened to almost genuine proportions. "Are the three of you going to the house meeting?"

"That was the plan, yeah," replied Zaruda, "before the littlest crusader here got all wand-happy." Trissiny gritted her teeth, but said nothing.

"Splendid. Our remaining two housemates are already below, speaking with Miss Van Richter. As my belongings have not yet been delivered anyway, I believe I shall postpone examining my room till afterward, since everyone else is ready."

"Sounds like a plan," Zaruda said cheerily, then prodded Trissiny in the back. "Well, you heard the wicked child of the underworld, Sparkles. We can't walk with you in the way."

Trissiny started moving, to get away from Zaruda if nothing else. Shaeine stepped in beside her, walking somehow even more silently than the rest of them on the thick carpet, and Trissiny fell to studying the elf sidelong. Her skin had an oddly matte texture that seemed to absorb the dim light in a way that human skin did not, but her straight white hair, which fell to her waist, was almost luminous. She wore a modest robe of green silk so dark it was almost black, trimmed in actual black, with patterns of spiderwebs in a different shade of black. Trissiny had never realized that black came in shades before.

Shaeine tilted her head slightly, catching her looking, and Trissiny flushed in spite of herself. "I really am sorry about that," she said lamely.

"You are a protector, and have the instincts of such," the elf replied smoothly with another diplomatic little smile. "And your reflexes are certainly impressive. No harm was done."

Nobody else found anything to say until they reached the parlor on the bottom floor. Passing through, Trissiny noticed for the first time that the staircase also continued downward from here. The tower had a basement, then? It would have to have been carved into the rock of the floating stalactite itself. Somehow, that was even more horrifying.

"Ooh, everyone's here!" squealed Janis from near the front door, clapping her hands. "My, *aren't* you girls punctual! Most years I have to go around gathering everybody up. Everyone, this is Juniper and Fross, our last two arrivals. Fross, Juniper, these are . . ." She pointed to each of them in turn. "Shaeine, Teal, Zaruda, and Trissiny. I know, that's not everybody's full name, I'm sorry. But! Since we're all here and ready, why don't you girls each find a seat and then we'll go about introducing ourselves! Go on, go on, get comfy! I'll be right back with a little something to nibble."

She bustled away down the hall to the kitchen, leaving the six girls alone. Five; to her confusion, Trissiny could only see one additional person in the room, but it was a person who made her blink to clear her vision, and then stare.

"*I'm* Juniper," she clarified, waving. "Good to meet everybody! Teal, wasn't it? Looks like we'll be sharing a room."

Juniper looked like the kind of woman dreamed up by lonely men, then drawn and printed on the covers of the sort of tawdry magazines Trissiny wasn't supposed to know existed. Her close-fitting, sheer dress did nothing to obscure a figure that was almost improbably curvaceous—an inch more bosom or less waist and she'd look like a caricature. Even that and her startlingly lovely face weren't her most eye-catching features. She had long, luxurious hair of a vivid green, and skin the shade of green-tinged gold that reminded Trissiny of new leaves in the early spring. Her eyes, incongruously, were an ordinary brown.

"Well," Zaruda said resignedly, "looks like I'm not gonna be the hot one after all."

"Oh, uh, hi," said Teal, who had to keep jerking her eyes back up toward Juniper's face. "It's, uh, good to meet you, too. Wow, you're . . . unusual."

"Thanks! You have a very interesting fashion sense." Juniper smiled earnestly at her. "Anyway, just so there's no confusion, I think that we shouldn't be more than friends, since we're going to be rooming together. I don't understand human relational politics very well yet, and I'd hate to blunder into a situation where somebody's feelings get hurt."

"W-what?" Teal flushed scarlet, then took a step back, waving her hands in front of her. "No, no, that's perfectly—I mean, of course, I wouldn't . . . that is, I don't . . ." She groaned and clapped a hand over her face. "Y'know what, I'm just gonna crawl under the rug here. Talk amongst yourselves."

A streak of light shot past Trissiny's face, making her jump backward, and came to a stop right in front of Shaeine, who again had to squint against the glare.

"Hi-hi-hi!" it chimed. "I'm Fross; I'll be rooming with you! Good to meet you! Wow, you're pretty. Can I touch your hair?"

"I would rather you did not."

"Oh! Right, personal space, sorry, I forget about that." The little ball of light fluttered backward with a faint buzzing of nearly invisible wings. "How's that? Better? Haven't got a feel yet for how close is okay. Big people are all different about it, and it's tricky with me being so much smaller, y'know? But I'll get it down! There's a lot of rules to remember; I'm working on it."

"You're a fairy," Trissiny said dumbly.

"Yup! Well, we're both fairies, but I'm a pixie."

"Great seas, you're tiny," Zaruda said in awe. "Why's a pixie need a room? Wouldn't you be fine with, like, a lily pad?"

Fross seemed confused by the question; she drifted sideways in midair, as though her concentration on her flight had slipped. "Students are supposed to have rooms. All students are required to live on campus, and the University provides housing. It's in the student handbook."

"You've *read* that? Mine's propping up an uneven chair back home."

"Of course I read it! All the rules are in there! How are you supposed to know the rules if you don't read it?"

"Easy, Fross," Juniper soothed, but the pixie began bouncing up and down in agitation, her voice growing shriller and more rapid with each word.

"What's the point of having rules if people aren't even going to know them? I'm still trying to wrap my feelers around the whole business and I can't be the only responsible person here and please tell me I'm not the only one who read the handbook!"

"I read it!" four voices immediately piped up.

Fross visibly calmed, her flight steadying. "Oh. Oh, good, okay. That's good." She zoomed forward directly into Zaruda's face; the princess jerked her head back, grabbing the hilt of her sword. "It's just you, then! Don't worry, I've still got my copy. We'll go over it later and I'll make sure you know all the rules, all right?"

"Great. Thanks. Sounds like fun."

At that moment, Janis returned, carrying a tray laden with a full tea set, as well as piles of tiny cookies and finger sandwiches. "Goodness me, are you girls all still standing around? Sit, sit, get comfortable! We'll just go over a few important facts, and then we'll all introduce ourselves and learn a bit about each other! Won't that be fun?"

Trissiny glanced around the room; the only comfort she found was that everyone looked as nervous and out of place as she did, with the exception of Fross, whose body language (if she even had any) was unreadable, and Shaeine, who wore serenity like a cloud of perfume.

"Yeah," Trissiny said weakly. "Fun."

CHAPTER 4

Trissiny was far from the only one clearly uncomfortable with Janis's forced attempt at a get-to-know-you party, but she was the first to make her escape, pleading the need for regular prayer. Hopefully her example would help liberate the others.

As always, she felt refreshed and calmer after time spent in prayer, not to mention blessed solitude. Even after half an hour, Zaruda had not returned to their room.

Trissiny considered going right to bed, but prayer left her feeling both serene and energized, and she knew from experience that sleep wouldn't come easily in that state. Where *was* her roommate, anyway? She really shouldn't get in the habit of staying out late this early in the semester, but it might be wise to make an effort to befriend the other girls of her class. After all, she *had* just walked out on them. Hopefully they'd understand the importance of prayer, but there was no reason to encourage hard feelings.

Satisfied with this reasoning, Trissiny belted her sword again and headed down the stairs.

She paused outside Teal and Juniper's door, which was now closed, but there was no sound from within, and after a moment she decided not to knock; years in the barracks had trained her not to infringe on anyone's privacy unless she had a specific need. They were probably all still down in the parlor with Janis.

The echo of voices was faint; sound bounced oddly off the curved walls of the stairwell and was deadened by the absurdly plush carpet, so it couldn't have been coming from far ahead. As she drew in sight of the third-floor door and beheld it standing open several inches, Trissiny determined the speakers had to be within. She was almost abreast of the door before words became audible.

"That's easy for you to say," Zaruda's voice declared loudly. "You don't have to room with her!"

Trissiny froze.

"Are we *still* talking about this?" Teal's voice groaned.

"At least one of us is," Shaeine said softly. Were they *all* in there?

"Come on, guys, look at this from my point of view. She's already almost stabbed Shaeine, tried to interrogate Teal at the meeting, and you should've seen the way she glared at me when I walked into my own room earlier. This may be funny for you, but I've gotta worry about getting a sword *amidships* while I sleep!"

"Um, I really didn't feel any hostility from her." Juniper's voice was nervous, uncertain. "But I'm not so adept at reading humans yet . . ."

Trissiny's heart pounded painfully. They *were* all in there, talking about her. Every instinct born of her training shouted at her to knock, or speak, or announce her presence somehow; eavesdropping was rude at the very least, and arguably a moral failing. But she felt frozen, listening to them.

"Nobody's going to stab you in your sleep," Teal said patiently.

"Okay, why doesn't somebody switch rooms with me, then! See how you like it. I asked Van Richter; she said the rooming assignments aren't set in stone and somebody always changes, every semester."

"I don't agree that Trissiny's intentions are hostile," said Shaeine calmly, "but it is early yet. I am not sure I would feel safe sleeping in her presence until I know her better."

"See?!" Ruda shouted. "How about you, June? Since you don't think she's dangerous?"

"Um . . ."

"Ruda, stop it," Teal said firmly. "You're being ridiculous."

"Yeah? Why don't *you* move in with her, then?"

"Absolutely not."

Shaeine's head swiveled suddenly toward the door. Rising smoothly, she glided across the floorboards to push it the rest of the way open.

"Is . . . is anyone . . ." Teal trailed off, her heart rising into her throat. Gods above, if someone had overheard their discussion . . . Janis would not be happy, to say the least, but if it was *Trissiny* . . .

"Nothing," said Shaeine, pulling the door gently closed. "I thought I heard . . . well. Sound echoes confusingly in this stairwell."

"Back to the subject at hand, then!" Ruda half sat, half lay sprawled in a corner, occasionally drinking from a bottle of whiskey. So far, nobody had bothered to ask where it had come from. "If you're so in favor of Trissiny, why're you so opposed to rooming with her?"

"Because, as I said, you're being ridiculous. More to the point, Ruda, you're being unfair. None of us know one thing about each other at this point, Janis's little game notwithstanding, and we know even *less* about Trissiny because she's not been part of this conversation."

"Cos she's too holy to hang out with us mere mortals," Zaruda sneered.

"Because she is a person with a sacred calling, and thus has an obligation to spend time in prayer," said Shaeine. "As do I. You may believe as you choose, but for me to condemn her as asocial due to that would be the height of hypocrisy."

"Besides, some people just don't like large groups," said Teal reasonably.

Zaruda snorted. "*Large* groups? Y'all should try sleeping below-decks in a storm sometime."

"Okay, I've gotta say, I am *completely* confused," said Fross, who was fluttering around the ceiling. "I thought Trissiny seemed nice!"

"Guys, I'm telling you, you'd know what I meant if you'd seen her earlier. All I did was come in the door and there she is, making fists and looking like she wants to kick me out the window."

"If I may ask," Shaeine interjected, continuing to arrange dark, silken tapestries along her walls, "did you enter your room the way you did mine a few minutes ago?"

"What's that got to do with anything?"

"Only that if you burst in, shouting and gesticulating with a wine bottle upon a highly trained warrior who doubtless feels as out of place and uncertain as the rest of us to begin with, some of the responsibility would fall on your head if she *had* struck you."

"Shaeine nailed it," said Teal approvingly, nodding at the drow, who paused in her work to nod back politely. "We are, all of us, in a new place, surrounded by virtual strangers, homesick and scared pantsless about sitting through class with the most dangerous individual in the empire tomorrow. I'll admit it, if nobody else will. I don't assume I'm a good judge of what any of you are really like, because I've only met you while we're all stressed as hell. Trissiny's in exactly the same boat as the rest of us." She sighed and sat down next to Juniper on Fross's bed, which the pixie had told them to treat as a couch since she didn't need it. "Ruda, just give it *time*. In three weeks if you two still can't get along, maybe we'll talk about redoing the room situation. But seriously, give her a fair chance before you start trying to upend the whole tower."

The pirate princess grumbled to herself and took a long pull from her bottle.

"And I'll tell you something else," Teal went on more sternly. "Your arguments are flimsy and your instinctive dislike of her is irrational. If I *were* to start making assumptions about people, I wouldn't start with Trissiny. It looks to me like you're trying to grasp for a sense of control because you're more comfortable fighting than trying to get along with people who're different from you."

"What did you call me?" Zaruda straightened from her slump, glaring.

"Actually, that seemed pretty spot-on," said Juniper. "Oh, don't look at me like that, you're so much prettier when you smile."

"I would not have put it so bluntly," added Shaeine, "but it is a common enough tactic among those of a warlike disposition. It is worth pointing out that, considering we are all here discussing Trissiny in her absence, it is not *she* who is chiefly guilty of hostile behavior."

Zaruda swept her glare around the room, but nobody backed down. Finally, she sighed, slouching back against the wall. "Three weeks, huh." She took another drink from the bottle. "Fine, we'll see. But you're all gonna feel pretty stupid if one of us turns up dead."

Trissiny paid no attention to where she was going. The paths of the University were well lit at night; on her previous trip through the campus during the daylight, she hadn't even noticed the glass orbs hovering unsupported over the paths, but in the darkness they put out a steady white glow that drowned out even the moonlight. She barely noticed them now.

She wanted to hunch over and wrap her arms around herself as she walked, but fought off the impulse. Proper posture was as much a part of her as her sword . . . as was the instinct not to show vulnerability.

No one had ever hated her before.

Mechanically, she put one foot in front of the other, staying on the paths but not seeing where they led. At the abbey she'd been a hero. Because of Avei's calling more than anything she'd actually done, but the knowledge of that disparity had driven her to work twice as hard, to make herself worthy of the attention. Even before the goddess had singled her out at fifteen, she had been well liked among the other initiates.

How had she offended everyone so badly in the course of one afternoon?

Trissiny raised her head and found that she'd wandered back to the open lawn she had seen earlier. Though she'd passed a few other students on the way, this place was empty now. Slowly, she made her way to the gazebo and climbed the three steps into its shade. It was darker here, with no fairy lamps nearby and the roof obstructing the stars.

So, this was what it would be like here. Mother Narny had tried to warn her that out in the world she would quickly meet people who resented Avei and all she represented, and would resent Trissiny by proxy.

She finally let herself slump into a bench, staring down at her boots.

She was a warrior. Her whole life was the expectation of battle. How could she let herself be so . . . hurt? It was just a few words from a few girls who didn't really know her. She swiped at her eyes; the tears weren't there, and she wasn't going to let them be. This whole thing was just stupid.

"You okay?"

Trissiny lunged halfway to her feet, gripping her sword, and the boy who'd spoken hopped back, raising his hands peaceably.

"Sorry! Sorry, didn't mean to sneak up on you."

"I . . . No, *I'm* sorry. I shouldn't have let myself be snuck up on." She sank back down onto the bench. "I'm fine, thank you."

"Okay, well . . . I won't bother you, if that's what you want, but I don't think Avei approves of lying."

She snapped her head up to glare at him. Something about him seemed familiar, though she couldn't place him and hardly knew that many boys anyway. He was a Westerner, with skin the darkest shade of brown she'd ever seen on a person, and curly hair that looked in need of a trim. The expression on his face was pure open friendliness.

"Do I know you?"

"Oh . . . sorry, I guess that was maybe a little presumptuous." He smiled ruefully. "It's just hard not to recognize you, what with the armor and all. I've been looking forward to meeting you since I learned we were both coming here this fall." The boy extended a hand to her. "Tobias Caine, Hand of Omnu. Toby to my friends, which I hope includes you."

"Oh!" Trissiny rose again, fully this time, and grasped his hand. "Oh, I'm sorry. I'd been hoping to meet you, too, Mr. . . . ah, Toby. I'm Trissiny. Avelea. Um, sorry, I'm just really out of sorts tonight."

"Yeah, I got that impression." Letting go of her hand, he hopped up the steps in one stride and seated himself on the bench opposite her, placing them on each side of the gazebo's entrance. "You don't have to do anything you don't want to, of course, but it's amazing how much it can help to just talk about what's on your mind."

"Don't worry about it," she muttered, slumping back onto her seat. "It's stupid, anyway."

He shrugged. "Maybe. Doesn't mean it doesn't matter. You should hear some of the stupid stuff *I* get upset about."

Trissiny cast about for something to say that would get rid of him. Omnu's followers were all about compassion, and there would be no shaking a paladin of that deity if he believed she actually needed help. She lifted her head; he was just sitting there, watching her. He had the kindest eyes she'd ever seen.

"Everyone hates me!" she blurted.

"That's hard to imagine . . ."

Still with a polite demurral half formed, Trissiny listened to herself babble on in growing horror; it was as if her mouth was done taking orders. "They do, though, everyone in my house. I heard them talking about it. That makes it even worse! I mean, what kind of person listens in on a private conversation?! I was raised better than that! But they were all talking about me and how they apparently think I'm going to murder them in their beds, and I was just, I don't know, *frozen*. And the worst part is, this is all so *stupid*! Why do I—how can I possibly even care about this? I'm a paladin; my whole life is going to be spent applying a sword to people who're going to hate me no matter what. It's just ridiculous that this bothers me so much. But it does, and now I don't even want to go back to my room . . ."

He just sat there, watching her and listening, his expression attentive without a hint of pity, until she finally trailed off and drew in a long, shuddering breath, trying to get herself back under control. She was *not* going to cry, damn it!

"That's rough," Toby murmured. "But first of all, there's nothing stupid *at all* about feeling hurt when people are jerks to you."

"I don't think they were jerks to me," she muttered. "I . . . I think they're *afraid* of me."

"Can I tell you what I think?"

She sighed. "Fine."

"It sounds to me like a misunderstanding. Whatever you did to set them off, they probably took somewhat out of context. I mean, come on. You're the Hand of Avei, champion of justice, protector of the weak. I *know* you didn't walk in there and say or do anything you meant as a threat. Speaking from experience, we paladins can take a little getting used to."

"We do?" She looked up at him miserably.

"If I remember right, you're from Viridill, right? Grew up at the temple there?"

"In the attached abbey, but close enough."

He nodded. "No offense intended, Trissiny, but . . . honestly, I bet you're a little sheltered. I was raised at the primary Temple of Omnu, but that's in Tiraas, a stone's throw from the palace itself. Literally, my friend Gabriel threw a stone onto the emperor's balcony once."

"Ooh, ouch," she said, wincing. "Is he still alive?"

Toby laughed. "Yeah, he's got a knack for getting out of the trouble he gets into. But my point is, I'm used to the politics and the fast pace of the capital. It's . . . Well, the first thing you learn there is that life is a bunch of confusing gray areas. It can be really hard to take a stand for what's important, and hold to it when you're surrounded by people who genuinely think nothing means anything and all that matters is power."

"You think that's what it's going to be like here?" Trissiny wanted to groan.

"No . . . I think the University is going to be a whole different tank of fish. More, uh, detectable shades of gray, maybe. Hopefully. But still, it's just not going to be as simple as only being around people who share your faith and your convictions."

"Great. So I'm naive as well as a menace." She sighed.

Toby stood up, walked over, and sat down beside her, resting a hand on her shoulder. She couldn't feel his skin through her armor, but there was something reassuring about the weight of it. "I wouldn't put it that way at all. You've just got a little adjusting to do. Avei's paladins have been a force for everything that's right in the world for thousands of years, and I know she didn't call you by accident. You'll do fine, Trissiny; remember you've got a goddess to help you through it."

He smiled at her, so warmly that she couldn't help returning it.

"Besides," he went on, "keep in mind your housemates are all as lost and scrambling to adjust as you and I are right now. I bet you anything when things start to settle down, you'll find out they didn't mean any harm."

She took a steadying breath and nodded. "I . . . may have exaggerated when I said they all hated me. Teal seemed to be, I don't know, trying to calm things down."

"Oh, that's right, you'll be rooming with Teal Falconer." He grinned, nodding. "That's good; she's a natural-born peacemaker. Yeah, I highly doubt Teal suspected you of anything nefarious."

"You've met Teal?" She let out a huff of breath. "Does *everyone* here know more about what's going on than me?"

Toby laughed. "Oh no, nothing like that; I got to spend some time with her a few years ago when she was at the cathedral in Tiraas. They weren't exactly giving her the run of the place, for obvious reasons; it's spooky going from your own cozy life to being cooped up by suspicious priests. We were both sort of in need of a friend."

Trissiny felt a perplexing stab of envy for her housemate; it must have been nice, getting to know Toby in a more comfortable place than this increasingly disturbing campus. Or had that really been comfortable? He didn't make it sound so . . .

"What was Teal doing cooped up in the Grand Cathedral?"

Toby winced. "I, uh, maybe I shouldn't have—"

"No, no, you're right," Trissiny said hastily. "It's none of my business. Sorry."

"Well, the thing is . . . Okay, I want to respect other people's confidence, but this *is* sort of paladin business. It might be best if you hear about it from me rather than . . . by surprise, somehow."

"I . . . sure, of course. Is she okay?"

"Teal has a demon inside her," he said, his expression intent and serious. "It was some kind of possession attempt that went wrong. She *is* okay, yes. She's got control of it. I know that's probably not how you were taught demon possession works, and your training is undoubtedly not *wrong*, it's just that Teal's . . . an anomalous case. But yes, I know her, and I can promise you she's safe to be around."

"Wow . . ." she breathed. "Yeah, I guess divine magic would burn a possessed person, wouldn't it? That'd be an awful surprise if someone was trying to heal her." Oh—actually, Trissiny *had* been channeling divine power right in front of Teal, who'd been visibly uncomfortable. One more thing she'd done wrong today, apparently.

"Exactly. Look, I may have said too much about this already; it's her business."

"No, I understand. That's fine, thank you for telling me. You were right, better not to be taken by surprise."

Smiling at her again, he stood. He really did have the kindest eyes . . . "Well, class starts early and Professor Tellwyrn is . . . legendary. Showing up half asleep probably isn't a good idea, so we ought to get to bed. I'm glad to have met you, Trissiny."

"You, too," she replied, then smiled hesitantly. "Thanks for listening, Toby. You're . . . a good listener."

"That's what I'm here for." He gave her that glowing smile again, then reached over to squeeze her shoulder one more time. "You're going to be fine. I promise."

She sat there, watching him stride away across the shadowed green. What a nice boy . . . Growing up in the abbey, one didn't get the best impressions of men. It was good to know the world had kind ones. She'd already met a few since leaving home, of course. But, she reflected, tilting her head as she watched Tobias make his way down the path, they weren't all that pleasant to look at . . .

Trissiny clapped a hand to her face. "Oh, good. That's great, Triss," she muttered. "Meet the only other paladin in the world and you immediately start drooling. Goddess, I'm worse than Zaruda."

Zaruda had apparently prevaricated about not packing anything but what was in the pockets of her coat. When Trissiny got back to her room, she discovered that half of it had been utterly transformed by colorful rugs, wall hangings, and throw pillows, all heavily embroidered and most with gilded fringes and tassels. It was as if the room had been turned into some kind of harem, albeit with maps tacked up onto the walls. Or at least half of it had. Zaruda had arranged her rugs on a very precise line along the floor, perfectly bisecting the room. Trissiny's side was still as sparse as ever.

The pirate herself was reclining in her bed, her face hidden behind an issue of *Varsity Princess*. She had finally removed her coat and hat; they currently decorated one corner of her wardrobe's open door. Seeing Zaruda in nothing but trousers and that ruffled wrap around her upper chest, Trissiny had to revise her impression of the girl as plump. She was short and had a curvy frame, yes, but her arms and abdomen showed solid muscle.

"Hello," she said carefully, receiving a grunt in reply. She sighed and began removing her armor, carefully arranging it on the floor beside her bed. "We'd better not stay up too late. Class comes early."

"Hm."

Trissiny paused for a moment, looking up at her roommate. "I'm not going to attack you or anything, you know. We're all here to learn. I don't want any problems."

"Yeah, you know what's good for that?" A pair of dark eyes appeared over the rim of the magazine, the blue gem glinting in the magic light of the fairy lamp. "*Stop creating problems.*"

Biting back an unhelpful reply, Trissiny stripped down to her shift and pulled back the thin blanket on her bed; Zaruda vanished behind the pages again. Trissiny padded across the cold floor, not stepping on any of the rugs, and pulled the wall lever by the door, plunging the room into darkness.

"*Hey!*"

"Good night, Zaruda."

There came a flutter of paper and a *thump* as the magazine was thrown into a wall. Trissiny climbed into bed and lay still, listening to her roommate's growling and shuffling as she crawled under her own blankets. She missed the barracks, the quieter sounds of the other girls. Girls she knew and trusted.

She would not cry. That would be *ridiculous*; she was a paladin. Trissiny lay there not crying until the sheer fatigue of it finally put her to sleep.

CHAPTER 5

Sharidan Julios Adolphus Tirasian, ruler of an entire continent, lounged on a settee on his balcony, dressed in a fairly modest robe of crimson silk. On the armrest beneath his hand sat a flat jewelry box, on which he occasionally drummed his fingers. Despite the awe-inspiring sight of his glowing city spread out at his feet, bristling with flashing scrolltower orbs and the factory antennae discharging lightning into the atmosphere; despite the soothing incense wafting from the door to the harem wing behind him and the soft notes of a harp playing nearby—in fact, partly because of that—his body was tense and his expression grim. He was not a man to shirk duty, but this one would be painful.

The piece of music came to an end, finishing on a long, ascending arpeggio. He drummed his fingers once more on the jewelry box.

"Beautiful."

"Thank you, my lord," murmured the woman, setting her harp down at her feet. She rose from the ottoman on which she had perched and approached him from behind, kneeling on the settee and beginning to gently knead the emperor's shoulders. "I would feel more flattered if my music soothed you as it usually does. You are one great knot of tension tonight."

Because you're touching me, he did not say.

"Tell me what troubles you, my lord," she murmured. There was no sultriness in it—that wasn't her way—but in spite of himself, despite what he suspected, his blood warmed at her voice, at the way her fingers glided along his skin. Not for nothing was she his favorite concubine. Gods above, this was going to be painful.

"What troubles me?" He felt his own shoulders tensing further as he spoke, despite her ministrations. "What *shouldn't* trouble me, Lillian? There's been too much progress, too fast. It's not just magical conveniences and technologies, or even weapons. Too many new ideas, too much travel and communication; the populace has been slapped in the face with the whole size of the world and the diversity of the people in it, and they're reacting about as well as one would expect to their children growing up learning dwarven philosophy and elvish ideas about sex and love." He sat up, leaning forward out of her grasp. "And the Church—may the entire Pantheon piss on their Archpope one at a time—has taken ruthless advantage to increase their own sway with the people. The Church and the throne have always existed in a careful balance. Now . . . It's tradition against progress all over the empire, but this time both sides are militarizing." The emperor stood up and began to pace rapidly. "I'm sitting atop a fault line into which every citizen of my empire is constantly pouring black powder and playing with fireworks. Yes, I am *troubled*."

"Well," she murmured, gazing up at him with limpid eyes, "if you don't want to talk about it . . ."

He halted, glaring down at her. Lady Lillian Riaje was tall and lean of build, almost elvishly so, though her bronze skin and prominent nose hadn't come from any elven bloodline. He usually preferred his women buxom and soft, but Lillian had always had a way of calming his tensions and carrying him away from his troubles that no other could rival. In light of what he'd recently learned, he now had to wonder . . .

"Perhaps you didn't hear me, my lady?"

"I heard you give a nice expository speech on current affairs, my lord," she replied, smiling. Her dark eyes glinted with mischief, in that adorable expression that made him find her charming, even when she said things for which he'd have other people banished. "It was well done, very succinct. But *those* troubles are simply part of the world in which we live, ailments like war, poverty, and disease. Nothing that should drive you into such a state. You have never hesitated to share your burdens with me before, my master . . . I begin to wonder if I've done something to displease you."

The emperor drew in a long breath and let it out slowly. "You . . . have never been anything but a joy, Lillian."

"There's an unspoken 'but' following that compliment," she replied after a pause. "Does this have anything to do with the four Hands lurking just out of sight?"

He didn't bother to ask how she'd known, and did his best not to betray any surprise, though he had a feeling she could read him much too well for such dissembling. The Hands of the Emperor were his agents of choice, his voice and touch throughout the vast realm, as well as the last line of defense protecting him, even here in his home. A diverse group of men hidden behind their homogeneous black suits, they had in common only their ferocious loyalty to the throne and the high degree of their dangerous talents. Facing a Hand of the emperor, one never knew exactly what his abilities might be, only that they were prodigious. He had chosen these four for their stealth; that Lillian had spotted them was more than merely troubling.

The emperor turned his back on her, staring out from the balcony. Directly before him, across Imperial Square, loomed the Grand Cathedral of the Universal Church of the Pantheon, flanked on both sides by the central temples of Avei and Omnu. Not visible, but its presence very much felt, was the Temple of Vidius beneath the pavement of the square itself. Avei had her stronghold in Viridill, as well, but this square was the center of divinity and worship in the empire. On its fourth border, the palace seemed . . . outnumbered.

"My expository speech, as you put it, was immediately relevant to the matter at hand," he said finally. "The Archpope has taken to moving more directly, and I am not yet sure what to make of it. Most recently, he has made troubling suggestions about you, Lillian."

"That's a novel approach," she said wryly. "Subtle, but perhaps effective. The girls in the harem may not have political power, but we do contribute to your well-being. At least, so I devoutly hope." Her laugh was a throaty ripple of music. "Besides, if he can cut you off from the chance to produce an heir . . ."

He scowled, twisting his mouth at the reminder.

The imperial harem had been built to house dozens; some of Sharidan's predecessors had filled it to capacity and more. He was not so self-indulgent; there were only seven women in residence, and three of them were attached to his wife. The emperor's concubines were, as Lillian pointed out, not a luxury . . . or at least, not entirely. The empire needed the Tirasian dynasty to continue, and there would be no heir from Empress Eleanora.

He counted Eleanora as his closest and most cherished friend, as well as his most potent ally in the shark pool of court politics; as such, he had chosen to respect the revulsion she felt at the prospect of sharing herself with any man. It was within his power to insist she perform wifely duties, but that was just not the kind of relationship they had. So she had her girls and he his; they were an odd little family, but a happy one. Yet there was still no sign of pregnancy in any of his mistresses. Lillian was correct. If the Archpope, or *any* of his enemies, could prevent that from coming about, they could throw the empire into easily exploitable chaos simply by removing him from the picture.

Eleanora had not been pleased at being excluded from tonight's business, but he needed her safe, elsewhere. Given how badly this could go . . . if anything befell him, she would have to hold the throne against those who would try to seize it. The empire's needs must come first.

"I'm taking precautions," he said quietly. "But I will not be bullied nor tricked into blundering. I am . . . alarmed by this maneuvering, and these escalations. The empire has always flourished with the Church and the throne both strong. We need that tension, the back-and-forth of power. Power unchecked is what tore this empire apart a century ago. Now, though, Archpope Justinian seems determined to . . ." He trailed off.

"To win," Lillian said.

The emperor nodded. "Yes. He either doesn't understand the nature of this game, or places his own ambitions above the greater good. I'm not sure which prospect I find more frightening."

"How to defeat an opponent whom you cannot actually afford to vanquish?" She hummed softly to herself. "That is quite a puzzle. There is one encouraging thing: Justinian will likely expect you to meet him on the same absolute terms—that, or if you fail to do so, believe that you haven't seen the true nature of his own game. Either way, perhaps it is you who can trick him into a misstep."

"I love the way your mind works." He turned to give her a sad smile. "Sometimes I regret not giving you a greater role in the palace. And not just you . . . Am I wasting valuable potential, keeping such clever women as . . . as pets?"

"I, for one, quite enjoy being a pet," she said blithely. "It's not for everyone, but I don't miss having heavier obligations. Milanda might like to have another outlet for her cleverness, I suppose . . . but by and large, we remain here because we love to be here." The humor faded from her features, and she simply gazed up at him, into him. "Because we love you."

It made the weight in his chest ache, because even if what he suspected proved correct, he knew that she spoke the truth in that moment.

"I have a gift for you," he said, bending to pick up the jewelry box from the settee.

"You didn't have to," she said softly.

"That's what makes it a gift, my lady. Please." Steeling his nerves, he held the box out toward her. Though he could not see or hear them, he knew the watching Hands had tensed, preparing to spring if it proved that they needed to.

"All I need is to be near you . . . but thank you. I can't refuse a token of love, now can I?" Lillian rose, giving him a sad little smile, and took the box from him. He stepped back twice as she turned it in her hands, thumbed open the catch, and opened it.

A burst of golden radiance exploded on the balcony with the intensity of the sun. Lillian shrieked in pain and went staggering backward into a potted fern, flinging the box away. It clattered against the balustrade, spilling a masterwork diamond necklace onto the stone floor. The priceless piece of jewelry lay in a jumble, glowing furiously; a faint sound like bells hovered at the edge of his hearing.

That necklace carried the most powerful blessing that his considerable resources could arrange, the kind of holy magic that one might expect to find on a paladin's sword, not a court lady's ornament. Lillian scrambled backward, deeper into the plant, glaring down at it.

There was only one kind of creature that was harmed by holy magic. Any demon would be blinded and hurt by that blessing, but only one of immense power could have caused it to erupt so fiercely.

The moment the necklace had blazed to life, the four Hands had plunged onto the balcony, two through the door into the harem, and the others out of nearby windows. In the space of a second, the first two had bracketed the fallen consort and covered her with a pair of wands and a battlestaff; the remaining duo positioned themselves between her and the emperor, both holding swords at the ready.

Sharidan felt something crack inside himself. He forced the pain not to show. Later, he would sit with Eleanora and grieve in peace. Now, a brave face was needed.

"That," said Lillian reproachfully, "was a discourteous prank, my lord." She carefully lifted herself out of the shrubbery, straightening her sheer robe and recovering a bit of dignity, though she kept well back from the blazing necklace. For all the attention she paid them, the two Hands and the firepower they had pointed at her might as well not exist.

"So, Justinian was right," the emperor said, then heaved a sigh. "There is going to be absolutely no living with him after this . . . Please don't do anything brash, Lillian. I've no wish to see you harmed, but it's clear I can't allow you to roam free any longer."

"You always were such a clever lad," she said fondly. He could just see her face past the shoulder of the nearest Hand. "You do better when you have time to prepare, though. Are we not past the point of pleasantries, now? You did not deploy your Hands without expecting to inflict harm."

"I am emperor," he said simply. "I've done things that pained me before. Today, even. And I will again."

"You and I both," she replied, and flicked both hands at the two men holding weapons on her. One was sent hurtling into space over the balcony's rail, the staff discharging a burst of lightning that cracked the stone at her feet; the other slammed into the wall of the palace with a nauseating *crunch*, wands tumbling uselessly to the floor.

Instantly, one of the remaining Hands bore the emperor to the ground, flipping the settee up into a makeshift barricade and tossing his liege behind it with one efficient burst of motion. The other lunged at Lillian, sword first. The Hand and the concubine were both cut from the emperor's view as he was unceremoniously shoved down, but he could not miss seeing the burst of flame that illuminated the balcony for an instant, nor hearing the man's quickly stifled scream.

Four of them should have stood up to almost anything! How had he underestimated her so badly?

A split second later, his last remaining Hand was yanked away with a cry of surprise, dropping his sword in the process. There came the sound of flesh striking flesh, then flesh striking stone. Then silence.

Sharidan snatched up the sword and rolled to his feet. It was obvious, now, how this was going to end, but he was determined to end it upright with a weapon in his hand, not cowering behind a couch.

The balcony had become a scene from a nightmare in the last few seconds. Everything was burned, ferns and flowers reduced to ash, rugs and pillows to smoldering scraps; Lillian's harp was a twisted, blackened shape resembling an unfortunate piece of driftwood. Three bodies lay where they had fallen, two wearing imperial black, one little more than a charred skeleton. All of it was illuminated sickeningly by the light of the gods, burning from that accursed necklace.

Lillian hadn't even a hair or a fold of her robe out of place. Ignoring him for the moment, despite the sword he held pointed at her heart, she heaved a soft sigh, then stepped over to the necklace, bending to pick it up. The intensity of its blaze grew in warning as she approached; when she touched it, a shrill whine of protest rose in his ears, and smoke began to curl from her fingers.

"This really is a stunning piece of work," she said calmly. He could hardly see her through the glow put off by the necklace now. "A fitting gift from an emperor. I believe I'll keep it, as a reminder of you, my lord. Since it seems I must leave you now." With that, she lifted the necklace to her throat and fastened its clasp behind her neck.

A chime like silver bells rang out, and the glow abruptly vanished. The necklace, still smoking slightly but now inert, lay fetchingly against her coppery skin. He blinked in the sudden dimness.

It hardly mattered now, given what was surely about to happen, but Sharidan's heart sank further. He had never heard of a demon powerful enough to *snuff out* a holy blessing.

"What *are* you?" he whispered.

She looked up at him, and he was taken aback by the pure hurt in her expression. "I wish you had less of the Church's nonsense poisoning your mind. Of all the things I've been called, Lillian Riaje will do fine. I am a woman who has shared your bed and your travails this last year, and has never done you any wrong." Again, she sighed. "Well, I can't blame you for this, not entirely. The world is what it is."

Lillian stepped toward him and he backed away, keeping the sword between them. "Stay back. Please."

Shaking her head, she reached out to touch the tip of the sword with one finger; the blade instantly drooped as though made of rubber. Sharidan stared down at it for a second, then, shoulders slumping in defeat, dropped the ruined weapon to the floor with a clatter. "Whatever you intend to do, I hope you'll do it quickly."

"Oh, Sharidan." Lillian shook her head, gliding closer. She lifted her hand toward his face, but let it fall again when he flinched. "I want you to know a few things. First of all, your dynasty *will* continue. And your heir will be beyond the power of the Church or anyone else to harm." Her lips curled up in a smile, and she placed a hand against her belly.

"Oh," he groaned. "Oh, *no*."

"Second . . . despite what the Church and the Pantheon have said these last millennia, I have never been humanity's enemy," she said, gazing intensely at him, "nor shall I ever be yours. I really will miss you, Sharidan. This last year has been the first time in so long that I've felt . . . happy."

She stepped back, and smiled at him again, sadly. "Goodbye."

Then she was just gone.

Roughly sixteen hundred miles northwest of Tiraas, at the rim of the space-altering magical prairie dubbed the Golden Sea, Professor Alaric Yornhaldt strolled through the halls of the Ultimate University in his dressing gown and robe. It was a habit of his when he couldn't sleep, to pace the corridors and ponder what lay below. Millennia of history lurked beneath this mountain, and though the University's master had as much control of it as a person possibly could . . . magic, especially magic of the slumbering, half-forgotten kind, was at its most dangerous when taken for granted.

This night, he thought sourly as he passed the door to Professor Tellwyrn's office, it was refreshing to be able to worry about his old standby of ancient forbidden magics instead of worrying about starting the semester with the University's president and professor of history absent, as he had for most of the past week. Tellwyrn had come traipsing in this afternoon, a few hours after the last of the students had arrived, looking disgruntled but not sullen. Long experience told him this meant that her quest had failed, and she'd taken a little time off to work out some of the disappointment. He wondered how much damage had resulted. Arachne typically left quite a mess in her wake when she decided to let her hair down.

Just as he came abreast of the study, an explosion occurred within that rattled the door in its frame, accompanied by a scream.

"*Arachne!*" Yornhaldt bellowed, his annoyance of a moment before forgotten. He grabbed the doorknob; locked, of course, and bespelled against his customary tricks. Backing up, he rammed his shoulder into the wood.

The door had held against the pyrotechnics but was not up to resisting two hundred forty pounds of frantic dwarf. It burst off its hinges and tumbled inward in pieces, Yornhaldt staggering in atop it.

His first sight was of Professor Tellwyrn, sitting on the floor against the far corner, her face blackened and glaring at him furiously. He relaxed; if she was angry enough to glare, she wasn't badly hurt.

"What have I told you, Alaric?!" she shouted. "*How* many times? If you hear knocking and screaming in here, I am either amidst a delicate experiment or masturbating, and your assistance IS NOT REQUIRED."

Professor Yornhaldt took a moment to straighten his robe, surveying the office. Papers were blown about and the chandelier hung crookedly, but nothing else appeared to be damaged except for the utterly pulverized scrying stand that had stood in the center of the carpet. It was now two cracked halves of a crystal ball, a charred map, and a few sticks of kindling. The carpet was going to need cleaning, too, if not outright replacing.

"We go through this every time you scream and I break in," he rumbled, "and I have yet to catch you doing either of those things. I *usually* find you either on fire or wrestling something you've accidentally summoned, and on one memorable occasion, glued to the ceiling. How in blazes did you manage to blow up your scrying equipment? There's not enough magic in that to light a candle."

"Hmph." She surged athletically to her feet, unable to repress a small smirk. Over the years Yornhaldt had grown adept at handling Professor Tellwyrn; the fastest way to soothe her annoyance was to give her a chance to boast when she'd done something clever. "Well, I discovered that you can significantly boost both the range and receptivity of a scrying attempt using the energy-to-matter component of a conjuration spell, with a few tweaks."

"You . . . you did . . ." He blinked in confusion, then a thunderous scowl began to grow on his face. "Arachne, that sounds like an excellent way to unintentionally conjure up whatever you were trying to scry on.

Which, I gather, was the interior of a furnace. Is this what happened the day you had this place knee-deep in venom-spitting saberfish?"

"Don't be absurd, I was making bouillabaisse." She half-heartedly brushed ash from her vest, then reached up to pat at her hair. "Besides, desperate times, inventive measures, and all that. I'm out of leads on the exploding girl problem, and I would prefer to pursue this without interrogating Miss Falconer, who has enough concerns of her own."

Yornhaldt's scowl deepened. "You used a *conjuration* spell to scry on *demons*? Woman, have you gone utterly *insane*?"

"No more than when last we spoke." She leaned down toward him. "How're my eyebrows?"

"Full of soot, but still there."

"Ah, splendid. It'd take all night to regrow them, and I can hardly start class without."

"Damn it, Arachne, take this seriously! If a student had done something so reckless, you'd toss them off the mountain! Are you *trying* to open a hellgate in your office?!"

She stepped around behind her desk, pulled open a drawer, and produced a hand mirror. "Nonsense, if I wanted to open a hellgate, I'd do it in the men's room in the music building. Have you *seen* what's written about me in there?"

"What were you doing in the—*Arachne*!"

Tellwyrn paused in rubbing soot from her face to peer down at him in exasperation. "What?"

Yornhaldt stomped over to the desk and leaned his fists upon its surface, glaring at her. The pose was less effective than it might have been, given that the desktop was at chest height on him. "What. Happened. Here."

"Oh, that." She flicked her fingers at him dismissively, causing a tiny puff of soot. "I was having a measure of success, at first. Scanning for current demon activity, since I wasn't sure yet how to combine my modified scrying spell with a time-bending spell, and that's the kind of thing that tends to break reality if you do it wrong." Yornhaldt clapped a hand over his eyes, which she ignored, continuing to scrub at her face while she talked. "I found quite a sizeable spike in Tiraas."

"In the capital?"

"Unless they moved the capital while I was frontier-hopping, yes, it's in Tiraas. More precisely than that I wasn't able to tell, which means it was in a warded location. Which means the Imperial Palace or the Grand Cathedral; I've cracked everyone else's wards. Cracked the palace wards, too, but they change them every few weeks. Sharidan has been annoyingly careful about security since the vodka elemental incident."

"Still think that was funny?"

"More so every year. Anyhow, I was trying to narrow my focus on whatever demon—and it had to have been a *really* big one, probably more so even than Vadrieny—when whatever it was did something very extravagant and the feedback blasted my scrying table."

Yornhaldt leaned back from the desk, stroking his neatly cropped beard with one hand. ". . . do you think we should warn the palace?"

"I guarantee they already know, and are dealing with it," she said, shooting him a sardonic look. "All that would do is raise awkward questions about why I was trying to scry on the palace. This new emperor is a pretty reasonable fellow, but his grandfather tried to have me kidnapped for that once." She sighed reminiscently. "Now *that* was a good time. Nobody knows how to throw a proper kidnapping anymore."

"Then what do we do?"

"We?" She cocked her head to one side. With half her face still smudged with ash and her blackened hair sticking up every which way, she looked like an inquisitive jungle bird. "*I* am going to back off and try a different approach in a few days, depending on when I have time. *We* are going to go to bed. We've got the freshmen first thing in the morning, and I want you alert for that, Alaric. I'll want your opinions of them right after classes. Oh, and also, I'll need to get Stew up here to fix my door, *apparently*."

He grunted. "Fine. As long as you're not going to detonate yourself again *tonight*, bed sounds very inviting. Who knows, I might actually sleep."

Tellwyrn heaved a melodramatic sigh. "I remember when we used to have fun, Alaric."

"The necessary cleanup after you've had fun just isn't in the budget," he said wryly.

"Yes, yes, fine, of course. I won't have time to fool around with it for at least a week anyhow, with classes starting up. I'll think of something more subtle for my next attempt. And now," she added gently, pushing at his shoulders, "go to bed."

"Promise me you will, too."

"Oh, no worries on that score. Omnu forbid I should have to face the little monsters at less than my best."

"Good night, you crazy witch."

"Night, y'old worrywart."

As Professor Yornhaldt strolled off toward his own rooms, he found he wasn't worried about the unknown horrors lurking beneath their feet at all.

CHAPTER 6

So I saw the other paladin this morning when I was out nosing around," said Gabriel. "The blond?"

"Yeah, Trissiny," Toby replied. "Left here, Gabe. Your *other* left, up the stairs. Yeah, I met her last night. Nice girl, very down-to-earth."

"Mm." Gabriel slouched along, hands thrust into the pockets of his sweeping black coat. It was a striking effect. Between the coat, his prominent nose, and tousled black hair, he looked like a self-important crow; though, Toby privately thought he'd be a lot better looking if he would stand up straight and dress more carefully. "Tall, too. Not bad looking, either, in a sort of gangly way. It's funny, the Hand of Avei not looking anything like the Avenic ideal."

"Avei has absolutely no interest in how pretty anyone is," Toby said wearily. "The so-called 'Avenic ideal' is just imperial society deciding that curvy, dark-haired women are attractive because that's what Avei happens to look like. I seriously doubt she's pleased to have her name attached to it."

"Yeah, well, no offense to Miss Trissiny, but I happen to think that ideal is pretty great." Grinning, Gabe finally removed his hands from his pockets and made a vulgar squeezing motion with them. "I like a lady with a little something I can sink my fingers into."

Toby came to a stop. They had arrived at the uppermost level of the University, which housed the administrative offices, the dining hall, greenhouses, and Helion Hall, their destination. He turned to face Gabriel directly, tucking the map into his pocket.

"You know, Omnu pays attention to what's around me. The gods don't watch everywhere all the time, but just from my schooling in theology I know that he makes a point to be aware of events in my vicinity."

"Uh, yeah, you guys are great together," Gabriel said, frowning. "Why are we stopping?"

"There's a paladin of Avei at this University, as we were just discussing, which probably means that Avei is keeping an eye on things here. Avei, goddess of war and justice, and of *women*. A goddess of the Pantheon, and thus predisposed *not* to give you the benefit of the doubt, Gabe. So maybe it would be smart if you *didn't* walk around campus loudly talking about girls like you're telling a butcher which cut of meat you like best."

Gabriel paled. "Ah, well . . . you didn't let me finish. I just think it's a shame, how society imposes such arbitrary standards on women. Good on Avei, ignoring all that when picking a paladin."

Toby snorted, turning and resuming his walk. "Nice save."

"Yeah, that's me. Slick as buttered silk."

The entrance to Helion Hall was up a short flight of broad marble steps, just left of the dining hall. Both boys paused in the foyer, peering around.

"This is a bit more like home," Gabe noted. "I was half afraid this whole place would be made of logs or something."

They stood in a handsome, vaulted entry hall with a glossy marble floor. Dark wood paneling was interspersed with fluted columns rising to a dome two stories up, which was inset with stained glass windows. In the center of the atrium stood a glass display case containing some kind of . . . broken shell of glossy metal, with a cracked glass panel attached. It looked almost like part of a machine. Toby leaned forward to read the label, then shied back; allegedly this was an Elder God artifact of unknown nature and purpose, confirmed inert. Weren't those famously *always* dangerous?

"This is *way* fancier than anything you or I ever saw back home, man," he said aloud.

"Which way from here? You still have that map, right?"

"I think that's a hint," said Toby, pointing. Opposite the door ahead of them was a hefty wooden desk, currently unmanned; on either side, hallways opened. The one on the left was marked with a small cardboard sign reading FRESHMEN with an arrow pointing down the hall to their left.

"Well, sure, if you're gonna go paying attention to stuff. Show-off."

Toby nudged him with an elbow, grinning, and received a good-natured jostle in return. Together, they strode off as the sign indicated. After only a few feet the left wall vanished, and they found themselves walking down a marble colonnade. Aside from the pillars holding up the roof, all that stood between them and a lovely, terrifying view over the side of the mountain was a chest-high fence of wrought iron.

"Oh good, an outdoor hallway," Gabriel groused. "Does it snow in winters around here?"

"I think we're too far north for that."

"Well, that's something. Does it *rain*?"

"Yeah. You can tell, because everything's not, y'know . . . dead."

"Sir, I believe I have spoken to you about throwing logic around when I'm being melodramatic."

The open walkway curved around the outside of the apparently round building. It terminated at a heavy-looking wooden door, which admitted them to their classroom. The boys found themselves at the bottom of a small amphitheater, with rows of small desks and chairs occupying two ascending levels. They entered near a little stage on which sat a lectern and another, much larger desk, which was against the opposite wall near the other door.

Their classmates had already arrived.

Trissiny immediately caught Toby's eye and gave him a bright smile, which he returned. Of the other girls, only Teal glanced up upon their entrance, also grinning delightedly at him. It was good to see them both in good spirits. The rest of the freshmen girls were apparently absorbed in a conversation taking place between the drow and a tiny fluttering ball of light.

"Three to one," Gabriel murmured. "I *like* these odds. It's like a buffet."

At that, though he had spoken barely above a whisper, the dark elf turned her head to fix Gabe with a chillingly neutral stare, and Toby fought the urge to slap his friend. Gabriel fancied himself a ladies' man, despite the preponderance of evidence to the contrary. Fortunately, the drow quickly turned her attention back to the conversation.

"I know it's not in the student handbook or any official University policy"—the pixie was chattering loudly enough to be plainly heard— "but I read and listened as much as I could about human customs from anybody who'd help me learn them, and yes, I know neither of us is human, but we're staying here now and it's only polite to respect their customs, and anyway I think this is a good one, right? I mean, it makes sense, right? So since it's our room, we can make it our own official rule: if anybody's having sex, they hang a sock on the door handle so everybody knows not to accidentally barge in on them."

"Fross," the drow said with serene patience, "casual sexual encounters are utterly out of the question for me for cultural reasons, and with all due respect, I doubt you will be able to find a physically compatible partner on this campus. This appears to be a nonissue."

"Also," added a girl in a huge hat and coat, one row down, "apparently boys can't even get in the tower." Toby thought she must be Punaji; her complexion was nearly as dark as his own. According to the roster—

"What do boys have to do with it?" Fross began buzzing around in agitated circles. "So if we never need to invoke the rule that's fine; that doesn't hurt anybody or cost anything, which is so much better than if it turns out that we need a rule and it's not there and then somebody ends up embarrassed or worse, right? I mean, we're new here and there's no telling what might happen and life is unpredictable and all, especially since neither of us *knows* all that much about the customs! You get what I'm saying?!"

"It's a comfort thing," said the green-haired woman softly. Right . . . the dryad. Toby had carefully read the class roster before he came, and the pixie wasn't even the most exotic freshman this year. "Rules help us know what's expected of us in unfamiliar surroundings."

"You present several compelling arguments," the dark elf said seriously, her eyes tracking her darting roommate. "I find your proposal agreeable. We shall consider it a rule."

"Okay. Okay, good." Fross slowed her oscillations, settling into a hover over the desk. "Okay, that's fine, then!"

Toby was still watching the dryad sidelong. *Two* fairies; he'd never met a fairy in his life, nor expected to. He hadn't even realized pixies were sapient, but here was one attending college. Still, he was more concerned about the green-haired woman. She had big brown eyes and skin a subtly golden shade. Also, she was so improbably voluptuous that even sitting down he thought she looked like the world of some horny artist.

Which was undoubtedly the reason for what happened next.

Gabriel swaggered up the stairs ringing the amphitheater and leaned against the dryad's desk, grinning. "Hi there. I'm Gabriel."

"Well, hi!" She turned to face him with a bright smile. "My name's Juniper!"

"Juniper, I have never been so delighted to learn anything in my life. So, did you invite all these people? I was hoping we'd have privacy." She laughed delightedly, but from the next row up, Trissiny lowered her eyebrows, staring hard at Gabe. The drow gave him another exceedingly calm stare.

Toby had to suppress a wince. Hassling female students was the quickest possible way to get on the Hand of Avei's bad side, drow were well-known to be matriarchal, and most importantly, *this was a dryad*. Wait . . . did Gabriel even know how dangerous dryads were? Crap, Toby had a feeling *he* hadn't even bothered to read the class roster; he should've warned his friend about this beforehand. He'd have to take the first opportunity—

His ruminations were interrupted when the door on the far wall opened and a slender blond woman strode in.

"Class rule," she announced. "Anyone not in their seat when I reach mine will be expelled. From a catapult."

Neither Gabe nor Toby wasted a second wondering if she could possibly be serious until after leaping into chairs; Fross, the pixie, became a streak of light that slapped into the back of a desk chair hard enough to set it rocking. Professor Tellwyrn—he hadn't seen her in person before, but it could be no one else—ignored all of this, turning her back to drop an armload of heavy books on the desk, then casually kicked the door shut. She strolled toward the podium, interweaving her fingers and flexing in a way that set her knuckles loudly cracking, and eight pairs of eyes (assuming pixies had eyes) silently studied the first living legend they had ever encountered.

She didn't look particularly impressive, and certainly didn't look three thousand years old. Tobias had met a few of the older elves in the course of his training, and though age didn't show on their faces, there was a serenity, a gravity to their every movement that his new history professor lacked. Arachne Tellwyrn was a slim woman with her blond hair tied back in a simple tail; she was pretty, but just in the way elves tended to be, with delicately pointed features and large, expressive eyes. Her ears came to the sharp upward points that marked her as a wood elf.

The professor halted next to the podium, resting a hand upon it, and slowly dragged her gaze across the room. Her eyes were vibrant green, striking even at a distance. Suddenly, she grinned lopsidedly, but it was not a humorous expression. There was something predatory in that smile.

"Who can describe imperial relations with the pirate states, with which the Tiraan Empire has treaties? Miss Punaji, do not answer. Miss Awarrion."

The drow lowered her hand. "Tiraas has similar treaties with the Punaji pirates of the Azure Sea in the east and the Tidestriders of the Grand Mere in the west. In fact, these treaties and their attendant imperial support are largely the reason those two nations have grown to dominate their respective territories. The pirates agree not to harass imperial shipping, and in return are not attacked by the empire. Both are expected to render aid to one another in the event of attack or disaster."

"Accurate, but shallow," Tellwyrn acknowledged, inclining her head. "From another perspective, the empire is in essence paying pirates to exclusively prey on overseas interests. How has this not provoked a war with other nations?"

"The Tiraan Empire is an expansionist power which consolidated its rule of this continent more than a century ago," Shaeine continued, still coolly impassive. "By entering into relationships with the pirates, which are dependent on them having a steady supply of non-Tiraan victims, the empire tacitly promises not to extend its control to foreign shores, which would make any ocean between them unavailable to the pirates according to the treaties. The empire gains maritime vassal states to secure its borders, other nations gain the assurance that Tiraas will not encroach upon theirs, and the pirate bands gain patronage and safe harbor on this continent's coasts. All parties incur costs, but ultimately benefit. It is a masterwork of diplomacy."

To Toby's left, the girl in the hat twisted her mouth as if tasting something sour, but Professor Tellwyrn nodded approvingly at Shaeine. That would be Zaruda Punaji, according to the class roster he'd read. If that was her actual surname, didn't that make her . . .

"Excellently reasoned," said Tellwyrn. "That's more what I expect from you, Miss Awarrion. Can someone explain how mortals have historically interacted with fairies? Juniper, Fross, do not answer. Yes, Mr. Arquin?"

"By staying the hell away from them," said Gabriel with a grin.

"How colloquial, Mr. Arquin. Care to expand on that slightly?"

"Well, everyone knows, or should, not to accept gifts from fae, or make any deals with them, or try to attack them. And to always be as polite as possible if you do meet one. But, yeah . . . honestly, the best policy is to avoid them as much as possible."

Professor Tellwyrn folded her hands behind her back, fixing him with a flat stare. "*Why?*"

"Professor?"

"There have been no wars against fairykind, no major interactions at all. Why this aversion?"

Gabe glanced over at Juniper; for once, his gaze stayed above her collarbone. "Because . . . we don't understand them. Most experts, I mean, most philosophers and mages *and* the diplomats who've tried, believe we *can't* understand them. They run on a whole different kind of logic, sort of like demons. They're extremely powerful and totally unpredictable. The only safe thing is just not to bother them."

"We're scary?" Juniper looked so hurt Toby wanted to get up and give her a hug, for the second it took him to remember *why* dryads in particular were scary.

"See, Mr. Arquin?" said Tellwyrn, smirking so condescendingly that Gabriel's guilty reaction to Juniper's distress vanished into a scowl. "You do know a thing or two, once it's pried out of you. I will remind you all for the record that just because scholars have concluded a thing does not make it so. Someone describe the nature of imperial relations with the drow city-state of Tar'naris. Miss Awarrion, do not answer. Yes, Miss Punaji."

Grinning, Zaruda lounged back in her chair. "As I understand it, the empire just went in and pretty much redid the place overnight. Put up sun crystals, like the dwarves have underground, taught the drow about agriculture, imported a bunch of soil and plants and stuff and basically turned their big empty cave into a place that can support itself with plenty of food without needing to raid the surface. I understand before the treaty with the empire, the drow valued food more than gold."

"That's an awfully generous move from a huge militaristic power, which was previously at a state of undeclared war with the Narisians and all other drow," the professor said dryly. "Are you maybe forgetting something?"

"Oh right. In return, both parties get peace, of course, and also Tiraas gets first dibs on metals and jewels and stuff out of Tar'naris, pretty much for free."

"Essentially correct. Tar'naris controls access to several of the continent's richest mineral deposits, for which it has relatively little use. To be more specific, by the treaty the Narisians have first access to their own resources, but deliver a yearly quota to the empire in perpetuity in exchange for the magic that makes their caverns verdant. And yes, to drow, access to plentiful food is a bounty whose value simply cannot be overstated. But Tar'naris is only one of three drow city-states controlling an egress from the underworld into imperial territory. Why does Tiraas not have similar treaties with the others? Mr. Arquin?"

"Because they're too crazy to deal with."

"How *eloquently* dismissive, Mr. Arquin. I don't suppose you'd like to add a little more detail to your analysis."

Gabe grimaced, but straightened in his chair, continuing. "Well, of the other two drow cities, one has refused a treaty like the Narisian one without saying why, and the others literally *are* too crazy to deal with. Or at least too aggressive. You can't do diplomacy with people who attack diplomats on sight."

"Again, more or less correct, though it would be closer to truth to say that the Akhvari explained their reasons for declining commerce and the empire failed to understand them. What has been the most significant drawback of normalized relations with Tar'naris? Yes, Mr. Caine?"

Toby lowered his hand. "Dwarves."

"'Dwarves' is not an answer, Mr. Caine. It is not a sentence, nor even a sentence *fragment*."

He shifted in his seat, repressing annoyance. "The dwarf kingdoms were the empire's biggest trading partners when it came to metals and stone. With the empire suddenly getting a lot of free minerals, they stopped buying, and the dwarven economy was hit hard. They've been . . . a lot less friendly since."

"Econom*ies*; the dwarves are hardly monolithic. But you are correct. Who can summarize what is known about demons? Miss Falconer, Mr. Arquin, do not answer. Oh, this should be good. Yes, Miss Avelea?"

"I prefer *Ms.* Avelea," Trissiny said firmly. She glanced speculatively at Gabriel. Everyone was now looking speculatively at Gabriel, except for Gabe himself, who was looking speculatively at Teal.

"I prefer not to be contradicted. Life is a succession of disappointments, Miss Avelea; embrace it. Your answer?"

Trissiny visibly gritted her teeth before replying. "Demons are the evil creatures native to the infernal plane, also known as Hell. They are servants of the dark goddess Elilial, who rebelled against the Pantheon, and for her crimes against the mortal races and the other gods was hurled into Hell, where she became ruler by slaughtering all who opposed her. All demons hate mortal creatures and constantly seek to enter the material plane to spread destruction in whatever way they can."

"That was better than the rant I was expecting. For future reference, Miss Avelea, reciting Church dogma in this class is no way to attain a passing grade; you'll be lucky if I don't make you eat soap. However, in this *one* case, the Church has the right of it." Professor Tellwyrn folded her hands in front of her, peering around the room as if to make sure everyone was listening. "Whether demons are constantly seeking to escape from Hell and invade us is up for debate; some experts even within the Church theorize that many of them accidentally wander in through hellgates and cause havoc much the same way a bear accidentally caught in a tavern would. But it is unquestionably true that most, if not all, demons are specifically hostile to life on this plane, and there is strong reason to believe the majority, if not the entirety, of Hell answers to Elilial. And they certainly *have* mounted a number of organized invasions, which were repelled only at great cost."

"You don't agree with the Church?" Gabe said, suddenly looking a lot more interested.

"Raise your hand, Mr. Arquin; we are not baboons. And the matter is not that straightforward. Religious institutions by nature view the world in simple, dichotomous terms, whereas the infernal plane is probably as huge and diverse as this one. Mortal excursions through hellgates have never gotten far, and we have only cataloged nineteen sapient and eighty-three other varieties of demons. We know less about what goes on in Hell than we do about what's under the ocean; it would be tremendously foolhardy to feign total understanding of it. Enough about that. Who has observations to share about paladins? Miss Avelea, Mr. Caine, do not answer. Yes, Miss Awarrion."

"Paladins are the designated servants of the gods," Shaeine answered, lowering her hand. "An individual is selected by a deity to serve as that god's Hand on this plane, which entails chiefly taking action when, for whatever reason, the god in question cannot or will not. Paladins gain a variety of powers and gifts from their patron, which vary by deity, but all called by gods of the Pantheon are able to summon holy light, which has healing properties to life native to this plane and is destructive to demons."

"A textbook answer, Miss Awarrion—incontrovertible, but lacking nuance. Anyone have something to add? I'm fishing for recent history. Mr. Arquin?"

"Yeah, paladins were supposed to be *gone*. At least until recently; there hadn't been one in twenty years, since the last Hand of Omnu died, and none had been called by any of the gods for more than ten years before that. Most people thought that since magic had advanced so much and most fighting is done with wands and staffs nowadays instead of swords and armor, they were pretty much obsolete and the gods had given up on the whole thing." He grinned wickedly. "Then boom, Toby and Trissiny are called out of nowhere, and the Church was caught with its pants down."

"Such a way with words you have, Mr. Arquin. You're not wrong, though, and the world is avidly waiting now to see if more paladins will be called again, and herald a new Age of Adventures." She snorted. "Gods, I hope not. Speaking as a retired adventurer myself, we managed to cause enough havoc without having ready access to cheap magical weapons. These days you can buy a wand for less than a horse used to cost . . . But that's a subject for another class."

She stepped behind the lectern and leaned forward on it, looking over the students slowly. Again, that diabolical smile spread across her face. "Welcome," she said, "to the Ultimate University."

"Ultimate?" Gabe looked around at the others. "I thought it was just called the University."

"*Hand*, Arquin." Despite her reproof, the professor's grin remained unabated. "Ultimate in both senses—as the preeminent university above all, and the *final* one. This is where I seek the solution to what I deem the final problem—mortal stupidity. You will find, children, that nearly all harm done in this world is through some combination of ignorance and idiocy, committed by people who fail to understand what's happening around them, and in particular, what they should do about it.

"It is *stupidity*, not malice, which is the root of all evil. This institution's true name is hidden; it is part of a potent fae geas laid upon this land at its founding. Only initiates of this University know its name, so you will find yourselves quite unable to share it with outsiders. In this way, you may recognize one another in the wild, as it were, which you'll find a very useful thing. Graduates of Ultimate University are the best and brightest, and definitely the most dangerous, people at large in the empire, and beyond."

She drummed her fingers on the lectern once, then straightened. "Since none of you are . . . any stupider than is understandable in your various situations . . . you'll *hopefully* have deduced the theme of my little question-and-answer session. There are other schools in the Tiraan Empire, several of them with academic standards that, I must acknowledge, surpass our own. The student body here is composed of . . . well, look at yourselves. Several of you are here for diplomatic reasons, rather than having been strongly encouraged to attend by the throne, but *all* of you have this in common: you possess the academic qualifications necessary to attend a competitive school of higher learning . . ." Her wolfish grin widened. "And you are simply too dangerous to be allowed to run around unsupervised."

Toby slowly lifted his hand; Professor Tellwyrn raised an eyebrow in his direction. "What happens to people who are too dangerous to be unsupervised but *don't* have the academic qualifications?"

"A complex question, Mr. Caine, and one which has as many answers as individuals to which it pertains. Later in your tenure here, you may find it needful to that very subject. For now, suffice it to say that you should be grateful to find yourself here and not there."

She stepped around from behind the podium and began to pace slowly up and down the stage. "Given the unique nature of our student body, we do things a little bit differently here. Book learning is all well and good, and you can expect to do a great deal of it, but our entire curriculum is strongly skewed toward the practical. This class, for instance, has been billed as History 101. Undoubtedly, you were surprised to find there is no textbook. Yes, I do expect you to learn some history, because understanding the past is a necessary first step in not blundering back into it, but in truth, this class will be an ongoing examination of the forces that move people, both as individuals and nations." She spread her hands wide, smiling more kindly around the room. "Why, in other words, do people do what they do? This is something you, in particular, will very much need to understand. You'll all go out into the world and be expected to have a great impact on the course of events. In fact, more of you than otherwise are going to end up leading large groups of people."

Tellwyrn folded her hands again and resumed her pacing. "You'll find this same emphasis reflected in your other courses, to varying degrees. Our music program is, in fact, designed to produce fully competent and accredited bards, individuals who are roving entertainers, diplomats, and, on occasion, mercenaries. As such, it covers a great deal that would horrify the music students at Tirasian University even to contemplate. Herbalism is a required freshman course rather than an elective, and could be more correctly called 'How Not to Have an Embarrassing Plant-Related Death.' On the other hand, martial arts are martial arts, and not much goes on there that doesn't elsewhere, though in that area our standards are toweringly high.

"The point is," she went on, coming to a stop, "everything you think you know about school, you can forget. Those of you who aren't familiar with imperial academic traditions are actually at something of an advantage here. All but one of your first-semester classes will be taken in the company of the people in this room. The eight or nine of you, depending on how you count, are a unit, my dear freshmen, so I suggest you begin getting used to one another. Which brings us to the homework. You will each have on my desk by tomorrow night a two-page paper, detailing in brief a general tactical analysis of each of your classmates, including strengths and weaknesses, and how you personally expect to be of assistance to them."

Tellwyrn smiled with much more humor at the flabbergasted expressions this produced. "Welcome home, kids. Class dismissed."

CHAPTER 7

"Hey."

"Mm?"

"You ever wonder why we're here?"

Rook paused in his eighteenth consecutive game of solitaire to peer up at Finchley. "Interesting. Now, is this an existential-type question, such as 'what is the meaning of life' or 'why did the gods see fit to place us in these bodies at this time in history . . .'" He reached into the unbuttoned collar of his uniform jacket to scratch himself. ". . . or more along the lines of 'why in fuck's name did the army assign us to guard this here empty box canyon approximately five miles west of nowhere's asshole?'"

"Our orders *specifically* prohibit speculation as to the nature of this assignment," their other companion growled, not looking up from polishing his army-issue battlestaff.

"Blargle largle blumble boo," said Rook airily, sweeping up his cards and beginning to loudly shuffle the deck. "Look at us, Moriarty. Five privates on two duty shifts assigned to a hatbox-sized 'fort' in the aforementioned empty-ass box canyon, with *no officers present*. Even by army standards, this whole thing is idiotic. I bet they *want* us to start ignoring orders. It's the only explanation that makes sense."

Finchley sighed, recognizing a new chorus of an old quarrel warming up. He leaned forward against the rail, not minding the way the entire structure vibrated; experience had taught him that it would probably hold, and if not, tumbling off the roof would at least alleviate the tedium. Their "fort" was little more than a wooden hut with a railed observation platform on top, occupying one end of the small box canyon. Behind it was the retractable rope ladder leading to the stairs *out* of the canyon. They really had nothing to do while on "watch" but to stare at the abandoned mine opening at the other end of the canyon, which they had been emphatically ordered never to approach.

"It was a practical question," he said, cutting off the gathering argument. "And don't glare at me like that, Moriarty, you know he's right."

Private Moriarty harrumphed and bent over his staff again, dipping his rag in the jar of polish. The thing already gleamed blindingly in the sun. The hot, hot sun . . . Finchley cast a longing look up at the trees rimming the canyon's lip. It must be so shady and cool up there . . .

"You better leave that thing alone or you're gonna rub all the magic out of it," Rook said, his customary sly grin creeping across his swarthy face. "How's about you go below and polish your *other* staff for a while? Might improve your disposition."

"If I bothered to report every flouted regulation or act of open insubordination that goes on in this wretched excuse for a base," Moriarty said woodenly, "I'd have no time to do anything but write reports. If not for me, Rook, you'd be running a still and a brothel here by now."

"That just isn't true, brother, and I'll tell you why." Rook tucked the cards into the pocket of his jacket and folded his arms behind his head, leaning against the rail. "This is an answer to your question, too, Finchley. See, my theory is we're part of some big experiment. I mean, seriously. Five privates, middle of nowhere, no officers? It makes no *sense*. And what the hell are these?" He lifted a hand to tap one of the clouded crystal orbs that surmounted the corner posts of the railing. "I think these are some kind of scrying equipment. I think they're studying how long it takes discipline to completely break the hell down when they don't bother to maintain it."

"That'd be useful for them to know if we ever go to war again," Finchley mused, shifting his staff to the other hand.

Rook nodded. "Exactly! See? He gets it! So yeah, *that* is why you chumps don't have the privilege of living in Rook's Hookerarium and Moonshine Palace. I figure they *expect* us to let the uniform situation slide a bit, but I try to keep my court-martial-worthy offenses to no more than three a day."

Indeed, of the three of them only Moriarty kept his navy-blue Imperial Army uniform to regulation standards. Finchley had, after the third week of not being checked up on by Imperial Command, stopped buttoning his jacket as a concession to the heat. Rook didn't even bother to tuck in his shirt most days, nor to lace up his boots properly, and only a truly epic tantrum from Moriarty had prevented him from tearing the sleeves off his coat.

"I think it's a hellgate," Finchley said.

"Hellgates are classified material," Moriarty all but shouted. "Speculating about them while *on duty* is a class four act of insubordination!"

"Oh, blow it out your ass, Moriarty," Rook said lazily. "And Finchley, get your head out of yours. If this was a hellgate, they'd have a platoon here covering it. With artillery and wizards."

"No, see, my dad *is* a wizard," Finchley insisted. "He does research for the Wizards' Guild. Almost all known hellgates are completely quiet, sorta like they're blocked from the other end or something. But gates that've been silent for years have been known to unexpectedly cough out a demon once in a while, so the empire wouldn't just leave them unwatched. But there's only so many troops and so much funding to go around, and with most of it on the frontiers around the Golden Sea and the deep wild, they can't possibly put full security on every single known hellgate; there are hundreds of 'em. But five soldiers, two or three on duty at a time with wands and staves? A couple blasts would do for most of the kinds of demons that might accidentally slip through. And this one being in the middle of nowhere, if Elilial was gonna invade or something, she wouldn't use this one."

"That," Rook said slowly, "makes a scary amount of sense. Well, fuck, I didn't want to ever sleep again anyway. Thank you *so* much, Finchley."

"If this conversation stops *now*, I'll forget I heard it," said Moriarty through gritted teeth. "Otherwise . . ."

"Otherwise you'll go and *tell* on us. I bet your schoolmarm *loved* you, Moriarty."

"I bet *yours* tried to drown you in the well!"

"Nope," Rook said, grinning, "but her husband did."

"Well. *This* wasn't here before."

The three soldiers lifted their heads in surprise at the new voice behind them, then as one, froze and stared in slack-jawed stupefaction.

Standing between their fort and the ladder, which offered their only chance of escape, stood a woman with skin of a dusky crimson, eyes that were swirling pits of orange flame, and a pair of ridged horns sweeping backward from the crown of her forehead. She wore an improbable black leather outfit, studded with steel rings and spikes of dubious utility, and with her feet on the ground, towered over their rooftop watch post by a good ten feet. That voice seemed like it would have been a throaty, sultry purr, had it not been powerful enough to rattle the floorboards.

"I see Sharidan has found my little bolt-hole," she went on with a sly smile. "Such a clever lad, that one. Though, honestly, his habit of putting soldiers at all my doors and windows is becoming tiresome."

"H-h-halt!" Finchley squeaked, though the apparition wasn't moving. He raised his staff and pointed it at her; the uncontrollable trembling of his arms would have killed his accuracy, had she not been so close and such a huge target. "Id-d-dentify yourself!"

"Oh dear, how rude of me." That smug smile widened to a grin; she had fangs as long as his forearm. "You would know me as Elilial, among other, less polite monikers. Incidentally, lads, you've built your little clubhouse right across my back steps, as it were. That's hardly neighborly."

All three of them were now on their feet, Rook after some awkward scrambling and nearly falling off the platform twice. Finchley and Moriarty had staves pointed at her heart; Rook couldn't reach his, but aimed his sidearm at her (and also Finchley's, which Finchley only just now realized he'd stolen at some point).

"Elilial?" Rook croaked. "Oh, bugger. I pictured someone less hot."

"Why, aren't you a sweetie," she cooed. Her breath smelled of a very confusing blend of sulfur and spearmint. "Suppose you just drop those things, boys? Surely you wouldn't shoot a pregnant lady."

A moment of silence held, while the goddess of demons eyed the three petrified imperial privates with unveiled amusement.

"Elilial," Moriarty finally said in a shrill squeak, "if that is your real name, you are under arrest on the authority of the emperor of Tiraas. You are commanded to stand down and submit to—to—to, uh, arrest."

At this, her grin widened to truly appalling proportions.

"Well, just look at you three," she purred. "Brave, loyal . . . *not* too bright. Exactly the way I like my boys. Makes me sad I don't have time to stop and play, but I have bigger fish in the fire. Take a nap, lads."

As though she'd flipped a switch, the three soldiers crumpled silently, dropping their weapons with a clatter. Moriarty began to snore.

Elilial shook her head as she stepped around the fort, heading for the old mineshaft. "Poor kids. You've seen what your superiors would rather no one knew was real, and that's usually a death sentence. Still, at least this time they won't have me to blame for the deed." In passing, she tapped one of the smoky crystal orbs with a fingertip; it exploded into powder.

And then she was gone, striding through a hole that opened in the air at the far end of the canyon and snapped shut behind her.

"So." Zaruda broke the slightly dazed silence that hovered over the eight of them as they navigated the University's paths. Toby was grateful someone did; he'd started to wonder if *he* should, but couldn't think of anything worth saying. "Anyone else have the distinct feeling they've accidentally been sent to the loony island and we're *all going to die?*" She tugged the lapels of her coat up around her ears, reached inside, and somehow pulled out a bottle of bourbon. "I've got that, a little."

"Well . . . sure, we're gonna die." Juniper seemed puzzled. "Everything dies, that's just science. But not, like . . . right *now*. Probably."

"She wants us to write essays about each other's weaknesses," Teal mused, "as some kind of bonding tactic. Does that seem completely ass-backward to anyone else?"

"Armies do something similar, at basic training," Trissiny said slowly. "Conditions are meant to be intense, and drillmasters make themselves into hostile figures. It encourages the soldiers to form a strong bond against any prospective enemies."

"My people use similar techniques in training," said the dark elf, as serene as always. "Though I am not an expert in military matters by any means, I don't believe soldiers are encouraged to pick at one another's failings."

"I'm not sure that woman is entirely sane," said Trissiny.

"Hah! You should talk." Zaruda took a long swig from her bottle, cocking a thumb at her roommate. "This one was up at buttfuck o'clock in the morning. Came back to the room an hour later, in full armor, looking worn out, and this just when I was getting up. Needless to say, we had us a discussion about shower privileges."

"I went for a run," Trissiny said defensively. "The main stairs up the mountain make for a good track."

"You . . . you ran down and back up the stairs?" Teal boggled at her. "In *armor?*"

"Of course in armor," Trissiny retorted testily. "People who expect to fight in armor should train in armor. The academic life is no excuse for me to get soft."

"Damn, girl," said Gabriel. "There's not getting soft, and then there's that."

"What do you know about demons?" she asked, half turning her head to stare at him.

His expression went flat. "I know to stay the hell away from them. What else does anyone *need* to know?"

"Hm." She turned away, absently fingering the hilt of her sword.

"I'm assuming, by the way, that somebody knows where the hell we're going," Zaruda said, peering around. The campus was lively and lovely in the midmorning sun, with students passing them on the way to their own classes. The eight freshmen had just descended a staircase to the next level down from the upper terrace and Helion Hall.

"We've got Introduction to Magic with Professor Yornhaldt," chimed Fross before Toby could reach for his map. "Derringer Hall, dead ahead! Follow me!" She flitted away down the path, occasionally darting back impatiently to the slower students.

They had progressed only another ten feet when a figure plummeted from above, landing directly into their path. "Well," she drawled, "isn't *this* just precious."

They stopped as one; Fross darted behind Juniper, and Trissiny gripped her sword, eyes narrowing. Zaruda snorted loudly and had a pull of bourbon. Blocking their way was a drow woman in denim trousers and a laced vest that left her muscular arms bare. She wore rectangular shades of black glass that hid her eyes, and her white hair was combed and gelled into a spiked ridge over the top of her head, the ends dyed a sharp green. Folding her arms across her chest, she sneered. "Another little rat scurries up from below, all prettied up and repressed half to death. Come to learn how to live without being waited on hand and foot?"

"Are you addressing me?" the dark elf among the freshmen said mildly. Shaeine nur Ashaele d'zin Awarrion, according to Toby's student roster; he had carefully memorized that and wasn't about to try pronouncing it until he heard her do so first. Upon leaving the classroom she had donned a dark cloak and put the hood up to shelter her face from the sunlight.

"Well, I wasn't talking to the pixie." The drow woman's sneer grew to an animal ferocity. "Let me guess, Narisian? Pampered pet of the empire, never had to work a day in your life? Word of advice, little bitch-pup—go home."

"Okay, I think that's just about enough of that," said Toby firmly, stepping in front of Shaeine—unsure who he was protecting from whom, but it seemed best to get between the two drow. "If you'll excuse us, miss, we have class."

She transferred her gaze to him, eyed him up and down, and smirked. "Yeah? And?"

"So this is what we're doing? We're hassling the freshmen now? Good, great. That's an excellent use of our time when we're about to be late for class."

Two figures appeared on the ledge of the terrace above, from which the drow had jumped—a grinning boy with sharp features and pale blond hair, who had spoken, and the dark-complexioned young man in the bone-decorated vest, who had sat over the arch yesterday giving out directions.

"Hey, guys," said the latter with a cheerful wave. "Finding your way around all right?"

"Until very recently, yes," said Shaeine.

"Yeah, sorry about her," said the blond. "I'd do something, but, y'know how it is. She terrifies me. Also, I'm hoping to sleep with her at some point."

"Fuck you, Chase," snapped the drow, glaring up at them.

"I'll pencil you in! How's Thursday at eleven?"

She bared her teeth and actually growled, then turned on her heel and stalked off.

"Tanq, do correct me if I'm mistaken, but Natchua's in our next class, right?" said Chase from atop the wall.

"That she is, my friend," his companion replied.

"Which is very much *not* in the direction in which she just departed."

"The sacrifices that must be made for a dramatic exit."

"Do you suppose we ought to be late, too? As a show of solidarity?"

"If by 'solidarity' you mean 'not setting off our insane classmate,' then your reasoning is sound."

"Seems like we've got a plan, then." Chase seated himself on the wall, dangling his legs over, and waved down at them. "Flee, little froshes! Flee whilst you can!"

"Yeah, okay." Zaruda shouldered through the pack and swaggered off ahead, the others trailing after her.

"Nice to see you again!" called Teal, waving up at Tanq. He nodded gravely in return.

Trissiny shook her head, muttering. "I really don't think I like it here."

Toby wasn't sure he was supposed to have heard that. He wasn't sure whether it would be better to pretend he hadn't or offer a word of comfort. Increasingly, he wasn't sure of a lot.

CHAPTER 8

Their first martial arts class with Professor Ezzaniel met on the big lawn on the University's middle level, near the gazebo. Having eaten early, the freshman class arrived long before the professor. To their mild discomfort, several other students were already lurking about the periphery of the lawn, obviously watching them. None came close enough to introduce themselves or offer greetings. Despite not yet being entirely comfortable with one another, the eight found themselves edging closer together under the scrutiny.

"So, you really packed away that chicken," Zaruda said to Juniper, who tilted her head in evident confusion.

"Is that bad? It was really good chicken! I've never had cooked food before, and Mrs. Oak is very good at cooking."

"Yeah, but . . . you're a dryad."

"Yeeesss . . ." Juniper looked even more puzzled. "And you're a human."

"I thought you nymphs were all vegetarians. Y'know, not eating Mother Naiya's creatures and all that."

"What? Where did you get that idea? You know how many things in nature eat animals? Including quite a few plants!"

"Oh. Uh . . ."

"And besides, almost all life forms exist by consuming other life forms. Plants are nourished by decomposition of dead matter in the soil, and are then eaten by animals. It's a vast, intricate web, and everything in it is food for something else."

"I . . . guess that's so . . . never really thought about . . ."

"What, you thought I'd value the lives of animals more?" Juniper planted her fists on her hips, frowning. Even that was pretty on her. "It's fine to kill broccoli and rice, but Naiya forbid anyone harm a chicken? Maybe you should get out more, Ruda!"

"Okay, okay, whoa now," said Teal soothingly, sliding between them. "It was an honest misunderstanding. I'm sure Ruda didn't mean any harm. And we all got to learn a bit about dryads. Everybody wins, right?"

"I guess so," Juniper said slowly, then suddenly broke into a dazzling smile. "I'm sorry, Ruda. I misunderstood what you meant. I'll get better at that, promise."

"Hmph." If anything, Zaruda looked even more annoyed than before.

"So, that's a pretty amazing sword," said Teal cheerfully, carefully moving to block Zaruda's view of the dryad. "Where'd you get that from?"

"Ah yes. My sword." Zaruda removed her hat, dropping it behind her; deprived of its shade, her face suddenly looked deadly serious. Slowly, she drew the rapier and held it out for them all to see. Sunlight gleamed along the blade and the gold of its hilt, while the facets of a dozen gems glittered brightly. In fact, the slender shaft of metal was oddly colored for steel—pale as moonlight, seeming almost to glow from within as the sun danced across it. "My grandfather was one of the greatest swordsmiths who ever lived. This . . . this was his final masterpiece, a great gift commissioned by the king of a foreign land. He labored on it for a year, and when it was done, the king's ambassador returned to collect the blade—but offered only a tenth of the promised price! My grandfather, of course, refused. Without saying a word, the ambassador stabbed him through the heart, and fled, with a dozen furious pirates on his tail." She let the blade fall slowly, resting its gleaming tip against the ground. "They did not catch him, for he used shadow-jumping to escape. But I swore to my father that I would take up this blade, and once I was strong enough and skilled enough, I'd hunt down that ambassador wherever he may hide, and end his life with this very sword."

She bowed her head in the sudden, heavy silence.

"Zaruda," Trissiny said hesitantly, "I had no idea. I'm sorry if I . . ."

"Nah, I'm just funnin' ya." Ruda lifted her chin and grinned. "I read all that in a book once. My papa gave me this for a sweet fifteen present. Isn't it sparkly? I think it's dwarf-made."

Trissiny went pale, then scarlet, stammering in apoplectic rage. "I—that—I—that—you—"

"Breathe," Teal murmured, placing a hand on her back.

"Good morning, students."

Professor Ezzaniel appeared almost as if by magic, striding toward them with the easy grace of a prowling cat. A tall man with a proud eagle's beak of a nose and a neatly trimmed mustache and goatee, his black hair just beginning to show silver at the temples, he was dressed simply in slacks, an open-collared shirt, and a coat with a saber belted over it, and he was carrying a large carpet bag.

"Good, no one has seen fit to begin their academic career by playing hooky. Most years, there's at least one. As I know each of you by name and your rather distinctive descriptions, we shall dispense with roll call and proceed directly to . . . theory." Ezzaniel placed the bag at his feet and folded his arms, sweeping his eyes across the group thoughtfully. "I understand that Professor Tellwyrn has you analyzing one another's strengths and weaknesses."

"Yeah," said Gabriel. "Is that, uh . . . normal?"

"'Normal,' Mr. Arquin, is a word you will find has little bearing on this campus and none whatsoever on your history professor. However, this dovetails nicely with a test of your analytical abilities, which I'd like to open our first class with. In your opinion, students, which of your classmates is the most dangerous combatant?"

Nobody bothered to answer, but everyone immediately turned to look at Trissiny, who straightened her spine and lifted her chin, saying nothing.

"Ah yes. A reasonable conclusion, but a shallow analysis. The focus of this course will be to give you the tools needed to preserve your life and health in a hostile situation, and based on my experience with teaching those new to the martial arts, I expect several of you will be surprised by the cerebral elements of this course. Combat is, to a great extent, in the mind. More than merely studying combat, we will also, chiefly on days when weather prevents meeting outdoors, study many of the dangers of this world and how to most effectively counter them. Knowledge is power; power is survival."

He stroked his goatee, smiling slightly. "To begin with, while Ms. Avelea is indeed a force you would be wise not to challenge, Miss Falconer is a far deadlier one. For that error I cannot blame you, as there are certain things I should imagine you have not yet been told. However, it *was* an error in judgment to dismiss Juniper. Given the choice, I personally would prefer to duel a paladin than a dryad."

There were several raised eyebrows at this, and Juniper looked uncomfortable, but Gabriel openly scoffed. "What? Seriously? I mean . . . look at her."

"Ah yes, because appearance is always a sure indicator of substance. I see we have a budding tactician in our midst." Zaruda laughed loudly, earning a glare from Gabriel. "Mr. Arquin, let us engage in a little test. You see that tree?" Professor Ezzaniel pointed at a towering oak that stood at the far edge of the lawn.

"Yes?"

"Good. Go over there and hit it."

He stared at the professor blankly for a moment. ". . . I'm sorry, what?"

"Is your hearing less than nominal? Do please tell me so up front; that will make a difference in the methods I use to train you."

"No, Professor, my hearing's fine," Gabe snapped. "I'm simply questioning what it tells me because it's hard to believe a teacher would say something so dumb."

"Belief is a crutch that cripples your faculties, Mr. Arquin. You are wasting your classmates' time. Get over there. Now."

With a long-suffering roll of his eyes, Gabriel turned and stalked over to the indicated oak tree. He paused beside it, looking back at the group as if to double-check that Ezzaniel could possibly be serious. The professor gestured for him to proceed. With a shrug, he lifted a hand and slapped the tree.

"Pitiful!" Ezzaniel shouted. "Once more, and pretend that you mean it."

Not even looking back at him, Gabriel straightened his shoulders and threw a punch into the trunk. He took a step backward, grimacing and shaking his hand.

"We can do this all day, Mr. Arquin," called the professor. "Let me see whether there's any meat in those arms at all, which frankly I begin to doubt."

This time, Gabe actually snarled at him, then drew back his fist and slammed it into the bark with a *thump* that was clearly audible all over the lawn. There were some scattered cheers from the onlookers.

"Very good, Mr. Arquin. You may rejoin us."

Gabriel stomped back over, glaring furiously and breathing loudly through his teeth. "Right. Fine. *Very* cute. Now, am I allowed to know the freaking *point* of that?"

"Quite." Ezzaniel folded his hands behind his back and turned to address the group as a whole. "This has been an example of the price of ignorance. As Mr. Arquin has just demonstrated, punching a tree is a painful and pointless exercise. The reason for this is physics—a tree is immobile, massive, and dense, especially in comparison with most of you. A dryad, students, is a magical creature, and thus physics alone fail to account for her full traits and capabilities. She has all the properties of a tree, but more conscious control of them. Being punched by a dryad is very similar to being struck by the full weight of an oak, moving at the speed at which she can swing her fist." One corner of his mouth quirked upward in a sly half smile. "Dryads are, for the most part, and making allowances for individual personality, not notably aggressive. They don't need to be; if you irritate a dryad, she will simply remove you from her personal space. This can extend for several miles, and she can do it with one blow."

Juniper, by now, looked positively mortified; everyone else was eyeing her nervously.

"Our first class, as you may have already surmised, will focus on gauging everyone's level of skill," Ezzaniel went on crisply. "More on analysis later. First of all, those of you with weapons, remove them. We will exclusively use safety equipment in this class. Miss Punaji, Miss Awarrion, come here, please."

Zaruda had already unbuckled her rapier and dropped it to the grass beside her hat. At his summons, she shrugged and swaggered over to him, grinning, with Shaeine gliding along behind her.

Professor Ezzaniel knelt to open the clasp on his battered carpet bag. "Within this bag are the practice weapons you will use for this class. Each of them is an enchanted item which will mimic the properties of a normal weapon but inflict no harm upon anyone, and there lies within sufficient variety to appease even the most exotic tastes. Simply put your hand inside, grasp the first object you find, and pull; you will produce a weapon appropriate to your fighting style."

"Neat," said Ruda, bending over and plunging her hand in. She straightened, dragging a wooden rapier from the bag, hilt first. Its design was basically the same as her own. She stepped aside to make room for Shaeine, who knelt, reached in with both hands, and pulled out a pair of matching scimitars.

"Heh, not bothering to defy the cliche, are we?" Zaruda asked, grinning.

"You used that word at lunch, as well," replied Shaeine, tilting her head inquisitively. "I am not able to infer the meaning from context."

"What? Cliche? That's, uh . . . You know how a phrase or idea or something is really awesome when it's first invented, but gets repeated so often everybody gets sick of it and it loses all meaning?"

"Ah yes." Shaeine nodded in understanding. "We call that a *drizzt.*"

"Enough chatter," Ezzaniel said brusquely. "Ladies, square off. Now, we shall observe the requisite etiquette in this class, so a duel will begin with a bow."

Still grinning, Zaruda swept into an elaborate bow, flourishing her rapier. Shaeine simply bowed from the waist, swords held loose at her sides.

"Very good," said the professor. "Begin!"

Zaruda lunged forward, the tip of her sword aimed for Shaeine's heart. It was slapped deftly aside by a scimitar, and the drow fell back, blocking each blow with small precise movements, allowing the pirate to push her around in a circle. Ruda, for her part, threw her weight into each thrust, seemingly tireless. Then, like a pendulum reversing its swing, they changed roles, with Shaeine pressing forward in a sequence of whirling, dancelike movements that forced Zaruda back, her rapier barely intercepting each hit.

Back and forth they went, first one way, then the other. The onlookers, both their own classmates and the other students on the periphery, watched avidly, the latter occasionally shouting advice and encouragement. As time went on, Zaruda's face grew sweatier and more frustrated, while Shaeine remained as collected as ever, despite her heavy robes and cloak.

"All right, enough," Ezzaniel finally called when a break occurred in combat. Shaeine stepped back, lowering her weapons, but Zaruda lunged at her again.

The professor was a blur in a stylish black suit. He bore Zaruda to the ground, her sword flying off in the opposite direction; after a brisk tangle of limbs, she ended up face-first in the grass with both arms pinned behind her back.

"When I call an end to combat," Ezzaniel said mildly, "combat ends. Is that entirely clear, Miss Punaji?"

Ruda lifted her head and spat out a few blades of grass. "That was amazing! Do that again, but slower. I wanna see how it—erk!"

"Clear?"

"Yes, clear, ow, ow leggo!"

Smoothly, he released her and stood. "See that you remember. Now, then. Miss Punaji, you were handed a sword as soon as you were old enough to lift one, set against an opponent roughly your own size or possibly slightly more and told not to die. Miss Awarrion, you have been carefully trained to exacting competency in a ritualized style of combat but never had to defend yourself in your life. Am I correct?"

"Correct," Shaeine said crisply.

"Wow." Zaruda got to her feet, brushing grass off her coat. "You got all that just from watching us fight?"

"I got all that because I know how Punaji pirates and Narisian nobility, respectively, raise their children. However, nothing I just saw contradicted my expectations. This is why I selected the two of you as opponents. One is all street-learned skill with zero technique, the other just the opposite. You can learn a great deal from one another, and I'll expect you to do so. Return your weapons to the bag, please."

He swept his gaze across the remaining students speculatively while they did so, then nodded. "Ms. Avelea, Mr. Caine, you know the drill. Weapons, then face off."

Toby pulled a simple wooden staff from the bag; Trissiny, having left her goddess-given armaments at the edge of the circle, produced plainer replicas of her shield and short sword.

"That's amazing," said Toby with a grin. "How'd you manage to pull that shield out? I'm pretty sure it's wider than the mouth of the bag."

"You know, I . . ." She looked down at the round shield thoughtfully. "I have no idea."

"Each year, I am surprised anew at the talkativeness of youth," Ezzaniel mused. "There is a time for conversation and a time for combat, and you confuse them at your lethal peril. Bow, and begin."

They did so, Toby with a simple bend of the waist, Trissiny saluting with her blade at the heart as she bowed. Then she surged forward, shield first.

Toby clearly knew what he was doing. His movements were swift, precise, and powerful, and he was not limited by a purely technical knowledge of the staff, but able to improvise when she tried to trip him up. His choice of weapon also gave him the advantage of reach, which he used well, trying to keep her at too great a distance to employ her sword. The one advantage she pressed was that he was clearly not accustomed to an opponent with a shield; rather than trying to hook his longer weapon behind her shield and throw her off-balance, as she had learned to do at the abbey, he simply beat against it to push her back when she closed in. And he never went on the attack. Trissiny chased him in a circle first one way, then the other, at first waiting for him to reverse the tide of their engagement, then growing increasingly confused when it never happened. It occurred to her that he might be trying to outlast her, which would be a good tactic. His conservative style forced her to expend a lot more energy trying to penetrate the wide range of his whirling defense.

"Enough," said Ezzaniel quite abruptly. "Cease."

Trissiny immediately stepped back, though she did not lower her shield, which at that moment had Toby's staff heading straight for it at blinding speed. He managed to rein it in at the last possible instant, and they exchanged a slightly awkward grin.

"Ms. Avelea," said the professor, "I'm afraid this class will be an utter waste of your time. Your level of skill is well beyond the scope of this level of study. Beginning next year I will place you in advanced courses; you are not nearly so skilled that I have nothing to teach you. However, given Professor Tellwyrn's insistence upon keeping the eight of you as a unit during this semester at the least, skipping a level is not currently an option. I may make use of your talents to assist your classmates."

"I'll be glad to help in any way I can, Professor," Trissiny said modestly, bowing to him. Behind her, Zaruda sneered and rolled her eyes, receiving an elbow in the side from Teal.

"Mr. Caine," Ezzaniel went on, "you are clearly not new at this either, but you have a long way to go. I saw several opportunities for you to end that contest using the superior reach and speed of your weapon. I cannot be sure, yet, whether your skill was simply inade-quate to the task, but I *am* sure that you lacked the initiative even to try. We must work on teaching you to employ some aggression."

"I don't do aggression, sir," Toby said quietly. "It's against Omnu's way. I train only to defend myself."

"Do you imagine, Mr. Caine, that you are the first holy warrior ever to lack a taste for violence? This is the great irony of your position, paladin. It will not always be possible to defuse conflict before it occurs. Once the weapons come out, there remains only one way to end violence." He stepped closer to Tobias, staring directly into his eyes. "*Finish it.*"

Ezzaniel turned and walked away, folding his hands behind his back. "If your role in life is that of peacemaker, you must resign yourself to the fact that sometimes, peace can only be made through force. Peace is a condition that *exists* only when those who hate to fight are better prepared to do so than those who love to. Furthermore, as far as finishing blows are concerned, it is very simple and very easy to kill. If you would learn to neutralize an opponent while doing them the minimum possible amount of harm, you must master the art of attack; master it more thoroughly than any killer ever needs to. Do you understand?"

"Yes, sir." Toby dropped his gaze, looking profoundly troubled.

The professor sighed. "All right, return your weapons. Fross, Juniper . . . we're going to have to skip your contribution to today's events. I am forced to design an alternative curriculum for each of you. Fross, in particular, will simply not be able to engage in physical combat, but that doesn't mean you have nothing to learn about protecting yourself. I will be working with Professor Yornhaldt to arrange your studies, but in the meantime, I do want you to pay close attention and learn as much theory as you can absorb from this class."

"Can do, Professor!" the pixie chirped.

"And Juniper . . . you won't have a strictly hands-off class, but for the time being, I'm not sending you against a classmate in a duel until I have a better idea of your level of skill and your ability to control yourself. I mean no insult, but the potential for catastrophic injury is simply too high."

"Okay," Juniper said in a very small voice, eyes downcast. Fross settled on her shoulder.

"Which leaves only two." He turned and raised an eyebrow at those remaining; Gabriel bared his teeth, still clutching his hand. "Mr. Arquin, Miss Falconer, choose your weapons."

"Sir?" Teal raised her hand. "I . . . can't. I'm an avowed pacifist."

"Then you will die by violence," said Ezzaniel curtly. "Pick a weapon, Falconer."

Her eyebrows lowered. "Perhaps you didn't hear me . . ."

"Perhaps *you* failed to understand *me* when I explained this very issue to Mr. Caine just now. Your convictions are not my concern; your ability to defend yourself is. Rest assured, Miss Falconer, considerable safeguards are in place in this class to prevent you from doing any harm to your fellow students, accidentally or on purpose. However, you *will* acquire the necessary skill to do so—or, more precisely, to prevent such being done to you."

"I would *rather* suffer violence than inflict it," she retorted.

"And once you have passed this class, that will be your business. Until you do, it is mine. I promise you, Miss Falconer, your compliance is not optional. I strongly recommend you offer it voluntarily."

Teal drew in a long, slow breath, then stalked over to the carpet bag and thrust in her hand. Moments later, she withdrew it, empty.

Ezzaniel rolled his eyes. "Close your fingers *around* whatever item you find, Falconer. Your stalling tactics are neither original nor acceptable."

"I *tried*!" she protested. "There's nothing in there!"

"Oh?" He raised an eyebrow. "Try again."

This time, Teal sank her arm in the bag up to her shoulder, making a show of rooting around for a full minute, before coming up empty.

"Reach in and pull out a quarterstaff."

With a sigh, she put her hand into the bag a third time, and almost immediately pulled out a staff just like Toby had used, possibly the same one. She blinked at it in surprise. ". . . huh."

"My, my. You actually *are* a pacifist. Most people will find a certain weapon that resonates with them, even if they have no knowledge of its use."

"Did you think I was kidding?" she snapped.

"I think you're an eighteen-year-old, and I have dealt with far too many of *those* to presume that you know your own mind.

Regardless . . . put the staff back, Miss Falconer. This is as good a time as any to begin working on open-handed techniques. Mr. Arquin, my apologies; this means you won't be starting off with a weapon, either."

"Whatever," Gabriel grunted.

"Square off and bow," Ezzaniel ordered. They did so, both looking unhappy and uncertain. "Begin."

Teal awkwardly raised both hands, bracing her legs. She didn't even form fists, and looked like she was trying to catch a ball. Gabriel just stood there looking at her, then at the professor.

"Did you two perhaps intend to sign up for a comedy improv class instead of Introduction to Martial Arts?" Ezzaniel demanded. "Fight. *Now*."

"I . . ." Gabriel looked back at Teal, who shuffled her feet, still watching him warily. "I can't hit a girl."

"Oh, by all the gods in the sky," Ezzaniel groaned. "I'd hoped to go at least *one* year without one of these. Very well, Arquin; fate has graced us with a remedy to your ignorance. Falconer, step back, please, since you're clearly only going to hurt yourself here. Ms. Avelea, if you would be so kind, go over there and punch Mr. Arquin in the mouth."

"Yes, sir," Trissiny said grimly, striding forward.

"What?! Wait! No!" Gabriel tried to scramble backward, tripped over his coat and tumbled to the grass, where he attempted to crab walk away from Trissiny until she got too close. Then he curled himself into the fetal position, arms over his head.

"*Ugh*," said their professor in tones of utter despair. "Avelea, stand down. This is like kicking a three-legged puppy with two lazy eyes. Well, at least I know who my *special projects* this year are going to be. Falconer, Arquin, I'm going to tell you this once—no grades are being assigned today, but if you keep up this hilarity, you will find yourselves failing my class, and thus repeating it. I am fully prepared to prevent you from graduating until I am satisfied that you are capable of protecting yourself, if that takes until you are my age and I am forced to teach from a rocking chair. Furthermore, Professor

Tellwyrn will back me every step of the way; feel free to go ask her if you doubt it."

He knelt to snap the carpet bag closed and lifted it. "The purpose of today was for me to learn what I will need to teach and to whom. Mission accomplished. All of you should have something to think about before we meet on Wednesday, at which time we will begin training in earnest. I cannot emphasize enough the importance of *being* earnest. If you are not capable of caring about your own self-preservation, then care about your grades. Until that time, you are dismissed."

With that, Professor Ezzaniel turned and strode away in the direction from which he had come, still with that easy loping step; it was as if he were part liquid. The freshmen stood—or in Gabriel's case, huddled—and watched him go.

Then Zaruda grinned broadly. "I *like* that guy!"

CHAPTER 9

"Well," said Gabriel, "I'm willing to call it. No one, anywhere, is having a weirder day than we are."

They stood awkwardly around the University greenhouse, where their first herbalism class was to be held, watching Juniper dart around in manic glee. She sniffed, rubbed her head against, fondled, greeted and, in a few cases, sang to every plant she came across, looking as delighted as a child in a candy store. Everyone else kept carefully to the paths and as far from the foliage as possible, due partly to the large sign that read IF YOU DON'T RECOGNIZE IT, DON'T TOUCH IT, but mostly to having watched Fross narrowly avoid being eaten by what appeared to be a daisy.

The greenhouse was a place of great beauty—not like back home in Viridill, but Trissiny appreciated greenery, and there didn't seem to be much native to this area except the amber tallgrass. In here, the profusion of plant life resembled a jungle. Green fronds were draped everywhere, vines climbed every available surface, and exotic blossoms made explosions of color in all directions. The air was damp and heady with the scent of earth and dozens of flowers.

"A bold assertion," Shaeine noted. "I think, with respect, that you underestimate the weirdness of the world."

"Uh, Trissiny?" said Teal nervously. "That vine is going for your foot."

"What? *Yipe!*" Trissiny leaped backward onto the path, almost bowling into Toby; the woody protrusion that had been creeping stealthily toward her boot slithered back into the underbrush.

Gabriel raised an eyebrow at Shaeine. "See?"

The greenhouse's heavy wooden door exploded inward, rebounding off the wall (luckily an interior wall, not a glass one) with a crash, and their professor arrived.

"BEHOLD!" he thundered, pausing in the doorway to strike a dramatic pose, before swaggering in the rest of the way. He was a tall, thinly built man with subtly pointed ears and flowing golden hair that fell nearly to his waist, dressed in painfully tight pants, glossy knee-high boots, and a lace-trimmed blouse that hung open halfway to his navel.

All of them stared at him, frozen, several with mouths open.

"I," he informed the eight stupefied students, "am Professor Admestus Rafe, master of plants and lord of this verdant domain! Lest you question my *utter dominance* of this subject, let me reassure you that an affinity with nature is in my blood. I am, as you can see, a half-elf!" He placed a hand just above his belt. "This half, from here up. Everything below is of the meatiest, manliest proportions, I assure you."

"*Gwuh,*" said Teal, bemused.

"I will be brutally frank," Professor Rafe intoned, stalking toward them along the gravel path, his hands clasped at the small of his back. "The warm, cozy security of this greenhouse is the greatest comfort you will experience in this class. To learn the lore of plants, we shall go where the plants are—the wild plants, the hungry, crawling children of Naiya's various drunken indiscretions with dark things born of an inebriated goblin's nightmares."

"Hey," Juniper protested. "You shouldn't talk about goddesses that way."

"SOME OF YOU MAY NOT SURVIVE." In the ensuing silence, Rafe examined them slowly with one eyebrow superciliously arched. Then, suddenly, he grinned. "Probably you'll all survive, but you're officially warned now; so, if somebody doesn't, you can't blame me. But seriously, kids, this is a lab work class; we'll do some stuff here in the greenhouse, but for the most part we'll be traveling. Occasionally by Rail to other parts of the empire—I hope nobody's got a weak stomach—but largely into the Golden Sea. I've got friends out there, and one *rarely* sees a tyran or minotaur this close to the frontier."

Rafe turned his entire body in a slow half circle. "So, let's see what I've got to work with this semester . . . hm, good, good, skinny but spry . . . Uh, I've got a sun-blocking oil you can use," he said to Shaeine. "We're gonna be in the sun a *lot*, and I don't know if your type burns or what. You, with the armor, you're gonna slow us down."

"I will *not*," Trissiny snapped.

"You totally will. You're wearing like half your body weight in metal."

"Would you like to step outside and have a footrace?"

Rafe threw back his head and roared with laughter. "Excellent! Stick it to the man, Avelea! Ten points extra credit!"

"I . . . wh . . . huh?"

"But seriously, the armor's not gonna work. If you want to wear it, fine, but don't whine to me when you sink in a bog. Let's see . . . nice hat, Punaji. Oh *my*." He eyed Juniper up and down slowly. "Any more like you at home?"

"Um . . . not *exactly* like me?"

"Splendid. Show me sometime; we'll have privacy. All righty, then!" Rafe clapped his hands together and rubbed them briskly. "Considering it's morally wrong to do actual work on the first day of classes, we're pretty much done here. Your homework! Before our next class, I expect you each to investigate the properties of grains by drinking something distilled from some. I am far too important to follow you around checking up on you, so you're on the honor system. Also, it has come to my attention that tomorrow morning you all have Introduction to Alchemy." In an instant his ebullient demeanor vanished, and he glowered at them so hard that Teal took a step back. "I will warn you up front that your instructor in that course is a blasted, swaggering troglodyte who is unworthy to suck down the oxygen of my magnificent greenhouse. Extra credit will be awarded in *this* class for pelting him with books while his back is turned. And with that, you are dismissed. Yes, oh great pirate princess?"

"Yeah, question." Zaruda lowered her hand. "Are you an idiot?"

"Ehh . . ." He made a waffling gesture with one hand. "I'll give you five points. Defying authority is less impressive when you're the second person in a row to try it. Nobody likes a brownnoser, Punaji. And now, ONWARD TO GLORY!"

Professor Rafe spun on his heel and charged out of the greenhouse, kicking up a spray of gravel. Seconds later, he popped back in, grabbed the door, and slammed it shut. They heard the muffled echoes of maniacal laughter receding into the distance.

"He didn't answer my question," Zaruda noted.

"Oh," Gabe said grimly, "I think he did."

Trissiny silently gripped her sword. It was the only source of comfort she had at hand.

CHAPTER 10

O ff to dinner, girls?" Janis said cheerily as she puttered about Clarke Tower's sitting room, applying a feather duster to the furniture. "Remember, just let me know if you ever want to eat in. Not that the cafeteria food isn't just wonderful, but we've a fully stocked kitchen here, and sometimes a lady doesn't feel up to facing the crowds. You know how it is."

Shaeine and Juniper had just entered the room from the stairs; Teal sat on the couch, strumming a soft melody on her guitar. She looked up and grinned without pausing.

"Pertaining to that," said Shaeine, "I have a favor to ask. Has anyone seen Trissiny or Zaruda?"

"Not since we got back," replied Teal, still playing. "If they're both up in their room . . . well, we maybe *should* go break up whatever's going on, but I'm not so sure it'd be safe to."

"Tut-tut, those girls just need a bit of time to get used to each other," Janis scolded gently. "Mind your head, duckie, let me just get the back of the couch."

"I see." Shaeine folded her hands together, causing them to vanish in the wide cuffs of her sleeves. "I need to visit the scroll tower office in Last Rock and dispatch a message to Tar'naris. I would greatly appreciate a human escort, if such is available. The more open-minded of imperial citizens, I find, react to my race with mere suspicion. I will be glad to pay for a dinner in town, as thanks."

"Oh!" Juniper bit her lower lip. "Oh, that actually sounds like a lot of fun, but I've already made plans this evening. I promised Mrs. Oak I'd be back at the dining hall for dinner, and then I have a date."

"Already?" Janis tittered. "But I shouldn't be surprised, you're such a lovely little thing. Just be careful, dear; a lady must mind her reputation."

"I'll come along," said Teal, her melody easing to a stop. "Mind if I bring my guitar? I've been wanting to have a go at playing the local taverns anyway; my parents never let me do it back home."

"I should be very grateful of the company," Shaeine replied, bowing to her. "And I never object to music."

"That's what I like to hear!" Grinning, Teal gently laid the guitar in the case at her feet and snapped it shut, then slung it over her shoulder as she stood. "I'm good to go whenever you are."

"I would not dream of making you wait. Shall we?"

Juniper watched, her head tilted inquisitively, until the girls had shut the door behind them, then turned back to Janis. "What about my reputation?"

They attracted some long looks from the townsfolk as they passed into the town proper, but no overt hostility. The citizens of Last Rock were doubtless used to unusual types, living in the literal shadow of the University; several offered polite greetings in passing, which Teal returned cheerily and Shaeine with a formal bow.

"Teal, I wish to ask what may be a personal question, but I desire not to offend. I do not yet understand the limits of acceptable conversation in imperial society."

"Ask away," she replied lightly. "I reserve the right not to answer, but I won't be offended by curiosity."

Shaeine's nod was a barely perceptible shuffle of her cowl. "In the dining hall, I heard two upperclassmen express fascination that a Falconer is in attendance this year. Are you of the nobility?"

"I . . . ehhh. Not as such." She made a wry face. "That is, a pedigreed aristocrat would be offended at the suggestion, but . . . partly because my family are richer than most of them."

"I see. Please forgive my impertinence."

"Shaeine, it's fine. If you tread on my privacy, I'll tell you, but questions aren't a bother. That's how people get to know each other after all."

"I will keep it in mind."

They walked in silence, occasionally nodding to locals. Last Rock was surprisingly busy, considering the hour; the sky was streaked with crimson shadows, the sun having long since vanished behind the mountain.

"Not very convenient of 'em to build the scrolltower office at the outer edge of town."

"Inconvenient for the University residents, perhaps, but not for the sake of commerce. It is, after all, adjacent to the Rail platform."

"I can hardly imagine anyone coming *here* just to send a telescroll," Teal grumbled. "Students and faculty probably give them more business than anybody stumbling off a caravan."

"Perhaps they take satisfaction in making us walk."

"I just bet they do. First Tellwyrn with her bloody staircase and then all these . . . fine people." She glanced around warily; nobody appeared to be close enough to listen in. "You know, we should visit town more often. It's rare I can walk among the proletariat and not be the center of suspicious attention."

"Honored to be of service," Shaeine said serenely. "Though, with respect, I would assume that your manner of dress did not signal an aversion to attention."

Teal kicked a pebble out of her way. "It's . . . maybe not so prudent. I suppose I'll have to up and grow out of it one of these days. I just . . . gah. It got to where I felt like I'd explode if I couldn't just be *me* and not what's expected of me. You know?"

"I confess that I don't. In Tar'naris, expectations are a fact of life, and the consequences for flouting them are not merely social."

". . . you must think I'm pretty shallow."

"Not in the least. I think your concerns reflect the world in which you live, and are shaped by pressures wholly alien to me." She turned her cowled head to look at Teal directly. "I am accustomed to the demands of a society with rigid gender roles; sometimes I think that integrating into a culture that lacked them would be easier than adapting to one whose roles are so utterly different."

"How so?"

"There is no word for 'patriarchy' in my language. Explaining the concept would incite either derision or violence, depending on circumstance. I am . . . given to understand that imperial society is not accepting of persons attracted to their own gender."

Teal sighed heavily. "It's sort of . . . regional. Depends on which religion is dominant, which pretty much depends on where you are."

"If the subject bothers you, of course I will not press."

"No, no . . . really, if anything, it's nice to talk with someone who's not just . . . tolerating me. I guess elves are okay with . . . with that?"

Shaeine cocked her head to one side. "Orientation is a human concept. Among elves, both surface and subterranean, refusing sexual contact with an entire gender is considered a sign of mental illness."

". . . wow. I guess I might not fit in so well in Tar'naris after all."

"On the contrary. You might not be welcomed among a plains or forest tribe, but my people have a more lenient view of the mind. Any condition which does not inhibit an individual's ability to contribute is considered a personality trait, not a problem. Drow do not waste resources."

"So . . . really? By that standard, elves would consider almost all humans crazy."

"Oh, we do."

Teal's laughter was loud and bright; Shaeine smiled at her in return.

The sun had set while they were in the scrolltower office, the crystal orb at its top already beginning to flash in the twilight as it sent out Shaeine's message. Back on the street, the drow left her hood down, and though most of the townsfolk had gone indoors, those who remained outside frequently stopped and stared. With the Narisian treaty barely fifteen years old, drow weren't a common sight anywhere in the empire, and their reputation as enemies of anyone who dwelt in the sunlight was millennia old. Shaeine greeted anyone who gave her a look with a bow and one of her polite half smiles, and nobody challenged them, but even so, Teal stayed close. Last Rock might be an open-minded place for a frontier town, but one never knew.

"I confess to a measure of excitement at this prospect," said Shaeine, sounding no more excited than usual. "The 'saloon' is a fixture of our popular fiction about the imperial frontier. I had hoped to visit one at least once during my stay on the surface."

"Really, you guys have popular fiction about the empire?"

"Have you never encountered popular fiction about drow?"

Teal winced. "I, uh . . . actually own a couple of novels. I figured they weren't very accurate . . ."

"Those I have seen tended to be quite erotic."

By this point, Teal's face was burning. "I've . . . heard that."

"Well, that is both an amusing irony and a basic fairness. Humans are often sexualized in my culture, as well."

"They . . . we . . . really?"

"Our standards of beauty emphasize that which differentiates us from our paler surface cousins," Shaeine went on serenely, "including muscularity and curvaceousness. Humans are more prone to both than even we. There are other cultural factors at play, especially the universal allure of the exotic. It's a fascinating topic; I will perhaps write a paper on it during my tenure at the University."

"I think I'd like to read that," Teal said wonderingly.

The Ale & Wenches cast a glow of golden light and a babble of happy voices across the square fronting the Rail platform, but they went nowhere near it. Finding the Saloon was simple enough, thanks to the directions the scrolltower operator had given them. Just approaching it, they could tell it suited Teal's request for a quieter venue; though, the cheerful sound of a slightly off-tune piano trickled out from the swinging wooden doors. This time, Shaeine went in first, pushing the doors wide, and stepped to one side once within to admit Teal.

It was a clean and well-lit space, its furnishings slightly shabby but clearly cared for. The decor had almost Shaathist sensibilities, with mounted animal heads on the wall and a full-sized stuffed bear rearing in one corner opposite the piano. The patrons filled the room with a cheerful but muted babble, which faded upon Shaeine's entrance as they turned to stare at her.

The two students found a table near the wall, by the bear, and slid into seats; already the murmur of conversation began to pick back up. A slender figure dodged nimbly around tables and patrons, sliding to a stop beside them.

"Hi there, ladies. What'll it be?"

Teal had to force herself not to stare; the waitress was an elf. Aside from the fact that elves seldom chose to live in human towns, they were usually too prideful to take on any kind of servant work. This woman, furthermore, had black hair, which was a striking rarity.

"Ah . . ." She glanced at Shaeine, who tilted her head slightly, indicating that Teal should proceed. "Just here for dinner. What's good?"

"Good," mused the elf, as though this were a foreign concept to her. "Now, do you mean good by the standards of the fancy-feasting imperial rich kids up at the University? Because I'm afraid we don't serve that here. Or what's good for someone treating themselves to a night out on a cobbler's wages? There's a whole spectrum of *good* to explore."

Teal found herself relaxing; the woman had a somewhat cheeky attitude, but she, herself, was right in her element when it came to banter. "Let me put this another way. What would *you* order?"

"Ahh, this one's got a mind. Well done." The elf smiled broadly at her, with a semblance of actual warmth. "That sounds to me like a steak dinner with the works. However, you being strangers, there's an obligatory gold check before anything that pricey comes to the table."

Shaeine reached into the folds of her robe, but Teal was faster, placing a small stack of imperial doubloons on the table. "This being cattle country, I can't imagine steak is too outlandish."

"Not nearly as outlandish as *that*," she replied, nodding to the coins. "Put those away; the losers around here can smell money. And to drink? I can't say I'd recommend the wine, but the beer is better than decent."

Teal glanced at Shaeine questioningly.

"Tea, please," said the drow.

"Coming up." The elf deftly pocketed a couple of coins before Teal retrieved the remainder of the stack. "I'm Principia; sing out if you need anything. Just don't call me Sippy unless you want a surprise in the bottom of your glass." With that and a wink, she darted toward the door at the back of the common room.

"That," Shaeine mused, "was an altogether unfamiliar experience. Doubtless local standards differ, but I am very unaccustomed to hearing insults and threats from servants."

"She was a little mouthy," said Teal, "but yeah, things are a little more relaxed around here. I suspect there was an element of elvish pride there; I'm honestly astonished to find one waiting tables. Though on the other hand, a waitress isn't exactly a servant as such."

"Hm. Her duty is to serve, is it not?"

"Maybe I'm imposing my own perspective," Teal admitted. "My family has servants; they're actually professionals with training and take a lot of pride in being attached long-term to one employer. Our butler would be pretty offended if I compared him to a saloon waitress."

"I see. I am not alone in being out of my element, then."

"You're a little further out, maybe." Teal returned her companion's smile. "But we can all stand to learn."

"That is always true."

Principia returned, carrying a tray with a full tea service; the china was coarse and unadorned, but not chipped. "Here we are," she said lightly, sliding it onto their table. "The good part will be along presently. Say, are you two new this year?"

"Yup," said Teal. "First day."

"Thought so. There's only one other drow up there, to my knowledge, and she lacks . . . social graces. Nice to meet you both." She grinned and slid away again, this time to check on another table.

"Would you excuse me for a minute?"

Shaeine nodded. "Of course."

"Thanks. Be right back." Teal slid from her seat and crossed over to the pianist, who was just finishing up a piece. He played with the exuberant imprecision of long practice and no particular talent; there was no applause when he finished, but saloon music wasn't really intended to hold an audience's attention.

"Evening," she said pleasantly. "That's nice work. You have live music in here all the time?"

"Well, not *all* the time, miss," he replied with an easy smile. "These fingers can't go every minute a' the day, and I've got the bar to run, too. But I like to play now'n again, when I can."

"A personal touch, I like it," she said, matching his laid-back good humor. "I have a guitar with me tonight. Would you mind if I played a song or two after dinner?"

"Sure, long as you keep it clean an' don't expect me to pay for the entertainment."

"Nah, it's just for the fun of it."

"Then consider yourself on the program, Miss . . . ?"

"Falconer. Teal Falconer. Thanks, I'll wander over after we eat. I've heard good things about the steak here."

"Jonas," he said with a smile, then nodded at her again, took a long pull of his drink, and turned back to the keys.

She barely made it back to rejoin Shaeine before Principia reappeared, this time balancing another tray laden with steaming plates. Teal goggled at her as she slipped back into her chair.

"Wow. Doesn't steak take *time* to cook?"

"Everything takes time, my young learner," the elf intoned, sliding plates in front of each of them, then grinned. "Things take *less* time when the owner of the establishment is obsessed with having all the latest magical doodads from Calderaas in his kitchen."

"It was my impression," said Shaeine, "that cooking times cannot be artificially accelerated without adversely affecting the product."

Principia glanced to the left, then the right, lifting her head and checking that her boss was absorbed with the piano. Then she leaned in close to them, one side of her mouth curling up in a mischievous smirk. "Can you keep a secret?"

"Sure," said Teal warily.

Principia's smile widened to a grin. "Me, too." She straightened up and dusted off her hands. "Enjoy your dinner, girls."

"I begin to see," said Shaeine, watching the waitress leave, "why surface elves customarily avoid serving work. They seem ill-suited to it." She examined her silverware, then peered at Teal's, which she had already picked up.

"Oh, um . . . Not what you're used to?"

"I am accustomed to a single knife as an eating implement."

"Wow, that sounds . . . messy."

"Potentially. I am struck by the irony that your society, and not mine, invented those portable items we had for lunch. On the other hand, we seldom have bread."

"Sandwiches? Yeah, those are handy. Here, just hold it like this. Don't worry about doing it wrong; it's just me here and nobody else is watching."

"But there is clearly a customary way to do it. There are no meaningless rituals, no matter how small; from such things is culture built."

Dinner was pleasant. Teal scooted her chair closer to Shaeine's to show the drow how to handle the silverware, and managed not to laugh at the intensity with which she approached this task. Their conversation was more casual, when they spoke, and chiefly about growing up in Tar'naris and Tiraan Province, respectively. They really were from totally different worlds, so much so that it hardly seemed to either that sentient people could truly live as the other described. Long pauses were devoted simply to chewing, however. Shaeine had never had a steak before. She strongly approved.

"How're we doing?" Principia asked, coming by their table as they were finishing up. Both girls were chewing at that moment, but Teal gave her a thumbs-up, getting a grin in reply. "Tolja the steak was good here. Hey, I wonder if you could do me a favor?"

Teal swallowed. "Uh, maybe. What would that be?"

The elf dipped a hand into her apron pocket and pulled it out, closed; a gold chain dangled from her fist at both ends. "You're freshman girls, so you'll be living with that new paladin, right? Trinity?"

"Trissiny," Teal corrected automatically. "Yeah, she's in our building."

"Trissiny, right. Totally knew that; I was just testing you." She winked and unfolded her fingers; in her hand rested a gold necklace, Avei's eagle symbol on a braided chain. "I do a little side business in trinkets and charms, and . . . well, I guess you could say I'm a big fan. Could you give this to her, please?"

"What kind of charms?" asked Shaeine.

"Oh, all kinds," Principia replied glibly. "Minor enchantments; I'm not a wizard. You can't put much on a holy symbol, of course, beyond a simple brightening charm. Not that I would, anyway."

"You're an Avenist?" Teal said in surprise.

The elf frowned at her. "What, you aren't? Avei is the protector of all womankind. No exceptions for pointy ears."

"I know, I just . . . I'd never heard of elves being . . ." Teal swallowed and reached for the necklace. "Yeah, sure, I can give this to Trissiny. I'm sure she'll appreciate the gesture."

"Prin," called the proprietor from across the room, "I'm not payin' you to stand around jawin' with the customers!"

"Whoops, the master calls," the waitress said with a roll of her eyes, then flashed Teal a brilliant smile. "Thanks, doll. You're a peach!" She whisked away to another table, whose occupants were calling for beer.

"I mistrust that girl," Shaeine said softly.

"Hm." Teal looked down at the necklace in her hand for a moment before tucking it into her pocket. "She's probably harmless; someone like Triss is bound to have admirers. Though I'm going to ask her how she feels about getting gifts for future reference. No point in making her uncomfortable."

"Indeed."

Teal caught the pianist's eye; he grinned at her and nodded. Nodding back, she picked up her guitar case and rose. "Well, wish me luck!"

"You don't need it," replied her companion, "but good luck."

He cleared the way for Teal to seat herself on the piano stool; he patted her shoulder once, smiling, then strode off toward the kitchen. She pulled out her guitar, gently plucking at the strings and adjusting the pegs. It had been in tune earlier but had been carried down a mountain since then.

"Hey, Ox, check this out," called a reedy man at the table nearest her. "A college student with a guitar! Will wonders never cease." He leaned one arm over the back of his chair, grinning at Teal. "How 'bout we make a bet, darlin'. If we ain't already heard all three o' the chords you know, your drinks're on me tonight."

"No bet," she replied. Her fingers lightly fell on the strings, and the guitar sang. A soft waterfall of notes poured forth, growing in volume and speed and climbing back up the scale, swirling about each other in a playful dance that distracted from their utter precision. Teal brought the sequence to a close with a relatively simple arpeggio, then winked at the man, who was now gaping at her. "I'd hate to take your money." Then she began to truly play, and sang.

She sang of a life that was peaceful and in order, suddenly upended by the arrival of a beautiful, beloved enemy; of the confusion of passion and frustration, of coming together and breaking apart until nobody knew where they stood. The song wove a bittersweet story of beauty and pain, the guitar adding its coppery voice. Silence fell all throughout the saloon as every patron stopped drinking and stared fixedly at the bard, many with mouths open. Principia leaned against the far wall, watching with a wistful smile; Jonas and the portly cook both leaned out from the kitchen. Shaeine straightened until she was barely still seated, her gaze fixed on Teal with an intensity she had never shown in class.

No one could have said how long it went on; time stopped having any meaning. Three more people arrived while Teal sang, but they didn't make it any farther inside than the door, immediately transfixed by the music. As long as the song lived, they were her prisoners. Teal never noticed, never looked up to see; her eyes were closed, her entire being wrapped around the guitar, coaxing the river of music from its strings.

And then it ended. The song came to a predictable close, as good songs do, the notes of the accompaniment winding to a conclusion for a few seconds after the words stopped and ended on a tonic chord, but still the audience leaned back as one at the severance of the invisible chains binding them in place. A tiny exhalation echoed around the room, as dozens of people in unison let out the smallest breath, each too soft to have been heard in isolation.

For a moment, silence reigned. Then someone cleared his throat roughly and began, "That was—"

"HEATHENS!"

The swinging doors burst open to admit a stooped figure in a severe black gown, leaning on two canes, her wizened old face contorted with rage.

"Evenin', Miz Cratchley," somebody said in a resigned tone.

"You should, every last one of you, be ashamed!" the old woman screeched. "Carousing and drinking and listening to devil music! This used to be a good town, a town that feared the gods, and then *SHE* came. Now there's poison in the streets, and honest human folks who can't say they don't know better have heads full of evil elvish ideas and would rather spend their nights in a saloon than a chapel!"

"Oh, brother," said Principia, just loud enough to be clearly audible. Teal, taking advantage of the distraction, quickly bent to put away her guitar.

"And YOU!" Miz Cratchley shrieked, pointing a cane at Prin, who stuck out her tongue in reply. "Shameless slattern! Walking filth, corrupting the young of this town! You, and all the deviants and lunatics up there on the hill, pouring down their poison like sewage! What is *that*?!" Her voice rose to a thin scream of rage as she caught sight of Shaeine.

"Now, Mabel," said the proprietor, striding toward her with his arms open. "You seem tired. Maybe it's time to head home and—"

"Don't you dare to touch me, Jonas Crete, not when you've opened your doors to the demons of hell itself!" Several of the locals stood up in alarm; Mabel Cratchley had actually begun to foam at the mouth, her eyes rolling wildly as she ranted. "Monsters and wizards and the forces of evil walk among us! You'll see what happens to a town that turns its back on the gods! YOU'LL SEE!" She flailed ferociously with both canes, swaying in place. "A great doom is coming, and woe to those who fail to repent! A GREAT DOOM!"

Then Shaeine was there, having slipped nimbly through the crowd. At her sudden approach, Miz Cratchley drew in a deep breath to unleash a bellow, her face twisting in incoherent rage. Before she could finish, Shaeine reached out and touched her lightly between the eyes with a fingertip.

Mabel Cratchley crumpled like a paper doll. Shaeine dived forward and caught her before she could hit the floor and eased her the rest of the way down, showing surprising strength for someone so diminutive. Gingerly letting the old woman's head come to rest on the floorboards, she placed a slate-gray hand over Mabel's forehead and closed her own eyes in concentration. Men rose to their feet on all sides and crowded around.

"I find no physical ailment," the drow said, "beyond the stresses of age. However, I am not as familiar with human anatomy, and problems in the mind are difficult to diagnose at best. Is this normal behavior?"

"No," rumbled a huge man in an old, faded Imperial Army coat. "Miz Cratchley is a lady of strong opinions, but I never seen her get like that. Never."

"Here now," someone said near the back, "what's the dark elf done to 'er? We oughta—"

"You shut the *hell* up, Wilson," Mr. Crete snapped. "The elf just saved her from prob'ly busting her own heart, and we all know it. Ain't nobody got time for your trouble-makin'. Tommy, run quick and fetch Dr. Akers. And Prin, you go get Father Laws and the sheriff."

"I'm an errand girl now?" Principia muttered, but did so. In seconds she was out the door, right on the heels of the boy who had exited at Jonas's first command.

"Is there . . . I mean, can we help at all?" Teal asked worriedly. She had worked her way around to the door and managed to squeeze in next to Shaeine.

"Best leave this to the professionals now," Jonas replied, scratching his head. He nodded respectfully to Shaeine. "You stopped her from doin' herself real harm there, miss, an' I appreciate that. But I think now we need to give her some space till the doc gets here. That means y'all! Everybody move back; let the woman breathe."

Grumbling, the crowd shuffled backward from the fallen old woman, only Jonas staying close to watch over her.

"Maybe we should just . . ." Teal trailed off, but Shaeine nodded to her, and they slipped through the swinging doors.

The huge man in the army coat came out right behind them. In the dimness of the moonlit street, his enormous mustache and bushy eyebrows made his size even more intimidating. "Ladies," he said, nodding respectfully to them, "if you don't mind, I'd feel better if you allowed me to walk you back to the stairs."

"I believe we are capable of looking after ourselves," Shaeine replied.

"Ain't what concerns me, ma'am," he said. "On average, one of you University kids is worth at least four drunk galoots in a scrap. But if it should happen that you *need* to 'look after yerselves,' there'll be real trouble after that. The kind that don't go away as long as anybody's left alive to remember it. Nobody in this town'll have a go at you if I come with."

The girls exchanged a look. "Um, yeah," Teal said at last. "We'd appreciate the company."

He nodded and fell in alongside them, and they headed up the street.

"How likely is it that there will be 'real' trouble, do you think?" asked Shaeine.

"Not very likely at all," he replied. "This here's a good town, full of good people. Folks who're more familiar with the outlandish than the average run o' frontiersmen, besides. You did a good turn for Miz Cratchley when nobody'd have blamed you for just lettin' her bust 'er own heart, and that's what most in that room will remember." He snorted, rather like a bull, causing his huge mustache to flutter. "But, only takes one idjit to wreck the peace for everybody. I learnt that in the army: if a given outcome is bad enough, you plan for it, no matter how unlikely it is to happen."

"That is a wise policy," Shaeine said approvingly.

He nodded. "I'm Ox Whipporwill, by the way, an' pleased to make your acquaintance. I hope this don't put you off visitin' the town."

"Oh, don't worry about that," said Teal, having regained most of her equilibrium. "Like you said . . . it only takes one. And there's a few like that in every town. Doesn't pay to let them upset you."

"Well said, miss, well said." They had kept a brisk pace; Ox didn't rush, but the easy reach of his enormous legs had them both making quick steps. In just a few minutes, they had reached the edge of town and the abrupt beginning of the steps up the mountain. He turned to face them and tugged the brim of his hat to Teal. "Ma'am, I surely did enjoy your singin'. I never heard nothin' like it before, an' I got to see the opera in Tiraas once. I do hope you'll come an' play for us again sometime."

"I'd love to," she said, unable to repress a grin of pleasure.

He tugged his hat again to Shaeine, receiving a bow in return. "Night, ladies. You have a safe trip home."

They had ascended almost to the height of the scrolltower before Shaeine spoke. "Your song . . . It is the strangest thing, but I cannot recall any of the lyrics."

Teal stumbled over a step, clutching her guitar case protectively against her body before regaining her balance. Then she sighed and continued trudging upward, not meeting her companion's question-ing gaze. "There weren't any lyrics, Shaeine. I was humming."

The dark elf's eternally calm face grew considerably more intent, the closest Teal had seen to a frown on her. "I was certain the song told a story. Now that I recall, I am not sure why . . ."

"I . . . It's . . . I didn't mean to . . . Ugh." She threw back her head, took a deep breath, let it out slowly, and said, "Her name's Vadrieny. My . . . partner. She has a kind of voice magic, really the only magic she can use . . . Sometimes, when I play, it sort of seeps out. I don't do that on purpose; I think it's cheating. A bard should be able to move an audience with the sheer power of the music itself, or nothing at all. But, we're . . . we're still working out how to exist together, and things like that sometimes happen. I can't control it. The only way to control the effect would be for me to let her take over, completely, which . . . is probably not a good spectacle to show a saloon full of cowboys."

Shaeine nodded. "I understand, then. Thank you."

After a dozen more steps, Teal spoke again, very softly. "Thank you, too. For not digging."

Shaeine turned her head and smiled, and this time there was no doubt at all of the genuine feeling behind it. "You will speak of it when you choose to. There is no hurry."

They climbed the rest of the way in comfortable silence.

CHAPTER 11

Images in crystal balls were always somewhat distorted by the shape of the thing; it was like looking through a soap bubble. The larger and clearer the crystal, though, the sharper and more comprehensible the image. That was why the four men met in the emperor's conference chamber rather than the little out-of-the-way nook in one of the palace's sub-basements, where they were accustomed to meeting. It was hardly less secure and had the advantage of the proper equipment to display what the Hand of the Emperor felt they should see personally, without the awkwardness of making several of the empire's more important personages crane their necks and squint.

On a brass stand in the center of the hulking conference table sat a pumpkin-sized globe of utterly flawless white quartz, a gift from the queen of Tar'naris. Viewed from any angle, its central body was all but perfectly transparent, but with a white haze around the edges—at least, when it was not in use. Now, the peripheral discoloration remained, but the scene within was of another time and place. Modern "crystal" balls of formed glass avoided this property, and they held less than ideal enchantments and showed paler, washed-out images with greater distortions due to the shape of the ball. On balance, the quartz made for sharper viewing. It had been a kingly gift indeed.

The four watched the recording in silence; the image in the crystal orb was the same no matter the angle from which it was viewed. There was no sound, but before sending the recording to them, the scryers had added floating words to the bottom of the image conveying dialogue. A ripple briefly distorted the scene when Elilial casually destroyed one of the scrying orbs atop the watch post, but the image cleared immediately. There was nothing much to see by that point, though, save the goddess walking away.

Once she vanished, so did the recording, and the four men leaned back in their chairs in unison. The black-coated Hand turned the crank beneath the table, and with a clacking of gears, the crystal orb descended back into its resting place within the heavy piece of furniture, the hidden panel sliding over it once it was secured.

"The men?" asked Quentin Vex, who headed Imperial Intelligence. As usual, he looked disinterested and half asleep, which they all knew to be an act; one did not get ahead in his field by being dull-witted, but one often could by pretending to be.

"They're fine," said the man across from him, a slender and diminutive figure in a plain Imperial Army uniform without any medals. General Toman Panissar disdained the indulgences that his position entitled him to; it was one of the things that endeared him to his troops. "Woke up within the hour, none the worse for wear. Not even much confused, though getting coherent reports out of them was a chore. All three have an amazing literary gift for botching even a simple incident report. This is the first time I've had a clear picture of what actually happened that day."

"Well, you've seen it now," said the Hand, who sat at the head of the table in the emperor's place. For nearly anyone else that would be a misdemeanor, at least, but Hands of the Emperor were his voice and spoke with his authority. Outside their own ranks, nothing was known of the process by which they were selected and trained, nor what powers they wielded or even how many there were, but their absolute and devoted loyalty was a cornerstone of imperial rule. According to rumor, these men had no names and no desires or even identities apart from their service to the emperor. This Hand was a balding man with craggy features, his remaining hair a dark brown that matched his deep-set eyes. "The view from the ground, so to speak, is significant, but Lord Quentin has more for us, I believe."

"Quite, and I'll forestall the obvious question that I know is at the front of everyone's minds," the spymaster said, slouching languidly in his chair. "It's her, beyond doubt. The visual identification is a complete match with Elilial's other recorded incarnations on this plane. That can be faked, yes, if someone had the skill and the haycart necessary to carry his balls around, but we've no shortage of corroborating evidence." He nodded to the Hand. "She was in the palace immediately prior to this incident, having planted herself among the staff—"

"Omnu's *breath*," Panissar cursed, then shot a guilty look at the fourth man at the table. "Ah, my apologies, Bishop."

Vex went on with an amused twitch of his lips. "—and we had our scryers point everything in their arsenal at the site the instant she set off the wards—which she did in a dramatic way. The hellgate was unmistakably opened from the outside, then closed from within, which I'm sure you know is extremely unusual. And it was done by *divine* energy. We can know for an absolute fact that this was the act of a god. As an incidental aside, our scans picked up traces of another scrying spell targeting the site, which we tracked to the vicinity of Last Rock."

"That woman," Panissar growled.

"That about sums it up, yes," said Vex, turning to the bishop. "We sent a briefing and a request to the Church immediately . . ."

"Indeed, yes," said Bishop Darling, putting on a polite smile. "His Holiness was apprised beforehand of events unfolding within the palace, having himself foreseen Elilial's involvement and warned the emperor. He communed personally with the Pantheon immediately upon receiving your request. The Archpope personally verifies that none of the deities with whom we have any contact entered Hell at that location. Several were keenly interested to learn that Elilial apparently had."

"They don't know things like that anyway?" Panissar asked drily.

The bishop shrugged. He was a new addition to their group, the previous Church liaison having retired quite recently, and this was his first attendance at their regular meetings. He was also, by at least a decade, the youngest man present. "What the gods do and do not know is a matter best not speculated upon. Of course," he admitted with a grin, "we do anyway. They are known to be able to hide their movements from each other, and Elilial, perhaps by necessity, is exceptionally good at that. To the point that I don't believe *we* would have been allowed to see this move on her part if she did not wish us to."

"I agree," said Vex.

"And that is where the matter stands, gentlemen," the Hand said, drumming his fingers on the table. "The Queen of Demons is on the move, and has an interest in the empire itself, specifically. Tiraan forces have fended off several of her minor exploits at various times in the last thousand years, but this marks her first direct move against our government that we know of."

A sober silence fell as they digested this, broken by the general. "What, exactly, was the nature of her interest in the palace?"

"That's classified," said the Hand stiffly.

"Seriously?" Panissar leaned forward, glaring. "Classified to *us*?"

"Sealed to the throne," replied the Hand. "I'm sure I don't have to tell you, General, that this is not a thing lightly done. The mere knowledge of what she was up to would rock the empire if it spread. Therefore, preventing its spread is our highest priority. Rest assured that His Majesty and the empress are tending to it with the full support of the Hands."

"What *are* we allowed to know, then?" Panissar shot back with heavy sarcasm. "Bureaucrats sending soldiers into battle with faulty intel is a recipe for dead soldiers and not much else."

"At this point, our priority should be preventing this from becoming a matter for soldiers," said Vex. "We can't match a deity for brute force. Our best chance is to play her game. No matter how powerful or how *beyond* us the gods are, an individual god isn't more intelligent or devious than a human is capable of being. Or am I wrong?"

"You aren't," said Bishop Darling, "though I may be forced, later, to deny admitting that."

"And so the game is on," the Hand said flatly. "I'd like to begin by sketching a profile of our enemy, if Bishop Darling will oblige us. You are the resident expert on the gods."

"I don't see this leading to anything but a sermon," said the general.

"Well, the high points such a sermon would hit are relevant." Darling folded his hands on the tabletop, gazing earnestly at them. "Queen of Demons, betrayed mankind, cast into Hell, obsessed with revenge against the Pantheon, and so on. All this is pertinent to her motivations, but I'm going to assume you've all managed to attend enough temple services to have heard it before. Unless someone wants to correct me? Good. I have, in fact, made something of a study of the records of Elilial's various gambits over the millennia, and I must remind you, gentlemen, not to fall prey to the most common misconception. She is . . . *situationally* associated with demons, not the goddess of demons. Elilial is more of a trickster goddess."

"You mean that she's sly?" the Hand answered, frowning. "That isn't news, Your Grace."

"I would say it is more that she's *gleefully* sly."

"That makes a difference?"

"It does indeed," said Vex.

"It means," Darling went on, "that she fits a pattern of behavior which better suits, say, Eserion or Vesk, than the leader of rampaging demonic hordes that the sermons tend to portray. In account after account, she has favored subtlety over brute force, and has never been gratuitously cruel except on the rare occasions when she had a god of the Pantheon at a disadvantage. She *really* hates them. When it comes to dealing with humans and other mortals . . . I would say that she seems to appreciate a worthy opponent. From her recorded comments alone, it's apparent she has quite a sense of humor."

"Humor," Panissar repeated incredulously.

The bishop nodded. "I am imposing my perspective somewhat here; as I said, I have made something of a personal study of Elilial's movements. It's a hobby, you might say. But my impression from this is that she tends to be less aggressive and more . . . playful."

"How certain are you of that analysis?" asked the Hand after a moment, in which the others silently digested this.

"Very. If you would like, I can bring you a selection of materials to read. None are actually classified by the Church, but most of the accounts are not widely published . . ."

"That's all right," the Hand said quickly. "I have enough reports to slog through. You're the expert; we'll take your word. That's why you're here after all."

"Of course."

"That being the case, it's a significant observation," said Vex. "A campaign against a con artist will play right into her hands if you try to approach her as a general; but, if you know what she is and how she works . . ."

". . . then the game becomes less one-sided," said Panissar, nodding. "Know your enemy. Unfortunately, if we are not allowed to know *what* she is up to, her personality profile is of little use." He pressed his lips into a thin line, staring at the Hand.

"This much I can tell you," the Hand replied. "Her actions suggest an attempt to place a puppet on the throne of the empire itself. The bishop's observations fit with her methods, in fact," he added, frowning in thought. "She killed four Hands, but only when they attacked her. She was left with a golden opportunity to assassinate the emperor himself, but offered him no harm."

Vex suddenly sat bolt upright in his chair. "The recording. She said 'you wouldn't shoot a pregnant lady.'"

"Omnu's *balls*," Panissar hissed, realization thundering down on him.

The Hand shot to his feet, slamming both palms on the tabletop and leaning forward to glare at them. "This matter is *sealed to the throne*. You will not repeat anything you have heard inside this room, even to each other, nor speculate further on the matter! Is that utterly clear?"

He did not relax even slightly until receiving a verbal acknowledgment from each of them.

"You were right, though," Darling noted. "That information would rock the empire. And I think we've seen the evidence of her willingness to use it. Dropping that hint just where it would get back to the people analyzing it . . ."

"I think," Vex said slowly, "you had better begin laying contingency plans for the rumor, at least, to get around."

"I believe that is *your* job, Lord Vex?" the Hand shot back, still visibly irate.

"Indeed, sir, and now that I have an idea what is going on, I may be able to actually do it." He sighed, slouching back down in his seat. "There's a method to countering rumor, if you get out in front of it. Of course, one runs the risk of spreading the very tale we want to suppress, if she doesn't, in fact, attempt to spread it herself."

"And so it begins," Darling said. "We second-guess ourselves and each other while she is out there, freely acting. This is exactly how trickster figures operate."

"What would you suggest we do about it, then?" demanded the Hand.

"Individually, I'd have to say we would be overmatched. As a group, however, I advise you each to simply be careful not to become bogged down in introspection. Trust your instincts and communicate clearly with the rest of us; between our various skills, I believe we have a good chance of countering her."

"So, you suggest we fulfill the letter of the reason for this group's existence," the Hand said flatly. "Thank you very much, Bishop."

"Don't take it to heart," said Vex with a grin. "He likes to have the last word."

"Let's keep this on track," said the Hand, still quite stiffly.

"Indeed," said Darling. "He reminds me of a smart-mouthed fellow I used to know in my younger days. Always had to make sure he was the head of the group, that one."

"But you forgave his trespasses and became the bigger person, as the gods would have it of us," said Panissar, rolling his eyes. "Yes, yes, we know."

"Actually," Darling mused reminiscently, "eventually I kicked the crap out of him and slept with his girlfriend. And then his sister."

A dead silence fell, the three of them staring at him. The bishop spread his arms in a gesture of benediction, smiling beatifically. "No one is *born* a priest, gentlemen."

"*Anyway*," the Hand said loudly, "all other things being equal, we are in the unenviable place of needing to await our opponent's next move before we understand enough of her plans to counter them. The purpose of this meeting is to ensure that each of the bodies represented by this group is aware of the situation, in communication with one another, and able to meet the threat as it arises."

"That's it, then?" Panissar grunted. "We wait?"

"We've little choice, General, unless you propose to invade Hell."

"I have, in fact, drawn up projections of that very campaign."

"Oh?" The Hand lifted an eyebrow. "And what did you conclude?"

"I can't imagine I would need to spell it out for you. Insufficient data to properly plan an attack, and even the Tiraan Empire hasn't the resources to wage war on an entire plane of existence."

"Then yes, we wait. In the meantime, there are two related matters that need to be addressed, pertaining to the security of this matter. First is the ping from Last Rock."

"We should just send someone round to put that damned elf out of our misery," Panissar said sourly. "You could see to that, couldn't you, Quentin?"

"It's been attempted," Vex replied with a dry smile, "by the best. The last time was by the empire itself. Tellwyrn sent the family signet ring of the then head of intelligence to Princess Sharina as a wedding gift. His hand was still in it."

"There is a policy in place to deal with Tellwyrn and those like her," said the Hand, "and it revolves around not antagonizing them without good and specific cause. The effort it would take to purge the empire of such troublesome individuals would leave our civilization in ruins. For the time being, we are simply concerned with keeping her out of *this* matter."

"Need we, though?" asked Darling. "It seems to me she could be a useful ally in this."

"The Tiraan Empire does not make *alliances* with individual citizens living within its borders!"

"You know what I meant. Tellwyrn's name crops up repeatedly in my readings of the histories of the gods. I rather think she knows many of them more intimately than their own priests. I'm sure all three of you are aware that she's almost certainly killed one herself. For all her apparent love of causing trouble for its own sake, she is a heroic figure in legend as often as a villainous one. And she's very likely been investigating this matter longer than we have."

"What?" The Hand leaned forward, frowning. "How?"

"There is the matter of the exploding girls. You're aware of it?"

"I wasn't," said Panissar, though Vex and the Hand both nodded. "Exploding girls?"

"Roughly three years ago, there were five confirmed cases of spontaneous human combustion," Darling explained. "All teenage girls. In each case, it was discerned after the fact that the victim had been attacked by a demon of extraordinary power, which attempted to possess her, resulting in the destruction of both demon and girl in all cases except one. The one successful possession was of Teal Falconer, who is, I believe, currently enrolled at the University in Last Rock."

"Blazing hell," Panissar whispered.

"Indeed," said Darling, nodding. "The Falconer girl has control, and the demon, Vadrieny, appears to be amnesiac as a result of the trauma of possession, and evinces no desires except to exist. After a *thorough* examination by the Church, they were issued a Talisman of Absolution. I can't imagine Tellwyrn is ignorant of the other events surrounding this student's condition, nor that she's let them go."

"She hasn't," Vex said. "She's been sniffing around the attack sites for the last year, despite our attempts to keep the business hushed up. You're assuming this is part of Elilial's current activity?"

"I'm not discounting Elilial's capacity to have multiple irons in the fire," the bishop replied, "but on the scale on which gods move, three years is *nothing*. I think it's a safe assumption that the matters are, at least, related. So not only is Tellwyrn already involved, and a person of useful capabilities who could *help*, but I think there's a good chance she's a leading expert on the matter."

"Bringing her in is absolutely out of the question," said Vex. "That, too, has been tried. It was . . . ugly."

"How ugly?" asked Panissar.

"Ever heard of the Ministry of Mysteries?"

"No."

"That's right, you haven't. Neither has anyone else, since they tried to hire Arachne Tellwyrn."

"Yes, let us maintain perspective," said the Hand. "Directly involving an individual with a legendary capacity of destroying everything she touches is not on the table."

"However, it's not impossible that we can make use of her, provided we maintain a *very* circumspect distance," Vex mused, "especially if she's already involving herself. Pointing Tellwyrn at Elilial would be a handy way to keep them both busy."

"I'll present the idea to His Majesty," the Hand said briskly. "The only remaining matter is our three witnesses, who I believe are currently being detained. Obviously, the most logical solution is that they be silenced—"

"No," Panissar said flatly.

The Hand scowled. "imperial security is a matter well worth the lives of three extremely underperforming soldiers . . ."

"The empire is *people*," the general snapped, "not some vast mechanism. The day this government begins to exist for its own sake instead of the benefit of its people is the day it needs to fall."

"General," said the Hand quietly, "you've picked a strange audience to give voice to borderline treason."

"Go tell the emperor, then. It's nothing I've not said to his face. I'm fairly confident, in fact, that he agrees with me. Those three boys may not be the best soldiers by any stretch of the imagination, but I want you to remember something. Faced with the most evil force in existence, their response was to draw their weapons and invoke their emperor's name. They will *not* be thrown away like inconvenient puppies. I will fight you with every resource I can muster if you try." He leaned forward, staring intently at the Hand. "I advise you not to force me to exhaust those I can legally use."

"Getting soldiers for those posts is tricky," Vex explained to Darling in the icy silence which followed. "Hellgate guard and such. We like to use men who've tested well above average on loyalty and devotion to the empire, but in the bottom rungs of every trait that makes them useful as soldiers. Loyal enough to be trusted, in short, but expendable in case whatever they're guarding acts up. It's not a common combination of traits, and well . . . it leads to complications like this when it comes time to actually *expend* them. This is why you don't name the goats you raise for meat."

"I . . . see," Darling said slowly. Panissar and the Hand were still glaring daggers at each other. "I might be overstepping my bounds, here, but I believe I have an idea."

"Go ahead," said the Hand wearily, leaning back in his seat.

"Well, it sounds to me like we have two problems," he said. "There's the matter of handling Professor Tellwyrn, who is probably inextricably involved in this already, without letting her botch our own efforts completely, or attempting to force her out of it, which we're assuming would backfire."

"Backfire *horrifically*, yes," sad Vex with a faint smile.

"And then," Darling went on, "we have three soldiers who frankly deserve medals, but who for security reasons need to be stuck somewhere that they cannot go blabbing and blow the lid off the whole thing."

"Yes," said Panissar. "And?"

The bishop smiled. "Sometimes, gentlemen, if the gods smile on us, two problems are the solutions to each other."

CHAPTER 12

A black-haired elf?" Trissiny repeated. "I . . . Wait, did she come up *here?*"

She studied the necklace lying in her palm as she walked; it was not hard to identify, and not merely because Avei's eagle symbol had been an omnipresent part of her life since birth. She distinctly remembered the pushy elf who had tried to give her this item right as she stepped off the caravan into Last Rock.

"She did not," said Shaeine in her soft, even voice. "I had to visit the scrolltower office in town. Teal was kind enough to accompany me. She approached us there."

"We stopped for dinner at the Saloon afterward," Teal added. "She's a waitress there, said she moonlights as an enchanter. Um, I'm blanking on the name . . . it was one of those polysyllabic elvish monikers."

"Principia," Shaeine supplied. "And I believe it is actually Old Tanglish. It comes from no branch of elvish with which I am familiar."

"Sorry," Teal said with a wince. Shaeine touched her lightly on the shoulder, earning a smile in return.

"I remember her." Trissiny carefully tucked the necklace into one of her belt pouches. She'd put it away somewhere when they were back at the tower; she did *not* wear jewelry. "She tried to give me this the other day when I first got to town. The hair is distinctive."

Shaeine and Teal exchanged a glance. "Really?" said Teal. "You mean you talked with her before? Because she seemed to have trouble remembering your name."

"She knew my name well enough when we met in person," Trissiny said slowly.

"A small deception," said Shaeine, "merely an attempt to underplay the degree of her interest in you to avoid raising our concern. A person of upright motives has no need for such tricks. It might be prudent to have that item examined by someone schooled in enchantment."

"I think you're right." The necklace suddenly seemed to weigh more heavily at her belt. "Thanks, Teal, Shaeine."

"I'd have brought it up last night, but we got back late-ish," Teal explained. "Your door was closed."

"No worries, this clearly wasn't urgent." Trissiny smiled at her before returning her attention to watching the path, mulling the matter of Principia and the necklace over in her mind.

The freshmen straggled toward their Tuesday morning class in a broken line, with Tobias silently bringing up the rear. Trissiny was increasingly intrigued by him but hadn't had much opportunity to strike up a conversation, and this didn't seem the time, either. Ahead of them, Gabriel strolled along between Zaruda and Juniper, flirting unabashedly with both. Trissiny was not well schooled in such interactions, but even she could tell that Ruda was egging him on for her own amusement. The girl was increasingly difficult to like. Juniper . . . was hard to read. She clearly enjoyed the attention, but at times she had displayed startling insights into what people were thinking, and at other times complete obliviousness to things others found obvious. It wasn't clear whether Gabe was getting anywhere with her. Fross flittered about excitedly, shooting ahead and then coming back to rejoin them, bobbing impatiently at their slow bipedal pace. She appeared never to stop talking, though the thread of her speech was often inaudible as she wandered out of range.

Ronald Hall was on the second-lowest terrace, just above the library. For whatever reason, it was a battlemented structure, clearly modeled after a medieval barracks, flying the University's banner from each of the four squat towers which stood at each corner. Trissiny felt a wave of mingled comfort and homesickness as they approached; the obviously militaristic style was reminiscent of where she came from, though why the alchemic sciences building had such styling was beyond her. Knowing what she did of Professor Tellwyrn, she was willing to believe that a lot of things on this campus had no purpose whatsoever.

She was looking forward to this class. The professor's name wasn't on her schedule, but if Rafe had some sort of vendetta against him, he must have at least some redeeming value.

Gabe darted ahead to open the door and hold it for the girls, bowing grandly to each as they passed and receiving a mixture of flirtatious and polite responses from the others; Teal ruffled his hair. Trissiny glared at him. He winked in response to that, and Toby had to ward off a likely confrontation by gently pushing her into the building.

The Ronald Hall foyer looked appropriate to the exterior of the building and totally unlike the other interiors they'd seen on campus, with well-trodden wood floors and stone walls decorated by weapons and shields, all of which had clearly seen active duty. Directly across from the entrance was the main auditorium; a note beside the doors informed them that this was where the freshmen Introduction to Alchemy class would be held.

Juniper and Fross wandered right in, seeing nothing amiss, but Ruda stopped in the doorway, gaping; Trissiny did the same beside her.

"Is there a problem?" Teal finally asked. Wordlessly, they parted, allowing the others to enter.

This room looked more academic in design and out of place in the roughness of Ronald Hall. Much like Tellwyrn's history classroom, rows of desks descended toward a dais at the bottom level opposite their entrance, accessed by doors on either end. Various alchemy paraphernalia was scattered about this and along the edges of the auditorium, though nobody gave it more than a cursory glance. Everyone was staring at the mural. It covered the entire wall behind the dais.

After nearly a full minute of silent contemplation, Teal finally spoke. "Is everyone else seeing what I'm seeing?"

Shaeine descended the steps gracefully to study the vast painting up close. "It appears to depict Professor Rafe . . ." She tilted her head slowly. ". . . shirtless, playing a lute and kicking a rearing dragon between the legs. Framed by lightning bolts. This is very good work; the brush strokes are exquisitely precise."

"I think dragons are bigger than that," Teal said weakly.

"I suspect this depicts an entirely fictional scene," added Shaeine with the same unflappable calm.

Gabriel snorted. "You *think?*"

"I thought Professor Rafe hated the guy who teaches this class," said Ruda, idly sipping from a bottle of vodka.

"Maybe he snuck in here to prank the classroom," said Toby.

"The effort involved would have been extraordinary," Shaeine replied, returning to the group. "As I said, though the subject matter is trite and the composition uninspired, the mural is a masterpiece in terms of technique. It would have taken considerable time and effort—"

She was interrupted by one of the lower doors flying open with such force that it rebounded off the opposite wall, its inset glass panel shattering. Professor Rafe himself burst onto the dais, flinging an arm outward melodramatically.

"BEHOLD!"

"You've gotta be shitting me," said Gabriel.

Fross almost fell out of the air in shock. "I have to *what?*"

Fortunately, Rafe missed this exchange, having turned to regard the damage caused by his entrance. "Oh . . . bugger. That's the third door this year. Arachne's gonna throw me off the astronomy tower again . . . Ah well." With a shrug, he tossed his head, sending his golden hair sailing about, and strode toward the center of the dais. "It's only to be expected. No mere edifice is up to the task of CONTAINING MY GLORY!" So declaring, he slammed his armful of books down on the lectern and grinned maniacally up at them.

"Dude," said Gabe, "are you on the shrooms?"

"Doubtless," Rafe intoned, "you ducklings are curious about yesterday's encounter in the greenhouse. I have it on good authority that that dastardly oaf Professor Rafe has been filling your heads with calumnies and lies about my fitness to hold this post. I think you will find, my children, that it is *he* and not I whose incompetence and moral turpitude will result in his expulsion from this fine seat of higher learning. It is only a matter of time."

"What the *fuck* is wrong with you?" Ruda demanded.

"Tell it like it is, Punaji!" he crowed, pumping a fist in the air. "Ten points extra credit! Anyway, it's quite simple. Academic rivalries are all part of the faculty experience at any fine university. You can't be taken seriously down in the faculty lounge unless someone else there hates your guts and spends their free time plotting against you. But woe is unto me, for there are none who DARE stand against the magnificence that is Professor Rafe!" He shrugged nonchalantly, beginning to leaf through one of the textbooks he'd deposited on the lectern. "But be not dismayed on my behalf, children! For such is my versatility and vigor that I, in addition to teaching multiple disciplines, am able to serve as my own greatest rival! Thus, you shall soon behold the inevitable triumph of the glorious Professor Rafe over the nefarious and cowardly Professor Rafe!"

"I will say it again," Ruda repeated, "what the *fuck* is *wrong* with you?!"

"All right, that's enough folderol, kids. Butts in seats; we're here to learn. Anybody who wants to hear me wax poetical about how awesome I am, my office hours are clearly posted. Now then!" He went on as they trickled into chairs, still staring at him askance. "In this class we will explore the exacting art of alchemy, the wonderful wizardry whereby the simplest of substances become the most magical of mixtures! Alchemy has practical potential that rivals that of conventional magic, but is far more logically organized and has a somewhat lesser chance of accidentally ending the world or teleporting yourself to the moon.

"We shall pursue an aggressive curriculum here! By the end of the quarter I fully expect you to be able to poison each of your classmates, and also to prevent your classmates from doing the same to you. By the way, and while we're on the subject . . . no spoilers, but . . ." He leaned forward over the lectern, grinning insanely. "Guess what today's lesson is!"

Trissiny repressed a groan; the rest of her classmates sat in stupefied silence. She really was starting to hate this place.

She was still clinging to the last shreds of her poise an hour and a half later; the rest of her classmates were left dazed and quiet. In front of Ronald Hall was a pleasant little garden-like area, a round patch of tallgrass and wildflowers that looked as if it had been lifted directly from the Golden Sea below, ringed by a circular path from which other paths branched off to other parts of the campus. A few benches were placed around the perimeter.

The eight freshmen came to a stop out of sheer lack of momentum, straggling to a halt once they were safely clear of the hall. Even Fross appeared subdued, fluttering around Juniper's head. Teal flopped on her back on one of the benches and covered her eyes with an arm.

"How is your stomach?" Shaeine asked solicitously, perching beside her head at the very edge of the bench.

"Better," Teal grunted. "Should be fine in a bit. Hopefully."

Ruda gave up on adjusting her hat and tossed it into the grass, growling. Her hair was still bright blue, but true to Rafe's word, the color was starting to recede, the roots already returned to her normal lustrous black. "Okay, yesterday I was at least half kiddin' around. But seriously, now. Are they actually trying to kill us?"

"My theory is this is all some kind of test," said Toby, scratching his enormous beard. According to Rafe, it would fall out overnight. "It would fit with what we've seen so far, and what I know of Professor Tellwyrn from . . . other sources. I don't think Ultimate University is the kind of place where they ease you in. Hopefully things will calm down once we've proved we can handle the pressure."

"You're assuming we'll prove we can handle the pressure," grumbled Gabriel, flopping down on another bench and cradling his burned hand.

"Is that the same one Professor Ezzaniel made you hit the tree with in martial arts class?" asked Juniper, sitting next to him.

He grunted. "Yeah, about that. Next time a professor orders me to do something asinine, somebody please remind me to pretend I'm left-handed."

Trissiny seated herself slowly on his other side, frowning in thought. Class had been a whirlwind of "demonstrations," most of which were interesting and some actually entertaining, but Rafe had certainly not taken it easy on them. Only she and the two fae were free of lingering side effects; they appeared to be naturally resistant to alchemy, and she had flatly refused to participate, going so far as to reach for her blade after Gabriel had tested the "Burn in a Bottle" to demonstrate the properties of artificial wounds. Rafe had given her an F for participation and then awarded her sufficient extra credit for defiance, which she was now (as he had not hesitated to tell everyone) setting the curve for the class.

"This is too . . . chaotic," Trissiny said. "Abuse for a purpose is patterned. Rafe is a lunatic, and Tellwyrn herself doesn't seem too stable. This may all *be* some kind of sick test, but even if so, I think it's just because the inmates are running the asylum."

"I'm—and I can't believe I'm saying it—with Stabby on this one," said Ruda.

"Thanks," Trissiny said sourly.

"Got your back, babe."

"Hang on to your britches, kids, our day's about to get even better," said Gabriel. Everyone looked up at him, then followed his gaze.

The drow with the dyed mohawk was striding up the path toward them. Behind her trailed Chase, the blond human boy they'd met the previous day, carrying a stack of books—probably including hers. He appeared to be trying to engage his companion in conversation, but Natchua was visibly fixated on the freshman class, wearing a gleefully intent expression.

Shaeine rose smoothly, gliding forward to place herself at the center of their group; the other drow would have to step between Toby and Fross to reach her. Indeed, Natchua seemed intent on her specifically, but she stopped short of surrounding herself. Chase stopped talking as they came within earshot, and was now watching everyone with the eager expression of someone who had purchased a ticket to a boxing match.

"Can we not, please?" said Toby. "We've just had a rather—"

"Yeah, I bet you've had a rather." Natchua smirked. "First class with Rafe, eh?"

"Second," he said.

"Ah, then you've found out about his multiple academic personality." She grinned, and Toby relaxed slightly. Trissiny forced herself to do likewise, following his lead; Toby seemed much more attuned to social tensions than she. Natchua's bearing was still aggressive, but it was a positive sign that she didn't launch right into threats and insults.

"Is he actually as crazy as he acts?" Trissiny asked.

"Kid, *nobody* is as crazy as Admestus Rafe. Nobody who can put on their own pants and doesn't drool when they're awake. He's definitely not all there, though. My theory is he tried to play the part of the madman for whatever reason and lost himself in the role somewhere."

"*My* theory is Tellwyrn tortures him regularly," Chase piped up. "Whips, chains, dripping water . . . Actually, she's probably got a better setup than that. I wonder if she takes bookings . . . ?"

"You goslings have barely seen the tip of the iceberg," Natchua said with visible relish, grinning at them all in a way that was startlingly reminiscent of Tellwyrn herself. "Still feeling good about coming to the grand and glorious Ultimate University?"

"Is there some reason you need to be a bitch about it?" asked Gabriel. "Do you have a condition or something?"

She actually laughed at him, loudly. "Boy, if anything *I've* said gets under your skin, you won't last a week here. The professors alone will eat you alive." She turned her wolfish grin directly on Shaeine.

"You especially. Are you feeling homesick for your fancy manor and army of servants yet?"

"I would ordinarily not presume to correct any person's manners in public," Shaeine replied calmly, "but your lack of decorum reflects poorly on us all."

"Oh, that's just priceless. Decorum, she says." She stepped forward; Toby eased closer himself, but Natchua didn't move within arm's reach of Shaeine, though she lowered her voice to a sneering hiss. "Maybe a rich Narisian kid can afford to care about decorum, but you're not there anymore. The surface is like the Deep Dark, little one. Eat or be eaten." She snorted, and turned her back. "We can discuss it further if you ever decide to 'correct' my *manners* yourself. As if you'd have the spine."

"That has already been seen to," Shaeine said evenly. "I told your mother."

There came a sharp indrawing of breath, followed by utter silence. Natchua froze; Chase looked like his birthday presents had all arrived early.

Few on the surface understood Narisian culture in any detail, but it was common knowledge that drow in general were matriarchal. It wasn't a reach, from there, to conclude that using the *M* word was the first step to a fight.

"What," Natchua said softly, turning slowly back around, "did you say about my mother?"

"I contacted her," Shaeine replied, then tilted her head. "Do you truly not recognize me?" Natchua just glared at her, nostrils flaring, and she let out a soft sigh of regret. "I see. I would have preferred to stay out of your business, but as your logical next move in protecting your charade would be to contact Tar'naris and cast aspersions on *my* character to undercut my credibility, I deemed it necessary to report your actions to your House immediately, as a simple matter of self-preservation. If I have done you harm for no reason, I deeply apologize." She bowed from the waist, which was a mistake; it meant she wasn't looking when Natchua let out a feral scream and lunged for her.

Trissiny was between them in an instant, catching the charging drow's weight on her shield and throwing her back, hard enough to send her tumbling to the ground, knocking Chase aside in the process. Natchua yelped, having landed hard on her tailbone and glared pure hatred up at the paladin.

"Don't," Trissiny said firmly.

The fallen drow scrabbled awkwardly to her feet, bunching her fists and falling into a combative stance.

"Do *not*!" Trissiny's voice cracked like a whip; she gripped the hilt of her sword.

Natchua drew in a long, hissing breath through her teeth, then abruptly spun and dashed away back down the path. Evidently dark elves could move as quickly as their surface-dwelling cousins; she was out of sight in two heartbeats.

"Ohhh, boy," said Chase, running a hand through his hair. "That isn't good. You've made her back off twice now. In public, no less! Next time she's gonna go right for somebody's jugular." Despite his ominous words, his face beamed with the glee of a child in a toy store.

"How did you get over there so fast?" Gabriel demanded. Seconds before, Trissiny had been sitting beside him on the bench.

"It's what I do," she replied, still watching the path down which Natchua had vanished as she slung her shield on her back.

"Let me see if I got this straight," Chase went on, still grinning madly. "You're telling me that Natchua, the deep dark drow from below, is actually from the same effete, civilized culture that produced *you*?"

"She is my cousin," Shaeine said evenly. "Our Houses have been allied for generations. We were never close, and in fact have met only a handful of times, but I am frankly surprised that she failed to recognize me."

"Ohh, but this is just too . . . I can't even . . ." Chase dragged a hand across his face, as if trying to scrub away his grin. It didn't work. "This whole edgy act she's been putting on for the last year . . . Gods on bicycles, I have no words."

"I do not presume to understand Natchua's motivations," Shaeine said, a hint of sharpness in her voice now, "but the kind and respectful thing a friend would do is leave the matter alone until you know her intentions."

"Oh, of course, surely." He bent and gathered up his dropped books; his grin was, if anything, broader now. "If you guys'll excuse me, I have to go and *not* tell every single person I know about this."

Chase strode off, whistling, down the path in a different direction from that which Natchua had taken. The eight freshmen watched in silence until he vanished down a staircase onto the lower level.

"I'm . . . um . . . I wanna say confused, but the word isn't quite confused-sounding enough," said Fross.

"So, that guy fits in pretty well around here," said Gabriel. "By which I mean, he's a dick."

"I truly did not intend to cause her grief." The merest hint of distress was audible in Shaeine's voice, all the more startling because she was ordinarily so composed.

"You were protecting yourself," Teal reassured her. "And it sounds like your reasoning was solid. I don't really know enough about your culture to guess how much trouble this'll mean for her, but . . ."

"Potentially a great deal," said Shaeine. "Her mother will in all likelihood recall her to Tar'naris. What awaits her there will depend upon her House's traditions, but I cannot imagine it being gentle."

"Really?" asked Gabriel. "I mean . . . sure, she's a mean-spirited little piece, but it doesn't seem *so* bad. People go off to college and reinvent themselves. It's almost expected."

"The expectations of my people are very different. We have lived for millennia scrounging the barest survival from the rocks of the underworld. Those who will not contribute to the best of their ability are not accorded a share of the resources needed for survival, and those who turn against their own are dealt with harshly, out of necessity. Such behavior cannot be allowed to spread. To come here, in imperial territory, and deny association with her House and city . . ."

"Yeah . . . I get that it's rude, at minimum," Gabriel said, scratching his head. "It's just, it seems like a pretty harmless sort of rebellion."

"The concept of adolescent rebellion is fairly unique to human societies, and not all of those," Shaeine said, a hint of sorrow hanging in her voice. "I gather that a human who disgraces her family is not placed in a spider box."

There was a moment's silence.

"Okay," said Gabriel finally, "I'll bite. *What* is a sp—"

"Exactly what it sounds like."

Trissiny slowly returned and retook her seat next to him, her head swirling with commentary that she was determined not to make. She had put her foot in her mouth plenty of times already. The ways of Shaeine's people sounded harsh, but if their existence was as grim as all that, perhaps they had their reasons. On the other hand, Tar'naris had become positively verdant since the imperial treaty. On a third hand, she could manage little sympathy for Natchua. Trissiny had been raised in what amounted to a barracks. She'd never lacked for love and care, but had also never lacked for discipline, and associated the shirking of one's duties with the worst kind of fundamental weakness of character.

Gabriel was still absently rubbing the reddened burn on his hand. "Here," Trissiny said, reaching over to take it.

"Hm?" He looked up at her in puzzlement, then his eyes widened. "Oh. Wait, don't—"

She had already clasped his hand between both of hers and concentrated. The warm, familiar glow of the divine grew around her—

A burst of acrid smoke rose from Gabriel's hand. He shrieked in agony, jerking away from her and tumbling over backward off the bench and accidentally kicked Juniper in the face on the way down, which didn't cause the dryad to so much as blink. She, like everyone else, was staring down at Gabriel where he lay, panting and clutching his hand.

"Wh— I don't . . . I'm sorry," Trissiny spluttered. "I was trying to help; that's never happened before . . ."

"Move." Toby brushed past her, and her heart plummeted still further at his curt command. She'd never heard him speak with anything but kindness. He knelt beside Gabriel, gently forcing him to relinquish his grip.

"The hell did you do?" Ruda demanded.

"It was just holy light!" Trissiny exclaimed, near tears. "It's a simple healing spell!"

"Juniper, do you know any healing?" Toby asked sharply. "Anything nondivine."

"I, uh . . . I don't really have . . . magic? It's more like, I'm *made* of magic. If he was *poisoned*, I can do something about that . . ."

"*Could it hurt him?*" Toby demanded, agitation clearly held barely in check by his veneer of poise.

"I don't see how." She knelt beside them; Toby had coaxed Gabe to a seated position.

Trissiny stared down at them, shocked and confused. Teal had approached and placed a hand on her shoulder; Zaruda was saying something snippy again. She was barely aware of either of them.

The light of the gods *healed*. There was no reason it should cause pain to anyone. Had she done it wrong? *Could* she do it wrong? The power wasn't hers, but channeled directly from Avei. What would have to be wrong with her to make it come out so horribly backward?

All at once, the hints clicked into place in her mind. Tellwyrn had all but spelled it out in class yesterday, but she'd been too obtuse to follow the reasoning through. There was one obvious and simple explanation. There was one type of being always struck down by the power of the divine.

Trissiny grabbed her sword, shaking herself free of Teal, and a glow sprang up along the scabbard before she even pulled it free.

"Demon."

The infirmary was built at the very edge of the plateau; its east wall was the east wall of the University itself, and the tall windows in it opened directly over a nauseating drop. The view was stunning, though.

It was a long room, wide enough to hold a row of beds along each wall with an ample aisle between them. The beds and nightstands were clearly handmade, elaborately carved of a strangely glossy, whitish-yellow wood that Trissiny only realized after careful examination was actually bone. Dreamcatchers hung over the head of each bed, every one unique, and on a long counter on the far wall were a number of elven ritual tools that she recognized from illustrations, none of which she knew the purpose.

The infirmary matron back at the abbey had bustled about briskly, often humming to herself; she was a comforting memory. The University's healer was somewhat eerie by comparison. She was a plains elf, with hair a shade of blond that was nearly white, and ears that protruded more from the sides of her head than vertically like Professor Tellwyrn's. Miss Sunrunner, as she had introduced herself, wore a simple dress of leather bleached nearly as light as her hair, dyed at the cuffs, hem, and neckline with organic patterns in green and pale yellow. She moved gracefully and in near total silence, which was disconcerting and left the students mostly to stew in their own awkwardness.

Gabriel and Ruda were both unhappy at being confined to beds; Trissiny privately agreed that his burned hand and her black eye did not require lying down, but Miss Sunrunner had been adamant as to how patients were treated. Trissiny herself sat on another bed alongside Toby, who hadn't spoken to her since the drama outside of Ronald Hall. She had mostly avoided looking at him; the sheer weariness on his face when she did made her feel horribly guilty. Fross buzzed around in obvious agitation, but at least she had finally stopped chattering. Long before that point her speech had grown so fast and high-pitched that no one could pick out any actual words.

It was almost a relief when Professor Tellwyrn breezed into the room, though her presence almost certainly heralded some administrative retaliation for them all. Brawling on University property was not an activity approved of, according to the student handbook.

"Congratulations, Punaji," she said lightly, moving down the aisle with a casual, strolling gait that somehow propelled her as fast as most humans could run, "you've won the first punishment of the academic year."

"What?" Ruda squawked, jerking upright and ignoring Miss Sunrunner's pointed throat clearing. "Me? I just— That's a load of— She started it!" She pointed an accusing finger at Trissiny.

"Ah yes, the battle cry of mature adults everywhere," Tellwyrn drawled. "Here's a bit of useful knowledge for you kids: the ley lines on this campus are carefully adjusted to suit my needs, which include scrying. This morning's events having been recent enough, I was able to get Professor Yornhaldt to show me a full replay on his crystal ball. He was so disappointed at having to do such a thing this early in the semester, the poor dear. I wish you could have seen those big puppy dog eyes he does so well. I'd show you, but I can't really pull it off. I'm told it makes me look homicidally insane."

"Which differs in what way from the norm?" Gabriel asked the ceiling without raising his head.

"Glad you're feeling better," Tellwyrn replied. "In any case, here's what I saw go down out there: Miss Avelea—"

"*Ms.*"

"Shut. Up. *Avelea* here found out about Mr. Arquin's little family secret and reacted exactly the way I'd expect a paladin to—by flaring up and going for her blade."

"See?" Ruda screeched.

"The next person who interrupts me is going to find themselves with a *good* reason to be in the infirmary."

"There will be no threats of violence here," Miss Sunrunner said firmly.

Tellwyrn heaved a sigh and shoved her spectacles up the bridge of her nose. "*As I was saying,* Trissiny then allowed herself to be persuaded to stand down by the intervention of Caine and Falconer. Since she is notably not attempting to murder Arquin in his bed, she has clearly come round to the understanding that a person with a human soul who has clearly done no harm—as he's allowed to run around freely and attend college—is not someone she needs to put down. Which is *also* how paladins usually react to nonviolent demonbloods, once they get over the initial shock. Despite her general stuck-up narrow-mindedness and trigger-happy ignorance—"

"*Excuse* me?" Trissiny all but shouted.

"You are, in this instance, excused. Despite these failings, our resident Hand of Avei is not a complete imbecile. Avei tends not to employ those, unlike some deities I could name. And that would have been that, except that *you*," she turned to glare at Ruda over her glasses, "decided to 'protect' Mr. Arquin by pulling your sword on your roommate."

"I—" Ruda broke off as Tellwyrn held up a hand.

"I am giving you credit for not having lethal intent," she said. "You were pretty clearly beating on her shield rather than going for flesh. Maybe next time you'll think twice about pulling a sneak attack on someone who's been drilling in combat forms since she could walk. For future reference, Miss Punaji, if you must pick a fight with a Sister of Avei, go for one of the older ones. They've been training long enough to neutralize you harmlessly. A neophyte Sister your own age is likely to kill you before she can figure out what else to do with you."

"So she got in a lucky shot," Ruda said sullenly.

"No," Tellwyrn replied, her voice suddenly silken, "she did not get in a lucky shot. Be assured I get reports from all your teachers, including Professor Ezzaniel. In any kind of fair combat, Trissiny would obliterate you. Aww," she cooed at Ruda's furious expression. "What's the matter, Punaji, does reality ruffle your pirate sensibilities?"

"Arachne," Sunrunner warned, "this is a place of healing. Behave yourself."

"So, yes, Punaji," the professor went on in a more businesslike tone, "punishment. Immediately following your last class of the day, you will report to Stew, the groundskeeper, and see to whatever tasks he assigns until he is satisfied with your work. He put a lot of effort into the campus over the summer, so there shouldn't be much to be done. With any luck, you'll even have time to sleep tonight."

"Professor?"

Tellwyrn lifted her gaze. "Yes, Fross?"

"Should I be punished, too? I mean, I did attack Trissiny. Sorry, Triss," she added for the fourth time since the incident.

"For purposes of this discussion, Fross, freezing someone's boots to the ground does not constitute assault. You may have saved Miss Punaji's life, in fact; I wouldn't be inclined to blame Miss Avelea too much if she had reflexively lopped off an arm."

"Am I in trouble, then?" Trissiny asked.

Professor Tellwyrn tilted her head. "For what?"

"Well, I . . ." She glanced guiltily over at Gabriel, who was still staring at the ceiling, and then at Toby, who was watching Gabe. "I did sort of start it."

"Avelea, if being naive and hotheaded were offenses that warranted punishment, this University and all others would essentially be forced labor camps. You *badly* need to find a better default problem-solving tool than your sword, but you didn't actually apply it to anyone except in self-defense. So no, you are not in trouble. At least not as far as the school is concerned. I can't say how long that condition will persist if you don't straighten up."

Trissiny ducked her head. "Sorry."

"To whom, exactly, are you apologizing, and for what?"

"I don't . . ." She shot another glance at Gabriel. Knowing what he was, it was a lot harder to feel bad for him. "I'm just sorry."

"Oh," Tellwyrn said acidly, "still harboring a bit of animosity there, are we? Splendid! For a moment I was worried we'd have to put all this idiocy behind us."

Miss Sunrunner had been busy with Gabriel while they talked, cleaning his burned hand and wrapping it in a poultice. She finished this just as Tellwyrn wrapped up her little speech, and cleared her throat loudly. "Tobias, since you're here, would you kindly come and heal Zaruda's bruise?"

"Gladly," Toby said, and indeed, he sounded very glad to have something productive asked of him.

"Hang on, now," Ruda protested. "Not interested. I've seen what that stuff does . . ."

"You saw what it does to a half demon," Miss Sunrunner said with wry asperity. "Unless there's something you *really* should have told me when you first came into my infirmary, a touch of divine magic will do you nothing but good."

"But . . . what if I don't wanna . . ."

"Zaruda Punaji, you lose the right to be irrationally stubborn the moment you fall into a healer's care. Now hold still."

"This really should take just a second," Toby said encouragingly, holding a hand over Ruda's black eye. She didn't stop grumbling all through the gentle glow of Omnu's healing light, though Trissiny knew for a fact that a cleric's healing was one of the most pleasant sensations a person could experience.

"Is there going to be any problem treating Arquin in the future?" Tellwyrn asked. "Avelea here seems to have gotten her head out of her ass, albeit somewhat belatedly . . ."

"Hey!"

". . . but there's always next time, and there'll probably be more holy types enrolling every year."

"Gabriel is quite resistant to most forms of damage, as a result of his heritage," Miss Sunrunner replied, "and apart from that, heals much the same way an ordinary human does. My default methods do not rely on divine magic, though I won't hesitate to make use of a paladin when I have two at hand. We won't have a problem."

"Still in the room, by the way," Gabe said.

"Well, that was less mystical than I was expecting," Tellwyrn mused. "Which I suppose is to the good."

"Really? You want mystical?" Miss Sunrunner turned to her cabinet against the wall and grabbed a ceremonial headdress made of a cow's skull with antlers attached, which was trailing strings of beads. Placing this on her head, she then snatched up an elaborately carved staff, its end bristling with feathers and more rattling beads, and shook it at Tellwyrn. "Shaman speaks! The boy's aura seethes with shadow and flame, a living touch of the dark beyond! Woe to those who gaze upon his spirit! But for any physical injuries, modern medical science is very good medicine."

"You don't need to be a brat, Taowi," Tellwyrn snapped.

Sunrunner rattled the staff at her again. "Whatever gets you out of my infirmary."

"Let this be a lesson to you, students—never hire a friend's kid. All right, you're all patched up and properly abashed, and you all have class. Move it along."

CHAPTER 13

Tellwyrn accepted their essays at the start of class the next day, and graded them right in front of the students. She stood at the lectern, calmly reading over each of the eight two-page papers and setting them aside in turn, while the freshmen sat staring at her in trepidation. It wasn't a very long wait; the professor didn't spend more than a few seconds on each page.

Then she sighed, stacked the papers neatly, and stepped out from behind the podium. "Well, as you doubtless managed to figure out, this has been a little getting-to-know-you exercise. The idea here is chiefly to give *me* an understanding of what I have to work with; I'm not somebody who teaches by the book, nor is anyone who understands how people learn. The weaknesses you perceive in those around you reveal a great deal about your own, which will tell me what I'm going to have to work on with each of you. So, mission accomplished."

She began to stroll calmly up and down the rows of desks. "Miss Avelea, you are a judgmental jerk."

"*What?!*"

"Worse, you're not aware of it. Mr. Caine, you're *also* a judgmental jerk. You *do* realize this, and in overcompensating you reduce yourself to spinelessness. Miss Falconer, you have lofty ideals and neither the guts nor the backbone to do anything with them. Miss Awarrion, you've a head full to bursting with academic knowledge and little notion how such things actually play out in the real world. That's a forgivable failing; it's what you're here to learn after all. On the same note . . ." She came to a stop between the desks occupied by the two fae. "Juniper, Fross . . . You don't understand mortal society, which makes it difficult to judge how you will engage with it as you begin to. We'll work on that as best we can. *Mr.* Arquin. You are an extremely clever young man."

"Aw, thanks, teach," he said smugly.

"You are nearly a tenth as clever as you *think* you are. The gap there will be what kills you. Try not to let it happen on my campus. Miss Punaji . . ." She heaved a sigh. ". . . grow up."

They stared at her in furious silence as she slowly picked her way back down to the podium and took her place behind it. "Well," she said at last, staring up at them over her spectacles, "you did the assignment, so I guess I'll have to pass you. Everybody gets a D."

The outcry from all sides was so heated that the only individual words audible were curses, and that only because Ruda yelled the loudest. Shaeine alone kept silent, though she raised an eyebrow sardonically at the professor.

Tellwyrn endured this gracefully for about ten seconds, then raised a hand and snapped her fingers. A thunderclap blasted through the room, accompanied by a rush of air that tipped empty desks backward and rocked all the students into silence, sending Fross careening against the back wall.

"As you go through life," Tellwyrn intoned, "you'll find that doing what you're told by authority figures is a path to mediocrity. *Opposing* authority figures in a knee-jerk fashion leads to a swift and brutal end. It is necessary to find a middle ground—and finding that means understanding the forces that move both individuals and groups, and how you can manipulate those forces to your advantage. Ironically, this is an art that hinges heavily on the elucidation of your own principles, the philosophical framework of your life that you must uphold to protect your identity as a coherent being. This is the entire purpose of this class. The ultimate point of this task was to show me how far along you already are. I can't say I'm impressed.

"Each year," she went on, beginning to pace again, "I start my freshmen off with an assignment along these lines, if not this one exactly. Something needlessly, extravagantly cruel, calculated to attack each person where they are weakest and drive wedges between them. In case you were wondering, the correct solution to this problem would have been for you to confer outside of class, then show up here this morning with no essays done and tell me where to stick my damned homework." She smiled grimly at them. "Don't beat yourselves up too hard. Out of forty-eight freshman classes which have started at this University, only six did the right thing, and of those only two did it in such a wrong-headed way that they fared little better than yourselves. For future reference, outside of Rafe's classes, attempting to lynch your professor gets you a B-minus at best, if I'm feeling benign enough to grant points for style and strategy."

"How much of what happens in this class is gonna be sadistic mind games?" Gabriel demanded.

"How many times, Arquin, must I tell you to *raise* your *hand* before speaking?"

"A day may come when I give a flying fuck what you think," he shot back, "but it's not this day."

"Aw, look who found his balls. Better late than never." She grinned diabolically. "To answer your question, which is a valid one, your performance today gains you a bit of leeway going forward; I will not be party to the kicking of helpless kittens. Though, and I guarantee this is not the last time you will think so, the purpose of these exercises *isn't* to break your spirits. However, I will not have you leaving my University having memorized a bunch of names and dates out of a book. *Understanding* is what I teach, and what I expect you to gain. To that end, there will be a great deal of what Mr. Arquin describes as 'mind games.' I will test you nearly constantly, in one way or another. You will acquire and demonstrate a capacity to think quickly, fluidly, and beyond conventional patterns, or you will keep retaking my class until you do. Is that what anyone wants?"

She tilted her head inquisitively, looking around at them, but no one offered a comment.

"Rightyo, then!" Tellwyrn said cheerfully. "The scope of history is nigh limitless, but for our purposes we're going to focus on comparatively recent events. The Tiraan Empire itself is an excellent, ongoing case study in everything a civilization can do right and/or horribly wrong, so we will begin our investigations with the empire's founding, a little more than one thousand years ago, and proceed forward from there . . ."

Ruda caught up to Trissiny as they were leaving Helion Hall.

"So," the pirate said with an elaborately casual air, "I've been thinking."

Trissiny forcibly bit back a snotty comment that sprang to the forefront of her mind. Malicious sass was *not* becoming conduct for a paladin. Even if directed at a . . . pirate. She looked at Ruda, showing acknowledgment, but held her silence and waited for the other girl to continue.

She gave Trissiny a smile that, to her credit, only looked about half forced. "Yeah, I'm maybe not so inclined to take Tellwyrn seriously . . . and less every time she talks . . . but like I said, I was thinking, and I have to admit she wasn't completely wrong. I was outta line; I shouldn't have taken a swing at you. I was being needlessly hostile and pretty much showing off."

"We all make mistakes," Trissiny said after the silence had stretched out enough that she was reasonably sure Ruda was done talking. She'd grown used to silence between them; they had managed not to communicate or acknowledge one another since the incident yesterday, which made for tense living conditions. Still, she wasn't sure that was worse than actually speaking with her roommate. "I accept your apology."

Ruda blinked, then frowned. "Did someone use the word 'apologize' and I missed it?"

"Well, what was the point of this, if not that?"

For a moment, she thought they were about to have another go; Ruda drew in a deep breath, swelling like an angry toad. She let it back out, though, without incident. ". . . all right, fair enough. I'm apologizing."

"You're forgiven."

"Yeah, good. Great." She eyed Trissiny up and down quickly. "Cos the scowl and the moving combat stance really scream forgiveness."

Trissiny set her teeth, choosing her words carefully. "Forgiveness is just that. As far as I'm concerned, there need be no recrimination between us for anything in the past. However, I would be foolish to simply forget that a person is prone to being needlessly hostile and *showing off* with a deadly weapon."

"That's good advice," Gabriel said brightly from behind them. Most of their class was still walking in a group, though Fross and Juniper had fallen far behind, talking between themselves. "What does that say about somebody who decides to murder a person based on what kind of blood they've got?"

"Oh, hey, this sounds like a great thing for you not to get in the middle of," Teal said quickly, taking Gabe by the arm and all but dragging him away. Toby followed them, glancing back once.

"Look, I am *trying*, here," Ruda practically growled. "It's not like diplomacy is a big part of the Punaji upbringing. Meet me halfway, maybe?"

"I am," Trissiny said woodenly. "You apologized, I forgave you. We're moving on."

"All right, so that's step one," she replied, managing another somewhat unforced grin. "Then I can teach you what pirates *do* know about diplomacy. How's about we grab a drink, my treat? I hear good things about the pub in town."

"I don't drink," Trissiny said coldly.

Ruda sighed heavily and shortened her stride, allowing herself to fall behind.

"Of *course* you fucking don't."

CHAPTER 14

Bishop Antonio Darling smiled and nodded to his neighbors as he glided along the sidewalk toward his home in the last glow of twilight, keeping his pace to a modest stroll, which allowed him to appear almost to float. Darling's image was carefully cultivated, from his emptily cherubic smile and his exquisitely coiffed hair to his ever-so-slightly effeminate hand gestures.

Everything precise, everything calculated.

The neighborhood reflected his own facade, with its towering brownstones behind ornate little gardens. Darling opened his unlatched gate, closed it behind him, and smoothly traversed the path to his front door—it, too, was unlocked. No thief in this city would dare have a go at his home.

After pausing on his step only to return a polite wave from Lady Ansovar across the street, he finally slipped inside and pulled the door shut, blocking out the city. Darling took in a deep breath and let it out slowly, savoring for a moment the quiet gloom. This little moment was part of his daily routine, a break from the overstimulation of his life, and a line of demarcation between two pieces of it.

His butler, of course, was waiting for him, her timing precise as always. "Good evening, Your Grace," she intoned quietly, standing at the other end of the foyer. "Everything is in readiness in the study for your evening appointment. I have taken the liberty of providing a meal." It was positively magical how she could convey a whole conversation's worth of disappointment and reproach without altering her expression or voice in the least. Of course, she knew he'd not bothered to eat.

The bishop leaned back against his heavy front door for half a moment longer. Just a little indulgence, a few seconds' peace and quiet . . . Then, smoothly and suddenly, as if he had never stopped moving, he levered himself back upright. "Splendid, thank you. Whatever would I do without you, Price?"

"I shudder to think, Your Grace."

Whistling, he bounded past her into the hall and up the stairs, this time moving at ground-eating stride now that there was nobody but the butler here to see. Darling took the steps three at a time, grabbed the banister to slingshot himself around the corner at the top, and flew down the hall to his study. Price followed at a more sedate pace.

He inhaled deeply of the lovely fragrance filling his study without pausing. His clothes for the evening were laid out upon his big, excessive mahogany desk, with a pita wrap alongside. The pita, he noted with amusement, occupied the exact center of the desk. Off to the side, a steaming carafe of coffee perched on an end table, providing the aroma that suffused the room.

Ah, coffee . . . How mystifying that something which smelled so divine could taste so much like axle grease steeped in hate. Darling had used the mind-enhancing drug as a secret weapon for several years now, being careful to indulge only at need and not build up a tolerance, much less a dependence. It gave him the boost he needed on days like this one, when his double life disallowed the possibility of enough sleep. Best of all, it was a purely natural drug, not magical or alchemical, thus not detectable by ordinary means. He had heard recently that one could buy the stuff in some of the more upscale tea rooms these days. He'd have thought it a more appropriate addition to the menu of shroom dens.

Darling roughly pulled off the expensive robe of his office and tossed it carelessly in the general direction of an armchair; Price swooped over, intercepting and deftly arranging it to drape over the back of the chair without wrinkling.

He continued discarding his inner garments, which she similarly rescued. Darling stripped down to his skivvies without self-consciousness; one's butler was, in some ways, more intimate than family. She had seen every inch of his skin at one time or another, and cleaned and sewed up a number of punctures and tears in it. Somewhere along the line he'd gotten over the fact that she was a fairly attractive young woman.

While Price reassembled his flurry of cast-off cloth into a neatly folded stack, he plucked the evening's suit from across the desk, careful not to disturb the sandwich in the process. He could do without her passive-aggressive throat clearing while getting himself into the proper mindset for the other half of his life.

The slacks were old, well worn, and bearing faint stains that were all but invisible against the black, yet added texture that was part of their character. The old tuxedo jacket was a little too loose across the shoulders and too long in the arms, exacerbating the effect of its frayed cuffs. Price had laid out his favorite waistcoat, the one in a black-on-maroon paisley pattern that managed to be screamingly tacky and understated at the same time. The final touch, the cravat, he draped around his neck, letting its ends hang untied down his shirt front. This one was powder blue and pale orange; it clashed with everything else in the outfit. In fact, it clashed with everything on the planet, including itself.

He kicked off his preposterously expensive loafers, plopped down in the room's other armchair, pulled over his worn, old leather boots, and began lacing them up while Price stepped over and saw to his hair.

They finished their tasks at nearly the same moment, thanks to the rhythm of repeated practice. He stood, and she stepped back, holding up a hand mirror for his inspection.

The transformation was complete. From scuffed boots and a shabbily loud suit to a nearly invisible layer of stubble and blond hair that was now heavily greased down and slicked back, he looked almost like a different person. It was as much in bearing and mannerism as attire, however, that personality was expressed. He stood loosely, his posture slouched and lopsided, lips always pulling toward a faint smirk.

"Smashing. Thanks, Price."

"Of course, sir." She set down the mirror and turned to retrieve a tray while he strolled over to the end table and picked up his carafe of coffee. It was always "Your Grace" when he was the bishop, but simply "sir," now. She understood.

He gagged slightly as he forced the concoction down. It had to have been some joke of the gods that such a useful and potent tonic had to taste so foul. Thanks to Price's typically precise timing, the coffee was cool enough that he could get it down in a series of gulps without having to unintentionally savor any, but it was not yet growing cold. For some reason, it was even worse cold. He felt the warmth in his stomach immediately; the growing alertness in his mind and senses would kick in about ten minutes hence.

Turning back around, he found Price waiting, the tray held in front of her. He deftly snatched up the variety of items proffered—several different coin pouches; two decks of cards (playing and tarot); a couple of flowers; knives for eating, throwing, and stabbing; lock picks, a magnifying lens, vials of alchemical solutions; odds and ends. Each he tucked away deftly in its proper place about his person.

With this final step complete, he was ready to go. Casually tying his cravat into a lopsided knot that didn't resemble anything commanded by the creed of fashion, he turned to the grandfather clock.

Price cleared her throat loudly. "You will find the pita sandwich eminently portable, sir, wrapped as it is in butcher's paper."

"Ah yes, of course," he said glibly, snapping his fingers and leaning over to snatch up the sandwich. "I'll leave my head behind one of these days."

"You are far too fond of it, sir."

"Love you, too. Don't wait up; it's gonna be a long night."

Busy rescuing his loafers from against the wall, Price didn't trouble herself to dignify that with a response. Darling turned the hands on the clock to 3:13 a.m., stepped back as the entire thing swung away from the wall with a soft hiss, then ducked into the dim space beyond, lit only by a single fairy lamp. With the ease of long practice, he began descending the wall-mounted ladder down a deep shaft, not at all inconvenienced by having only one hand to use. Bites of the sandwich disappeared as he climbed down. Above, once he was past the lip, the clock slid shut, sealing him in.

Darling had been so proud, when he'd had it installed, of his sewer-access escape route leading to the second-floor study. How original, how cunning! Nobody would think to look for a tunnel to the sewers from the second floor. He had fairly quickly come to the realization that no one would think of it because it was a damn fool thing to do. Anybody doing a thorough search of his home would find it anyway, and any parties likely to be up to such a thing in the first place would probably know exactly where it was going in. He had simply outsmarted himself and guaranteed a long, dark climb at the beginning and end of each of his outings.

Ah well. Live and learn.

At the bottom, he set off down the path, as familiar with the tunnels as he was with his own chambers, and waited until he was around the first corner to toss the last of the sandwich into the vile-smelling water. Honestly, had she really expected him to eat while walking the sewers? The stench pervaded everything except his own boots, which had been alchemically treated to prevent it from clinging. He'd be able to taste nothing but the offal of the whole city.

Situated as it was on an island right at the mouth of a river, Tiraas had an incredibly expansive sewer system. As long as it wasn't flooding, there was ample space to walk along the banks of the channels which flushed its detritus out to sea. This made it a popular means of travel, storage, and other less savory business for those citizens who didn't care to explain their movements to the military police.

He let his mind turn, getting into the proper state for tonight's business, paying little attention to where he walked. His feet knew the way.

Having emerged from the sewers not far distant, Sweet strolled through the slums, whistling, and though even his shabby suit was a mark of wealth in this environment, no one troubled him. He returned called greetings and smiles, winked flirtatiously at the women no matter how worn down they appeared, and exchanged respectful nods with toughs lurking in the mouths of alleys. It was all about reputation.

The Glums, as the Lower Western Ward was called by its inhabitants, was practically next door to Darling's house. This neighborhood was a veritable chasm dug into the island's bedrock so that it didn't spoil the view of the city walls from his wealthy neighborhood above; it simply would not have done for him to be seen walking there, however.

He did not care for the symbolism, or his complicity in it, but . . . It was all part and parcel of the double life he led, and why he made a point to circulate a bit tonight, despite the fact that he was out on business. A fellow couldn't afford to forget where he came from.

The Pink Lady was the only pink building he'd ever seen; it was actually built of pink marble, not painted, though its once fine stone was long since pitted, scarred, and stained. If the sign hanging above the door—with the words of the establishment's name worked into the form of a reclining, voluptuous woman—didn't clearly indicate the nature of the business, the scantily clad women loitering about its facade did. As Sweet approached, one of the furtive-looking men lingering in the area apparently concluded negotiations and hustled inside with a slender girl on his arm.

His arrival was quickly noticed.

"Sweet!" squealed a short, plump girl. She hopped nimbly down from the banister, on which she had perched, and sauntered toward him. The cry was taken up by others; they shifted en masse to meet him, like a flock of seagulls spotting food. Across the way, a couple of well-dressed young men who'd clearly been working up their courage to approach scowled.

"Ladies!" He swept off an imaginary hat and executed a ridiculously elaborate bow, to a reception of titters and coquettish smiles. The girls clustered about him, several babbling all at once while the less forward hung at the edges of the throng, and a few new ones who didn't know him watched, mystified, from the safety of the porch.

Brothels were hardly a booming business in Tiraas, or in most parts of the empire; people did not line up to pay for what they could get free. However, there were always those who, for one reason or another, weren't welcome in a temple of Izara, and where a market existed, someone would take advantage. Unfortunately for those in the business, it meant that the clientele of a brothel were almost always the worst possible kind of people. Prostitutes led a harsh existence, and all too often a tragically short one. Their misfortune, however, made them very useful. They were often the first to hear of it when something truly ugly was moving in the city, and were frequently privy to the most interesting sorts of secrets.

The Pink Lady's matron took care of her girls by hiring only girls she could afford to take care of. She served a niche market, and thus managed to cater to wealthy patrons with particular kinks— and wealthy *young* patrons sowing wild oats, like the lads across the street—rather than the muddle of the drunken, diseased, and depraved who frequented most such establishments. There wasn't a human girl among the lady's stable; Sweet found himself towering over a throng of dwarves, gnomes, half elves, and even two full elves, both of whom managed to look depressed despite their best efforts at the industry's mandatory coquettishness.

"You've got some nerve, mister, swaggering in here like you own the place after we've not seen a hint of you in weeks," the dwarven girl declared, planting her fists on her hips. She smiled, though, and Sweet grinned back. The others fell quiet; she had seniority.

"Aw, Rose, you can't hold it against me! I'm a busy man—people to see, stuff to steal. You know you're the only one I love." This brought a round of guffaws and cackles, but Rose only grinned up at him as he tucked a silk flower behind her ear.

Sweet continued handing out presents while he got the news. For the sake of goodwill, he had something for everybody—candies and paper flowers, if nothing else, but coins for those who had something worthwhile to tell him. It was a time-consuming process, slowed down by banter and chitchat, but that was all necessary. The girls were plenty accustomed to being bribed; taking the time to be *nice* bought him the extra consideration that was his bread and butter. He joked, flattered, flirted, handing out his little gifts with amusing sleights of hand, and never groped or made lewd suggestions. They loved him.

Little of the gossip was particularly interesting to him, but at worst this was an investment in maintaining his contacts here, and thus worth the time. He picked up tidbits about the movements of other cults in the Glums and the richer neighboring districts, some potentially useful leads to follow up concerning business deals, both legitimate and not. He'd pass that along to the Guild, serene in the knowledge that such careless players deserved to be robbed. The one bit of bad news was that Missy was entertaining a client, which meant he'd need to double back here later in the evening; he couldn't afford to wait that out right now, but couldn't risk her goodwill by hobnobbing with her girls and not paying his respects.

There was a certain necessary timing to these things; the girls couldn't be away from their business too long, so he began making his goodbyes before Rose had to start hinting. As the others drifted back over to their stretch of sidewalk, waving and catcalling all the while, he caught the dwarf's eye and tilted his head toward the corner of the building, receiving a wink in return.

Sweet strolled off, paused right at the edge of the next structure, and lounged against the brickwork. Some of the Pink Lady's girls glanced over curiously, but knew better than to involve themselves, especially when Rose sashayed over to join him.

"I noticed your new arrivals," he commented, nodding toward the two elves. They were huddled together in the shelter of the porch, miserably failing to be alluring despite the clearly borrowed dresses that overemphasized their assets.

"Aye," Rose said, sighing as she followed his look. "The twins. Flora and Fauna."

". . . seriously?"

"Oh, get down off yer pedestal, Lord Fancy Pants," she scolded, smirking. "My mam didn't name me Rose, and yours *sure* as hell didn't call you Sweet. Unless she was trying to set you up for a hard time."

"Fair enough," he said peaceably, raising his hands in surrender. Also, twins? They might have been, he supposed. He hadn't spent much time around elves and didn't find it easy to tell them apart. There was only so much possible variation within the spectrum of lean, blond, sharp featured, and large eyed. "They don't seem terribly excited."

Rose frowned, shooting another look at the porch. Their conversation was well within the range of elven hearing, but the alleged twins didn't so much as glance their way. ". . . they aren't gonna make it," she said grudgingly. "It's been almost two weeks now, time enough for even the most stubborn girls to start adapting. But . . . they won't eat enough, they cry every night, and they're scaring off the johns. Even the customers eager to get their mitts on a real elf will shrivel up if she's obviously disgusted by 'em. Well, except for the few that's into that, but them two sure as hell won't play *that* up properly. Word's gonna start getting around before much longer, and then Missy can't afford to keep givin' 'em beds. Fair breaks my heart, and me thinkin' nothing could anymore. It's like watching flowers wilt."

"Mm. You still know how to get me a message at need, right?"

"You and that Guild of yours, aye." She grimaced up at him. "You know my feelings about that, but . . . hell, Light knows there's nothing else we can do for the girls, if they won't shape up."

He couldn't tender this offer to any of the others; they would immediately want to know why he hadn't offered *them* a place with the Thieves' Guild. He actually had offered to sponsor Rose—she had a quick tongue and deft fingers—but she'd been mightily offended at the idea. Apparently, to dwarven sensibilities, prostitution was a more respectable pastime than thieving. He'd been too mystified to be insulted.

"We don't get many elves, but they've been some of our best," he said. "Frankly, I'm amazed to see elves even willing to have a try at your line of work."

"Dunno what they're runnin' from, but it must be a doozy," she said thoughtfully. "Aye . . . your lot might be a better fit for 'em after all. But you *know* what Missy'll say about you tryin' to poach her employees."

"Why, my sweet Rose, you *wound* me," he protested, deftly tucking a silver coin into her cleavage. "I would never so much as *dream* of hiring away talent she's actually using. If it comes to the point where she's out to get rid of them, though . . . You might remind her that a pair of dead elves aren't nearly so useful as a pair of thieves who think fondly of her as the one who first gave them a roof and a chance in this city."

"I might at that," she said wryly, adjusting her bodice. What they both immediately realized, and that Missy would not, was that a pair of prideful elves in a position of strength were far more likely to hold a grudge against her for snaring them into degradation. Missy was as canny as anyone in her business, but not terribly insightful or far-sighted.

He gave Rose a cheerful wink, politely declined the insincere offer of a "freebie," which she'd have punched him in the balls for trying to accept (every society had its little rituals), and proceeded on his way as she turned back to her work.

There had been a time when Sweet's life consisted almost entirely of making his rounds throughout the city. Each night he would head out to a different district, hobnobbing with people of every class and culture. As his increasing duties within the Guild and then the Church had commanded more and more of his time, however, he'd drawn back his operations, and now focused on the Rim and the poorest neighborhoods, deciding that his time spent seeing to the bishop's business gave him as much exposure to wealth and power as he could stand.

He didn't even have time or energy to go out every night anymore, and tonight he had someplace to be. Out of stubbornness, and due to the fact that even his presence would help prevent his reputation from fading further, he kept his path to the Rim, circumnavigating half the city on his way to the Guild's headquarters on the opposite side instead of cutting straight across. He was careful to be seen, but kept his interactions to the most important cogs in the vast machine of the Tiraan underworld, rather than stopping at every pawn shop, brothel, back-alley moot, shroom farm, burlesque, and hidden Eserite shrine, as he preferred to do. Just the sheer volume of greetings he received and returned threatened to slow him down, but he pressed on. Still, it took a few hours to make the full walk. By the time he neared his final destination, he could feel the boost of the coffee beginning to wear thin, and had decided to take the straight route on the way home.

It wasn't truly dark anywhere anymore, even in the gloomy slums, which were sandwiched between the city walls and modern factory districts. The lightning of magical discharges crackled from towering antennae, casting an eerie glow for blocks around and filling the air with a sullen snapping. Passing close to several of these, he felt the tingling along his skin and in his scalp, where even his greased-down hair tried to stand up. A brisk business was done in some such districts in antistatic charms of variable effectiveness.

What impact all the loose energy had on the health of the inhabitants was hotly debated in certain intellectual circles, but for the Rim's dwellers, it was just another fact of life. The poor had too many concrete worries to fuss about vague possibilities.

He arrived with a light but steady stream of more well-dressed patrons at a small cul-de-sac bordered on three sides by a sprawling structure of white marble that would have looked almost ecclesiastical if not for the brightly colored banners and multihued fairy lights bedecking its surface. Though the people he passed on his way to the doors were mostly residents of even finer districts than this one and dressed in a manner that far surpassed his own in taste and quality, he received not so much as a disdainful glance. Regardless, anybody coming here knew very well what a shabby individual like himself would be doing in the place, and that it would be most unwise to antagonize him.

Sweet tipped a wink to the burly guard at the door, who only nodded respectfully to him and held it open, ushering him into the opulent interior without a word. The extremely well-dressed lord and lady who arrived at nearly the same time paused politely, allowing him to go first.

Organized gambling was technically illegal in Tiraas. The Thieves' Guild had not discouraged this, for the sake of the monopoly it granted them. Even the empire would not challenge the rule of a god in his own territory, no matter that it took place in defiance of the empire's laws and on its very doorstep.

And so, there was exactly one place in the city where the wealthy and powerful could congregate to indulge publicly in several of humanity's favorite vices, enjoying the style of luxury to which they were accustomed and without fear of any legal repercussion—the Imperial Casino, the not-so-secret headquarters of the Guild and the central Temple of Eserion, the god of thieves.

Gambling, after all, was just stealing on the grandest scale when you ran the games.

Sweet swaggered in as if he owned the place, receiving respectful bows and smiles from the staff and curious looks from the patrons scattered about the atrium. He didn't linger, though, setting out for the gaming floor, and none of the Imperial Casino's employees moved to intercept him, even to so much as offer a cocktail. They knew his ways well enough to anticipate at a glance whether he wanted to chitchat or get after his own business . . . even still. It had been over a year since he'd left his duties here to accept the role of bishop, but these people were, after all, functionaries in a temple.

They didn't quickly forget the habits of their previous high priest.

CHAPTER 15

L ate in the afternoon, after classes were out, Trissiny found Teal on the big open lawn by the gazebo where their fighting course was held. The paladin was returning from a jog down the mountain and back up—midday wasn't the ideal time for such exercise, but she needed to clear her head, and running tended to attract less attention than sword drills, even if it was on the University's abominable staircase. It had been a cool day, though, and she hadn't pushed herself. She was barely sweating.

She paused in the shadow of the gazebo, watching Teal clumsily try to practice a few things the martial arts instructor, Professor Ezzaniel, had laboriously tried to teach her. Even having taken off her tailored coat, Teal really wasn't dressed for exercise. For some reason, she wore cheap rubber sandals that flapped loudly with every step, in a bizarre contrast to her expensive-looking suits; they were certainly not doing her any favors here. Trissiny cringed, watching the girl make clumsy, disinterested parodies of punches without paying the slightest attention to proper form or stance. At least nobody else was around to see her.

Apparently, Teal had about the same opinion of her performance. She stopped what she was doing and stood there for several seconds. Just as Trissiny was about to turn and be on her way, Teal sighed so deeply that the paladin could see her chest rise and fall even from this distance, and trudged over to the gazebo. Teal plunked herself down on the steps and rested her face in her hands.

Trissiny was on her way over to join her before she'd decided to move.

She sat down beside the other girl. Teal didn't look up, though Trissiny's approach hadn't been quiet. She wasn't sure what to say, how to begin, and so the silence stretched. It was not an uncomfortable silence, though; sometimes, having a person nearby was all you needed. She'd been there herself.

"I can't do this," Teal said at last.

Trissiny bit back her knee-jerk reaction, which would have been very unhelpful, reminding herself that not everyone had grown up in a barracks. *Most* people hadn't.

Fortunately, Teal continued without Trissiny needing to say anything. "I hate violence. I can't *stand* it. Even play fighting, like what we do in class, it makes my guts clench up and . . ." She drew in a breath and let it out slowly. ". . . and that's not even the worst of it. I've got a . . . that is, inside me, there's . . ." Teal scrubbed a hand across her face. "Well. Suffice it to say that me getting used to aggression is a very, very bad idea. Sometimes I think my pacifism is the only thing keeping me from being an authentic menace to the world. I went to talk to Professor Tellwyrn about getting excused from that class as a conscientious objector or something."

"How did that go?"

"She laughed at me," Teal said sourly. "Then griped at me for wasting her time, and called me . . . some names."

"She did what?" Trissiny straightened up, frowning. Just who had put that woman in charge of a school?

"To be fair, that last part was as I was leaving," Teal said hastily, "and I don't think she knows that I understand elvish. It's just . . . Even putting my own problems aside, that attitude terrifies me. Why does everyone in the world think it's so damn *crazy* not to want to hurt other thinking, feeling people?" She glanced sidelong at Trissiny. "Oh, forget it. Look who I'm talking to."

"Excuse me?" Trissiny raised an eyebrow. "You do realize that the Sisters of Avei, among other things, protect the pilgrims and shrines of gods who don't allow violence in their followers? We prepare for war because someone needs to. I guarantee you have *never* heard an Avenist condemn you for being a pacifist."

Teal flushed. "I'm sorry. You're right, that was a stupid thing to say. I'm just frustrated and stressed, and taking it out on the wrong person. Sorry."

Trissiny studied her thoughtfully for a long moment, then stood. "C'mon, get up. I want to show you something." Teal hesitantly followed suit as Trissiny stepped away, giving them some room to move, then turned to face her. "Okay, throw a punch at me."

Teal got a long-suffering look on her face. "Triss, what was I literally *just* talking—"

"*Slowly*, if it helps you. Don't actually try to hit me, just demonstrate how the action would look."

She pursed her lips mulishly for a moment, then shook her head and stepped forward, pushing out her fist in an exaggeratedly slow motion.

Trissiny grabbed her wrist, hooked her other hand behind Teal's elbow, and spun, tossing the other girl to the grass.

Lying face-up on the ground, Teal heaved a sigh. "Great. Thanks. Thank you. I don't get nearly enough of this in class."

"Stop complaining for a moment and *think* about what just happened," Trissiny said, a smile tugging at her lips. "I didn't strike you. You landed quite gently; you're not even winded. I only had to put any muscle into it because you were throwing a pantomime of a punch; if you'd *actually* been trying to hit me, I would have simply used your own energy to move you out of my way." She bent over the fallen bard, extending her hand. "Self-defense doesn't have to be about inflicting violence. It can be about deflecting violence, turning it back on its user. Or, potentially, about taking all the violence out of a situation."

Teal allowed herself to be pulled upright, her forehead creasing in a thoughtful frown. "Then . . . you're saying Ezzaniel's full of it when he goes on about nonviolent self-defense being a crock."

"*No*," Trissiny said firmly. "He's never said it's not possible: he said it's prohibitively *hard*, and he was dead on. It is *always* easier to inflict damage, that's why most schools of fighting start by teaching that, and then move on to the subtler, more complicated approaches. Different martial arts are more than just different sets of movements, Teal; they're built on different philosophies. The eagle style I learned is based on the idea that the goal of a fight is to eliminate your opponent's capacity to fight. You'll be defeated if you do any less; you become a monster if you do more. However, the fact is the most efficient way to neutralize a foe is almost always to kill or maim them. We eschew both cruelty and hesitation."

"You get a kind of cadence in your voice when you talk about it," Teal said with a smile, "like you're reciting something."

Trissiny shrugged, her expression rueful. "That happens when you've heard the exact words enough times. Look, there are elder Sisters of Avei who can disarm and incapacitate a soldier without so much as ruffling his hair, but that is true *mastery*. It builds upon a lot of very violent technique, and I personally am nowhere near that level yet. I do, however, know enough that I would rarely need to kill someone to defeat them, unless they were obsessively trying to kill me. I think Ezzaniel is encouraging you not to think along those lines because, honestly, the only athleticism you seem to have is in those harp-strumming fingers."

"No offense taken." She grinned.

"The point being, starting you off on the hardest possible approach isn't going to be any decent teacher's first choice. But . . . if you are *serious* about this, if you acknowledge up front that you're setting yourself up to have to work harder than anyone else in the class, and you're willing to bust your butt to do it . . . I think we can persuade the professor to back down and let you. I'll help you as best I can. Plus, you have another classmate who's in a position to help you out even better than I ever could."

Teal perked up. "Shaeine?"

"*Really*?" Trissiny raised an eyebrow. "Have you *ever* heard of drow hesitating to use force?"

"Well . . . I just thought, Tar'naris being pretty peaceful . . ."

"The Narisians are civilized, not soft. Before the treaty, they used to raid the surface for slaves." Trissiny shook her head. "I was talking about *Toby*. After our fight in that first class, I did some reading on the Omnist monks, and their fighting style is pretty much exactly what you're looking for. They use it mostly as an exercise form, and only occasionally for self-defense. Sun style *has* no offensive moves. Its whole objective is to neutralize an opponent without doing them any harm. It's going to be a *very* difficult thing to learn from the ground up"—she smiled gently—"but I can't imagine that Toby would be unwilling to teach you. Anything that brings a little less violence into the world will make an Omnist happy."

Teal was already looking a lot more chipper. "I'll talk to him next chance I get. And . . . you were serious? You'll help me, too? I don't know if I can ever really thank you properly . . ."

Trissiny held up a warning finger. "I meant what I said, Teal— this is going to be *hard.* You'll have to work outside of class, a lot, and work harder *in* class. Ezzaniel is likely to hold you to a higher standard if you commit to this. My time is yours, if you make the commitment, but I will expect you to *hold* to it. I will not waste my time on a disinterested pupil."

Teal nodded firmly. "You have my word, I'm in it for whatever it takes. And seriously, Triss . . . *thank* you." She grinned again, shuffling her feet into a cringeworthy approximation of a fighting stance. "Now . . . show me how you did that."

Night had almost fully fallen by the time they left the broad lawn, with only a reddish tinge lingering in the sky above the rooftops to the west. Most of the light was from the fairy lamps, which lined the campus's paths; the lawn had little illumination, and Trissiny had called a halt to practice due to darkness.

She was increasingly impressed with Teal. The girl was as winded and obviously as tired as expected for someone in unimpressive physical shape who had just spent an afternoon exercising, not to mention her expensive suit was now rumpled, stained by sweat and grass, and actually torn in a couple of places, but she had stuck to it with a rugged determination that Trissiny found as surprising as it was impressive. There was a lot more to Teal than music and snark, apparently, which made her feel more optimistic about having committed to train her.

They met Shaeine and Gabriel at the nexus of paths leaving the lawn, to Trissiny's surprise.

"Hey there," Teal said brightly, waving and lengthening her stride to join them, despite the slight limp she'd picked up in the course of their training session.

"Good evening, Teal," the drow replied with one of her polite, little smiles. "Are you quite all right?"

"Oof, yeah, I'm fine. This one's quite the taskmaster," she said with a grin, nodding at Trissiny. "Good at what she does, though! I feel almost ready to stand off against an alley full of thugs."

"*Please* don't try that," Trissiny said firmly. She was sweaty enough to need a bath once she got back to her room, but nowhere near as disheveled as Teal.

"I concur," added Shaeine. "I would much prefer you uninjured."

"It was a joke. I was joking. Calm down, guys, I'm not a *complete* idiot, usually."

"What are you two doing together?" Trissiny asked curiously, glancing at Gabriel. He had remained silent through this whole exchange, staring flatly at her.

"We are returning from the library," Shaeine replied. "Gabriel was kind enough to help me access the upper shelves. I fear I am not tall even by elvish standards."

"Don't they have a librarian to help with stuff like that?" asked Teal. "Or at least stools or ladders or something?"

"Yes, but I found the librarian to be . . . how shall I put this . . ."

"A fuckin' creep," Gabe supplied, scowling. "Ruda and Fross were with us earlier, but that was before Ruda tried to flirt with him and he basically called her a whore. We barely talked her out of drawing steel on him. Now Ruda's gone into the town to get good and drunk, and the pixie went along to keep an eye on her." He rolled his eyes. "I'm sure nothing can possibly go wrong."

"He said that?" Trissiny demanded. "To a student? That is *intolerable!*"

"I thought you didn't like Ruda," said Gabe flatly.

"That is *completely* beside the point. A man in a position of authority has *no* business treating female students like—"

"Gabriel may have exaggerated the exchange a bit," Shaeine cut in soothingly. "It was a far more passive form of aggression. His exact words—"

"Don't," Gabe said quickly, grimacing. "Nobody needs to hear it again, and there's really no point in trying to reason with a cranky paladin."

"What does *that* mean?" Trissiny demanded, rounding on him.

"Oh, don't give me that wounded face," he growled, his grimace hardening into a glare, "or at least save it for someone we don't *know* you'd rather kill than talk to. 'What are you doing together,' my ass. Like you thought I was gonna drag her behind a bush and suck her blood out."

"You are being needlessly aggressive, Gabriel," Shaeine noted. She always spoke calmly, but suddenly seemed to be trying to project calm into the conversation by force of will.

"No known demon species does that," Trissiny said coldly, ignoring the drow. "And Shaeine is a cleric. I would actually like to see you try to harm her."

"Well, Trissiny, I've misjudged you." Gabriel gave her a grin that was all teeth and no humor. "Here I figured you were too craven to admit your murderous impulses in public. My apologies. I give you points for integrity, bitch."

Teal and Shaeine both lunged into action, the bard wrapping her arms around Trissiny and the priestess grabbing Gabriel by the arm and hauling him backward a few steps. It barely averted disaster.

"WHAT DID YOU SAY TO ME?!" Trissiny roared, stepping forward despite Teal's attempts to dig her heels in.

"Damn it, Gabe!" Teal yelled. "Do *not* throw gendered insults at a Sister of Avei! What kind of death wish do—" She cut off with a grunt as Trissiny effortlessly hooked a hand under her arm and threw her to the grass for the umpteenth time that afternoon.

Gabriel yanked himself out of Shaeine's grasp and stalked toward the seething paladin, baring his own teeth in a snarl. "You *heard* me. You know what, Trissiny? I have done *nothing* to you, or near you. I've done nothing to *anybody*. All I ever did was get born, which believe me, nobody asked me my fucking opinion about beforehand. I am sick of being spit on and treated like a rabid animal for *no fucking reason*."

"No reason?" she snarled right back.

"Guys, that's *enough!*" Teal tried to jump between them, but Trissiny just pushed her back out.

"You're trying to pick a fight with me out of nowhere, and you have the *gall* to act like the victim here?"

"Yeah, this is really coming right the hell out of nowhere," he spat back. They were now inches from each other's faces. "After you burned my hand, then went for your sword on me like *I* was the one who did something wrong, and now you're acting like me *walking a classmate* home is some kind of . . . of crime against humanity!"

"You. Are. A. *Demon!*"

"I'm a *person!*" he screamed. "And if I wasn't, I'd rather be a demon than a fucking *hypocrite!*"

"*What?!*"

"Oh, here's the great and noble paladin, protector of the innocent," he raged, waving his arms, "keeping us all safe by jumping up everybody's ass when those of us who weren't raised in a convent act like *normal* human beings. Thank the gods we have Trissiny here to let us all know how much better she is than the rest of us mere mortals!"

Teal's continued attempts to calm them were not only ignored, but all but inaudible beneath the shouting match. Shaeine had stepped back, and was alternating between watching the combatants carefully and scanning the environs for help. They seemed to be alone, for now, but it was only a matter of time before the raised voices drew attention.

Trissiny could feel herself losing control, feel her hard-won discipline cracking and letting the anger take over. Worse, she couldn't seem to stop it; worst, she wasn't certain it was wrong.

"I have *never* held myself above others," she snarled at Gabriel, "which you would know if you'd paid any attention to me instead of the—the—the *cartoon* of me you have in your head. I have to wonder what you're so guilty about that you have to cast the paladin as a villain in whatever drama you think you're playing in!"

"My *best friend* is a paladin, you self-righteous asshole! He's never threatened me, or overreacted to me, or acted like I'm less than human. He also doesn't make a habit of *burning* me just to prove a point!"

"I was trying to *help* you!" she shrieked. "Excuse me for embracing the light of the gods that protects us on this realm! If the purest form of energy in our world is so painful to you, why don't you just go somewhere you belong?"

"Damn you and your attitude, I belong *here*! I am not less than you, I'm not evil, and I don't deserve to have to put up with this bullshit! If you don't want to have a problem with me, why don't you try not being such a *cunt*?!"

Teal clapped a hand over her face.

"That," said Trissiny softly, "is too far." She drew her sword.

Gabriel reflexively hopped backward from the blade, but then forced himself to a stop, sneering at her. "Well, there we see your true colors. You really can't deal with anything except by killing it, can you?"

"This has indeed gone too far," Shaeine said. She was serene as ever, but her voice held iron command that none of them had yet heard from her since they'd met. "You two are behaving like errant children. This must *stop* before real damage is done."

"I'm just standing here," Gabe shot back, spreading his arms as if to embrace Trissiny, sword and all. "Just existing. We're just now finding out how much of a problem she has with that."

"You want to stand here?" Trissiny pointed the blade at him. "Then let's see you *stand here*."

A pure, golden glow sprang up around her, its intensity enough to illuminate the lawn. Gabriel screamed in pain and stumbled desperately backward out of the radius of her aura, covering his face with both hands.

Teal leaped away from the light, looking frantic. "Trissiny, stop it!"

Trissiny stepped closer to Gabriel, forcing him backward. "He goes on, and on, and *on* about how he belongs here just like anyone, but show a bit of the divine to him, and we see the truth. What kind of *thing* can't bear the light of the gods? Divine light is purity and healing, and *what does it do to you?*"

Gabe let out a long, animalistic sound that started as a groan but morphed into a serpentine hiss halfway. He parted his fingers to glare at her. His eyes were totally black, with no whites or irises.

Despite the tension holding her entire frame, Trissiny felt a shiver race along her spine. She had read and heard warnings, been told about the face of the demonic, but had never before seen it in person.

"And the real face emerges," the paladin whispered.

"Stop it!" Teal shouted desperately from a safe distance.

"Trissiny, you *must* end this," Shaeine snapped. "You are *torturing* him. Is this how Avei commands her paladins to behave?"

"I'm beginning to think you're right," she replied. "This is foolish. I should end it."

She slashed at Gabriel with the sword. He bounded backward, but screamed in pain as the weapon put off a fierce blaze of light, even the glow singeing him in passing. It wasn't a human scream. He stumbled as he landed, but regained his balance and snarled at her again. In the light of her aura, his face was twisted, fangs sprouting from his mouth, scaled ridges appearing along the backs of his hands, eyes fathomless pits. There was no reason or hesitation left in them.

The paladin and the demon lunged for each other simultaneously; sparks flew as they collided with a barrier of silver light that sprang up between them.

"This cannot happen!" Shaeine said firmly. "You've already pushed him too far, Trissiny. *You* must be the one to draw back and bring this to a stop!"

"That's what I'm doing! *Get out of my way!*" She darted for the side of Shaeine's conjured barrier; it shifted, following Shaeine's pointed finger, keeping her separated from her quarry. Gabriel, however, dashed the other way, whipping around its back edge with the agility of a jungle cat and lunging for her side. Trissiny barely got her shield up between them and threw him backward; she followed up with a thrust for his heart, but he flung himself back with the momentum of her throw and skidded out of range, before gathering himself to lunge again.

The silver wall of light darted between them again, and this time slammed into Trissiny's face, shoving her backward. At the same time, Teal leaped onto Gabriel's shoulders, trying to wrap her arms around him. He snarled and threw her roughly to the side.

"Teal!" Shaeine shouted desperately. "You need to get help! I can hold one of them, but not both, and whichever I incapacitate will be vulnerable!" As she spoke, she gesticulated, swatting first Gabriel and then Trissiny with the wall of light; it served to keep them apart for a few more precious seconds, but both were incredibly agile and single-mindedly fixated on getting to each other. It was as if they could no longer even see anything but the enemy ahead.

"It'll take too long . . ." Teal grimaced, climbing back to her feet. "All right. Hold Trissiny back."

Then she exploded.

The eruption of flames coalesced into a pair of immense, burning wings; a corona of fire wreathed her head. She stepped resolutely toward Gabriel, a creature of flame and scything talons, with eyes that blazed like portals into hell . . . and still wearing Teal's dapper suit.

"Gabriel." The archdemon Vadrieny's voice was music, as though an entire choir were speaking in flawless harmony. The distant corner of Trissiny's mind not occupied with the enemy in front of her thought it seemed wrong for such beauty to come from the demonic. Vadrieny did not immediately succeed in getting Gabe's attention, however; just as he tried to lunge around Shaeine's barrier, she reached out with one clawed hand and seized him by the collar. "Gabriel! I know you're still inside there. You need to calm yourself. We are your friends. You don't want to do this."

He thrashed in her grip, unable to shake her; finally, he reached back to grab her hand and wrenched himself free by ripping the fabric of his coat where she held it, then spun and drove his fist directly into her nose.

Vadrieny didn't move to dodge or block, taking the blow with a grimace of annoyance. "You didn't want to do *that*, either," she said, and backhanded him halfway across the lawn.

They were separated; that was all Trissiny needed. The archdemon could be worried about *later*.

She charged at Gabriel while he was down, shrieking in frustration as Shaeine's barrier zipped into her path again. Vadrieny gave one flap of her fiery wings and leaped over the lawn to stand beside the fallen half demon, getting herself in position seconds before Trissiny—having feinted left and then pivoted around the shield when Shaeine moved to respond—arrived.

She opened her mouth to speak, but Trissiny was not about to give this a chance; she drove her sword directly at the archdemon's throat. Vadrieny swatted the blade away with one set of claws; it rang like a bell and emitted a blast of golden light where she touched it.

"*Ow*," the demon complained, and punched Trissiny in the chest.

Her breastplate absorbed the worst of the impact, but she was flung backward and hit the ground in a skid, sliding a good fifteen feet away.

"This isn't going to stop until at least one of them is out of the picture," Vadrieny stated, turning to point at Shaeine. "Try to calm that one down. I'll deal with him."

So saying, she bent, grabbed Gabriel by both lapels, beat her wings once, and sent them both shooting into the sky. They were out of view in seconds.

Shaeine stared up at the sky, at the streak of fire that was so rapidly vanishing into the distance, her expression blank as usual, but more flat than serene now. Tension held her body rigid as a statue.

Trissiny bounded upright, rounding on the drow in a fury. "*Why did you—*"

A silver shield flashed through the air and knocked her back down.

There was no thought, no motive, no hesitation. There was only the rage, and the enemy before him.

He clawed frantically at the massive talons holding him by the throat, to no avail; their strength was far beyond his. She stared at him from an arm's length away, those hateful orange eyes that were nothing but pits of flame in an otherwise human face. Her expression was implacable, cold. She didn't hate him, didn't fear him. It filled him with fury.

Striking her did nothing. She didn't even close her eyes when he tried to jab at them with his fingers, and the hellfire within was so intense that he jerked away, feeling the burn in his hands even from the depths of a berserker state in which there was no Gabriel Arquin, only his unleashed rage and the infernal genetic memory that drove it. His skin was—should be—impervious to any damage, yet she burned him. That angered him further.

Up they went, her massive wings of flame beating like a hummingbird's, filling his view with fire and depriving him of any sense of context. He couldn't have seen the context, anyway, not with an enemy before him on which to focus. Yet, he couldn't do anything. She was just carrying him upward; she wouldn't fight or flee, wouldn't acknowledge his fury. He was helpless; he was ignored. That angered him most of all, constantly stoking his wrath until it seemed his very skin would rupture from the effort of containing such primal, savage rage.

But that didn't happen, she didn't relent, and they were alone with only each other and the whistling wind. Snarling and slashing at her, he did not even notice when the wind faded away; he noticed nothing until she let go.

His enemy released him, pushing off and shooting backward. He reached for her frantically, but she was instantly beyond his grasp. Even in the grip of his mindless fury, battle instinct told him what should happen. He would begin to fall. That was worth nothing unless she got below him, but he instinctively aligned his body anyway to control his descent.

The descent never began.

The lack of air meant nothing to him, as he was running on pure infernal magic now; the cold was enough to hurt, but pain did not slow him, either. However, as physics failed to act as they should, as he slowly rotated in place instead of falling properly, a tiny part of his awareness perked up to study his surroundings, and in the next moment, awe crept through the rage, finally beginning to diminish it.

Below, he could see the edge of the world.

It was *round*.

Stars blazed on all sides, more than there had ever been in the sky, in a sky that was bigger than the sky should be. The ground was distant, and he could see its circular rim, hazy with atmosphere. The land was green and gold, brown and gray, flanked by endless seas of blue, and between himself and all of that drifted titanic banks of cloud, looking positively flat from this height.

How long had she carried him?

He drifted, kicking and clawing at nothing and having no apparent effect on his momentum. Helplessly, he slowly pivoted to bring the world out of his view. Beyond him, against the jeweled sky, a reddish streak was circling about in the near distance, diving toward him. His rage sharpened back into focus at its approach. It was her. His enemy, the thing of fire and claws. Her speed was incredible. Hardly had he recognized her distant form before she slammed into him again from above, talons latching back around his throat and pushing him downward.

He tried to scream his rage at her, but there was no air in his lungs to express, no air through which sound could move. He flailed, punched, scratched, as helpless as he'd been before. It was intolerable. It was maddening.

But this time, it was different. This time, he began to burn.

The old lizardfolk shaman sat atop his rock as the third day faded to darkness. He was too old for this; he knew it in the cracks creeping around the edges of his scales, in the stiffness of his bones, the way his body rebelled at this effort. Yet, there was no other. His apprentice was not yet ready to undertake a vision quest. The people needed guidance; he had to seek the gods' will.

So here he had sat, as the cycles of sun burned into him, filling his body and spirit with energy, to be cooled and bled away during the desert's harsh night. Several times rattlesnakes had come to bask with him, but had not bothered his motionless form. Coyotes had sniffed about, but left, choosing to respect the sanctity of his quest. The creatures of nature understood . . . Yet this time, there were vultures. First a lone specimen, then a second. Now, at the end of the third day, a third joined them. Scavengers had never circled on his previous quests.

They knew. He was too old for this.

The world turned, nature cycled around him, driving weakness from his body, seeking to pluck loose his spirit into the realm where lay all wisdom. He had done this before, but his body was weaker now. He only sought to survive to give the people the answers they desperately needed. If the pursuit of this vision claimed his life after that, it was a cost he would embrace. The shaman only needed to cling until the vision came . . .

A star fell.

He knew all about shooting stars. They were important omens. This one, however, was different. The stars that fell slashed across the sky, covering only a tiny span before burning out, lasting a mere second if that. This one continued to fall, as if driven downward by some greater force than gravity. He blinked both sets of eyelids to clear his vision, then focused upon the star as it plummeted. It did not burn up. This was no simple act of nature's cycles, but something from beyond. Something *sent*.

His eyes tracked it steadily until the star struck the desert, miles toward the horizon. Though its fall had been silent to him, now he heard the thunder of its landing. An immense wall of dust was thrown up by the impact, rushing outward with a sound like the rage of a storm.

He stood, slowly. His muscles wailed in agony at their stiffness, but he had no time for complaints and ignored them. The wall of dirt and debris was rushing toward him, across the expanse of the desert. For the first moment, he thought he might be overtaken, but it dissipated too quickly, the heavier particles falling to earth, the sound and movement trailing off. Two full minutes after the impact, the last edges of the shock wave reached him, as a hot wind and a rush of dirty air. He shut his inner lids to protect his eyes.

The horizon was still fogged with dirt and sand where the star had fallen, but he did not stay to study it; his duty here was over. Stiffly, slowly, he turned and limped away, eager to return to the tribe with what he had learned. Despite his body's failures and complaints, he forced it to hasten.

Never had the gods sent so clear or so dire an omen.

A great doom was coming. The people must go.

Vadrieny beat her wings slowly, driving away the airborne dust and dirt. Soon enough, she had created a clear space in the base of the crater they had just made.

Gabriel lay at her taloned feet, limp and unconscious, and fully human. Every scrap of clothing he wore had been incinerated by the reentry, but his demonic heritage had protected his body from the heat and impact. That, at least, had been enough to beat back the demon in him. Though his eyes were closed in exhausted sleep, she could see from the lack of scales and subtler skeletal distortions that his demon blood slept again.

"*So* much trouble," she said, the loveliness of her layered voice echoing across the desert. "Lucky for you, I have a soft spot for kids with demon issues."

Kneeling, she gathered him into her arms. Then, with a great pump of her wings, she took off, carrying him back toward Last Rock.

CHAPTER 16

I t was a thing of beauty, really.

Not the imperial itself. All white marble, gilded furniture, and red plush carpeting, accented by stained glass and actual *frescoes*, it was a faux-royal monstrosity on the inside, albeit an unusually loud and bawdy one. Sweet had little use for such ostentation; when he'd run the Guild, he had frequently hammered home the point that anyone who flaunted their wealth was a mark whether they knew it or not. A *thief* who acted that way was looking to change places on the food chain.

Its *business* was another matter. A gambling den of any kind was a standing long con: a use of illusion and social pressure to part people from their money without resorting to any kind of force, which (best of all), relied on the greed of the victim to work. People who were content with their lot, who had no inclination to get something for nothing or take an apparent opportunity to put something over on a fellow citizen, were all but impossible to con. The richest class of the imperial capital were almost terrifyingly easy. Night after night they came, frittered away impossible sums of money on games that didn't even have to be rigged to offer them no realistic chance of winning, and every night *they came back*. It was beautiful. For the sheer elegance of it, Sweet could forgive the Casino's ostentation.

Besides, this place pretty much funded the Guild's operations by itself. They were thieves, disciples of Eserion; they stole as a way of life, as a spiritual discipline, and to an extent because their presence kept more dangerous criminal elements from arising. They weren't necessarily very profitable.

Sweet strolled casually across the gaming floor, navigating around roulette wheels and tables hosting a variety of card and dice games, smiling and waving to people he recognized. Well-dressed citizens who doubtless thought themselves his social betters politely stepped out of his way, and pulled aside newer patrons who apparently didn't know yet how the Casino worked. He noted familiar faces and unfamiliar ones, and out of sheer force of habit kept an eye out for trouble. The Casino wasn't his to run anymore, but he couldn't help doing a quick visual sweep to ensure everyone was doing their job.

Only some of those present and working were members of the Thieves' Guild. The men and women running the tables, definitely, as well as the girls chosen for their looks who changed money for chips behind barred windows along one wall. The guards were a mixed bag. Burly men in dark suits or the imperial's red-and-gold livery kept watch throughout the building; they were mostly hired on, with a leavening of actual thieves among them to keep them honest. Several doors and sensitive locations had other sorts loitering near them, however; more shabbily dressed men and women who had in common a lean and hungry look that did not belong among the imperial's clientele, some openly carrying weapons. The choice of different kinds of guards helped the patrons differentiate doors they weren't supposed to enter from doors they absolutely did not want to try entering.

"Care for a drink, sir? On the house."

Sweet drew up short, startled, as a tray of cocktails was thrust in front of him by a winsome, dark-haired young woman who fluttered her eyelashes at him. Not one he knew, of course, or she wouldn't have gotten in his way while he was obviously going somewhere. Like all her fellow servers, she wore a low-hemmed and high-collared sleeveless dress that was almost painfully tight; it kept the waitresses from being visual competition with the dancers while making them nearly as alluring. More so, in his opinion. Still, he had no time for flirting this evening.

"Not tonight, love," he said with a wink, sliding a doubloon out of his sleeve and setting it on her tray. "People to do, things to see, you know how it is."

Grinning delightedly, she bobbed a skillful curtsy without disturbing her tray and turned, swishing off into the crowd. Sweet gave himself a moment to watch her go, then resumed his own trek.

In a shadowy alcove disguised as a small grove of artificial trees—the decor in this place was over the top—two men lounged on either side of an unimpressive wooden door, the bigger one cleaning his fingernails with a knife so elaborately evil looking that Sweet was sure it would break in half if he actually tried to stab somebody with it.

"Thumper!" Sweet said cheerily to the other man, who resembled nothing so much as a salesman in his fancy but inexpensive suit and slicked-back hair. "They still letting you work here?"

"Eh, give it a week," he replied easily, but Sweet did not miss the momentary tightening of his eyes, the slight flare of nostrils. Still a lot of anger in this one, and very likely still enough to impair his performance. Well, it wasn't Sweet's problem anymore. "They're expecting you; go on through."

The bigger man had straightened quickly at his approach, and now appeared somewhat tongue-tied. Sweet recognized him, vaguely, a knee-capper who'd been only just raised to the most junior level of Guild membership at the time Sweet had left his position for the Church.

"I, uh, yeah, it's an honor to . . . I mean, go on through, Mr. Sweet, sir," he added unnecessarily, sketching a clumsy bow.

"At ease, soldier," Sweet said sardonically. Thumper grinned with actual humor this time.

"Yeah, he's new. I'll work with 'im."

"Glad to hear it. Stay sharp, gentlemen." Pulling the door open, he slipped between them and into a dimmer, quieter space.

Sweet strolled through the darkened halls more quickly, now that there was nobody around for him to interact with. At this time of night, not many people would be in the Guild's headquarters on business; night was when thieves were out in the city, hard at work. The relatively few who actually lived here were mostly at work on the Casino floor, and most who used these offices to do business kept to daylight hours.

Along an exterior hallway, hang a left, cut through a small meeting chamber, down another stretch of hall, then down two flights of steps. A couple more turns and he was at his destination.

Down here, the stone halls were rough-cut and rounded from their great age. The Imperial Casino was an old building, only repurposed by the Guild within the last century, but even it had been built upon the foundations of a much older temple. Exactly how old the lowest levels of the Guild's headquarters were nobody seemed to know, but the stonework was as worn as anything in Tiraas, and the iron accents corroded in some places to nearly nothing. Down here, torches provided the only light. They could certainly afford fairy lamps, but in the Guild's heart of hearts, the thieves did not try to make things easy or comfortable for themselves. That would have made for weak thieves.

The chamber he entered was expansive, opening before him and plunging twenty feet to the floor, with a narrow path surrounding its upper edges. Below, novices and some very junior Guild members practiced a variety of skills—climbing, sparring, opening locks, all under the watchful eyes of more experienced trainers. Sweet smiled fondly down at the spectacle, but didn't descend the narrow stone steps to the training floor or pause to watch. He moved swiftly around the perimeter of the upper level to a door directly opposite the one through which he'd entered.

This room was longer and narrower, and also more cluttered. The ancient stonework was all but concealed by maps, charts, and wall hangings; pigeonholed desks lined its edges, interspersed with bookcases containing ledgers and scrolls by the dozen. It was considerably better lit, with fairy lamps hanging from the ceiling, and even had a long stretch of mismatched bits of carpet along its center, between the rows of desks. Most of these had been worn to an embarrassing state by years of foot traffic.

He found the room now unoccupied, save for one person.

"Look who finally showed up," Style said sharply, rising from the overseer's chair—the only one with any padding, or armrests—and swaggering over to him. "Afraid to show your face around here while you're behind on your tithes?"

"Style, we gotta do this *every* time? The big guy gets the first cut of every copper I bring in. You know it, he knows it, the boss knows it. When have you ever succeeded in skimming off me? Save it for the newbies."

"It's the principle of the thing," she said with a grin, then swept him into a hug as soon as she got close enough. "Good to see you around again, Sweet. Damn, though, you're all gristle and bone. Doesn't that butler of yours feed you?"

"Well, gods know she tries," he replied, matching her grin as he pulled away. Style was dolled up today in the Punaji fashion, with a heavy leather overcoat and preposterous wide-brimmed hat that bristled with feathers, plus giant clunking boots. Underneath, she wore only a pair of harem pants in a screamingly loud pattern and several yards of ruffled silk wound around her chest. It was a new look for her, but then, all her looks were new. He'd wondered many times in the past how she managed to feed herself, given how much she spent on clothes. It definitely worked out for her, though; Style was a horse-faced woman and brawny as any dockworker, but had no trouble at all finding men to share her bed. Living proof that it wasn't what you had that mattered, but how you worked it.

"Seriously, though, I'm not late. Not very early, either, which begs the question, where the hell is the boss? He's usually lying in wait for me."

"Usually is, yeah." Her grin widened, and he began to smell a rat. "Care for a drink, Mr. Sweet, sir?"

He spun around, stepped back, and gaped. The pretty waitress who'd accosted him above stood smiling flirtatiously up at him, batting her lashes and proffering her tray, which still had his doubloon sitting amid the glasses.

"What the—" He shot a perplexed look at Style; how the *hell* had this girl gotten down here? Style, though, was trying and failing to contain laughter. He narrowed his eyes, peered more closely at the simpering girl, then swore. "Damn it, Tricks!"

Style let out a bray of amusement, giving up the fight, and the illusion melted. The girl's posture and facial expressions subtly shifted, and suddenly Sweet was looking at a short, slender man in extremely skillful drag and a lot of makeup, grinning up at him. "That's another one for me!"

"You are a pain in the ass," Sweet scolded. "We *know* you're good, dammit! You don't need to put on a show every time somebody comes to visit!"

"Oh, let me have my fun." Tricks tossed the tray casually down on a nearby desk and pulled off his wig, further ruining the illusion. "I certainly don't get much of it, what with trying to keep all you goons in line. It's good to see you again, though. You know, you're allowed to come visit, Sweet. You don't have to wait till we've got business to discuss."

"I know," he said with a grimace. "You're not the only one with too much on his plate, Boss. If I had the time . . ."

"Yeah, yeah, the time." Tricks had unfastened the high collar of his dress as they spoke, and now reached behind his neck, grasping a string there, and pulled. In a swift, oddly disturbing display, the false breasts attached to it popped out of his neckline, and he casually tossed this apparatus to Sweet. "As always, it's wasting. I will require you to hang out for a bit and catch up after business . . . but we better see to that first."

He strolled off toward the closed door at the opposite end of the room, pulling a rag from within one sleeve and wiping makeup from his face as he went. Sweet draped the fake boobs around Style's neck and followed, grinning at the swat he received on the back of the head.

They strode through single file, Style pausing to shut the door behind them. This room was completely bare of furnishings or decorations, lit only by four fairy lamps, one in each corner. Its sole content was the towering statue of Eserion against the far wall, surmounting a small fountain which gurgled softly. Gold and silver gleamed faintly within the water. The three thieves approached solemnly.

Sweet pulled an imperial decabloon from within his coat, pausing to press his lips against the golden gryphon inset into the platinum coin, then placed it gently in the fountain. Tricks touched his coin gently to his forehead before dropping it in; Style tossed hers, winking up at the statue as it splashed down. As one, they bowed to the idol, then stepped backward three times from it before turning to face each other again.

"All right, Sweet, what have you got for me?"

Sweet heaved a sigh. "Seriously, Boss, can you lose the dress? I can't take you seriously like this."

Tricks gasped in mock horror, fanning his face with one hand. "Land's sakes, he just wants to see me in the altogether! A *true* gentleman wouldn't stare so at my decolletage!"

"I'm keeping a wary eye on your decolletage, all right; otherwise Style'll club me with it."

"Oh, for fuck's sake, this is like having kids," Style growled. "Will you two settle down? Banter after the meeting; we've got shit to do."

"Right, right," Sweet said peaceably, winking at her, then his expression sobered. "Well, the news isn't great. Things were proceeding more or less according to plan, but then a new player entered the game and everything's gone to hell."

Tricks frowned. "Who?"

"Elilial has officially made the opening moves of a campaign against the empire."

Style spouted off a few choice epithets, while Tricks's expression grew grimmer. "You mean, more of a campaign than what she and the Wreath have been up to in general for lo these many years."

Sweet nodded. "Planted herself in the palace and got *very* close to the emperor himself, then swaggered through a hellgate a few days later in a manner calculated to tip off Imperial Intelligence, and prevent the Hands from keeping it contained. There's . . . more, but it's sealed to the throne."

"So?" Style snorted. "Spill."

"Heel, girl," said Tricks. "Sweet's taking enough risks to keep us in the loop here. The Hands have some kind of fairy witchery up their sleeves; when something's sealed to the throne, they'll know immediately if somebody unseals it. Then we'll be ass-deep in Hands within the hour."

"And you'd need to find yourself a new inside man," Sweet said dryly. "It's a hell of a thing they're sitting on, but *shouldn't* affect us directly, any more than it will the rest of the empire. I'll do my best to warn you out of any danger if it comes up. Anyhow, I hadn't even got to the best part yet. It seems the Archpope was the one who warned Sharidan about Elilial being in the palace, and provided the means to root her out. So the Church has counted coup, the throne's lost face, and now . . ."

"Oh, let me just fucking guess," Tricks groaned.

Sweet nodded. "Justinian's fondest desire has now been approved. The Universal Church is forming its own independent military." Style's swearing intensified; he had to raise his voice slightly as he continued. "They have permission for a small, elite force, adequate to defend the Church's holdings and carry on some antidemon operations. Not enough that the Church can take or hold territory, but . . . it's something. The biggest immediate change will be that the Sisterhood of Avei isn't going to be responsible for securing Church holdings anymore. Justinian is one step closer to being his own political entity. It'll take him some time, at least a year, I'd think, to get this thing up and running smoothly, but it's going to happen. I don't see how it can be pushed back at this point."

"There wasn't *anything* you could do to stop this?" Style complained.

He sighed, for once permitting his inner bitterness to show openly in his expression. "I greased most of the wheels myself. Remember, I'm Justinian's inside man, too, and I'm good at making connections. Even with imperial approval, there were roadblocks in place; I managed to disappear a few of them."

"What the fuck?!" Style roared, her face darkening with rage. "What the incandescent donkey *fuck*? Isn't this what we sent you in there to stop from happening? This *specific exact thing*? And now you go off and—"

"Settle, Style," Tricks said firmly.

"But he—"

"*Settle*." His voice grew sharper and she subsided, glowering. "Hon, you know I love you, but this is why you're my enforcer and I'm the boss. You don't have a knack for subtle. If Sweet pitched in to help this thing along, that means there was nothing he could've done to stop it."

"You didn't have to fucking *help* it!"

"Yes, I did," Sweet said grimly, "because that game was over; we'd lost, and I had to think of the next one."

Tricks nodded. "If he'd tried to get in the way, or even just refused to help, Justinian would know that Sweet doesn't have his back, and that'd be the end of him ever learning anything useful or being in a position to take action. *Now*, he's earned some trust, gotten closer to the Archpope, and might be able to throw the next round our way."

She glared back and forth between them, then suddenly deflated, kicking the ground savagely with one booted foot. "Well . . . just . . . *fuck*, is all."

"Pretty much," Sweet agreed. "The upside is my gambit *did* succeed. I'm getting more face time with His Holiness, and he's hinted at involving me in something else he's cooking up. But I'm afraid I just didn't work fast enough or gain enough trust ahead of time to put a stop to this when it was still possible."

"So what's his next play?" asked Tricks.

Sweet shook his head. "Don't know yet. I also don't know what security he's got. I *do* know he doesn't have anything like seals to the throne to let him know automatically if he's been betrayed. That's fae business, and the Church still refuses to have anything to do with *that*, even all this time after the Enchanter Wars. In the meantime,

I'm doing my best to make myself useful with smaller tasks that won't affect the Guild or the big guy's interests. Just basic brownnosing, but it's paying off. I want to be in the best position possible when the next big thing goes down."

"Right," said Tricks, still frowning. "Keep me posted."

"Always."

"Okay, wait," said Style. "So Elilial's up to something big, right? Can we use that? At the very least it seems like it'd keep the Archpope busy . . ."

Tricks was already shaking his head before she finished speaking. "It's just one more hand stirring the pot. A clever operator, which Justinian *is*, can turn that to his advantage. Remember what I'm always telling you about running a con? *Misdirection.* Anything that creates chaos is potentially useful, if you know how to use it."

"Feh. I'll stick to breaking kneecaps, thanks."

"The trouble is we don't yet know the extent of Elilial's plans," said Sweet. "Not her timetable or even more than the broadest strokes of what she actually wants. She's making a play for the imperial government, sure, but my instinct tells me that's a feint; she has always been obsessed with the gods of the Pantheon. Right now, though, everyone's waiting to see her next move."

"Right. So when she moves, *we* move, and hit the Church while they're not looking."

"Style," Tricks said patiently, "we do *not* have the manpower or resources to 'hit the Church.' You're talking about one of the most powerful institutions on the planet, with the backing of dozens of deities."

"We hit Justinian, then. Don't tell me that wouldn't help; no other Archpope has been half the pain in the ass he is."

"A direct attack on the Church is not happening," he said firmly. "There are too many ways we can lose and no real way to win. We just don't have the *power* to take out Justinian—nobody does. A sitting Archpope is as invulnerable as it's possible for a human to be. No, this is a game of maneuver. We need to weaken Justinian and *keep* him weak until he goes away. You're right that he's the problem here, him and his ambitions."

"And trying a sneak attack on someone right when they're at their most alert for trouble is a horrible idea," Sweet added. "Remember, everyone's on tenterhooks, waiting for Elilial's next play. Maximum possible security by everyone, everywhere. No, we wait. When the next step of the game is in motion we'll have to move fast, but it'd be a critical mistake to move too early." He turned to Tricks. "With that in mind, wait till you hear about the possible *other* player getting involved."

"Oh, for fuck's sake," groaned Style. "Who *else* can possibly stick their nose into this that matters enough for you to worry about? Naphthene? Fairies? Orcish revanchists? Arachne Tellwyrn?"

He winced.

". . . you have got to be fucking kidding me."

Succinctly, he sketched out the history of the exploding girl phenomenon three years ago, including the presence of Elilial's child in Tellwyrn's camp and the evidence of Tellwyrn tracking the Demon Queen's movements. "By the last meeting of the council there wasn't a concrete plan in place, but it looks like the empire's leaning toward trying to passively use Tellwyrn to run interference with Elilial. She appears to be doing that anyway, so it becomes a matter of discreetly helping her along."

"Risky," Tricks said skeptically.

"Yes." Sweet nodded. "But I think it's actually a solid idea. If you look at her movements historically, Tellwyrn gets *really* aggressive with people who try to put something over on her, but I don't think she'll fly off the handle at a good faith offer of aid. In fact . . . I think we may want to look into it ourselves."

"*Too* risky for my blood," Tricks added, a note of warning entering his tone.

Sweet held up a hand. "Hear me out. At the meeting, I floated the idea of using the three soldiers who witnessed Elilial's manifestation as a peace offering, and General Panissar went for it. The empire is stationing them at Last Rock. On the grounds of the University itself."

"They're putting *troops* on Tellwyrn's property?" Style said, aghast. "She'll go berserk."

"This isn't troops, it's three guys who apparently aren't even any good at their jobs. They're being placed there under an old law that allows the empire to quarter soldiers in civilian institutions at the host's expense during a crisis. Bad as that sounds, in *practice* it means these guys will have nothing but their staves and the clothes they're wearing; they'll be dependent on Tellwyrn's hospitality for everything. In short, they are *no* threat to her. They're a peace offering, a little gesture that the empire wants to open a relationship."

"And best of all," said Tricks thoughtfully, "they're an opportunity we can use. We can watch this to see how she reacts with no stake in the outcome. Nice work, Sweet."

"I do what I can," he said modestly.

"This means I'm gonna want someone reliable in Last Rock to keep an eye on things as they develop. The hell I'm leaving this up to Keys."

"Why," Sweet said dryly, "you mean you don't find Principia just a *joy* to work with?" Style snorted loudly.

Tags were both a practical necessity for protecting a thief's real name and a spiritual rite within their faith. Upon elevation to full membership, a thief was tagged by their primary trainer in one of the Guild's few actually religious rites; the working name thus bestowed would serve not only to identify them within the Guild, but signify their approach to Eserion's service.

Keys had been so named for her nigh-preternatural ability to get into and then back out of places she was not supposed to be. And not just places, but situations, even arguments . . . She would pop in out of nowhere and deftly weasel her way back out once she had what she wanted. The utility of this trait for a thief was obvious and considerable, but occurring as it did in someone who was allergic to authority and usually working her own agenda, it made her a nightmare for whoever was responsible for keeping her under control. Principia's assignment to Last Rock had been her own request three years ago, when Sweet was still running the Guild, and he'd been delighted to have her out of his hair. Plus, there was the hopeful prospect that she'd irritate Tellwyrn and cease to be his problem for good.

The Guild had a standing policy of not messing with powerful individuals who tended to be vindictive, so the only qualification for the Last Rock position was that the person holding it should be willing to not do anything, which suited Keys down to the ground. Now, though, they actually needed someone reliable on the scene, which complicated matters considerably. Based on the dark look Tricks was giving him, the current boss had followed this thread of thought all the way to its logical conclusion.

"I'll find somebody," Tricks sighed, running a hand through his hair, still mussed from the wig. "Got a couple of ideas . . . Anyhow. Unless you've got something else of crashing urgency to report, Sweet, there's a little something *I* need to tell *you*."

"Oh?" Sweet glanced back and forth between them. "See, now Style is grinning. That makes me nervous."

"As well it should," said Tricks with some amusement of his own. "We've been approached directly by . . . an interested party. One who wants to open talks, and asked to speak with you specifically."

"Me?"

"You." The boss grinned fiendishly. "And best of all, this request comes with an endorsement from the big guy himself."

That brought Sweet up short. Eserion was a hands-off sort of god. On the rare occasions when he gave explicit instructions to the boss of his Guild, it meant something big was brewing.

"I hope you're well rested, brother," Tricks went on, "because you've got another appointment coming up."

CHAPTER 17

Tellwyrn ignored them for a good half hour.

The office was dim, illuminated only by moonlight from the windows behind the professor and a single fairy lamp under a shade, which directed its light straight onto the desk, where she scratched busily away at an old-fashioned parchment with an equally old-fashioned feather quill. The paltry lamp left the four students in relative gloom, and ominously backlit Tellwyrn herself. Such tricks of staging and pageantry didn't exactly come naturally to her, but she hadn't lived for three millennia without picking up a few. The combination of the lighting and the awkward wait applied exactly the amount of pressure she wanted to these four young fools.

Trissiny had refused the proffered chair, standing at parade rest with her gaze fixed on empty space at a point behind and to Professor Tellwyrn's right. She had been kept in that pose for far longer than this before and was fully content to stay there, stone-faced.

Of the others, only Shaeine looked similarly at ease, standing behind Teal's chair with her customary serenity unruffled. She kept one slender hand on the bard's shoulder.

Teal slouched in her chair, staring emptily at the floor in front of the desk; ironically, of the four of them she seemed the most trauma-tized by the day's events. Her suit was still grass-stained and rumpled from her earlier exertions with Trissiny, but appeared to have suffered no damage at all during Vadrieny's brief rampage, though her rubber sandals had gone missing at some point, leaving her barefoot.

Gabriel sat to her right, purposefully putting the other girls between himself and Trissiny. He, too, slumped in his chair, but where Teal seemed exhausted and depressed, he mostly looked sullen, and perhaps somewhat embarrassed. Though the robe he wore was securely tied, he clutched it closed with both hands. He'd not been given time to put anything else on.

So far, about what she expected from each of them.

The minutes stretched on, marked only by the ticking of a wall clock and the scratching of Tellwyrn's pen, and occasional sighs from Teal or Gabriel. The latter showed increasing signs of impatience as time passed, lifting his head briefly to glare up at Tellwyrn, but he didn't go so far as to say anything. It wasn't as if there was any ambiguity over why they were in trouble, nor any suggestion that it was undeserved.

"There we go," Tellwyrn said quite suddenly, causing Teal to jump in her seat. She pushed the parchment to one side, neatly returning her quill to its holder on the desktop. "Sorry to keep you waiting; I had to draft a letter explaining all this rhubarb to the empire, and it's best to do such things sooner than later. Generally speaking, I require that they keep their noses out of my University and its business, but matters become different when a couple of my students create exciting new craters on imperial territory. Can't deny the imps have something of a legitimate interest. *So*, I'm left to explain matters in a way that doesn't make it sound as if I've completely lost control over you lot. Fortunately, as a college professor, my life is full of examples of bullshit in essay form. Given Miss Avelea's involvement, I'm putting it down to an act of the gods. I doubt Avei will bother to contradict me—she owes me a favor."

Trissiny shifted her gaze to Tellwyrn's, frowning, but the professor merely folded her hands in front of her and put on a warm, friendly smile that made all four of them shift backward slightly. "Well, then," she said pleasantly, "what an interesting evening this has been. I have to say I'm curious how Gabriel was forcibly rendered unconscious and inert. Hethelaxi are notoriously resilient; even a half blood shouldn't have buckled under anything but divine magic."

"We hit him with the planet," Teal said listlessly. Shaeine squeezed her shoulder.

"I guess that would do it," Tellwyrn said dryly after a moment's pause. "Out of curiosity, did Vadrieny aim for that desert, or was she just aiming for *down?*"

Teal raised her eyes, tilting her head to the side for a moment as if listening to something. ". . . for the desert. Nobody was there."

"Good. That takes care of one of my concerns. *However*, matters are not so simple as that. Even a desert may have people in it, either passing through or in some cases living there. Quite apart from people, they are surprisingly rich in plant and animal life, a big swath of which you two just incinerated." She tilted her head to stare at Teal over the rims of her spectacles. "Of much greater concern is the implications. Dropping indestructible objects from orbit would be a *fantastic* new way of waging war, which we are spared only because most of the people who'd be willing to do such a thing are not aware that 'orbit' is even a concept. The last thing the world needs is for them to get any ideas." She drew in a deep breath and let it out slowly, her expression growing grim. "Do *not* do that again. *Ever.* Am I clear?"

"Yes, ma'am," Teal whispered, dropping her gaze again.

Tellwyrn stared at her for a long moment. Then she spoke again, her voice deliberately more gentle. "Are you all right, Teal?"

The young bard hunched her shoulders, not raising her head. She still spoke barely above a whisper. "I . . . hate violence."

"I know. Professor Ezzaniel has *detailed* opinions about that, which he seems to enjoy sharing with me." Tellwyrn shook her head, expression rueful. "But if anything, this incident only goes to prove that you *need* to develop a middle ground. Right now your options for dealing with aggression are to stand there and take it, or unleash an unstoppable force of hellfire. If you can't get away from an attacker or put him down, it *will* get to the point that Vadrieny forces her way out on her own to protect you. You do understand that, right? And why this is not an acceptable state of affairs?"

Teal nodded mutely.

"With that said . . . you did well. You separated those causing the disturbance and pacified the one whom you *could* pacify without doing him permanent harm. A number of points about the execution could have been refined, but all things considered, I am impressed. I'll be giving a very favorable report to your parents and to the Church. I haven't heard about it specifically, but knowing the priesthood as I do, I'm assuming you need every bit of help you can get keeping them off your back."

"Thank you," Teal said softly.

The professor nodded and lifted her eyes to Shaeine. "As for you . . . same goes. I'd have been *more* impressed if you managed to put a stop to that without resorting to force, but I'm willing to grant that may not have been possible. Could have done better, in short, but your instincts and your strategy were both solid, Miss Awarrion. Would you like me to keep your House appraised?"

Shaeine bowed slightly. "Thank you, Professor, but if that is meant as a kindness, I would rather you did not. I concur with the first part of your assessment. My mother, however, will not be impressed that I failed to end a confrontation through diplomacy."

"As you like, then. For my part, neither of you are in any trouble here. Which leaves *you two*."

In spite of themselves, Gabriel and Trissiny glanced at each other, then immediately averted their eyes, neither of them looking at Tellwyrn, either.

"I wish I could say this is the worst thing a group of freshmen has ever done in their first week on campus," Tellwyrn went on in a pleasant tone. "Just for dramatic effect, of course. If I'm to be honest, though, it doesn't even make the top ten. Our admission standards being what they are, I've had some *inventively* pernicious little bastards matriculating here. I will say, however, that tonight's events may well be the *stupidest* thing I've ever seen happen at this University. And that, children, is a much greater offense in my eyes."

Her voice had grown increasingly stern as she spoke, and finished on nearly a growl. Tellwyrn paused to draw breath and collect herself.

"I make allowances for exceptional circumstances. Hell, there's not a student at this school whose circumstances aren't exceptional; that's why you're all here. But the *one thing* I will absolutely not tolerate is mindless behavior. You will *think* before you act. This is not up for discussion. That goes for everyone on the campus, but honestly, out of all the students here you are the *last* two who can afford to behave this way.

"You,"—she pointed at Gabriel, glaring—"are going to have people watching you for your entire life, just waiting for an excuse to decide you need to be put down like a rabid animal. How you've managed to live for eighteen years without wrapping your head around this concept is utterly mystifying to me, but it stops now. Walking up to one of the few people on the campus who both poses a serious physical threat to you and has a motivation to act on it and *deliberately* pushing her over the edge is . . . it's just . . . Gods, I don't have *words* in this language for the sheer idiocy. I'm almost regretful that I have a responsibility for your welfare, here. A creature with *your* survival instincts frankly deserves to die."

"Yup," he said bitterly, "so I've been told. Glad to know whose side you're on, Professor."

She stared at him for a long moment, blinked her eyes once, then smiled sweetly. "You just bought yourself an extra homework assignment on top of disciplinary action, Chuckles. Hit the library, do the research on imperial law governing demonbloods, and by this time tomorrow night be back in this office and present an oral report on the legal statutes which give me the prerogative to *execute you on the spot.*"

Tellwyrn shifted her gaze to the one person she had not yet addressed, and spoke very calmly. "Trissiny, *one* of us is going to wipe that smug look off your face." Trissiny instantly schooled her features while the professor went on. "I'll be honest: I'm going to go a bit easier on you, because nothing I can do or say will be half as serious as what you get from Avei the next time you call on her. Best to do that as soon as possible, by the way; she gets cranky if you make her wait."

"Goddesses do not get *cranky!*"

"It's amazing to me that you can say that, having actually met the one most prone to it," Tellwyrn said dryly. "Oh, calm down, you're swelling up like a bullfrog. If Avei needs you to defend her honor, she'll tell you so. In the meantime, consider the fact that you are responsible for carrying both her reputation and her plans in this world, and allowing yourself to be provoked to violence by a shrieking idiot who wanted nothing more than to get a rise out of you is a *catastrophic* failure—of both strategy and morals. As someone who has met a few dozen Hands of Avei over the centuries, I can assure you that if that's the limit of your self-control, you're going to have a short, undistinguished career and a rather pitifully brief existence."

She drummed her fingers on the desk, glaring at both of them in turn. "You two simply cannot act like this. There are too many forces arrayed against you, and too much riding on your shoulders. You don't *get* to be angsty, mad-at-the-world teenagers. It's not an option. As such, since I perceive that the basic problem for both of you is facing individuals who make you uncomfortable without acting out like overstimulated ferrets, and because I believe that punishments should always carry lessons, here's what I'm going to do. Starting tomorrow night, you will both report to Mrs. Oak in the dining hall immediately after dinner. You're on cleaning duty. I will inform her that there will be no splitting up of tasks, either. You will work side by side, and demonstrate a capacity to work together. Furthermore, you will damn well *get along*."

Tellwyrn grinned wolfishly, savoring the rising alarm in their expressions. "Kitchen duty will end when Mrs. Oak and I are both satisfied that you're either friends or have learned to act like grown-ups in the presence of someone you don't like. If there are any further outbursts of *any* kind, any evidence that you are not only failing to learn this lesson but backsliding, your proximity will be gradually increased until the problem is solved, one way or another. I assure you, kids, I will not hesitate to *chain you together at the wrist* if you don't get your act together under your own power. I've done it before."

"Are you completely out of your damn—"

"That is *totally* unaccept—"

"*SILENCE*!" Tellwyrn thundered, jolting to her feet and slapping both her palms on the desk. All four of them jumped back, including Shaeine. The professor glared at them with teeth bared, leaning her weight on the desktop. "You squandered your right to complain when you tore up my campus in a breathtaking act of mutual stupidity. I will not *have* this kind of idiotic behavior. Not from you, not from anyone! You're here to learn how to be stable, effective people in a hostile world. So help me, you kids are going to get an education if it *kills us all*!"

They stared at her, wide-eyed, for an infinite moment. She let them hang in suspense, staring them down as the seconds dragged on. Then, with deliberate abruptness, Tellwyrn sagged back into her chair and waved a hand dismissively at them. "All right, I have spoken. Get out, all of you. Go to bed. *Except* you, Arquin. Stay a moment."

Teal gave Gabriel a sympathetic grimace and a squeeze on the shoulder as she stood to go. In silence, the three of them filed out, Trissiny pausing to shoot one last, disdainful look at the professor before pulling the door shut behind her with more force than it required.

Gabriel shifted uncomfortably in his seat. Tellwyrn had fallen back into an unnerving stillness, her elbows propped on the desk and hands folded in front of her face, obscuring her mouth. She stared expressionlessly at him over the rims of her glasses.

A minute ticked by, then another, without a word spoken.

"That is a predatory look," he said finally. "I can't decide if you want to eat me or screw me."

Very, very slowly, she raised one eyebrow.

"I said it out loud, didn't I?" he mumbled.

Tellwyrn shook her head. "The thing that gets me, Gabriel, is that you appear on paper to be so *smart*. Not necessarily of the bookish variety; though, speaking as an educator, that is one of the less important kinds of intelligence. You're sort of witty, you think quickly, you exhibit good lateral thinking and decent social skills—your knack for offending women notwithstanding. Why is it, then, that you insist on being such a *bonehead*?"

Gabriel heaved a deep sigh. "I gotta be me."

"Just for your edification, neither of the two options you mentioned is on the table so long as you're my student." She stood, stepping around the side of the desk, and walked over to a closet door. Opening this, she began rummaging around within. "I noticed your choice of attire . . . prior to your current situation, that is. The black trench coat. Shows good fashion instincts; it's hard to go wrong with a good longcoat. Practical, attractive, and it goes with anything. The choice of a black one is maybe a *tad* trite. I grasp the image you were trying to project . . . though maybe it would be smarter for a half demon *not* to try to be intimidating."

"Yeah, I was pretty fond of it," he said bitterly. "Saved up the whole summer doing odd jobs to buy that . . . but whatever. Dunno why I expected I'd be able to keep anything nice."

"*Ugh.*" She turned back around, carrying a folded heap of fabric in both hands, and kicked the closet door shut with one heel. Her expression was disdainful. "You have *got* to drop that self-pitying griping, Arquin. If you won't be moved by the fact that you sound like a dumbass, let me assure you that girls are not attracted to whiners. Confidence and a sense of humor will get you much further than pity. Though a sense of style doesn't hurt, either. Here."

She tossed the fabric to him; he caught it somewhat clumsily, unfolding it and then having to stand up to shake it out completely. It was a trench coat, made of corduroy in a shade of green so dark that it verged on black in the dim office. Heavy bronze buttons inscribed with dwarven runes were its only decoration.

"Black, while timeless, is a bit trite, as I said. It's also not as stealthy as people like to think; truly black objects are rare in nature, and it tends to stand out in darkness. You're much better off with very dark shades of primary colors. Blues and reds, but that'll work, too." She nodded at the coat in his hands.

He stared down at it, rubbing his thumbs over the coarse fabric, then looked back up at her. "I . . . you're loaning this to me? I dunno when I can afford to replace it . . ."

"I don't loan people things, Arquin, and if you want my advice, you shouldn't, either. That's a good way to lose possessions and friends in one fell swoop. No, that's yours to keep. I have a habit of collecting trophies from beaten enemies, which sounds impressive until you realize that it's little more than a recipe for clutter. That one belonged to a pirate lord from a century or so ago. It's weatherproof, has a light armor enchantment that'll protect against some physical and a lot of magical damage. Also the standard bag-of-holding spells on the pockets." She tilted her head thoughtfully. "Now that I think on it, the guy I took that from was one of Zaruda's ancestors. It probably would be wise not to mention that to her."

"I . . ." He swallowed, keeping his eyes on the coat. "I don't know what to say."

"Your problem is you never let that stop you from opening your mouth. For starters, you could try putting it on."

Nodding, he did so, rather awkwardly as he tried to keep one hand on the front of his robe. Soon enough, though, the dark green coat was settled over his shoulders; he was surprised to find it a nearly perfect fit. Even his old coat had been somewhat loose on him in comparison.

"There," Tellwyrn said with satisfaction. "I thought that looked about your size."

"Do you know what the buttons say?" he asked, fingering one.

"Yes. From top to bottom: Beer, Honor, Family, Ham, Intelligence, and that last one is a kind of meat pastry they used to make in Svenheim that I don't think I've seen in a few decades. Dwarven runes were trendy a while back; humans often tacked them onto things without getting them translated. There is some truly embarrassing centennial architecture in Tiraas."

Finally, he lifted his eyes to hers almost shyly. "Thank you."

Tellwyrn waved him off. "All other things being equal, a sense of style is a very important thing to have. Losing your coat, at least, was one part of tonight's doings that I can't blame on you." Taking him by the elbow, she steered him gently toward the door. "Off to bed with you, now, and don't forget your assignments."

Gabriel paused right before opening the door, looking back at her.

He managed a hint of a grin. "So, uh . . . what about after I'm not your student anymore?"

Again, she raised an eyebrow. "Remember what I was saying about you being a bonehead?"

". . . right. I'll . . . show myself out."

"Do."

Silence reigned until they were well out of Helion Hall, where Tellwyrn's office was. Once the three had put space between themselves and the building, Teal came to a stop, with the others following suit. She took a deep breath, wiggling her bare toes in the grass, and tilted her head back to look up at the stars. Fairy lamps ringed the nexus of lawn bordered by the hall, the cafeteria, and the admin building, but they weren't powerful, leaving the girls with a clear view of the night sky. At the moment, there was no sign of anyone else in the vicinity.

"Well," Teal said after a moment's quiet, "this sure has been an evening."

"I retrieved these for you," said Shaeine, and pulled a pair of blue rubber sandals from within a fold of her voluminous robes. They were completely destroyed; the thongs had been snapped, one had an enormous puncture from Vadrieny's talon in the middle of the sole, and the other was torn nearly in half.

"Ah . . . yeah." Teal grimaced. "And now you know why I wear those dumb things. Actually, something about Vadrieny's aura protects my clothes from damage when she comes out. Even the wings don't burn holes in my shirt or anything. I don't think they're entirely . . . physical. But, yeah, those claws don't fit in any kind of shoes, so whatever's on my feet gets pretty well obliterated. I actually really *like* a nice pair of shoes . . . It got downright heartbreaking to see them get shredded every time. I'll just throw those away . . ."

She reached for the sandals, but Shaeine smoothly tucked them away again, giving her a bow and one of her polite, little smiles. "Not at all, I believe you have had enough to deal with tonight. I'll deposit them when we return to the tower."

They had turned to face one another directly as they spoke. Teal opened her mouth again, looking like she wanted to protest, when she caught sight of Trissiny from the corner of her eye.

The paladin had stopped along with them, and was staring at the ground, her posture rigid. She had one hand on the hilt of her sword in a white-knuckled grip; her other hand was clenched so tightly into a fist that her entire arm trembled.

"Triss?" Teal said hesitantly. "You okay?"

"What do you think of me?" she asked quietly, not raising her eyes. The other two girls exchanged a glance.

"I'm not sure what you mean," Teal said slowly.

"It's a simple question."

"Without context, it is anything but," Shaeine replied. "In the broadest terms, Trissiny, I have enjoyed getting to know you."

"Triss . . ." Teal trailed off, not certain what to say.

"Well?" Her voice rose slightly. "Triss, what? Am I overreacting? Have you actually not *noticed* Tellwyrn jumping on my case every chance she gets without any provocation? Or Ruda doing the same?" Her sword whispered faintly as she pulled a few inches of it from the sheath. "Zaruda Punaji is nothing more than a swaggering fool. I can ignore her. I can't exactly brush off Tellwyrn, since she's in charge, but I can live under a vindictive lunatic if I must. But I draw the line at being *attacked* by a demonblood in public and shrugging it off with a smile!"

"No one here contests that Gabriel was the instigator, or that he was unjustified," Shaeine said gently. "I, for one, am curious as to his motivations; that struck me as the act of a person in a great deal of inner pain. But remember, Trissiny, that it was you who first used force."

"Do *not* lecture me about force," Trissiny snapped. She pulled more of the sword free, glaring. "I've studied the art of war since before I could read. War is in the mind—it's in any contest of wills. A half demon who screams obscenities in my face out of nowhere is someone who won't hesitate to draw blood, and doesn't need a reason. Well, I do, and I promise you this: the next time Gabriel Arquin *gives* me one, I am going to finish him off."

"Put away the weapon," Teal ordered, her tone implacable but soft.

Trissiny glanced down at her sword and blinked, apparently surprised to see her hand in the process of slowly pulling it free. She shoved it fully back in the scabbard and removed her hand from the hilt.

"And don't be so eager to forswear the prospect of mercy," said Shaeine quietly. "If it helps, I concur that you have not been treated fairly by some. Since you spoke of the art of war, however, remember to consider the motivations of your opponents. Zaruda is fairly obviously acting out of insecurity, and I think most of what Tellwyrn does is calculated to pressure us into adapting. Gabriel could benefit from a great deal of discipline, it's true, but not at the expense of your compassion."

"*My* compassion?" Trissiny bared her teeth. "I am the Hand of the goddess of *war*. Some peop— Some *creatures* do not deserve mercy."

"Compassion isn't about what anybody deserves," Teal said sadly. "Triss, you're angry right now. Please think before you commit to any—"

"*Of course I'm angry!*" Trissiny snarled, throwing her arms wide. "I don't even know what I'm *doing* here! I should be out in the world doing some *good*, not attending this ridiculous school, and I am *through* taking abuse from wretched people who don't deserve a minute of my time! And now you're talking to me about compassion as if that has anything to do with anything. Have you ever heard of anyone beating an enemy through *kindness*?"

"All right, that's *enough*." Teal turned to face her full-on, meeting the paladin's furious stare. "Have I heard of anyone prevailing through kindness? I'm a bard, Trissiny. The stories are *full* of people doing just that."

"Stories! Of all the—"

"No!" Teal snapped, thrusting a finger into Trissiny's face; the paladin reared back in surprise. "It's my turn to talk now! You want to know about winning through kindness? Three years ago, I was taking a walk in the woods, minding my own business, when someone opened a hellgate inside my *brain*. Can you even imagine what that would feel like? *I* can't, and I *remember* it. I think you'd need a whole set of senses that humans don't possess just to appreciate the amount of pain that caused. And *then*, something came through it."

She stepped backward from Trissiny, clenching her own fists at her sides, but holding the other girl's stare. "I have tried, over and over, to describe what it was like. To my parents, to all those priests and imperial agents who wanted every detail. There just aren't any words. To have something *inside* you, something that's so much unfathomably *bigger* than you are. Your body burning up and being shredded at the same time because it can't hold all that power, your whole identity being crushed within your own mind by the pressure of some colossal, alien intelligence trying to take root in your brain. I was *burning alive*, and I could barely even feel that anything was wrong with me, because her mind was all I could sense.

"And she was in worse agony than me. I could feel her pain at being crushed into something that couldn't hold her more clearly than I could feel mine at being crushed *by* her. She was . . . screaming. It wasn't a sound, it was like the *concept* of a scream, as a pure thought, filling my consciousness. Confusion, betrayal, agony . . . I could barely feel myself at all. I could only feel *her*, and all she could feel was anger and pain. So I . . . I gave her a hug."

Teal shrugged, a gesture of helplessness, and actually laughed softly, though tears were sparkling in the corners of her eyes. Shaeine, off to the side, stared at her fixedly. Trissiny seemed frozen in place.

"Not a physical hug, obviously, since it wasn't a physical thing. There was barely enough of my mind functioning at all, certainly not enough I could have hoped to understand what was going on. I just . . . I felt how she was suffering, and I opened up. Tried to embrace her, offer what little comfort I could. I did *that*, and only that, for . . . I don't know, it must have been several hours. It took a long time for us to sort ourselves out."

Slowly, and without fanfare, she shifted.

A spark ignited deep in Teal's eyes, expanding until they were filled entirely with fire. The blazing wings unfolded from behind her as her hair blossomed into flame, and her posture shifted subtly with the transitioning of her feet into birdlike talons. Six-inch claws of black bone extended from each of her graceful fingers. In the end, Vadrieny simply looked like Teal with extra features, touches of fire and wicked claws. Standing still, it was apparent that her hair and the feathers of her wings weren't actually flames, but glowed orange from within as though formed of fire, an effect emphasized by the way her long mane gently waved about her head as though moved by an underwater current.

"I couldn't tell you which of us was in more pain," she said softly, and even just speaking, her voice was like a choir, like a dozen women speaking in perfect harmony. "I couldn't feel anything except how much it hurt, just being on this plane, within this body that couldn't hold me. The only thing I could feel outside my own agony was that . . . that thread of compassion. It was a lifeline, and I grabbed it and hung on. I clung to her even as pieces of me broke away and dissolved. I could feel myself fracturing, and . . . I was terrified." She shivered, closing her eyes momentarily, those wings shuddering behind her. "My whole identity vanished. Who I was, everything I'd done, my memories . . . gone. All the power that should have been mine slipped away. All I managed to hold on to was my name. I could have tried to fight it, tried to grasp it all, but that would have killed us both, though I didn't realize it at the time. I didn't realize *anything*. All I knew was that the world was nothing but agony, but I was trapped in it with one tiny, little presence that offered me love. I accepted it. She gave me enough courage to let it all go . . . and that saved us."

For a long moment, the demon and the paladin stared at each other, then Vadrieny shook her head. "I don't understand love. It makes little sense to me. But I don't argue with results. You know we weren't the only ones? Whatever sent me to this realm sent others, into other girls, and every one of them died. Demons and girls both, burned to nothing. Teal saved us, because when her whole identity was being burned away, the only instinct she had left was to *love*. So yes, Hand of Avei, I follow her lead when she wants to use compassion. I don't *need* to understand it to know it works. Love is *stronger*. It's not as quick as force, not as immediately satisfying, but it succeeds absolutely in the long run when other methods turn against themselves."

As gradually as she had come, the demon retreated back within. Flames died away and claws withdrew, until only Teal stood there, blinking in the lamplight. She reached up to brush away tears, but still managed a smile at Trissiny. "So yeah . . . I pretty much do believe in the power of compassion. You can think of it as another kind of strategy. All it takes, really, is a little patience."

There was absolute stillness for a moment that seemed to stretch forever. Trissiny clenched her jaw once, opened her mouth as if to speak, then closed it, and glanced to the side.

Teal stepped forward, slowly, raising one hand. "Trissiny . . ."

"I need to pray," the paladin said curtly, then turned on her heel and stalked off in the direction of the campus chapel.

Teal was left staring after, still with the hand reaching out to her. After a moment, she let it fall, and sighed. "Well . . . I tried."

Shaeine stepped up and placed a hand gently against her back, smiling. "Let her cope, for now. This isn't over. It is as you said; it takes a little patience."

CHAPTER 18

The University's chapel was nondenominational. Its stained glass windows depicted all the Pantheon gods, plus Themynra, and for some reason Khar, but these were only artistic works; there were no holy sigils on display, not even the ankh of the Universal Church, and Trissiny sensed no blessing of divine magic laid upon the building itself. This had to be the first place of worship she'd ever seen where the grounds weren't even consecrated.

She had no idea why such a thing would even be done, but it was adding to her growing conviction that this whole campus and its irascible founder were one big exercise in nonsense, and a waste of her divine mandate.

Trissiny strode down the center aisle at a speed that just barely conceded anything to the dignity of a place of worship. There wasn't even a pulpit or altar, just an elevated platform at the end of the room opposite the door. She reached it in a handful of long strides and knelt before the stairs, bowing her head.

Avenism was more inclined toward action than contemplation, but she *did* know meditative exercises. It was not for these that she now reached, instead searching within herself for the glow that was always there. The harmonious brilliance of Avei's divine power, and beyond that . . .

The goddess herself. It was a paladin's privilege to call upon their deity's direct attention, a privilege she had been warned not to invoke frivolously. And so Trissiny did not make that demand, hovering instead in that space of awareness, her mind brushing against the reality of Avei's existence. It would be the goddess's decision whether this warranted an answer.

She did, this time.

Not in a full incarnation, but her presence was a pressure upon reality, a consciousness connected to power which seemed to push against Trissiny's very existence, leaving her keenly aware that she only survived the direct attention of such a being because Avei took great care to protect her. Though no physical body appeared, nor even a glow of divine light in the dim chapel, the goddess's voice resonated powerfully through the air all around, sourceless and omnipresent.

"That was a disappointing display, Trissiny."

The mortification of it was such a crushing weight she could almost have thought Avei had inflicted it on purpose. But no; cruelty was not in Avei's nature. Trissiny only felt like she was being ground into the floor because . . . she felt like she deserved to be.

"I know you chafe under my orders. You are the first in the line of my Hands in eight millennia to be sent to an institution of learning instead of straight into battle. You question the value of this."

"It's not for me to question any of your decisions, Goddess," Trissiny blurted.

"She who cannot bear to be questioned ought not be obeyed. You may ask for explanations, Trissiny, and you should. Orders must be followed, but they can be followed better if understood. Tonight you allowed an enemy to provoke you into lashing out. This time it was by a young fool with nothing on his mind but his own angst and perhaps an unconscious death wish. Had it been a wiser foe, such a tactic could have been used to place you at a lethal disadvantage. If you do not control yourself, child, you will be controlled by your enemies."

Trissiny cringed, physically. It was gently delivered, but the rebuke struck deep, because she could immediately see the truth of it.

"I . . . see how . . . that is right. I am sorry I failed you, Goddess."

"This is why you have been sent to study before being sent to fight, Trissiny. Not because you are weaker or more foolish than your predecessors; do not think that. Even so young, already you outshine some. It is because the world has changed. A paladin in the old style could not succeed in this era. You must learn to think—to think deeply, quickly, and unconventionally. Arachne, flawed creature that she is, can teach you this better than anyone."

"I . . . I am trying to trust," Trissiny whispered, "but I truly don't believe that woman is *sane*."

"Do not absorb too much of her worldview; she is a moral vacuum. Do, however, absorb her wisdom. You have been taught to view the world in black and white; Arachne sees many shades, not only of gray, but of blue and orange. Your challenge is to keep a mind just open enough that your brain does not pour out."

"What . . . what is it I don't know? I've been trained all my *life*. For fifteen years as a novice Sister, for three more as a paladin . . . I don't understand, Goddess. Why *here*? What is it I'm still lacking?"

"Keep an open mind about what you have already learned, not only what you will in the future. My Sisterhood does not know how to train a paladin to contend with this rapidly evolving new world, and so they trained you for the battles of a century past. Consider this, Trissiny. According to the doctrine in which you have been drilled, what you faced tonight was a demonblood driven to mindless anger—an immediate threat to the lives and souls of all in the vicinity, which must be ended, immediately, by whatever means are necessary. According to other doctrines, including the perspective of your fellow paladin at this very school, tonight you faced a confused young man in great inner pain who was no threat to you at all, lashing out in emotional outbursts which could not have harmed anything but your feelings. Had you succeeded in destroying him, Trissiny, that would have been an offense which would carry massive consequences, not least of which would be your own grief and guilt."

She physically could not hang her head any lower from this position, which was frustrating. It really felt like she ought to.

"Between these two options, you chose the wrong one. Yet that is not the failure in which I am most disappointed. Your error was in seeing only that simple choice, instead of the countless shades of truth, the innumerable divergent actions available to you. The world will be more like this now: the dilemmas subtler and more complex, their consequences more far-reaching. You will need to face such trials and navigate them carefully. It is not in you that I am disappointed, Trissiny, not as a person. You are what the Sisterhood made you to be . . . and I need you to be more. Do not forget their teachings, but add to them. Do not let Arachne teach you what to think, but learn from her how to think."

"I don't . . . I am not . . . sure I understand . . . what that means."

"You have only just arrived, child. This is a school; understanding is exactly what you will gain here. Do the work, and give it time. I have faith in you."

Trissiny inhaled deeply, trying to steady herself. "I will not disappoint you again."

So she desperately hoped.

"To that end," said the goddess, *"I suggest you take advantage of a prime source of insight and counsel which has been placed in your path. I do not speak of Arachne, this time, but one of your classmates."*

"You mean . . . Toby?" she asked.

There came a faint pulse, a ripple in the sensation of psychic pressure that was Avei's presence on this plane; it seemed to suggest amusement. *"No doubt Tobias Caine is worth listening to, or he would not have been made a paladin. But no, I do not generally advise you to absorb too much of the perspective of Omnists. No, on the contrary . . ."*

At eight members, this was one of the smallest incoming classes in the University's history; between that and its gender imbalance, the boys' dorm was nearly uninhabited, with Gabe and Toby having occupied adjacent beds down at one end. So Toby currently had ample room to pace, and he made full use of it.

"She tried to *kill* you?"

"It wasn't her fault," Gabriel repeated wearily, now sitting slumped on the edge of his bed, still in nothing but a borrowed robe and his new coat.

"You keep saying that. We keep going back and forth between these two points, and, like . . . You *see* how I'm having trouble reconciling them, right?" Toby came to a halt right in front of him, spreading his arms in worried exasperation. "Come on, Gabe, *talk* to me. What the hell *happened*?"

"It was my fault," Gabe insisted, staring at the floor. "I . . . I dunno, man. I'm just not . . ."

It wasn't in Toby's nature to push, but he could recognize when something had to be pushed. He could believe a stereotypical Avenist with a sword would have tried to murder his half demon friend, but having known Trissiny for a few days, it was hard to imagine the tense, awkward girl doing such a thing. Even in their previous scuffle, after her initial reaction she'd immediately decided Gabriel wasn't a threat and backed down, and Toby had thought that would be the end of it. But if there was any chance of whatever had happened tonight flaring up again . . .

"Okay, how about this," Toby said, seeking calm within himself and putting it into his voice, hoping to share some with Gabriel. "Let's back up. What happened first, like right before that? What led up to it?"

That actually seemed to work, bringing a little more energy back to Gabe.

"Oh, well, I was walking back from the library with Shane . . . uh, Shayeen . . . Um, the dark elf girl. No matter how many times I hear her pronounce it, I can't figure out what vowel that is."

"It's called a triphthong. Tanglish doesn't have any, that I can think of. You should ask Teal about pronunciation; she speaks elvish."

Gabriel nodded, perking up a little further at the continued diversion. "Yeah, okay. Anyway, um, *Shaeine* is actually really nice. I thought she was stuck up at first, but turns out she's just quiet. Funny, though! Really got that deadpan sarcasm down."

He paused, and Toby nodded encouragingly, holding his peace.

"We . . . ran into Teal and Trissiny and . . . and I . . ."

Gabriel trailed off again, his eyes falling back to the floor, and slumped his shoulders once more.

Toby gave him a minute, and when he continued to say nothing, sat down on the bed at Gabriel's side. There, he waited.

"I don't know why I did it," Gabe finally said, raising his head. He looked . . . confused. "I just . . . I *lit into* her. I think . . . Hell, *I* might've tried to kill me if I went off like that at me. Um . . . you know what I mean. I dunno, Toby, I genuinely don't. I've never gone after someone like that."

"No, you haven't," Toby agreed quietly. "Our whole lives you've been almost unreasonably patient with people who are assholes to you. It's really noticeable, because you can't seem to shut your yap about any other subject under the sun."

That brought a weak little half-grin to Gabriel's face. It faded quickly, but it was something, at least.

"Man, though. The things I said to her. It was like . . . like it *all* came boiling up at once. Eighteen years of this shit, and I've never *dared* say anything to anyone. My dad always drilled that into me, that I can't afford to seem like a threat or . . . well, you know what'd happen. But why at *Trissiny*, though? She's gotta be one of the only people alive who's personally a physical threat to me. And she didn't even *do* anything to me! I mean, she burned me, but that wasn't on purpose; I know she was just trying to help. I just . . ."

"Maybe . . . that was it?" Toby suggested. "You just snapped."

"It was so weird," Gabriel whispered. "It was like I was watching somebody else pick a fight with a paladin. I couldn't stop it. Just me riding in the head of some fucking dumbass trying to get himself killed. I don't understand it, man."

He stood up abruptly, and now they had changed places—Toby perched on the edge of the bed, Gabriel pacing up and down the floor.

"And now," he said, his voice rising in pitch, "I have to worry about when the *next* time I fly off the handle will be! Is . . . is this a demon thing? Hethelaxi are known for berserking, but I've *never* had something like this . . ."

"Lots of things can trigger a dissociative episode," Toby said, still using his voice to project calm. His friend clearly needed some right now. "Like, a truly unhelpful number of possible things. And I only know that much from my basic meditation studies; I'm far from the kind of expert who'd have answers like that. But I *do* know that simple stress is one of them . . . And also that if you don't have an established history of it, this is probably a one time thing. Everything's up in the air right now, Gabe. Just getting properly settled in here will help a lot, I bet."

"Well, even if that's true, now the Hand of Avei thinks I'm an unstable maniac full of demon blood, so . . . *that's* a ticking clock on me, all right."

"Granted, I wasn't there to hear *exactly* what you did to her," Toby said with a smile, "but Avenist or not, I don't think Trissiny's all *that* unreasonable. We're all strangers to each other still, but one of the things we *do* know about her is that she can look beyond her own prejudices. Remember? When she found out your secret, she panicked, and then immediately calmed down and wasn't going to do anything. I bet nothing at all would've happened back then if Zaruda hadn't . . . uh, helped."

"You always do like to see the best in people." Gabriel sighed.

"I see the *good* in people," Toby corrected. "Make your apologies and give it a chance, Gabe. I bet she will, too, once everything's calmed down. And don't catastrophize, man—you said yourself that Teal and Shaeine were both trying to intervene. *They* didn't think you deserved to die. Obviously Tellwyrn didn't, and she kinda gets the last word around here. In the worst case, she'll plant her big magic foot on things until they do calm down, one way or another."

He stood up, more slowly, and Gabe halted his pacing.

"It will be okay," Toby insisted, still smiling. "Look, it's late. I can see you're too keyed up to crash. Want something to eat? The cafeteria's closed but there's gotta be someplace around here we can scavenge a snack."

"Ugh. I think I'm too tense to digest anything right now," Gabriel said, grimacing.

"Want a hug?"

"Oh, come on, Toby, you know better than that." Turning his head to scowl at the windows, Gabriel held his arms out wide. "You can't just go around *hugging* your guy friends, man. I've got my manly pride to consider." Arms still spread, he made a beckoning gesture with the fingers of both hands. "What do you think I am, some kind of human being with feelings or something? Sometimes I can really tell you were raised in a monastery."

"Yeah, those monks really messed me up," Toby agreed, grinning and embracing him. "I dunno what your excuse is."

Gabriel hugged him right back. "I dunno, the demon thing excuses a lot. Well . . . right up until it doesn't."

"I believe in you, Gabe. I'll say this for you—you don't usually make the same mistake twice."

"Right, so, don't verbally assault a sword-happy paladin for the second time. That's an important tip. I'll get right to work on that."

"Please do."

CHAPTER 19

Darling couldn't help noticing that he had never noticed this place before.

Positioned in the Steppes, an upscale mercantile district, which had been formed into a series of terraces rather than flowing with the gradual slope of the ground as most of Tiraas did, it was a little over a quarter of the way downhill from Imperial Square in the opposite direction from his own home. He had been here many times, both as Sweet and on the more aboveboard business of the Church, and knew it well, yet the Elysium was an unknown sight to him. From the outside, it could have been any upscale tea room or winery, with an understated sign bearing its name and nothing else to distinguish its modest facade. This was *exactly* the sort of place that should have caught his interest many times before.

Of course, there were enchantments that could conceal a place from those who were not invited, or who were not looking for it specifically, or based upon any number of other variables. They were complex and expensive spells, though, which raised questions about what was hidden behind them and who would bother to place them there. Luckily he knew who he was here to meet, which answered several such questions, but he could not shake the feeling that he wasn't being told everything.

He paid close attention to this feeling. It had saved his life repeatedly.

Thus, he loitered for over a minute on the sidewalk, studying the plain stone construction, the tastefully gilded sign—and wondering what "Elysium" meant, aside from sounding vaguely elvish—the wrought iron bars on its curtained windows and bordering the stone staircase descending to its subterranean entrance, above which only a single fairy lamp contended against the after-midnight gloom.

With a sigh, he finally descended the stairs. At the bottom was a clean little nook containing an elegant stone bench and the entrance. The Elysium's door was of redwood, polished to near luminosity, offset by clouded glass panels and a brass handle. Darling rolled his neck, straightened his shoulders, double-checked his aloof smile (in place and operating normally), then pulled the door open and strode in as though he owned the place.

It *was* a pub, an almost offensively fancy one. A more expensively appointed space he had rarely seen outside of the mansions of the rich; everything was dark-stained wood, with accents of marble and gilt, with silken tablecloths and draperies, surmounted by a chandelier of actual crystal, which glowed without benefit of candles. The room was tall, easily a story and a half, with tables scattered widely enough that those sitting at them would have relative privacy. A bench lined the wall adjacent to the street above, a long bar lined the other immediately to his right, and at the rear of the room a short flight of steps rose to an elevated nook containing a lavishly appointed booth, at which his "date" for the evening waited.

Darling didn't immediately fix his eyes upon her, however, first taking stock of the room's other inhabitants. The Elysium was sparsely inhabited at the moment. Closest to the door was a woman in an Imperial Army uniform, sitting at the bar; she glanced up at him when he entered, then returned to nursing her drink, clearly dismissing him as unimportant. She was also, he noted, quite pretty—tall and strongly built, with black hair drawn back in a severe ponytail which cascaded down her back in an avalanche of curls. Women could and did serve in the Imperial Army—the empire's goddess of war being also the protector of women, there was no discrimination by sex among the armed forces. Most women who wanted to be soldiers joined the Silver Legions, though. Still, this wasn't the first female imperial soldier he'd ever seen. The legions didn't take everyone who applied, and besides, there were always the patriotic, the irreligious, and various other outliers.

Like the soldier, the bar's other denizens gave him barely a glance before returning to their own business. In the corner opposite the door, a burly blond man dressed as a laborer and a slim man in the black coat of a Church priest were hunched over a game of chess; they ignored him entirely. A young couple was canoodling in another corner. He made a point not to stare. The mix of people in here made little sense to Darling—judging by the rich trappings and extravagant magical security, not to mention the company *he* was to keep this evening, he'd have expected lords and ladies, high priests, possibly even the better class of criminals. Soldiers, preachers, farmers . . . The list of incongruities continued to grow.

He nodded respectfully toward the alcove at the back and moved forward to approach it.

"Evening, Antonio! Punaji Sunrise, right?"

Darling blinked in surprise, turning to look at the bartender, who had been hidden behind the soldier from his position at the door. This was a face he knew *very* well—lean, swarthy, with shaggy black hair and perpetual mirth lurking about the eyes. On the bar before him was a drink, a layered confection of different liqueurs and syrups that cost far too much and took far too long to make, which was exactly why Darling habitually ordered it. The man pushed it gently toward him.

For a moment, his mind went blank at the sheer enormity of the implications. Then, the pieces snapped into place, and he cast another swift glance about the room. The soldier, the farmer, the dark man . . . of course. No *wonder* he'd never seen this place before. None of them looked up to acknowledge him, but the woman took a contemplative sip of her whiskey on the rocks as his eyes slid across her. Realization did nothing to lessen his unease—if anything, it did the opposite.

Then he was back in character, the interlude having taken a sliver of a second that few humans could have noticed, and the bar's occupants surely had. "You remembered!" he said cheerfully, stepping over to collect his drink. "Should I be flattered, or concerned at the prescription?"

"Prescription, bah." The bartender waved him away, grinning. "Worst you'll get from that thing is a sugar rush. Best go on, your date's waiting."

"Aren't they always," he said vaguely, tilting his drink toward him in toast, then turning to resume his course.

He ascended the steps carefully to the alcove. Quentin Vex sat above, at one side of the table, but Darling ignored him for the moment; it would not have done at all to greet him first. Instead, he bowed deeply to the person who had asked him here.

"Your Majesty."

Empress Eleanora Sultana Tirasian was, needless to say, a strikingly beautiful woman. She was also a crafty and formidable individual who was known to have little regard for looks—her own, at least. The reality was, however, that one did not marry onto the imperial throne without being something of a showpiece. She certainly was that—tight curls of sable hair, deep mahogany skin, black eyes that glinted like daggers. She was tall and fell right into the combination of "slender yet curvy" that occurred so often in cheap novels and so rarely in biology. Indeed, she might have suited the so-called Avenic ideal perfectly, except that she lacked the strong build of a woman who worked and/or fought for a living. Eleanora was a noblewoman and born politician; she had never run two steps in her life, nor lifted anything heavier than a wine bottle.

"Bishop," she replied coolly, not inclining her head in return. There was probably no one in the world to whom she would bow. "Please, join us."

"My thanks, Your Majesty," he said, then set his drink on the table. Taking one of the gilded chairs by its back, he slid it around and seated himself at the side of the table, opposite Lord Vex, rather than directly before her as indicated. She raised an eyebrow, and even the normally somnolent Vex straightened slightly at this flagrant breach of protocol, but the hell he was putting his back to that room full of . . . *them*.

Eleanora flicked her eyes once to the main floor of the bar, then smiled very faintly. Darling took this for a sign of understanding; she was far too savvy to accidentally betray her thoughts with careless gestures.

"How may I be of service, Your Majesty?" he asked once seated.

For a moment she just looked at him. There was a stillness about her, a piercing intelligence in her gaze, that threatened to ruffle his equilibrium. As both Sweet and the bishop he was accustomed to the presence of dangerous people and rarely met anyone who penetrated his calm. Something about her, though . . . Eleanora had certainly *not* become empress because of her looks.

"I am in need of a priest," she said finally.

"I am flattered," he replied, "and somewhat perplexed, I confess. Surely you could have your pick of the services of any priest in the empire?"

"I have," she said dryly, "and it is to my great fortune that my pick of priests *is* available to me, as I think you know that many are not." This was skating close to the dangerous topic of the rivalry between Church and throne, a subject he was eager to avoid in this of all company, but she went smoothly on. "The gods are fond of reminding us that no degree of mortal power entitles any human being to a greater stake of their attention, but the reality is as you see it here. For the leaders of the empire, certain little courtesies *are* extended, to our great gratitude. One such is access to this . . . sanctuary. When it is deemed needful."

Again, she glanced past him to the bar area, and he did likewise. The barman winked.

"Here," the empress continued, "we are effectively outside the world and its concerns. Its bloody never-ending *politics*. Here I can forget for a moment about being empress, and you can relax the tension that leading the multiplicitous existence you do must cause. Neither of us need pretend that we don't all know *exactly* the nature of my relationship with the man I call husband." She leaned forward slightly, holding his gaze. "I can approach you as a woman with a spiritual problem, seeking help from a cleric who happens to be the leading expert in this topic."

"All right, then," he said slowly. "Is there . . . something you would like me to steal?"

The corners of her eyes crinkled very slightly in amusement, but she quickly mastered her expression and spoke a single name. "*Elilial.*"

"Ah," he said ruefully. "I'm afraid I was never one for kidnapping, but I'll see what I can do."

Vex cleared his throat. "I believe I warned Your Majesty that the bishop fancies himself . . . amusing."

"He *is*," the empress said, not taking her eyes off Darling, "but I would prefer that we be serious now."

"My sincere apologies, Your Majesty." Darling bowed to her from his seat.

"She was in my *home*," she said, and from beneath her iron self-control there whispered hints of ferocity, barely contained. "She shared a bed with the man I think of as a brother. We talked, shared meals, even games." The empress clenched her jaw momentarily. "I once let her rub my shoulders. She was *remarkably* good at that."

Darling put on and held his very best sympathetically attentive face. In truth, this was a situation he had little idea how to handle. He was unaccustomed to that feeling; handling people was his specialty.

"Among the theologians who have studied Elilial extensively," Eleanora went on, "most are so heavily wedded to Church dogma that every other word from them is a sermon in miniature. But Lord Vex tells me that you are something of an expert on her movements as well. More importantly, he suggests that you see her as an individual, not an . . . incarnation."

"You know what invaded your home," he said softly. "You want to understand *who*."

"Precisely."

Something tingled at the back of Darling's neck, a sensation with which he was well acquainted—risk, and opportunity. "What, specifically, would Your Majesty like to know?"

"First of all . . . how did you come to devote such time and study to Elilial?" Apparently, she wasn't one to come right to the point, but then, few politicians were. "It seems a peculiar hobby for an acolyte of the god of thieves."

"On the contrary," he said smoothly, simply running with it, "the cults of Elilial and Eserion have many similarities. Sometimes I am tempted to conclude that ours are the only faiths which inherently value *subtlety.*"

Below, one of the chess players—the thin man in the dark coat—cleared his throat. Darling carefully did not betray himself by glancing at him.

"As for why . . . I have often thought that the Church's approach to warning people against Elilial's schemes has done more harm than good. So much effort put into portraying her as the destroyer, the deceiver, playing up her relationship to the demonic plane without ever mentioning how *that* is happenstance caused by the Pantheon and not her own choice. It warns the faithful and the casual away from seeking her out, yes—well, most of them—but leaves people frighteningly vulnerable to her when she *does* choose to move among us."

"How so?"

"She's a thief," he said, warming to his subject. "A con artist, a trickster. All theatrics and misdirection, someone who plays as many parts as the job requires. You could say that from a certain perspective, I empathize with her. More to the point, I understand the broad strokes of how she operates, and why telling people that she's some kind of slavering monster is the worst possible thing we can do. The Black Wreath is older than the empire by a wide margin, older than the Church, and while it's damnably difficult to track their movements, we know they've never suffered from a lack of membership. That's because Elilial, when she wants to be, is just so bloody *nice.*"

"Nice," Eleanora said flatly.

"I think, Your Majesty, that you are in a position to know that better than most, if you'll pardon my saying so."

She held his gaze silently for a moment, then glanced to one side in thought, and nodded slowly.

"And so we shoot ourselves in the foot," he said. "People meet this fearsome Queen of Demons, and find her warm, charming, rather funny, in fact. It throws everything the Church has taught them about her into question. That, by association, throws *all* the Church's teachings into question. Thus, she gets one fingernail into their minds and knows exactly how to work that until she has a loyal convert, willing to die for her."

The empress narrowed her eyes slightly. "Funny?"

"People are always so surprised when I say that," he said wryly. "Yes, she has quite the sense of humor. Was that not apparent when you met her?"

"I didn't merely 'meet' her. I knew her well for several months, or so I thought." She pressed her lips into a thin line. "And yes . . . she did, in fact, have a sardonic wit that Sharidan and I both enjoyed. In hindsight, I've been second-guessing everything I remember about her in light of what I now know."

"Don't do that," he advised. "It's a trap. You are, by reputation, both perceptive and clever when it comes to people. Elilial is *certainly* sly enough to use that against you, but that doesn't mean everything she said or did was a deception. Encouraging you to think it was gives her a kind of invisibility. If nobody *believes* what they know about her, they don't really know anything, do they?"

She kept her gaze to the side, frowning slightly in contemplation. Vex sipped at his own wineglass, staying silent. Darling sat, not reaching for his Punaji Sunrise, allowing the empress to think.

"How certain are you of the things you know? Why is it you believe you know better than most of the Church's theologians?"

"Simple scholarship, Your Majesty," he said modestly, refusing to back down from her intent stare once she returned it to him. "There are over eight *thousand* years' worth of materials about Elilial's movements to sift through, much of it muddled by simple time or tainted by the agendas of millennia of history. Not to mention that some incarnations of the Black Wreath have been quite adept at spreading misinformation. I simply hired a bunch of university and seminary students to sort through the information and single out the bits that met a good historian's standards of believability. Thirty of them, for over two years . . . There really was a *lot* of material. In the end, only the tiniest amount could be considered reliable. That tiny amount was merely the work of another couple of years for me to study through, and the picture it painted of our girl was remarkably consistent."

"Our girl?" Eleanora raised an eyebrow.

"Forgive me," he said contritely. "If one spends enough time studying somebody's life, one tends to feel oddly . . . proprietary. No matter how horrifying the subject matter may be."

"Hm." Whatever she thought of that, her face gave nothing away. "She had ample opportunity to harm Sharidan, myself, and many of those closest to us. As far as we can tell, she did not."

"That is consistent," he said, nodding. "Historically speaking, she only harms particular people, for specific reasons. If anything, I'd say she's more careful about collateral damage than some deities of the Pantheon."

"Really. Regard for others?"

He leaned back in his chair slightly, frowning in thought. "No . . . and yes, but no. It's wasteful, inelegant. A *good* con artist uses only the lightest touch and leaves as little trace as possible. A good knee-capper relies on the threat of force rather than the use of force; you have to beat a few people down now and again to establish that you can and will, but nobody could do business if everybody were constantly attacking each other. It becomes . . . a code of honor, so to speak, a set of best practices that all *good* scoundrels follow, irrespective of any affiliations or moral leanings they may have. In time, that can be internalized to the point that causing unnecessary pain is troubling to the spirit, like a twinge of conscience. Not true compassion, but . . ." He groped silently for the word. "An ethic of restraint."

"Again, you speak of her as you would a member of your Guild."

"I think she'd do very well in the Guild. This business of infiltrating an organization in human guise . . . The recent events in the palace are not the first time she's done this. I'd be totally unsurprised to learn she has *been* a member of the Thieves' Guild at one point."

Below, the bartender laughed aloud, but did not look up from wiping the glass he was working on, and ignored the irritated look the soldier shot him.

"To move this back to my original concern . . . how likely do you think it that she left some trap behind, some delayed way of harming my family?"

"Not very likely at all. At least, that would be wildly out of character." He drew in a breath slowly, looking down at the table. "Your Majesty, I'm not certain how to phrase this with any delicacy . . ."

"Then don't concern yourself with delicacy," she said firmly. "I'll neither swoon nor demand your execution if you ruffle my feathers."

"Very well," he said gravely, keeping amusement hidden only through a truly heroic effort. "Everything in the histories suggests that Elilial's attachments are quite real, at least to her. She's been known to discreetly watch over people with whom she has formed relationships through deception, giving assistance when they need it years after their part in her schemes is over, sometimes avenging them when necessary."

Eleanora narrowed her eyes. "You suggest she is truly a caring person, deep down."

"I am not sure I'd go that far," he hedged. "No . . . My perception has always been that she's a *lonely* person. Her only real peers are the gods she turned against, and who cast her into Hell for it. She's down there with nothing but demons for company most of the time. All things considered, I have a hard time seeing her as particularly softhearted, but able to form real attachments? Maybe even desperate to do so? That I have no trouble believing."

"Then . . . with regard to my family . . ."

"I am not sure how much of the story I know," he admitted, "but from the basics that I do . . . If there were any hostility, any animosity there, you'd know already. If she behaved toward you and yours with affection, that affection is likely to be sincere. Oh, she'll use you in her schemes like she does everyone else, and I know I needn't tell you how these schemes in particular could well kick the very empire right out from under us all. But on a personal level? No, I don't believe your family has anything to *fear* from Elilial. If anything . . . should you ever find yourself in truly desperate straits, you might find yourself with a very unexpected protector."

There was silence. In the stillness of the chamber, the very soft voices of the two in the other corner were almost intrusive; the echo of a chess piece being set down seemed to reverberate.

"That should be encouraging," Eleanora said at last, "but if anything, I find myself even more disturbed."

"I know what you mean," Darling said with perfect sincerity. "This is why I am always careful to study Elilial and her people from a safe distance. Reading old stories, rather than interviewing those of the Wreath we've managed to capture. It's terrifying, how easily she can suck you in."

"We still have no imperial heir, nor any sign of one forthcoming," she said abruptly. "The court physicians are positive that the problem is not with Sharidan. But then, they say that about each of the women in his harem, as well, and it defies reason that *someone* hasn't ended up with child by now. He's quite energetic. You will repeat that to no one."

"Repeat what? Your pardon, Your Majesty, I'm a trifle deaf on this side."

"Good. Elilial has twice hinted broadly that *she* is now carrying his child. Once to his face, once to three hapless soldiers who, luckily for them, had no idea what she was talking about. Is there any chance she is lying?"

"Of course. *Lying* is the better part of what she does. I'm the most likely person—except the Wreath themselves—to give credit to Elilial's better traits, but even I won't try to present her as anything less than an inveterate deceiver. Before the fall, she was simply the goddess of cunning. The other gods didn't turn their backs on her *then*, and that's when they considered her an ally."

"But on the other hand . . ."

"On the other hand, yes, she has birthed seven demigods that we know of. *One* of whom is currently attending classes in Last Rock, after the rest perished in . . . an event of unknown cause. All my knowledge is historical, Your Majesty; there's almost no guessing how an experience like that would change a mother's personality. Not for the better, I should think."

The empress's mouth twisted in dislike, but she simply went on in the same calm tone: "Could she have been responsible for the childlessness of the other women in the palace?"

"It does seem consistent with her apparent scheme, but . . . I'm sorry, Your Majesty, I'm glad to share my insights into what Elilial is *likely* to do, based on what she's done in the past, but as to what she *can* do . . . nobody can really help you. The one thing we *know* she is very good at is concealing her movements, a trait which extends to members of the Wreath. Just as priests of Omnu have that calming aura, and Izarite clerics get the uncanny ability to discern someone's emotional needs, invested followers of Elilial gain the gift of hiding their movements. Even from the gods."

There were no fewer than three small sounds of activity from the floor below. He reflexively froze for a moment.

"Which, obviously, makes any other powers they possess . . . particularly unknowable."

"Just so, Your Majesty."

"You have been very helpful, Bishop Darling," the empress said, leaning back in her seat. "Not that my mind is put at ease, but I feel I can worry constructively rather than generally now."

"I do what I can," he said modestly.

"Well, that is another question," she said in a mild tone that instantly made his hackles rise. "Rather like Elilial, it is a curious conundrum . . . what you *can* do, and what you are likely to do."

"I beg your pardon?" he said politely. His mind was racing at the shift of mood. Vex, still silent, was watching him fixedly through half-lidded eyes. Eleanora's attention was less subtle, and there was a hint of a satisfied smile hovering about her mouth that he didn't like at all.

"Tell me, are you acquainted with Bishop Syrinx?"

"We have spoken in passing," he said, tilting his head to the side in a gesture of innocent curiosity. "I can't say I know her well."

"She is possibly the *worst* Avenist I've ever met," Eleanora went on conversationally, not even flinching when the soldier set her whiskey glass down hard on the bar. "Vindictive, underhanded, and altogether a better politician than a priest. But if I do say so, she makes an excellent bishop."

"I begin to wonder if I should feel offended."

"There is an interesting layer to the power struggle in this city, you see. Not just between the throne and the Church, but between the Church and the disparate faiths it is supposed to collect under its aegis. So many of their doctrines contradict one another outright that the Archpopes have always been forced to dance a *very* delicate line, keeping a unified doctrinal front."

Darling nodded pleasantly, refusing to glance at the door. He knew this, she knew he knew it; *everyone* who was a player in this game, or even just a somewhat educated cleric, knew it. She was giving a monologue, like a villain in a novel. This was not a good sign; Eleanora Tirasian was clever enough and ruthless enough to make an *excellent* villain. Vex, even less encouragingly, had begun to smile. Both of them had a theatrical streak.

"This results in things like the bishops," the empress went on, still in that conversational tone. "By and large, they are a consistent bunch. Crafty, better at rising through the ranks of religious hierarchies than at practicing any actual faith. I imagine their respective high priests were just as glad to get rid of them, and they make *excellent* pawns for Justinian. And then there is you."

"I'll have you know I fit in splendidly with my colleagues," he said mildly. "I get along with everyone."

"I know you do, Sweet. You are everybody's friend." Her eyes bored into him; he refused to react to the use of his tag. "This city is just lousy with people who owe you favors, or simply like you enough to *do* you favors, which has been the secret of your success. And that is what makes you stand out among your fellow bishops. You are actually a really *good* priest of Eserion."

"You're going to make me blush!"

"It may just be that Eserion's cult is an inherently unusual one," she went on, ignoring him, "where most of the gods direct their followers to some beneficial end, or what they believe to be one; disciples of the god of thieves are sent to go out and *steal* things. So I have to wonder . . . Why would the Guild send their once high priest to the Church?" She folded her hands primly on the table and smiled pleasantly at him. "What, exactly, are you supposed to steal?"

Darling made a show of glancing back and forth, then leaned in close. "Can you keep a secret?"

Still smiling, she raised an eyebrow.

He grinned. "*Everything.* Every damn thing, down to Justinian's fuzzy slippers. It'll be the heist of the millennium."

"I believe I asked you to be serious."

"So you did, and so I was. And *then* you attempted to maneuver an avowed thief into a corner. I'm curious, Your Majesty, what response you expected that to get."

"There is a question here, Darling, about loyalty. I am intrigued by you on a number of levels, but it is hardly possible for me to take any action with regard to you before I know with whom you stand. Is it the empire? The Church? Your god, or the gods in general?"

"This I know about gods," he said, picking up his untouched drink. The layers had begun to blend into each other after long minutes sitting idle. "I am fully aware of and grateful for their gifts to us. But gods, like people, are individuals, with their own personalities and agendas. They *are* people, however fundamentally different. And like any other group of people, they can be a right bunch of bastards."

Her eyebrows climbed at that, and a deathly silence fell over the room. Darling raised his glass to her in toast and focused his attention, reaching for that inner glow deep inside himself.

They were not encouraged to draw on it; thieves had little use for it. But Eserion, for good or ill, was a god of the Pantheon, and he and his followers were therefore entitled to certain benefits—including the healing light. Channeled through his hand, it caught the liquid in the glass, blazing from each of the slightly muddied layers of the drink and causing it to glow like a stained glass fairy lamp.

"Those who have my loyalty know it. Those who *would* have my loyalty can earn it, in the usual ways. To them, and to you, Your Majesty . . . good health." He smiled at her, sipped his drink, and turned to look once out at the bar. It was a look he'd had ample occasion to practice on Guild business—not quite a challenging look, but more than simple acknowledgment. It was a look that said "Yeah, I see you, what of it?"

The gods were looking back at him, and most were smiling. The exception was Avei, who had swiveled around on her barstool to give him a look of weary disdain. Eserion, behind the bar, laughed aloud as he added a splash of whiskey to her glass. In the corner, Izara's eyes twinkled merrily, brightly enough to be visible from across the room; beside her, Vesk, the god of bards, lifted his hands and patted them together lightly in a silent ovation. Both the chess players were staring at him now, Omnu with a gentle smile, Vidius wearing a grin of wry humor.

The empress, when he turned back to her, looked decidedly less amused. "And I am left to wonder, still, at the *exact* nature of your apparently considerable interest in, and sympathy for, a certain goddess of cunning."

"Oh," he said softly, "so *that's* it, then."

"I have the Black Wreath running rampant in my empire and in my city," she went on, "more so than we had previously imagined. Aside from recent shenanigans in the palace itself, an entire cell of them recently popped up in a little flyspeck town, with a suicide summoner and dwarven technology that we've never seen before.

Unfortunately, Arachne *bloody* Tellwyrn demolished them before any useful questions could be asked, but the fact remains, they're growing bolder, and stronger; at the same time their mistress is up to something *well* beyond her usual antics. This, obviously, is not acceptable."

"Obviously," he said dryly. "But if you'll pardon my narcissism, what does it have to do with *me*?"

"Imperial Intelligence are the best in the world at what they do," she said, absently patting Vex's wrist, as one might acknowledge a favored pet, "but they face certain stark limits against the Wreath. To say nothing of the inherent challenges of chasing after diabolists, we have no effective counter to Elilial's gift of stealth. The Church doesn't either, and while they are better equipped to contend with demons, they lack any personnel with the skill Lord Vex's people have in this kind of skullduggery. Besides, I obviously cannot trust Justinian or any of his lackeys."

"What, you don't think I'm his lackey?"

"I don't know *whose* lackey you are, if anyone's," she said evenly. "And that is where you may be exactly what we need. You said yourself that the Thieves' Guild is very like the Black Wreath in its operations and general outlook."

"The Guild is not going to start a war with the Wreath."

"For innumerable reasons, obviously, no. But a man whose loyalties are stretched multiple ways to begin with provides deniability to all his putative masters."

"Ahh," he nodded, smiling, "now I see. If *I* were to go chasing after the Wreath, they wouldn't know against whom to retaliate. Very clever. Quite elegant, really."

"I'm glad you think so."

"Of course, I'm absolutely not going to do it, but I do appreciate the merits of the idea."

"I think you mistake my intentions," she said with a smile. "You spent what had to have been most of your earnings in your first years as bishop, not to mention the years in question on a colossal research project just to build up a working understanding of Elilial's psychology. Strange behavior, for a thief."

"What, a man can't have hobbies?"

"No. People like you . . . and like me . . . do not have hobbies, we have *obsessions*. One singular obsession for each of us, really, which fills our lives and colors every activity we undertake. You are an information man, Sweet, a connection man. You wanted to know the Dark Lady's ways for a reason." Her smile widened a fraction of an inch. "You're hunting her."

"Or perhaps," he offered, swirling his glass idly, "I'm looking to join her. She *does* run a most admirable outfit. Perhaps I already have."

"And what would you do if you had? Wage war on the gods? Overthrow the empire? No, Darling, she has nothing you want. You want the *chase*. We are talking about the single most challenging prey that has ever existed. I think if you ever manage to *catch* her, you'll find yourself at a loss."

"You presume to know me well, Your Majesty."

"Indeed so. And perhaps I am wrong." Still she kept that smile, but her eyes burned with intensity. "I am not threatening you, nor will I ever. I'm not asking you to do anything. I am extending an offer."

He raised an eyebrow.

"How is it the organized criminals always put it in the novels?" she mused. "You've done me a favor today. Perhaps someday I'll be in a position to do you a favor. Especially if it leads to progress in uprooting the Black Wreath from my city."

Darling matched her smile. "Your Majesty has a fertile and eloquent imagination."

"Thank you," she said sweetly. "But my offer stands: whatever aid I may lend you, should you need it in hunting the Wreath." With that, she stood. Vex and Darling did likewise, as protocol demanded. On their feet, she was shorter than he, though not by much. Whereas most women of her breeding and upbringing would never miss a chance to look up at a man through their lashes, Eleanora tilted her head to gaze at him directly. "And, of course, should you decide that your loyalty lies against the empire . . . I will not bother to threaten you then, either. You are a most valued subject, Antonio Darling."

"There are not words in our inadequate mortal language for my appreciation of your acknowledgment, Your Majesty," he replied, bowing deeply.

"Thank you for your time, Bishop."

He took the dismissal for what it was, backed up a step, and descended the stairs.

The gods were all watching him.

He nodded to Eserion, and then tipped Avei a wink. For just a second he thought something very bad was about to happen to him, but Izara let out a peal of delighted laughter from across the room, and the goddess of war wordlessly turned her back on him.

He didn't breathe again until he was back outside, and not deeply until he had climbed the stone steps and stood safely on the streets of Tiraas. Already, the tense atmosphere within the Elysium was starting to fade like a dream.

Darling wondered, as he started walking, whether he would still be able to see the sign if he turned around. He didn't check. His mind was already furiously at work, teasing apart the details of that conversation.

None of this made sense. The empress had as much as accused him of having divided loyalties, offered her support, and then dismissed him. Those actions were contradictory. Why? One didn't just baldly come out with such details right in front of the person one suspected of double-dealing, especially if one intended to secure that person's aid. Traitorous people could be incredibly useful, but only if you knew they were traitorous and *they* didn't know you knew. This disarming honesty . . . This was no way to play the game.

Unless . . .

Darling frowned as he walked, letting his feet carry him home by muscle memory.

. . . Unless the game was not going in your favor, in which case the best move available was sometimes to introduce a little chaos. Forcibly change the board, realign the players, knock a few pieces out of place. It might improve your position, or might not. It was a gambit for when no sensible actions could lead to victory.

The Wreath, the gods, Elilial, Tellwyrn, the Church, the cults *within* the Church . . . all swirled around and within the empire, nipping at it from all directions. And, he now realized, the empire, or at least its empress, believed it was losing.

Interesting.

CHAPTER 20

So, what do you think of my odds?" Gabriel asked.

"Well," Juniper said slowly, "it seems like either Professor Tellwyrn is crazy, or maybe just wrong, *or* you just couldn't find what she sent you there to find. So, y'know, the way she likes to play mind games with people, I'm guessing the second one."

Gabriel sighed heavily. "Damn it . . . that's what I thought." He shrugged, scowling, and folded the paper on which he'd scrawled his notes and citations and stuffed it in the pocket of his new coat. "But I went over it and *over* it, and even asked that asshat librarian for help. imperial law is absolutely dead clear: anybody with human blood is legally human under the law. If I don't commit a crime, nobody's allowed to hurt me. The only way she can legally *execute me on the spot*," he said, the last few words in a sneering imitation of Tellwyrn's voice, "is in self-defense. I don't *get* it. She's setting me up for something; that has to be it."

"Maybe," the dryad mused, "that *is* the trick. There's no legal reason for you not to act like anybody else. Like, a hidden moral lesson?"

"Hm. So we're in agreement that there's a hidden trick of some kind?"

"Well, ch'yeah. I've got class with her, too, y'know."

He grinned at that. "I like your way. But . . . damn it, this is *Tellwyrn*. What's more likely, a hidden moral lesson or a hidden trap?"

". . . I see your point."

The fine weather had continued to hold; indeed, it seemed the dry country of the prairie wasn't prone to much besides clear skies and warm sun. It was enjoyable, certainly, but Gabriel was starting to feel twinges of homesickness for the interminable rain of Tiraas. Still, the company made up for a lot. He and Juniper were ambling slowly through the campus, not really going anywhere in particular. After the day's classes and a further two hours on his part squirreled away in the library poring over legal texts, he badly needed to stretch his legs and enjoy the fresh air. The company of a gorgeous girl in a short, sheer sundress just made everything seem brighter and more beautiful.

"Well, the hell with it," he said, stretching his arms over his head. Amazingly, he wasn't even hot, despite the hearty sunshine; the coat's weatherproofing enchantment clearly applied to more than wind and rain. "It's a sunny day, I'm strolling with a pretty girl, it's hours yet till I have kitchen duty with our resident stabadin . . . and did I mention strolling with a pretty girl? Because that makes up for a lot."

Juniper smiled up at him, a mischievous expression that was more than half smirk on her face, but it faded just as suddenly as it had come, leaving something like puzzlement hovering around her large brown eyes. "Gabriel . . . I'm having a little trouble wrapping my head around all the customs here, and I don't want to offend, so . . . um, you'll let me know if I say something wrong, right? And not hold it against me?"

"Sure, June, what's on your mind?"

She bit her lower lip for a moment. "Well, I'm just trying to figure out what to do here. Cause you obviously want to have sex with me, but you haven't *asked*. Did I do something wrong?"

He choked and very nearly did a spit-take, which was all the more impressive because there'd been nothing in his mouth.

"And I think that'd be really fun," Juniper went on earnestly, causing him to trip while standing still, "but I didn't want to ask you, either, because there are rules about men and women that I just can't figure out, and nobody will *explain* them to me. Shaeine told me to ask the humans, but when I do, Trissiny starts ranting about feminism, and Ruda just tells dirty jokes. I haven't tried Teal yet, but she's not even into men, so I'm not sure what she even knows. See my problem? I sort of get that female humans aren't expected to be *forward*, and okay, honestly, it seems pretty silly to me, but I want to respect the culture, y'know? Does that make sense?"

"I think I need to sit down," he said weakly, glancing around. The nearest bench was thirty feet down the path.

"And now I've upset you," she said, chewing her lip in earnest. "Darn it, this is exactly what I was afraid of. Cause even aside from issues about what's expected of women, there are issues of what's expected of men, and *that* I think I understand a little better. You're supposed to make the overtures, right? It's the whole hunter-warrior thing, it's very primal, and I *respect* that. I really didn't want to make you feel . . . Aw, I'm doing this all wrong."

"Okay, whoa, hold up," he said, taking her by the shoulders. She was starting to look genuinely upset. "Yes, there are rules, and yes, they're pretty much as silly and arbitrary as you think, but I swear to you, Juniper, no guy will complain about you making the first move. Hell, guys *dream* of being approached by a woman like you."

"You're not mad?" She gazed up at him with limpid eyes.

"Mad?" He swallowed. "No . . . I am not . . . uh, that."

"Oh, thank Naiya," she gushed, beaming. "I didn't want to cheat you out of anything. I mean, I really don't object to being your first, at all. In fact it'd be an honor."

"Whoa, wait, what?" Gabriel backed up, holding up his hands and frowning. "What do you mean, my first?"

"Yeah, I actually would really like to try that," she said brightly. "I've never mated with a virgin before. I bet it's interes—"

"Now you can stop right there," he said firmly. "I'll have you know I'm a witty and stylish half demon from the world's most cosmopolitan city. Girls go *crazy* over me. You really think I've never had any opportunities before now?"

"Um," she said, nonplussed, "okay . . ."

"Besides, we went over this in Yornhaldt's class, remember, when Ruda asked about witchcraft? Virginity, as a magically significant state, is an old wives' tale. It's nonsense; it doesn't make any difference at all."

"Well . . . uh, technically, that's not really . . ."

"Look, I'm just saying, if you're worried about offending people, maybe don't throw around accusations about a guy's manhood like that!"

"Okay!" Juniper raised her hands in surrender. "You're not a virgin. There's no such thing as virginity. But just for, you know, *reference*, dryads have senses specifically for . . . well, magically significant states. What's magically significant to me, I mean. So, uh, lying to me about anything sexual is pretty much a waste of time."

He stared at her for a long, tense moment, then suddenly sagged where he stood, dropping her gaze. "That's not fair. He *said* it wasn't really a thing . . ."

"Well, in Professor Yornhaldt's class we're still doing the unit on arcane magic," she said helpfully, "which is a whole different type of deal. Fae magic is . . . honestly, I'm not sure I'd even call it magic. It's just what we do."

"Sorry I snapped at you," he mumbled. "Fuck . . . this suits the week I'm having. Why am I so good at pissing people off?"

"Gabe," she said gently, "I'm not mad." He finally lifted his gaze as she stepped close enough to him that they were nearly touching. Juniper was smiling up at him, amused. "Look, I've been exploring the campus a lot since we got here. I know a wonderfully private little spot where we can go and make love. If you're up for it."

Gabriel swallowed once, heavily, then had to clear his throat before he could speak again. "May I be honest?"

"I would prefer that, yeah."

"I am *so* up for it I may have trouble walking there."

Juniper laughed delightedly, taking him by the arm and setting off. He let himself be pulled.

"Hello," Shaeine said politely, nodding as Trissiny fell into step beside her. She nodded back, opening her mouth to speak, but closed it mutely.

They walked in silence across the entire width of one of the University's terraces, before turning right, ascending a stone staircase, and continuing back in the other direction on a path that would eventually lead to the dining hall. The layout of the campus was unfriendly toward the goal of getting anywhere efficiently, a fact which Trissiny actually appreciated. Despite the lack of battlements, it would be an easy structure to defend from invaders; the terraces and numerous switchbacks created ample choke points and opportunities to ambush from above. There were actually ways to get directly from one point to another, but not all students felt equally about squeezing through tiny alleys, crawling under bushes, and scrambling up dirt inclines. Neither she nor Shaeine had much interest in such, when it was easier to simply budget one's time to allow for travel.

"Forgive me if I am impertinent, but something appears to be on your mind," Shaeine said, her voice as calm as ever. Her expression was obscured; with the afternoon sun still high, she had her heavy cowl pulled forward.

"I don't . . . I'm not good at . . . talking to people. At least, not at broaching uncomfortable topics . . ."

"Do you know anything of the political structure of Tar'naris?"

"I actually don't," Trissiny admitted, puzzled by the apparent non sequitur, but not ungrateful.

Shaeine's hood bobbed as she nodded. "The organization of Houses is common to all drow societies, as is infighting between them. In most cultures, particularly among the Scyllithene drow who live in the deep underworld, a House is a self-contained political entity. In Tar'naris, however, our queen has reorganized the city so that each House provides one essential service. Agriculture, defense, construction, magic . . . In this way, Narisians avoid the constant civil warfare that plagues most of our kind. To attack a House is to attack an essential point of the city's infrastructure. In the unlikely event that any matriarch were mad enough or foolish enough to do so, the queen and the other Houses would instantly move against her."

"Interesting," Trissiny said sincerely. It actually did sound like a very functional system.

Shaeine nodded again. "House Awarrion serves as the city's diplomatic corps. We arbitrate disputes within the city and serve as the queen's voice and face to the outside world. This is what all of my family are trained for, specifically, from birth." Her hood shifted so that she faced Trissiny somewhat more directly as they walked. "You may think of me as an ambassador and negotiator, Trissiny. I am very conscious of the difficulties people face communicating across differences in perspective, and I'm trained to bridge those gaps. Above all, I will not take offense unless it is plain that you truly mean to give it. Please, I would have you speak your mind."

Trissiny mulled for a moment, selecting her words carefully. Shaeine made no sound to hurry her along.

"Last night," Trissiny said at last, "when I knelt to pray over the day's events, Avei manifested to me in the chapel." She grimaced. "It . . . wasn't one of the more pleasant conversations I've had with her . . . but, well, most of that is irrelevant. Of course I'm ready to do anything she commands me to, but . . . She, in essence, seemed to suggest I should make friends with someone. And I . . . have no idea how to go about doing that."

Shaeine cocked her head to one side. "Gabriel?"

"I don't think she cares much about Gabriel. No . . . I was referring to you."

"I *see*."

There was more emphasis and emotion in those two words than Shaeine normally expressed, but Trissiny couldn't quite discern what emotion it was exactly. Fortunately, the drow continued before she had to think of something worthwhile to say.

"I have been trying, as I have time, to familiarize myself with the theological history of the surface world, but eight thousand years of lore are not easily condensed, and the Universal Church has codified much of it in service to its own political agenda. As such, I am in no position to make assumptions about what you may or may not know. Are you aware of the reason my goddess is not a member of the Pantheon?"

"I . . . no, not really. Themynra and Khar were mentioned in passing, but Mother Narny just said they were nothing we needed to worry about." She kicked a pebble out of her way with more force than it probably deserved. "I'm sorry if that seems rude; I don't mean it to."

"The expectations taught to us in childhood are a powerful thing."

Trissiny nodded. "*My* goddess said, specifically, that if I find myself opposed by a cleric of Themynra, it's a sign I should reconsider my actions."

"How flattering," said Shaeine with a note of wry humor. "According to history as I was taught it, Themynra was an ally of your gods during the Elder Wars, and upon the formation of the Pantheon she was offered a place among them. She declined, largely in protest over their treatment of Elilial."

"*Elilial?!*"

"Before the Pantheon, during the wars, three goddesses formed the strategic core of the rebellion against the elders: Avei, Themynra, and Elilial. At least, this is history as my goddess has taught it to us."

Trissiny stopped walking in sheer disbelief. Shaeine came to a halt alongside her, continuing her tale. "The goddesses, respectively, of strategy, judgment, and cunning, were in effect the mind of the rebellion, and each a formidable warrior in her own right. We remember them as the Three Sisters."

"*Sisters?*"

"You seem shocked."

"Elilial is the goddess of *demons*."

Shaeine held up a finger. "Ah, but you are mistaken. She is the goddess of *cunning*. Each deity is tied at the core of her or his identity to a *concept*, something which roots their power in the nature of the world. Elilial is the *queen* of demons, because she now resides on their dimensional plane and is sufficiently powerful enough to command the obedience of Hell's populations."

"That's . . . that's hair-splitting. The point is, Elilial has been at war with the Pantheon and all its members since they overthrew the elders, and then she tried to turn on the others and destroy humanity."

"And does it shock you so that such enmity now comes from such closeness before? Your cult call themselves the Sisters of Avei; you address one another as 'sister,' I understand. Is this so?"

"Yes," Trissiny said tersely. "What of it?"

"Just that you surely understand the nature of such a relationship. The bond between sisters is not easily broken, because it does *not* break; if tested more cruelly than it can bear, it twists, transforms into a bitterness like no other. Seen in this light, in context of the closeness the three once had, does not the present status quo make *more* sense? Elilial's hatred, Themynra's detachment?"

"Avei isn't hateful *or* detached."

"I think you know well how discipline and duty can sustain us when other motivations falter. It does not strain my credulity at all that the soldier could carry on when the judge and the trickster could not."

Trissiny was silent for long moments, parsing these insights. Eventually she began moving again, and Shaeine fell into step with her.

"Are you . . . that is, do you have plans to meet with anyone over dinner?"

"Teal and Ruda usually join me, but it is not a *plan*, per se."

"If you don't mind, I'd like to hear more about this."

Shaeine reached up and eased her hood back just enough to alleviate the shadows around her face and reveal a faint smile. "You have enjoyed our conversation? And wish to have more?"

"Very much. I think I could learn a lot from you. I mean . . . if you don't object."

"And that, Trissiny, is how you make friends."

CHAPTER 21

This is almost criminal, how much crap there is to deal with. They actually make poor Mrs. Oak do all this *without* help? How does she manage when nobody's being punished?"

Trissiny ignored him, stoically washing dishes. Gabriel wasn't entirely wrong; the pile of detritus that resulted from the feeding of a hundred-odd people was taller than either of them, but she had never been one to be intimidated by work. If anything, she would have found the monotony rather soothing, if not for his constant patter.

Mrs. Oak just grunted at him in passing as he mentioned her, stomping back over to the ovens, which she was scrubbing out by hand. If she felt any particular way about Gabriel's commentary, she gave no sign. The woman uncannily resembled a tree stump in a stained apron. Almost cylindrical in shape, she had a flattish head crowned with a thatch of wiry brown hair, a face composed entirely of horizontal lines and folds which all but hid her eyes, and beefy arms dusted with dark hair and old scars. If she had more expressions than the disgruntled one she now wore, there had been no hint of it thus far.

Getting no response from his last foray, Gabriel tried again as he swabbed at a plate with a threadbare towel. "What do you reckon the odds are we'll be outta here before midnight?"

Trissiny shot him a sidelong look, not pausing in her scrubbing. She was washing, he drying, and so far they were still on the flatware.

For all the complaining the boy was doing, he looked to be in annoyingly good spirits. His posture was relaxed and carefree, and he couldn't seem to keep the grin off his face. It was, she decided, ominous.

"What are *you* in such a good mood for?"

"Me? Oh, nothin'. I just had a *really* good day. Well, good afternoon, actually. Okay, to be precise, a good hour and a half." He glanced over at her, as if expecting to be prompted for more. When she refused to look up from the dishes, he finally burst out. "With Juniper!"

"Oh," Trissiny replied, filling the word with the full weight of her disdain.

"What, you've got a problem with Juniper, too?" That, at least, seemed to finally puncture his bubble of happiness.

"None whatsoever, I like Juniper just fine. She's one of the more consistently kind people on this campus. Of course, even if I were interested in women, I wouldn't go to bed with her."

"Wait, you're *not*? I thought all you Silver Legion types were supposed to be les—" He cut himself off, a syllable too late.

For the first time since they had begun, Trissiny paused in her work, bracing her hands on the edges of the sink. She drew in a deep breath, then very slowly let it out, relaxing the sudden tension in her shoulders with visible effort. Then, making no further comment, picked up her rag again.

"In hindsight," he mused, "it occurs to me that since we're supposed to be learning to get along, repeating rumors about Avenists is probably not gonna be my best approach."

"I bet you discover a lot of baldly obvious things in hindsight."

"Yeah, that right there is a big improvement."

Trissiny went back to ignoring him, and for about two minutes was able to work in blessed silence, scrubbing plates clean and passing them to him to be dried. The *slosh* of water, the *chink* of porcelain were their only accompaniment. She almost dared to believe he would let up . . .

"What's your big problem with me sl—uh, dat—um, *being* with Juniper, then?"

"No problem. By all means, do that." She glanced at him again, carefully keeping her face neutral; he was watching her suspiciously. "Of course, a *smart* man would do some research on dryads before sticking anything of his into one, but that is clearly none of my business."

"I do believe, Trissiny my dear, that the overall lesson of the last few days is that I am *not* a smart man."

"We agree."

They got through the rest of the plates in relative peace, by dint of making no conversation. Gabriel, though, would not be repressed for long, and made another stab as they began on the cups.

"Does it really bother you that much?"

"Many things bother me. Pick one."

He sighed. "I meant me being half . . . blooded."

"You have full agency regardless of your heritage," she said immediately. "Demonbloods have been known to go their whole lives without harming so much as a mouse. No, I take no interest in your bloodline."

"Well . . . that's good, I guess."

"The fact that you are an arrogant, belligerent, self-entitled, disrespectful *fool*, however . . ."

"I think I see where this is going."

". . . makes the fact that you have hellfire in your very veins a matter of immediate concern."

"Yup, there it is."

He let the silence hang for a few more minutes before speaking again, in a more subdued tone.

"I'm sorry."

She shot him a glance. "Excuse me?"

Gabriel paused in wiping, leaning his head back to look up at the ceiling, and heaved a sigh. "For . . . well, all of it. Especially for calling you names, that was a really shitty thing to do. I'm sorry for getting in your face in the first place. I was reacting to stuff in my head, not anything you'd done. I just . . . I was an asshole, and I actually do really regret it. So . . . sorry."

She stayed still for a few seconds, peering at him from the corner of her eye, before realizing that she had paused in her work, and resumed scrubbing. "Apology accepted."

". . . just like that?"

"Yes."

He grinned. "So . . . we're all right, then?"

"Of course not," she said scornfully. "You're still the person who *did* all that. I see nothing to suggest you won't turn right round and do it all again. Words are easy, Gabriel. I choose not to hold grudges for my *own* sake; it's exhausting and morally deficient. That doesn't mean you've earned any trust, or respect."

"Well," he replied after a moment, picking up his towel again, "how . . . refreshingly honest."

Mrs. Oak came over to collect an armload of plates and trundled off with them to the cabinet they called home. She did not speak to or acknowledge her two enforced helpers for the three trips it took to pack them all away. Gabriel held his peace until she finished and went back to her own cleaning.

"So, apparently they hold a big harvest dance down in the town every year. Not that there's much of a harvest; Last Rock does business mostly in trade and cattle. But hey, it's a dance! People need to relax once in a while, let their hair down."

He grinned at her; she carried on ignoring him.

"So?" he prompted.

"So?"

"So, you wanna go?"

Trissiny set down the cup she was working on, hard enough to earn a warning growl from Mrs. Oak.

"Gabriel," she said stiffly to the wall behind the sink, "I think I may be suffering from hallucinations. I could *swear* I just heard you ask me to go to a dance with you."

"That's not a no."

Finally, she turned fully to face him, pulling her sopping hands out of the dishwater. She hadn't worn her armor or shield for this task, for obvious reasons, but carried her sword belted at her waist, and had to repress an urge to place a wet hand on its hilt.

Gabriel stepped back from her fierce expression, holding up his hands placatingly. "Now look, just hear me out. Tellwyrn wants us to get along, right? We can either spend who the hell knows *how* long doing this crap every night without killing each other until she decides the point is made, *or* we can do something a little more proactive to demonstrate how chummy we are. What, I ask you, is more chummy than dancing?"

"You're insane." She snorted, turning back to the dishes. "Anyway, that wouldn't work. Tellwyrn isn't going to fall for an obvious ruse."

"That's the beauty of it," he said, resuming his own labors alongside her. "We *can't* fake this. Even if we're only pretending to like each other for one night, that's us collaborating on something. If we can get through it without breaking down into yelling or fighting, the point is pretty much proven. Or do you *really* wanna spend the whole semester on kitchen duty?"

"Aside from the company, I rather enjoy this. At the abbey we were all expected to work to sustain the place; it makes you feel like part of the community. Here, all I do is study, train, and attend classes. I've been feeling more and more like a . . . burden. This is comfortable. Homey."

"You are *so* weird."

"I'm not the one who wants to go dancing with me."

He had the gall to laugh at that, as if she were joking with him. "Okay, fine, so you like doing dishes. Think, though. Remember that horseshit essay assignment where apparently the only right answer was to *not* follow the instructions? You've gotta think like your enemy. Tellwyrn rewards initiative and . . . let's say, lateral thinking."

"Is Tellwyrn our enemy?"

"She has her good points," he said a little grudgingly, shooting a glance at the door of the kitchen where his green coat hung from a peg. "But for purposes of *this* problem? She's the thing we need to work against."

"I don't see why. As I've said, this situation is fine with me."

"And what makes you think *this* situation is going to be the end of it? You really believe she's gonna let us get away with coasting, with mediocrity?" He let that hang in the air between them for a moment. This time, Trissiny's lack of response was because she didn't have one. "No, I'm talking about dances and thinking about strategies, because I'm pretty damn sure if we don't come up with something extra to deal with this, she will. And I really, *really* would rather not end up chained to your wrist."

"That was hyperbole," said Trissiny without conviction. "She wouldn't *actually* do that. It's completely crazy."

"If half the things I've heard about that woman are true, there's *nothing* she wouldn't do, and not much that she can't," he said grimly. "We're talking about one of the only people known to have *killed a god*."

"What?!" Something heavy and cold clutched at her gut; it was an absurd thought, but looking at his face, she had a terrible feeling he wasn't speaking in ignorance for once. "That's not even possible."

"Look it up," he retorted. "The Church doesn't like it getting around—obviously—but I'll bet you anything the story's not hard to find in *this* school's library. The point is . . . Yeah, I know you don't like me. I'm not gonna claim you're my favorite person in the world, either. But we dug ourselves into this hole, and nobody's gonna dig us back out. Personally, I'd rather do that with an evening at whatever kind of hick-ass hoedown they throw around here than . . . wait to see what Tellwyrn cooks up."

Trissiny realized that she had stopped working again. The water was growing cold and scummy anyway; she reached into it to pull the plug, watching the suds swirl down the drain around the remainder of the cup. She didn't speak until more hot water was running to refill the sink.

"I'll consider it."

"That's all I can ask, I guess. Well, except maybe . . ." He grinned at her expectantly, getting only a raised eyebrow in return.

"What?"

"Come on, there was some mutual responsibility for all this. We're having a moment, just like in the stories. I apologized, so now you . . ."

"I did not act in a manner best reflecting upon my calling," she said coldly. "I regret that." With that, Trissiny turned a cold shoulder to him and resumed her scrubbing.

He sighed heavily. "Yeah. Great. Good talk, Triss."

Professor Tellwyrn read over the imperial proclamation a third time, even more slowly than before. At this point, she wasn't absorbing any new information; it was simply for dramatic effect. It was also rather petty, she knew, since the three soldiers standing in front of her were no more to blame for any of this than a rabbit was for the snare it stepped in. Still, *someone* had to suffer for this, and Sharidan Tirasian wasn't here.

Finally, she lifted her eyes and stared at the men over the rims of her spectacles, slowly drumming her fingers on the paper bearing the imperial seal, now resting on her desk.

"Do you know what this says?" she asked finally.

"Yes, ma'am," replied the one on the right. Private Moriarty. Dark Western complexion, proudly stiff posture of a man for whom standing at attention was a nigh-spiritual rite. Polite, too . . . this would be Mr. By-the-Book. Of course, devotion and a love of regulations didn't make one a good soldier. He wouldn't be here if he were.

On the opposite side of the lineup, Rook, the guy who managed to look like he was slouching even while standing at attention, cleared his throat. "Professor, I respectfully ask that you not explode our heads. 'Specially Moriarty's. The stick up his ass'd shoot right out and punch a hole in your ceiling."

"I will take that under advisement," Tellwyrn said gravely as Private Moriarty clenched his jaw and Finchley, the third one, swallowed. They were afraid of her, even Rook. Maybe especially Rook; she knew his type well, joking in the face of what he thought was doom.

Good.

"It seems you're to be staying with us," she went on in a mild tone. "Now why do you suppose that is?"

The trio exchanged glances.

"Ma'am, if we were the types to ask ImCom what the hell they were thinking, honestly I think we'd've started with the empty box canyon in the middle of the wilderness," Rook offered.

Tellwyrn ignored him. Also Moriarty, who was clearly too preoccupied with presenting the image of a respectable soldier to do any independent thinking. The third one, though . . . Private Finchley had orange hair, a smattering of freckles, and the pale complexion of someone who must spend half his pay on sun lotion if he managed to serve in the army and not be burned to a crisp by exposure. Moreover, there was something about the set of his eyes that reminded her of the students who aggravated her the least. Especially in the way they narrowed slightly when prompted by a question. This one was a thinker.

He noticed her studying him and swallowed again, somehow managing to go even paler.

"Something on your mind?" Tellwyrn asked him directly, still in that calm tone.

"What we . . . That is, the events at Outpost C9-121 are strictly classified," he said slowly, "but General Panissar himself told us . . ." He glanced sidelong at Moriarty. "He, uh, hinted that it would be all right if we talked to you about it."

"According to Lord Vex, you are granted provisional security clearance on this *one* issue," Moriarty said stiffly.

"Provisional security clearance," Tellwyrn mused. "I do believe that's one of the more idiotic things I've ever heard of. Rather defeats the purpose of having things secured in general, doesn't it? It sounds like the sort of made-up-on-the-spot nonsense they'd tell a person who can't function in the blind spot between regulations and necessity."

Moriarty gave no sign of understanding her implication, but Rook snorted a laugh.

"So it's politics," Finchley went on, frowning in thought. He grew more confident as his attention drew into his own mind. "Legally you can't be involved. Off the books . . . the empire is willing to accept you as a player, extending an olive branch. Shit, this is way over my pay grade," he added under his breath, then started and flushed, abruptly remembering who he was talking to.

"Not bad," Tellwyrn murmured approvingly. "Not bad at all. Better than I was expecting, anyhow. So, you three are de facto imperial ambassadors, without any of the training, competence, or diplomatic privilege. That's quite a promotion from monitoring one of Vex's little shoebox deathtrap forts. Or, rather, a sidestep. Out of the absurd frying pan into the equally ridiculous fire. This must be a rather trying week for you."

"I want it known up front that I will not be swayed by money," Rook intoned. "Beer and girls, sure. I'll sell you my mum's bones for those, but financially? My honor has no price. I'm sure my colleagues will say the same." Moriarty closed his eyes and squeezed his lips shut, visibly repressing a response.

Tellwyrn didn't validate his posturing with a response. "So. You three met Elilial, then."

"Met her?" Rook grinned broadly, reaching around Finchley to punch Moriarty in the shoulder. "*This* crazy bastard tried to *arrest* her!"

"Don't touch me," Moriarty growled.

"And how did that go?" Tellwyrn asked, intrigued in spite of herself.

"How do you think it went? She knocked us the *fuck* out!" Rook said, incongruously gleeful.

"Stop." Tellwyrn held up a hand, then pointed at Finchley. "You. Recount the series of events."

He gaped at her for a moment, then shut his mouth, glancing from side to side at each of his fellow privates.

"While we're young, please," Tellwyrn snapped.

"Aren't you, like, three thousand?"

"Private Rook, do you know how many pounds of pressure are necessary to break a human femur?"

He gaped at her.

"It's a trick question," she went on, grinning. "It depends on how long you're willing to spend at it. And I assure you, I have *all* day." That was one of her favorite threats—always so effective that they'd probably already forgotten she'd *just* demanded they hurry up. Tellwyrn gave that a moment to sink in before returning her gaze to the man in the middle. "Finchley. Report. *Now.*"

As she suspected, receiving an order in a superior officer's tone galvanized Finchley's training to overcome his natural wishy-washiness. He spilled out the details of their encounter with the Queen of Demons in a thorough if rather disjointed fashion, helped along by commentary from Rook. Moriarty remained silent throughout, thankfully. It was something of a chore to sit through, but Tellwyrn had absorbed crucial information from even less reliable witnesses, and anyway, the story was a short one. It was impossible not to get the gist of it.

"But why would she do that?" the professor murmured to herself after Finchley trailed to a halt. Elbows on her desk, hands folded in front of the lower half of her face, she stared through her spectacles at a point in empty space past Moriarty's shoulder. "Stealth is what she *is*. Nobody catches Elilial in the act unless she intends them to. But *you* three? Why do *you* matter enough to warrant a visitation?"

"Hey, no offense taken," Rook said lightly.

"The scrying orbs," Finchley said, frowning again. "Remember, Rook? You thought Imperial Command were monitoring us through them. It actually *was* a hellgate watch, though, so it probably wasn't us that ImCom was watching. One was broken when we woke up . . . She wanted the empire to see. *We* didn't matter; she was just . . . setting it up. Letting the message get sent through the right channels."

"So," Tellwyrn said more briskly, "here you are, and here, it seems, you will be staying for a while. I'll expect you to learn and adhere to the same code of conduct that applies to my students. This is a dry campus; you will not drink or *be* drunk here. If you must pickle brain cells, go to the town and do it; they'll be delighted to take your money. Unlike the students, however, you may *stay* in town until you're sufficiently dried out to walk a straight line. I don't want to see you drunk on my campus. Clear?"

"Yes, ma'am!" they chorused.

"The other item of particular note to you three is that you will not interfere with the education of those who are here to get one. I don't mind you fraternizing with the students; they aren't prisoners. I'll even tolerate romantic relationships between you and them, *unless* it begins to interfere with their academic careers. Despite what the storybooks tell you about true love—beginning with the delusion that that's a real thing—I can and will separate you in the most permanent manner possible.

"Any harassment of female students will, if I'm feeling lenient, result in your immediate expulsion from the mountain. I do mean *immediate*, and it won't be down the sloping side. Or, if I'm in a more vindictive mood, I'll simply hand you over to our resident Hand of Avei. Understood?"

Finchley and Moriarty repeated their affirmation, looking progressively more intimidated, but Rook perked up visibly.

"The Hand? She's *here*?" He grinned. "Awesome! I'll have to pay my respects. What's she like?"

There was a moment's baffled silence.

"*You're* an Avenist?" Finchley finally demanded.

"What, you aren't?" Rook frowned at him. "Either of you? Come on, how can you not follow the goddess of war? What kind of soldiers are you?" At that, Moriarty clenched his jaw and began to physically swell with repressed fury.

Tellwyrn slapped a hand down on her desk, regaining their wandering attention before this could develop into something truly annoying.

"As luck would have it, there are only two boys in this year's freshman class, so I have a heavily underoccupied male dormitory in which to stick you. I'll have someone show you there. In fact, I'm expecting him any time now."

"Only two boys? *Fantastic!*" Rook grinned maniacally. "So the ratio of girls is about . . . uh . . . that is . . . Of course, I'm speaking strictly of my admiration of the lads' good fortune. Not out of any *personal* interest. I wouldn't dream of . . . Well, you know."

She stared at him evenly.

". . . that is a predatory look," he mumbled after a long pause. "I'm not sure if she wants to eat us or—gn." Rook broke off with a grunt as Finchley jammed an elbow into his ribs.

"So, um, Professor," Finchley said somewhat desperately. "What is it you would like us to . . . ah, *do*?"

"Do?" Tellwyrn turned her gaze on him. "How should I know?"

"It's just . . . we're to be *stationed* here, but . . . there are no officers present, and we weren't given any orders except to be . . . ah . . . stationed. I'm just wondering what our duties will be."

"The hell if I care," she said. "Don't cause a ruckus on my campus, and you can spend your days playing poker or learning piano for all it matters to me. If the army didn't give you anything to do, I certainly don't have a stake."

They exchanged another series of dubious glances.

"But," Moriarty began, "what if—" He was interrupted by a knock at the office door.

"Ah, what timing," Tellwyrn said dryly, then raised her voice. "Come in, Mr. Arquin."

The door opened and Gabriel poked his head in, peering around its edge. He frowned on seeing the three soldiers.

"Gentlemen," said Tellwyrn, "you will kindly wait in the hall till I'm done here, which I don't expect to take too long. Then Mr. Arquin will escort you to your new residence."

"Wait, I'll what?" Gabriel said. "What's their new residence?"

"*Your* residence. In case you failed to notice, which I'm not going to rule out at this point, you and Mr. Caine are living in a suite meant to house ten."

He scowled at the three privates. "Who *are* these guys?"

"The comedy relief," the professor said, "so you can give it a rest. Outside, boys; you'll have plenty of time to get to know Gabriel later."

They filed past him and out the door; he watched with a frown as they went, then turned back to Tellwyrn. "What's going on?"

"imperial politics. You're going to be ass-deep in it soon enough, I expect, but that's a headache for another day. Right now, I believe you have an assignment?"

"Yeah, well . . . sort of." He pulled a slightly rumpled sheaf of paper from an inner pocket of his coat and unfolded it. "I took citations of every legal textbook I could find that mentioned demonbloods, and according to *all* of them, what you asked about is . . . Um, it's not. Legally you *don't* have the right to execute me, under any circumstances. If I were attacking you with deadly force, you might be excused for using deadly force in return, but . . . that's it."

She stared at him for a long moment. "And that's all you've got?"

"That's all there *is*." His voice rose with annoyance.

"Do you recall your question a few days ago about . . . Let's see, how did you put this; it was rather poignant . . . Ah yes, 'sadistic mind games?'"

"Yeah, I had a feeling this was gonna be one of those." He refolded the paper and stuffed it back into his coat. "Let me guess, I failed to find the trap."

"Fortunately for you, I don't apply the results of punishment assignments to your grade in my class; I just break your fingers if you don't do them. So you're still passing. You did the work . . . well, half of it."

"What the fuck was the other half?!"

"The *assignment* was to prepare a report on the legal statutes that allow me to kill you. There were two things for you to research there—you, and me. You only did one."

He stared at her for a moment, then glanced furtively back at the door, behind which waited the three imperial soldiers. "Do . . . Are you an imperial agent?"

Tellwyrn threw back her head and barked a laugh. "Ohh, that's rich. Really, I'm gonna have to remember that one. Seriously, though. Ever heard of Designation: Zero Twenty?"

"Um . . . I think maybe at one point . . ." He trailed off under her stare. "No."

"It's a code used by Imperial Intelligence," she explained. "Part of Quentin Vex's new system of categorizing threats to the empire; before he came along, the relevant classification was Class Zero Personified Event. Standards for identifying a Zero Twenty are a little vague, as

the spooks like to leave themselves some room for interpretation . . .
but basically, it refers to an individual who is immortal, sufficiently
powerful that even the full resources of the empire could not easily
put them down and, while not directly *hostile* to the empire, prone
to being . . . difficult." Professor Tellwyrn leaned back in her chair,
smiling smugly at him. "My personal designation is Z20-136. *Do*
keep that under your hat; I'm looking forward to seeing the look on
Vex's face when he finds out I know it."

"Wow," he said dryly.

"You think you're being ironic, but after some thought I believe
you'll realize how 'wow' that is. What this means, legally, is that a
person designated a Zero Twenty becomes a walking act of the gods.
They are not regarded as a sapient being by the empire, but a force of
nature. You don't jail a typhoon or execute an earthquake for treason
after all. So if I heal someone, they had a miraculous recovery. If I *kill*
someone, they died of natural causes." She spread her arms as if to
embrace the office. "*Legally*, this University just sprang up out of the
ground like a patch of mushrooms."

"Hell, that wasn't even two subjects to research," he said. "Only
thing that matters here is *you*."

"*No.*" Tellwyrn sat up straight glaring. "No, dammit, Gabriel! You
need to think about *context*. So the empire won't intervene in every little
thing I do or hold me responsible as they would just about anyone else.
That doesn't mean they'll let me wander around doing whatever the
hell I please. So, I'm a walking natural disaster. How does the empire
respond when a natural disaster hits? What does it do?"

"I guess," he said slowly, "it depends on the situation."

She pointed a finger at him. "Bingo! It depends on the situation. So . . . what's the situation? What response is merited? Big bad
Tellwyrn has just offed some whiny half demon. What reaction does
this get?"

"'Whiny' is a little strong," he muttered.

"If I were to kill someone important, or a large enough group of
people, that would pretty much require an imperial response. So the
question becomes, how important are you? If you die, *who cares?*"

"My father," he said immediately.

"Ah yes, your father. I'm sure *that* would make an impact on imperial policy. A washed-up ex-soldier, discharged for 'gross indecency.' Which is a bit of a catchall, as they don't have specific regulations to cover doing something with a hethelax demon that results in an offspring. Sounds like 'gross' was the operative word there. I can practically hear his old army buddies telling him to be glad the evidence of *that* lapse in judgment is gone. Worst-case scenario, he decides to come up here and avenge you and I have to waste two minutes dealing with it."

"I *know* what you're doing," he snarled.

"Oh, is that what you think?"

"You're just trying to make me angry!"

"Gabriel, look at yourself," she said dryly. "I'm not *trying* anything; you're pretty angry. Seriously, though, who else?"

"Toby," he shot back. "*Toby* cares what happens to me."

"Yes, Toby. The chosen Hand of a god whose core teaching is unconditional compassion, a boy who happens to think of you as a brother. That, and your only blood relative, is all you can muster? Doesn't look encouraging."

"*Juniper* likes me!"

"Oh yes. *That*." Tellwyrn wrinkled her nose in disgust. "I did hope you'd go at least a week without plunging into more trouble . . . No, I'm not even going to get into that right now; you can learn all about dryads on your own time. Suffice it to say that yes, Juniper would probably miss you, and no, she wouldn't do anything about it. So . . . where are we, then? Gabriel Arquin is dead, and it just doesn't *matter* enough for anybody to bother dealing with the one who did it. Seems kind of sad, don't you think?"

"Is this *really* the point of this whole thing?" he demanded. "So you can make me feel like shit? Or did you just want to brag about how you can do whatever you like around here?"

Professor Tellwyrn planted an elbow on her desk and leaned her face into her palm, displacing her glasses. "Arquin . . . seriously. This has got to stop. Your first response whenever anybody challenges you is to complain about it, instead of *thinking* about what it *means*." Lifting her head, she pulled the spectacles off and tossed them down carelessly on the desk, staring up at him almost sadly. "I'll spell it out for you—you cannot carry on as you have. Too many people are going to want to take a piece out of you just for being what you are, and you just *can't* fight them all off, no matter how skilled or dangerous you become. You need *friends*. You need for there to always be someone willing to back you up. You've got the raw material for that; I told you as much last night. Funny, sort of charming, generally well-intentioned, intermittently clever. But it's a long road to developing personality traits into a useful skill set, and in this case it begins with you learning to *stop pissing everybody off*."

Silence stretched out in the office while he shuffled his feet, staring down at them. Tellwyrn let him, remaining still in her pose. Finally, he lifted his eyes again, and spoke much more softly.

"That was the point of this . . . whole assignment? You want me to be *nice?*"

"Nice is a starting point," she said mildly. "Frankly, it won't get you far. Being *useful* would be better. There are a thousand ways to go about it, but in the end, you just need to *matter* to people. Build connections, create an identity as someone the world is better off having, with people willing to vouch for that. You're safer at this University than probably anywhere else on the planet, but right now, the path you're on, you'll be lucky to live long enough past graduation to collect your diploma."

". . . any advice?"

"For the very basics?" She smiled, and adopted a gentler tone, now that he was clearly listening and taking her seriously. "Talk less, listen more. You have an irritating habit of making everything about you. Try focusing on the other people around you, learn about *them*, make them the focus of your interactions. You will be flabbergasted how popular you become, and how quickly."

"Really?" He perked up.

"All right, that's enough of that for tonight. Run along, Arquin. Show those soldiers to their new lodgings, introduce them to Toby.

You might take this as a golden opportunity to practice what I just told you—those three lads have no idea what a boneheaded pain in the ass you are. Make a good impression."

"Yes, sir, ma'am, sir," he said, saluting crisply.

"Cute," she replied. "*Out.*"

CHAPTER 22

As if to prove that nature itself bore him a grudge, vast improbabilities aligned such that neither the region's interminable rains nor the discharges of the city's magical factories blotted out the sky on the morning that, a little after seven, Bishop Darling's bedroom drapes were flung open. Brilliant, hateful sunlight burst in upon his peace like a stampede of buffalo.

"GRAAAUGH!" he roared, coming awake in the most unpleasant manner he could remember. Sleep-addled, Darling tried to throw off his blankets with one hand while pulling them over his head with the other, succeeding brilliantly in entangling himself. "PRICE! What in the fell hell are you doing?!"

"Good morning, Your Grace," his butler said crisply, stepping away from the windows and beginning to swiftly lay out a suit from his wardrobe.

"What *bloody* time is it?"

"Nearly two hours before Your Grace's customary breakfast. You have a visitor. I took the liberty of installing her in the downstairs parlor."

"Visitaaaaaaaaarh." The word was mangled by an enormous yawn, but at least he finally managed to extricate himself from his blankets. "Her? Who in Omnu's flaming name would be daft enough to barge in here at this hour?"

"One of the young talents at the Pink Lady, a Miss Rose."

He blinked, then frowned. "Wh . . . Rose knows how to get in touch with me. There are *channels*, procedures. She also knows damn well better than to show up here."

"Indeed, Your Grace has spoken positively of her wits and discretion. The young lady appears quite distraught. I gathered that the circumstances must be exceptional and took the liberty of awakening Your Grace, lest the matter should require immediate attention."

"Right," he said, shook his head to clear away the fog of sleep, and then repeated more firmly, "right. Good thinking, Price. I'll dress, you brush."

"Very good, Your Grace."

He tossed aside his silk pajamas and stuffed himself into one of Sweet's better suits, an only slightly shabby outfit in royal blue and maroon. Price darted about him like an efficient hummingbird, sorting his sleep-tousled hair into a semblance of a proper order.

"Shoes?" he asked, looking around for them, as they finished this joint task. Price handed him a pair of slippers. ". . . really?"

"Laces are a relatively time-consuming prospect, Your Grace. Perhaps we ought not leave the young lady to wait too long."

Darling rolled his eyes, but dropped the slippers to the ground and stepped into them. "She's not gonna *steal* anything, Price. The girl's not an idiot."

"As you say, Your Grace."

"You are *such* a snob. You know that?" Rubbing the last traces of sleep from his eyes, he strode to the door.

"As you say, Your Grace."

Price managed to barge in front of him diffidently—butler training really was astounding—and by the time he had reached the bottom of the stairs, was in position to open the door of the downstairs parlor for him with a bow.

It was the less impressive of the rooms in which he entertained guests, but only Bishop Darling's guests were entertained here; Sweet went to where the people were, rather than bringing them to him. As such, the room's thick carpet, ornate wallpaper, expensive furniture, and assortment of art and knickknacks made it probably the most sumptuous room this guest had ever visited.

She was standing with her back to the door, studying a silver idol of Eserion that stood over the mantel, which was about two feet above her head, treating him to a view of a pleasingly plump backside and an upper back left almost entirely bare by the uniform of her trade. Gods above, had she come in the front door? There'd be hell to pay with the neighbors . . . Rose jumped like a startled rabbit on his arrival, though, spinning to face him, and he felt a twinge of alarm. She was ordinarily one of the most unflappable people he knew. She had to be in her line of work.

It grew worse as he took in the sight of her face. Tears had melted her makeup into a hideous mudslide, and apparently hadn't stopped flowing. She looked . . . It was hard to pin a name to the emotion ground into her features, but it was clearly something on the ragged edge of trauma.

"Sweet," she cried desperately, taking a stumbling step toward him. "I'm sorry, I know I shouldn't've come, I'm sorry, but I-I-I didn't know what to do! She's dead, it's such a mess . . . Oh, *Light*, she's dead, it was just *awful*, I never saw anything like . . . I never *imagined* . . . And there's police and Imps all over, and the girls are all a wreck, and Light, I hated to leave 'em, but I didn't know what to do; you're the only one I could think of . . ."

"Rose!" He crossed the room in three long strides and knelt to take her gently by the shoulders, holding her gaze with his own. In ordinary circumstances it was one of the rudest possible things you could do with a dwarf, short of pissing in their beer. Rose, though, was clearly on the edge of an utter breakdown. She collapsed against him, dissolving in sobs, and he rocked her gently, heedless of what the mix of mascara and snot was inevitably doing to his suit.

"It's okay, doll, you're safe right now. I need to stiffen up for just a bit, though, all right? We've gotta figure out what to do, and I can't help you if I don't know what's up. Price, fetch us some brandy?"

"Immediately, sir."

Gently, he eased her back. "Can you hold on for just a bit longer for me, love? I know you can; you're the strongest person I've ever met." She nodded, gulped, and gasped for air, choking back another sob. "That's my girl. Now start at the beginning; tell it slow. What happened? Who's dead?"

Rose gulped again, and drew in a shuddering breath, staring up into his eyes. "It's Missy, Sweet. She . . . It was murder. They *butchered* her!"

Heavy curtains shrouded every window and door, obscuring the chamber in a dimness broken only by a single light—a modern fairy lamp sitting on the floor against one wall, the harshness of its glow softened by a paper shade. In eras past, it would have been a brazier, and the smoky illumination of such a fixture might have better suited the crowd of people standing in silent patience, obscured by their ash-gray robes. But that was then, and this was now, and they used what was at hand.

Those who by faith and need alike lived in the shadows well understood the value of appearances, and when not to bother with them.

One curtain stirred as the door behind it was opened; sickly purple light flashed about its edges for a moment, accompanied by the breeze trying to move through the shrouded opening. For a second, the scent of sulfur and ozone wafted out along with the dull light of magic.

But the light faded immediately, the airflow ceased, and the door was pulled shut with a solid *thunk*. And then the curtain was whisked aside, and the last of their number strode into the room.

"My friends! Our patience is rewarded."

The robed warlocks of the Black Wreath turned as one, waiting for the pronouncement of their mortal leader.

He was *not* in traditional robes but a white suit, which made him seem like a walking lantern in this dim room. His dark, almost black complexion and lanky build spoke of Onkawi heritage, though his accent was Tiraan, and his skull practically gleamed, bald as an egg, until he placed atop it the wide-brimmed flat hat he'd been carrying.

One did not wear one's hat when conferring with one's goddess, obviously.

"The Dark Lady's gambit was a success," the high priest of the Wreath proclaimed, striding forward into the center of the room with careful, mincing steps like a patient stork on the hunt. "She has what she needed from the emperor; that which she wanted set in motion is now moving. Elilial has returned to the seclusion of her realm for now. The next moves are ours."

"What are our orders, Embras?" asked one of the robed figures, her voice a soft alto.

"Our eternal mission carries on as it always has," Embras Mogul declared, stopping in the center of the room and beginning to turn slowly in place as he spoke, addressing the entire crowd of his followers. "Indeed, I cannot overstate the urgency—the alignment is drawing closer, and you all know the disastrous setback we suffered three years ago. But for the moment, matters proceed according to plan. We will watch for opportunities, as we always do, and seize them as they come. In this breath of relative calm, however, we are to busy ourselves with *retribution*."

The soft whisper of fabric as the robed figures stirred faintly was the only response. They awaited his instructions, tense and alert.

"The Tiraan Empire, with its countless grasping fingers and limitless ambitions," Embras continued quietly. "The Universal Church and its Archpope, Justinian, that spider lurking untouchable at the center of his web and pulling every string. That bombastic meddler Arachne Tellwyrn, with her absurd school and ancient pattern of thrusting herself into the business of the gods. And most recently . . . perhaps most intriguingly . . . the priest. The *bishop*, the Eserite—the one who plays the Church and the empire and the Thieves' Guild against one another, and now has decided to make himself the expert on Elilial's own movements. Darling."

He completed one full revolution and tugged the brim of his hat, lowering it so that only his smirk was visible.

"Of the thousand and one irons we have in ten thousand fires, *these* are the principal suspects—the likeliest parties to have interfered in the great summoning which we carried out with such care. One of these is surely behind the loss of the Dark Lady's daughters. We will watch them, prod them oh so carefully into movement . . . see what they do, and what they give away. And when we discern *which* of them is guilty of this crime; we will teach them the true meaning of *remorse*."

Robes rustled again, a bit louder this time, the assembled warlocks stiffening in hungry anticipation.

"Well, it wasn't Tellwyrn," one man said, lifting his head just enough that a heavy beard was visible beneath his hood. "For the past three years she's been running hither and thither, trying to figure out for herself what happened and who did it. And I doubt the Lady would have permitted Vadrieny to attend that University if Tellwyrn had murdered her sisters."

"Do not underestimate that sorceress, Bradshaw," Embras admonished, turning to him with a wagging finger upraised. "No one, no matter how powerful, survives for three thousand years by picking fights and then throwing fireballs at them. The fact that Tellwyrn has cultivated such a reputation for lacking subtlety only proves the subtlety of which she is capable. Just for example, making a show of investigating a crime is a downright *traditional* way of concealing the fact that you committed it. Or, being Tellwyrn, she could well have forcefully disrupted a mass summoning of archdemons just because she happened to notice it occurring, and then spent the next few years trying to figure out what happened and why. No, she is on the list. Not my favorite suspect, either, but . . . we'll see."

"Are we to intervene in Vadrieny's education, then?" asked the woman who'd spoken first. "Beyond what we are already doing?"

"Orders with regard to Vadrieny have not changed," Embras replied, his tone grave. "She was the least of her sisters and was rendered amnesiac by the trauma, besides. Much as I'm *slavering* to figure out how the hell she survived when six much stronger and smarter archdemons did not, there's nothing she can do for her mother's plans in this state, save become a target. Elilial wants her discreetly watched over and otherwise left alone, to live in whatever way she and her . . . host deem best. Except, of course, with regard to her reeducation in what it means to be a princess of Hell. And since you brought it up, Vanessa, how is that going?"

"I am even less optimistic than I was," she admitted, a tinge of annoyance entering her voice. "It might prove best to wait until she's out from under Tellwyrn's thumb and approach her directly. Working with an outsider proxy is . . . Embras, I increasingly think that Eserite elf is going to stab us in the back."

"Well, that fails to shock me," he drawled. "Do you think so for specific reason, aside from the fact that stabbing everyone in the back is Principia Locke's entire personality?"

"She's made first contact with Teal and Vadrieny. I have managed to watch her closely enough to observe that much. And she *used* that contact to attempt to weasel herself into direct communication with that paladin, Trissiny. I warned you about trying to play games with Eserites, Embras. I was willing to make use of Locke because using *us* to screw over everyone *else* would appeal to her, but if her actual goal is to cozy up to the Avenist, it's likely she only wanted a connection to the Wreath as something to hand over for credibility."

"And so it goes." Embras chuckled. "Well, we haven't invested enough in dear little Prin to be at risk, no matter what she does. Besides, it was before any of our time, but the Wreath owes her a comeuppance for the shenanigans she pulled during the Enchanter Wars, anyway. I'll get to thinking about a suitable way to rap her little knuckles, but in the end, it's a low priority. The Church, for now, is an uncrackable nut, and the Dark Lady's business with the

Silver Throne is just that—*her* business. We'll continue shadowing Sharidan's agents, but make no aggressive moves against the empire without clearing it first. I don't want to risk endangering the Lady's plans. How are we handling their reactions so far, Rupi?"

"Imperial Intelligence retaliated after the Lady's . . . escapade in the palace," replied another woman in a thick Punaji accent. "They all but had to. We've lost quite a few of our lowest-ranked members in the last few days, Embras—no one important or hard to replace. That could mean Intelligence doesn't know any of our higher-value assets, *or* that they want us to *think* so, the better to watch our own next moves. Quentin Vex is annoyingly competent; I would not take him lightly."

"So far, so good," said Embras, tipping his hat to her. "Well handled, Rupi; stay the course and stay out of their way. For now, there's no point in playing tag with Intelligence. The empire, the Church, and Tellwyrn are all frustratingly difficult to work a fingertip into . . . But *fortunately*, our fourth prospect has an absolute genius for rattling everyone else's cages without getting his own fingers pinched. I have a feeling if we prod an interesting reaction out of *him*, it'll cause the most fascinating shock waves among our other targets, with minimal risk to us."

"Right, Darling," grunted Bradshaw. "I shouldn't have to tell you that Eserites are dangerous in a way the other Pantheon cults are not, Embras, but I'm repeating it anyway because I know how you get when you scent opportunity. We don't even understand what game that one is playing, only that he's unpleasantly skilled at it."

"What do you want us to do?" Vanessa asked quietly.

"Keep on as you were, and inform me immediately if anything interesting comes up," Embras ordered. "I shall do likewise. For the moment, leave Darling to *me*. I have a few . . . ideas. Once I've seen him in action, seen him *pressed*, I'll understand how to goad him into a misstep. And that just might be the flick of the wrist that topples the whole house of cards."

He strode suddenly the rest of the way across the room, arriving in front of a bank of thick curtains against the wall opposite where he'd entered; from here, Embras turned and could see all the assembled warlocks at once without having to swivel around to face each in turn.

"I know I do not have to remind *you*, my friends, of the deadly peril of complacency. Nor will I minimize the catastrophic failure that was the loss of the Lady's daughters, nor the consequences from which we are still reeling. But we have recovered from that fumble and stolen a march on our enemies since. Now, the Dark Lady's plans proceed apace; all rival players are tripping each other up while failing to catch our trail, and it is the Black Wreath who have the initiative. For now, this game is ours to lose."

"Remember we're not the only ones making assertive moves," Bradshaw urged, "nor is ours the only deity doing so. We are the first Wreath in a generation who may have to worry about ending up on the wrong end of a paladin's sword."

"Oh, I promise you, I have not forgotten about those kids." Embras chuckled. "But then, I wouldn't say I'm *worried*. That, too, is a gambit that can be turned against the gods themselves. Remember the truth is on *our* side, Bradshaw—and what is a paladin but a person trained to value truth, and then made to serve a lie? When the moment is right, all we have to do to turn the Hands of Avei and Omnu, and any of the *others* who resume calling paladins against their masters, is shine a light on the Pantheon itself."

Grabbing the curtain, he yanked it aside with a flourish, and brilliant sunlight burst into the room through the broad bay window, causing several of the Wreath members to emit muffled protests and most to shield their eyes.

It was an unusually bright day in Tiraas, nearly devoid of the city's normal cloud cover. The Wreath's current lair afforded them a glorious view across the city, bristling with ancient minarets and steeples amid modern flashing scroll towers and factory antennae emitting lightning into the bright sky. Farther still, the outer walls rose around the edges of the city, each venerable tower now holding up a late-model mag cannon.

"A great doom is coming," Embras Mogul of the Black Wreath stated, gazing out across the imperial capital with a cold smile. "But not for us."

ABOUT THE AUTHOR

D. D. Webb is the author of the Gods Are Bastards and Only Villains Do That series. In his free time, he enjoys writing fantasy stories, playing the violin, and being sad. Webb resides in the Pacific Northwest with two elderly cats.

JOIN THE FELLOWSHIP

follow us on our socials

 podiumentertainment.com

 @podiumentertainment

 /podiumentertainment

 @podium_ent

 @podiumentertainment